I0639726

# The Psychic's Heartwish

## Heartwishes, Volume 6

Daisy Dexter Dobbs

Published by Department of Daydreams, LLC, 2023.

THE PSYCHIC'S HEARTWISH

**First edition. February 9, 2023.**

Copyright © 2023 Daisy Dexter Dobbs.

ISBN: 978-1587850882

Written by Daisy Dexter Dobbs.

This book is spiritedly dedicated to all those who march to the beat of a different drummer. To the free spirits, the mavericks, the rebels—and those suffering from Imposter Syndrome. To all the wonderfully odd, quirky people. The daring nonconformists and gutsy misfits. Those who boldly color outside the lines. All the magnificent wizardly creatives. The kooky, madcap, unorthodox and the unconventional. All hail the avant-garde bohemians; the independent thinkers; the eccentrics. The kind; the caring; the compassionate. The cockeyed optimists who focus on the bright side. And to those who thrive on making others smile and laugh.

You are my people.

# ABOUT THIS BOOK

~<>~

More than anything, Kady Malone wants to heal the rift in her family. She starts the herculean task by inviting her snobby, elitist cousin Lorraine and her brainy new fiancé to dinner. When Lorraine accepts the invitation but includes a lengthy email full of stipulations and conditions, Kady is insulted. How dare Lorraine suggest Kady's incapable of hosting a simple dinner party? Detesting romance novels, Lorraine warns bookshop owner Kady not to discuss those *cheap, tawdry bodice rippers* over dinner. Kady's further instructed not to embarrass Lorraine by bringing up anything mystical, like crystal balls or, God forbid, parading her rescue dog, Izzy, around. For heaven's sake, what's wrong with Kady being proud of her adorable tarot-card-reading psychic dog?

Dressed in a purposely bizarre co-mingling of garish fortuneteller and debutante socialite garb, Kady wonders if it's childish to antagonize Lorraine by hosting the most bodice ripping, psychic-themed dinner party ever? Perhaps. Deserved? Definitely.

Although Kady's mischievous plan has all the ingredients for success, she's thrown for a loop when she meets science professor Rylan Kilpatrick, who isn't the stuffy fuddy-duddy fiancé she expected. Their mutual attraction is electrifying and forbidden, throwing Kady's world into utter chaos when she gazes into her crystal ball.

*Heartwishes, Book 6: Quirky bohemian warmhearted heroine, brainy magnetic knockout hero, mean girl drama queen, beloved ostracized disowned cousin, abundant humor, suspense, fantasy, wondrous wish, and a pair of precious reincarnated dogs. This guaranteed HEA romcom can be read as a standalone but is better appreciated when read in order.*

# Chapter 1

"THIS IS MOLLY," Aladee Malone told her sister-in-law, Kady. "She likes cheese, carrots, hamburgers and ice cream, so she's definitely not a vegan like you." She chuckled. "Her favorite activities are eating, sleeping, and playing with children. She prefers a family with kids."

"Well that definitely lets me out," Kady Malone noted. "Cute little thing though." She bent low to reach through the cage and rub behind the dog's ears.

Searching for her first dog was more difficult than Kady had imagined. They were all so precious, she was tempted to scoop them all into her car and take them home...to her small apartment. Fortunately she had Aladee with her to help clue her in on which dog would be the right one for her.

There was nothing like looking for a rescue dog with someone who could communicate with animals telepathically. No matter how many times Kady witnessed her new sister-in-law's astounding ability, she still found it mindboggling. It was only one of the amazing traits her brother Nevan's new wife possessed. Kady was still getting used to the fact that Aladee was a bona fide nymph.

She couldn't help rolling her eyes at the implausible reminder. A nymph...with concealed wings, no less, that Aladee had, thank goodness, learned to mostly control now so they didn't just flip open at the most inopportune times.

Nope. No one could ever accuse Kady of having a mundane life.

As they walked they stopped to engage with dogs along the way before Aladee stopped in her tracks, grinning from ear to ear.

"You've found her?" Kady asked. "The right one for me?" Kady looked at the tiny dog in the cage, feeling a slight pang of disappointment because she didn't feel a sense of connection to the small creature...plus she wasn't especially a fan of chihuahuas, which she was fairly certain this dog was, because Kady had been bitten by a non-stop yapping one as a child.

"Um...no." Her wide grin still evident, Aladee said, "I've just been advised not to be rude by passing by without us acknowledging Miss Chowa here." Aladee thumbed toward the chihuahua. "She enjoys wearing jewels, fashionable harnesses for her walks, and prefers homemade gourmet meals to bagged or canned pet food. Don't try to give her green beans...she'll barf them all over your floor to teach you a lesson."

"My goodness, Miss Chowa's certainly persnickety, isn't she?" Kady said through laughter. "Unusual name. How did she get it?"

"She says she loathes the name. Detests it. The family's little boy couldn't pronounce chihuahua. Once he came out with "Chowa" the family thought it was adorable and it stuck, much to Veronica's infinite disdain."

"Veronica?"

"Mmm-hmm, Chowa considers herself a Veronica. She's annoyed her adoptive family was making her into a clown rather than the princess she deserves to be. She made the family aware of her dissatisfaction on a regular basis by depositing well-deserved clumps of poop and puddles of pee where they couldn't miss them."

"Yikes." The corner of Kady's lip hiked into a smile as she eyed the little dog with its head held high in a royal manner. "So I guess there's no question as to why little Chowa ended up in Glassfloat Bay's no-kill shelter. You think she'd rather stay with a family than—"

"Chowa says absolutely not," Aladee cut in. "She's waiting for the right person to come along. They must be childless, stylish, and appreciate Veronica's obvious attributes. She says she'll know the right person when she sees them." After a small hesitation, Aladee added, "She says you're not it."

The small dog proceeded to turn its back to them, presenting her royal butt.

Kady broke into spontaneous laughter. "I'd say Princess Veronica is very perceptive. We definitely wouldn't make a good match."

They studied each dog until Aladee stopped in front of another cage. "Ooh, this one called to me, Kady...by name! She said she's meant to be with you, and that you already know about it."

"Is that so?" Bending close to the cage, resting her hands on her knees, Kady smiled at the darling little black and white dog with the big *please-take-me-home* eyes. When the dog's small paw tapped against the cage, begging for Kady's attention and remaining there until Kady acknowledged the pup, Kady tapped back. Stroking the little paw, she smiled.

"Well you're a real cutie pie, aren't you?" The little dog was clearly doing its best to look and act irresistibly adorable, even seeming to do a wobbly little dance for Kady.

One of the women from the shelter stopped by. "She's a real sweet dog. We're not certain but we believe Lady is a bocker."

"What's a bocker?" Kady asked, thinking the dog was cuteness personified.

"Part beagle and part cocker spaniel."

"She's definitely a bocker," Aladee confirmed. "Poor little thing has been here more than three months already because nobody wants her."

The woman's head snapped up and her eyebrows pulled together. "That-that's right. How did you know that?"

Clasping her sister-in-law's arm, Kady gave it a gentle squeeze. "Aladee is just one of those people with a close connection to animals," she said before Aladee had a chance to say she was a nymph who communicated telepathically with animals, possibly making the dog shelter woman think they were nuts. "Probably just a feeling she had."

Catching on, Aladee smiled and offered a companionable nod. "Right. Just a feeling, that's all. You probably get them too, working with all these dogs every day."

"Oh...yes, I understand what you mean." The woman's facial expression eased until the angst was replaced by a pleasant smile.

"Well I think Lady is just perfect," Kady said, feeling a special connection with the captivating little dog. There was something special about her Kady couldn't quite put her finger on. She just had an inner knowing that Lady was the one for her. "I think we'd be a wonderful match."

"Before you make a decision," the shelter woman advised, "you should know that one of Lady's back legs is shorter than the others, giving her a limp, and making her sort of wobble when she runs."

"Which is why she hasn't been rescued yet," Kady surmised. "Aw, the poor little thing." Lady did her best at that moment to pluck the strings of Kady's heart, succeeding splendidly.

"Yes, unfortunately," the woman said. "Lady tumbles down a lot as she tries to keep up with the other dogs. But she's got plenty of spirit and determination, as well as a very sweet demeanor."

"Can I speak to you for a moment?" Aladee asked and Kady nodded, excusing them before they stepped a few feet out of the woman's earshot.

Speaking in a subdued voice, Aladee said, "Her name is Izidora Meszaros...Izzy for short."

Kady scrunched her face. "The woman from the shelter?"

"No, the dog."

"What? Aladee, that's not possible. Your animal tuner thing," Kady tapped her temple, "must be screwed up or something. Meszaros is the last name of the family I stayed with while visiting Budapest, remember? I told you about it. You're probably just confusing—"

Shaking her head, Aladee insisted, "I'm not confusing anything. When you were there did you have a palm reading from an old grandma?"

Kady nodded slowly. "Well yes, but—"

"And were you told to expect a good soul named Izidora, described as a female with a limp, to come into your life?"

Nodding again, Kady's eyes went wide. "Holy macaroni..." Leaning in close, she whispered, "Yes but...how could you possibly know that? I thought you said you weren't a psychic."

"I'm not. Izzy told me."

"Whoa...okay, wait...what?" Kady massaged her temples. "You're making my head hurt, Aladee. I don't understand any of this. What's going on? How could a dog in a shelter here in Oregon know anything about what happened between me and the Meszaros family—especially things that specific—when I stayed with them at their bed and breakfast in another country?"

"Izzy also told me your angel grandma, Bekka, arranged for her to be here at this shelter—just for you."

"Oh...that makes me so happy." Looking heavenward, Kady whispered, "Thank you, Grandma Bekka." Taking a deep breath, she fought against the deluge of happy tears threatening to spill.

"Would you like me to take Lady out of her cage so you can visit with her more closely and get to know her?" the woman from the shelter called to them, startling Kady who was in deep confused-concentration mode. "That way you can inspect her leg too. Plus I have a report from our vet that you might like to see."

"Yes, I'd like that," Kady answered. "Thanks."

"Let me just get her cleaned up a little bit and I'll bring her out to you."

Once the woman left, Kady returned her attention to Aladee. "Okay," she began, "so when I was in Budapest, one of the old gypsy grandmas gave me a reading and offered the same information that you just confirmed." She sucked in another deep breath. "Listen, it's no secret that I'm a great believer in otherworldly events but I have to admit, Aladee, that this is way over the top, even for me."

"Gypsy..." Aladee said haltingly. "I'm still trying to learn all of Earth's idiosyncrasies but...isn't that considered a racial slur now? I thought people resent being called gypsies."

"That's what I thought too," Kady agreed, "but the family I stayed with explained to me that the Romani or Roma people are—"

"Do you mean Romanians?" Aladee asked.

"No," Kady shook her head, "that's something entirely different—Romanians are people from Romania, while Romani and Roma people are..." She threw up her hands, completely flummoxed. "I don't know, it really gets confusing. Like sometimes gypsy is capitalized and sometimes it's not." She offered a helpless shrug.

"Anyway, many gypsies and non-gypsies consider the word a slur because of the negative connotations now connected with it, but then others, like the Meszaros family I stayed with, are extremely proud of their rich Gypsy heritage and teach their children to be proud of their background."

"When I communicated with Izzy telepathically," Aladee said, "she told me she was a proud gypsy in a former life. And she still considers herself a gypsy."

"Whoa!" Kady's eyes grew wide. "Hold on a minute...you mean former life as in..." she looked left and right, then whispered, "Izzy was human? The dog used to be a person?" Kady's head shook back and forth slowly as she digested the information. "I mean, I'm open to the concept of reincarnation but...no...uh-uh...no way."

"Yes indeed." Aladee gave a knowing smile. "That's what Izidora told me. She also said she went through her human life with a limp. She was a fortune teller—kind of like you, Kady."

"Holy—"

"In fact, Izzy claims she still is, which is clearly one of the reasons you two share such a close connection."

Unable to say anything intelligible, Kady muttered her disbelief beneath her breath.

"Izzy purposely chose to live this life as a canine," Aladee explained. "As soon as she spotted you here at the shelter she knew you two were meant to be together. Her dead Meszaros ancestors confirmed it."

"Dead Meszaros ancestors..." That had Kady chuckling. It was all so crazy beyond belief it made her head spin. For someone who prided herself about being open-minded, she was having a difficult time accepting all this. However...she couldn't deny the special connection she felt with Izzy, as soon as she'd spotted her.

With an acquiescing sigh, she said, "I have to admit that I felt it too. The old gypsy grandma who gave me the reading in Budapest was a Meszaros family member. She predicted that a kind old soul with a limp would come to live with me one day." Shrugging, Kady said, "I assumed she meant one of my relatives when they got elderly and infirm."

Clawing her fingers, Kady pressed her fingertips against her head before releasing them outward, mimicking an explosion. "Pshewwww," she made the sound to go with her action. "Seriously, Aladee, my mind is blown."

Nodding her agreement, Aladee agreed, "It *is* rather unusual."

Unable to help it, Kady fell into full blown laughter.

Wrapping an arm around her sister-in-law's shoulder, Aladee reminded Kady, "Are you forgetting about all the totally unbelievable things that have occurred in the Malone family, starting with the heartwish rings, angels, ghosts, genies—"

"And *nymphs*," locking gazes with Aladee, Kady cut in, finishing her sentence. Arching one eyebrow, she flicked her wrist, adding, "Etcetera, etcetera. I suppose when you think about it, a gypsy fortune teller reincarnated into a dog isn't really any weirder...right?"

Holding each other's attention for a long moment, the two of them finally cracked up in laughter, just as the woman from the shelter brought an eager tail-wagging Izidora Meszaros to her delighted new owner.

# Chapter 2

## *Sunday Morning*

~<>~

"WELL KATHLEEN Doolan Malone, I've got to hand it to you," Astrid Malone told her daughter. "I can't remember the last time anyone in this family has been able to keep a secret so well. We've all been pumping each other for information," she chuckled, "but it seems everyone's as clueless as I am. So when are we finally going to learn what this," Astrid waved the artsy printed brunch invitation, "is all about?"

"Soon. It's not just one surprise, it's a few." Kady, thoroughly enjoyed being able to pull this special day off without anyone being the wiser. Using her psychic abilities, she'd discerned this morning would be a perfect time to bring everyone together to celebrate the good news she was about to share.

"Aren't those invitations beautiful?" Kady asked. "Sabrina designed them. I explained what I needed and, knowing how much I love paisley and purple, she incorporated them to create the front of the card as well as the inside border." Turning to her sister-in-law, Kady blew her a kiss. "Thanks again, Sabrina."

"My pleasure. I can't wait to see what this is all about!"

Bekka House, the family home and gathering spot, was full, evidenced by all three leaves secured in the long, oak dining table. With everyone Kady had invited, they'd be elbow to elbow at the table if it weren't for the fact that the guys were glued to their football games on TV in the family room.

She'd set up a long folding table for them so they could grab their breakfast sandwiches and slices of Kady's brother Nevan's Irish pork pie to eat in front of the television. Since Nevan owned

9

Half Potato Pub, he'd provided an assortment of craft brews for the guys, and Kady added a big self-serve urn of coffee.

In the dining room, Kady's three sisters, Delaney, Laila, and Reen sat on one side of the table along with her mother, while Kady's sisters-in-law, Aladee, and Sabrina, plus Sabrina's sister, Annalise Griffin, the owner of Griffin's Café, sat on the other side.

Kady reserved seats close to her spot at the head of the table for Glassfloat Bay's dynamic real estate sales team, Saffron Devington and Monica Sharp Griffin who hadn't yet arrived. Newlywed Monica had married Annalise and Sabrina's brother, Hudson Griffin, last year.

Completing the lineup at the dining table was Nancy Sharp, Monica's mother, who positively glowed. Her happy demeanor was so rewarding after overcoming her serious addiction problems, and nearly losing Monica to cancer. With dental implants replacing her drug-damaged teeth, Nancy no longer hid her mouth when she smiled. Previously a dysfunctional duo, mother and daughter were the picture of a loving, caring family unit now.

As the women sipped their beverages, some choosing to lace their coffee with Kahlua, or their tea with brandy, they munched on a variety of mini-scones from Laila's bakery, The Great Pretender. Over their conversations, shouts and groans could be heard from the family room where the guys were camped out.

Kady's two brothers, Gard and Nevan, her stepdad, Tore, and her three brothers-in-law, Varik, Zak, and Drake, were camped out in the family room. During the commercial they shared their joint frustration that Oregon didn't have its own NFL team. Half the guys there rooted for their hometown team, the Chicago Bears, while the others cheered the team closest to Portland, the Seattle Seahawks.

Red Devington, Kady's cousin and Saffron's brother, had traveled to Glassfloat Bay with his life partner, Lonan, in answer to

Kady's invitation. It was the first time the family had seen Red since he moved to Mount Olympus—yes, *that* Mount Olympus—last year and was designated an immortal minor god. Sorely missed, the hearty, welcome reception they received was no surprise.

Red and Lonan, aficionados of opera, ballet, museums, and the arts, seemed to be enjoying themselves as they strived to understand the game the avid football devotees tried to teach them amid all their boisterous cheering, roars, and growling. They weren't alone in their lack of knowledge of the game. Reen's husband, Professor Drake Slattery, shared Red and Lonan's creative interests and was in the same boat. Drake knew as much about football as he did about any sport...practically nothing.

The children were downstairs in the playroom where the family's regular babysitters kept them occupied.

There was nothing Kady loved more than a house full of loving friends and family enjoying their time together. The feeling of joy was almost palpable, creating just the right ambiance she'd hoped for to make her announcements.

After a quick trip to the kitchen, Kady returned with champagne.

"Ooh, the pricey stuff," Delaney noted. "Must be something special."

"It is." Kady poured glasses, letting the guys know they could help themselves if they wanted any. It wasn't a surprise that most chose to stick with the craft brews instead.

Picking her phone up from the table, Kady sent off a couple of texts. When the doorbell rang, she called out, "It's open, come on in!" In walked Monica Sharp Griffin and her husband, Hudson, brother of Annalise and Sabrina. They both sat at the table, with Hud being promised he could join the guys within a few minutes.

The newlyweds were so obviously in love. Kady thought the secret smiles they exchanged were adorable.

Coming upstairs from the finished basement, Saffron Devington walked to the table, cradling something in a small blanket.

"Kady!" Astrid's face was a mask of delighted surprise. "You adopted a baby?" As Astrid rose from her chair, Kady touched her mom's arm, stopping her.

With gentle laughter, she said, "Nope, it's not a baby. However...someone here just might have something to share with you all that has to do with an anticipated bundle of joy." She nodded at Monica, who stood with Hud at her side. Monica's smile was so bright it practically lit the room.

"It's us!" Monica said with an excited giggle as she caressed her midsection. "Hud and I are having a baby. I'm due in five months. Every single one of you wonderful people," Monica's bottom lip trembled and a tear coursed down her cheek as Hud held her close, "have been so loving and supportive after all that's happened, including my miraculous healing from cancer, that Hud and I wanted to share our very happy news with you first."

Joyous congratulatory wishes resounded throughout the room.

"A year ago I didn't think I'd still be alive, much less married to my soul mate and having our baby. Thanks to your generous, unselfish heartwish, Reen, I'm healthy, thriving, and I'm going to be a mommy."

"And I'm going to be a grandma!" her mother, Nancy said, elated.

"How can I ever thank you, Reen?" Monica went to Reen and they embraced, crying happy tears.

"Just by being happy, Monica," Reen answered, "and by enjoying your life to the fullest."

"Will you be our baby's godmother, Reen? Please say yes."

Clapping her chest, Reen broke into a joyful, teary grin. "I'd be honored."

"We just learned it's a little girl," Monica said. "We're naming her Reenan Saffron Griffin, after my friend of the heart, Reen, for obvious reasons, for my mom, Nancy, and for my dearest friend, Saffron." By now all the women dabbed at tears with their napkins.

"I don't know what to say," Reen said. "That's a beautiful name and a beautiful gesture, Monica. Thank you."

"Reenan," Hud repeated with an ear to ear grin. "Get it? It's a combination of Reen's and Nancy's first names," he explained. "Pretty cool, huh?"

"Very cool!" Astrid rose from her chair, drawing the happy couple into her arms for a hug. "Before you go traipsing into the family room to join the guys, Hudson, there's one thing I need to do first."

Lifting his hands in surrender, he chuckled. "I know, I know…"

"It's another Kodak moment," everyone chorused around the table amid laughter while Astrid reached into her cavernous purse and pulled out her vintage Kodak Instamatic camera. Special moments never escaped Astrid's photo taking opportunity.

Once Astrid was satisfied she'd captured the right poses, she informed Hud he was free to join the guys watching football.

Her smile reached her eyes as Monica told him, "You can fill the guys in on our good news at halftime." Hud nodded before planting a sweet kiss on her cheek.

A tiny bark came from the bundle Saffron held.

"Oh! It's a puppy!" Sabrina said.

"Perfect timing," Kady said. "Let me introduce you to surprise number two." Taking the bundle from Saffron's arms, Kady held the small dog up. "Everyone, this is Izzy. Izzy," Kady beamed a mile-wide smile, "this is everyone." Switching to babytalk, she held the dog close, lightly jostling it. "Isn't she just the most precious little thing? Yes you are." She received a lavish face lick in return.

"Now I understand why we're meeting here at Bekka House for Sunday brunch instead of our usual spot." Astrid took her newest granddog from her daughter's arms. "As sweet as you are, Annalise, and as much as you adore dogs, I doubt you'd be too thrilled to have a puppy running around your café."

"I suspect my customers might object to tufts of dog hair topping their cheddar omelets." Annalise chuckled.

After significant cooing and cuddling, Astrid reluctantly passed Izzy to Reen's waiting arms. "Is she a rescue dog?" Astrid asked.

"Yes, from Glassfloat Bay's no-kill shelter," Kady said. "But...I first learned about Izzy while I was in Hungary." She received the surprised and confused reactions she'd expected.

"Don't keep us in suspense," her sister-in-law, Sabrina, said. "What happened?"

"You had some sort of psychic connection with the dog while you were traveling?" Laila guessed.

"I only have psychic connections with people." Kady smiled. "Aladee's the dog whisperer in our family."

"So what happened in Hungary?" Annalise asked.

"It was the last place I visited on my overseas backpacking trip. My favorite places to stay were always the rooms in people's homes that they let to travelers. Meals were almost always included. Good homemade traditional foods you don't find in restaurants. The meals I enjoyed most were when I was invited to eat with the families. I met so many wonderful people and learned so many things that way."

"So you stayed with a family in Budapest?" Delaney asked.

"The Meszaros family," Kady said, "in their ancestral home which has been there for hundreds of years. They keep building onto it, similar to what we've been doing here with Bekka House."

"Imagine what this place will look like in a hundred years," Laila said with a dreamy look. "Private passages and hidden staircases galore."

"And private reading nooks filled with books," Annalise added.

"The family I stayed with included parents, grandparents, great-grandparents, plus children of all ages. The food was," Kady's eyelids fluttered closed, "amazing. I confess to ample cheating on my vegan way of eating. The stuffed cabbage rolls were outrageously good. The Dobosh tortes? To die for. Multilayers of impossibly thin cake with fillings of buttercreams, caramel, chocolate...I'm salivating just thinking about it."

"If your genes didn't keep you naturally thin," Saffron said, "you probably would have gone up a good three sizes."

Checking the jeans she wore and patting her thighs, Aladee's eyebrows furrowed. "Jeans keep us thin?"

Amid gentle chuckling, Astrid explained, "Consider that one more bit of colloquialism you have to learn." Nevan's wife had come a long way since she took up residency on Earth from Mount Olympus, but it was tough learning the thousands of sayings Americans were used to.

"I emailed you the Meszaros family's recipe for Dobosh torte," Kady told Laila.

"I don't know if I'm up to the task."

"Oh please." Kady gave a dismissive wave. "Laila, you're the best baker I know. Even without using my psychic abilities," she winked, "I can safely predict we can all expect to enjoy Dobosh tortes this holiday season."

"I'd love for you to do that, Laila," Delaney said. "I'll write one of my Delaney's Diary articles about you and the Meszaros family's food traditions."

"Perfect," Kady said. "I took plenty of notes and made recordings too. I have lots of good material for you, Delaney."

"Izzy is adorable." Reen nuzzled the little dog, making babytalk. "She seems so comfortable and at ease with all of us already. Do you know what kind of mix she is? Part cocker spaniel, maybe?"

"She's a bocker, part beagle and part cocker spaniel," Kady said. "Sometimes they're called speagles."

"I've never heard of bockers or speagles. Too cute!" Monica leaned over to scratch the pup behind the ears. "Did you learn that from the Meszaros family?"

"No, they didn't know. The vet at the shelter told me he suspected it and I could do a DNA test to confirm but it wasn't necessary because I have something much better than a doggy DNA test, I have—"

"You have Aladee!" Saffron cut in, making a *Tada!* gesture toward Nevan's bride.

"That's right!" Delaney laughed. "I mean, all Aladee had to do was ask the dog, right?" Closing her eyes, she shook her head back and forth. "Honestly, it's going to take me a hell of a long time coming to terms about my sister-in-law's ability to communicate with animals."

"It comes naturally to me." Aladee offered a nonchalant shrug. "I've been doing it all my life. All nymphs have that ability."

"Of course they do," Delaney teased, still chuckling. Clasping her sister-in-law's arm, she gave a warm smile. "I don't mean to laugh or make fun, Aladee...it's just that it's *really* difficult to get used to your amazing skills. Let's face it, not everybody in Glassfloat Bay has a nymph from Mount Olympus in the family."

"I take no offense," Aladee assured. "Nevan explained the habit of teasing and what it means. He's quite the expert at it himself in fact."

"You know my son well." Laughing, Astrid bit into a mini-scone. "Oh, honey," she said to Laila, swallowing her mouthful, "this one is scrumptious. Is that spiced chai flavor? And are these little chips butterscotch?"

"You're spot on about the chai spice, and close about the butterscotch," Laila said. "Salted caramel chips, and I added spiced pecans."

Astrid's eyes fluttered shut. "If only these were part of your bakery's lower calorie offerings I'd be in seventh heaven."

"Well start flapping your angel wings, Mom, because they are." Laila chuckled as she watched her mother's eyes pop wide.

"No!" Astrid said, her mouth still full, which was unlike her. Covering her mouth with her hand, she laughed. "Sorry, I couldn't help it. I'm absolutely stunned."

"Unbelievable." Reen bit into one herself. "Fabulous."

"The salted caramel chips are sugar-free," Laila told them. "And I used part sugar and part sugar alternatives for the dough. The hardest part when making scones is reducing the fat content while still maintaining the buttery texture people expect."

"You aced it, Laila." Annalise reached for another scone.

"Careful not to let Izzy get any," Kady cautioned. "They're not good for her."

"Izzy," Reen said thoughtfully. "Cute name. Why did you choose it?" She passed the dog into Delaney's waiting arms as Delaney wiggled her fingers in invitation.

"It's short for Izidora." Kady beamed a bright smile. "Izidora Meszaros."

"Well, that's a mouthful," Sabrina noted with a chuckle. "How did you come up with that?"

"You won't believe this—" Kady started and everyone at the table laughed.

"Yes we will," her sister, Laila assured. "We know you and Aladee, remember?"

"The one thing we know not to expect from you and my new daughter-in-law," Astrid said, "are bland, mundane responses. No doubt you're going to tell us Aladee communicated with Izzy telepathically, right?"

Scooting forward in her chair, Kady grinned. "You should have seen it. I knew my own intuition would be strong when it came to choosing a dog but combined with Aladee's skills, it was infallible. There were more than a dozen dogs when we went and," she breathed a hefty sigh, "I wanted to take all of them home, but," she shrugged, "well, you know..."

"Tell them about your grandma," Aladee urged.

"Oh, right! Izzy communicated that Grandma Bekka is responsible for us finding each other."

"So Mom's been at it again, hmm?" Astrid's eyes misted and she smiled. Looking up, she added, "Thanks, Mama."

Glancing around the table, Aladee smiled. "Izzy revealed to me that she..." she paused for dramatic effect, "is a reincarnated human."

"Come on," Sabrina tsked, "you're just making that up."

"Truth. Scouts honor." Kady raised three fingers of her right hand with her thumb holding down the pinky.

"You weren't in the scouts, dear, that was your sister, Delaney," Astrid reminded her, which was met with laughter.

"A reincarnated human. That's...I don't know," Laila's expression twisted, "cool but weird. I don't know if I want to come back as a dog. No offense, Izzy."

"She says none taken," Aladee related with a smile. "It doesn't happen to everyone, only if the soul chooses it. The closest friend Izidora Meszaros had while human was her own beloved dog. Izidora was a gypsy in her former life. Both she and her dog were gifted psychics."

"Wait..." Astrid scrunched her eyebrows, "Izzy's dog was a psychic too? I consider myself broad-minded, Aladee, but the dog being a psychic and Izzy being a reincarnated human?" She pressed her lips together. "I don't know."

"I understand," Aladee nodded, "it's a lot to ponder."

After more discussion, questions and answers as the women sipped their liqueur-laced coffees and munched on scones and pastry-wrapped breakfast sausage, Aladee became teary-eyed.

"I can't begin to tell you all how much I love this," she said. "It's so wonderful.

"What, honey?" Astrid placed her hand on her daughter-in-law's arm. "The spiked coffee or the food?"

"No, being here with all of you." Aladee gave in to soft laughter. "It's going to take time to get used to being part of a big family. You've all made me feel so welcome. Thank you." The women offered their assurance that they were delighted Aladee was one of them now.

"You're are all so creative," Aladee noted. "Laila with her baking. Reen, with knitting and crochet. Kady with her psychic abilities, and Delaney with her amusing *Delaney's Diary* column and books."

"Don't forget about your mother-in-law. I'm extremely creative too." Astrid had a teasing gleam in her eye. "I've perfected the art of being able to successfully hide all my treasured collectibles."

"She means her secondhand junk," Reen clarified with a snicker.

"You're one to talk." Kady elbowed Reen. "You're just as bad as Mom. Maybe worse."

"Me?" Fluttering her eyelashes, Reen's hand flew to her chest, making Kady laugh. There was no way Reen could deny Kady's claim after Reen had artfully decorated hers and Drake's entire house with secondhand finds.

"It's so cute," Laila teased her sister, "how you can so perfectly playact the role of a *normal person*," she made air quotes, "who isn't a diehard junk collector...someone who doesn't haunt thrift shops, and garage sales, and estate sales, and—"

"Okay, okay!" Reen's hands lifted in contrite surrender as she laughed. "Point taken."

"What is it you all collect?" Aladee asked.

"Oh my dear," Astrid's expression turned blissful, "just wait until garage sale season starts in the spring. We'll introduce you to the many joys of rummaging through people's discards. You have no idea of the wonders that await you."

"Mom's talking about garbage picking," Kady joked. "She excels at it. As they say, one man's trash is another's treasure." Her hand flit through the air in a nonchalant wave.

"Okay, Miss-I-Collect-All-Things-Hippie-and-Flower-Child-Related," Reen teased Kady, with Astrid joining in her laughter. "Not to mention all the incense sticks, the crystals, the hanging beads," she counted on her fingers, "and the rest of the useless New-Agey stuff you search for. Don't try to pretend you're not as hooked as the rest of us."

"Well, after all, it *is* the Age of Aquarius." Kady winked.

"So when we do this secondhand shopping," Aladee began, looking none too eager, "we will pick through people's garbage...and pay them for it?"

Hearty chuckling spread around the table.

"Ouch. Aladee has just described us all, ladies," Kady admitted.

"That would definitely be Drake's definition," Reen said about her husband, "as well as our brothers."

"Tore's the same way," Astrid said of her husband, the girls' stepfather. "He's kindly offered to use his no fail organizational skills for all my collectibles." After pausing for effect, she explained,

"His helpful suggestion is using a blowtorch to scale down all my precious finds."

"I'm convinced the men in our family must talk," Reen said, "because I've heard the same *helpful* suggestion from Drake."

"Remember the fun you had shopping at the mall for the first time, Aladee?" Kady asked. With a ready smile, Aladee nodded. "It's like that, but better because you can find awesome things that aren't available in retail stores. It gets addicting."

"I'm sure I'll enjoy it immensely." With an uncertain expression and valiant attempt at a smile, Aladee added, "I look forward to learning how to appreciate the value of other people's garbage." She was clearly too new to the family to feel comfortable being anything but polite. Kady figured they'd have her broken in soon.

"Does Nevan enjoy garbage shopping too?" Aladee asked of her new husband.

There was a burst of laughter.

"Nevan's going to kill us," Kady noted aloud. "Your husband's got an undeniable distaste for garage sales, thrift stores, and estate sales, Aladee."

Kady decided it was time to present the rest of her news. Nodding at Saffron, Kady stood and lifted her champagne glass. Saffron did the same.

"I told you there were several reasons for our brunch today. I'm pleased to report that my dream of owning a bookshop is now a reality."

There were surprised gasps of delight.

"And I'm happy to announce," Kady continued, barely able to contain her joy, "that my dear cousin and good friend, Saffron Devington, is my full business partner and co-owner of Cherished Pages Bookshop. Please join us in a toast! Pregnant Monica—your glass contains sparkling apple juice." Kady grinned, while also filling Nancy's glass with juice as Nancy held it aloft to indicate her preference for a non-alcoholic drink.

Kady clinked her glass against Saffron's while everyone around the table clinked theirs together, toasting "*Cheers!*"

"That's sensational!" Astrid said. "How could I not know this?"

"We worked hard to keep it a secret, Aunt Astrid," Saffron said. "I had a lot to tie up with my real estate broker before everyone found out."

"No more real estate?" Reen asked.

"I'll keep my license so I can still practice, but selling real estate's no longer my career."

"Saffron and I had a long heart-to-heart," Monica said. "After my near-death health scare last year, my priorities changed. Significantly. I've been a hard-hitting, dedicated real estate agent for years now, but after my healing experience I realized I no longer have that killer salesperson instinct." She smiled. "Listing and selling properties no longer gives me a feeling of satisfaction."

"I immediately understood how Monica felt because I'd been feeling the same way," Saffron said. "So the timing was perfect. You need to develop an aggressive personality to compete and succeed in real estate. While I'd developed the necessary skills to thrive in the business, my heart isn't in it anymore. Once I'd confided in Kady about my love of books, my nearly becoming a librarian, and my dream of owning a little bookshop, *boom*, we set things in motion."

"And *voila*!" Kady boasted a smile. "With our combined skills, abilities, and love of books and reading, we know we can operate a successful, thriving business—loving what we're doing at the same time."

"Congratulations to you both!" Delaney lifted her glass to them again. "This is just the sort of news I'm always looking for to add to my column."

"Count on me for your art and graphics needs," Sabrina offered. "I'm designing websites now too, so I can help with that. Did you guys see the site I created for Nevan's Half Potato Pub?"

"Great job!" Laila said.

"Nevan loves it," Aladee agreed. "You're such a talented artist, Sabrina."

"I know you like a retro feel, Kady, and I have, oh..." Astrid's smile stretched wide, "just a few vintage knickknacks and items you might want to use, if Saffron's on the same page, of course. Don't worry, Saffron, I won't be offended if you'd rather I didn't help."

Coming to Astrid's chair, Saffron bent to capture her aunt in a loving hug. "I'd love to have your participation. Throughout all the trouble with my frustrating family, you've never been anything but kind, supportive and encouraging to me and my brother. I love you for that and appreciate it more than you'll ever know."

Quickly waving her hand through the air, Astrid said, "Oh now you're going to make me cry." She tightened their hug, offering Saffron the love and positivity Astrid was known for.

"I'm here for all your catering needs," Annalise chimed in, raising her hand. "Whether it's a big affair, or a small luncheon, whatever you need."

"Thank you so much, Annalise," Kady said, with Saffron echoing her remarks.

"Have you considered including a little coffee and scone area for your customers?" Laila asked with an expectant smile. "With some cute ice cream table and chair sets set up in a corner?"

"Being the best damn baker in the Pacific Northwest," Saffron noted, pointing at Laila, "you, my cousin and friend, are already on our list."

"I've been making bookmarks for years and giving them as gifts," Monica's mother, Nancy, said. "I'd be happy to make some for Cherished Pages."

"They're really eye-catching," Monica said. "Unique designs." She reached over, clasping her mother's hand.

After exchanging smiles with Saffron, Kady said, "Well that settles it. There's no possible way you and I won't have the absolute best bookshop on the Oregon coast, partner." Reaching across the table, the pair shook hands.

# Chapter 3

~<>~

"I WENT TO THE bank last week and met with Uncle Walter about taking out a small business loan for our bookshop," Kady said. "You know how he loves to talk." She made a jabbering motion with her fingers. "I just let him go on and on, impressing me with how much he knows about anything and everything related to money and banking."

"Walter?" Astrid bristled visibly at the sound of his name. "But why? Tore and I already told you we'd be happy to loan you whatever you need. Do you really want to be indebted to Walter Devington, especially after everything that man did to his son?" Astrid shuddered, then shifted her attention to her niece. "I'm sorry, Saffron, I don't mean to offend. I know he's your father, honey, but..."

"Trust me, Aunt Astrid, I'm fully cognizant of my father's frustrating and appalling traits. There's no need to apologize whatsoever. Dad and I haven't been on the best of terms since he disowned Red. I mean, really...what's there left to say? The man is stubborn as an ox."

Astrid reached over to squeeze Saffron's hand. "I'm sorry about the rift in your family, dear. I'm sure it's not easy." Astrid's eyes narrowed as she looked off into space. "Walter Devington," she said again with another shudder.

Kady's suppressed laughter surfaced. "You make it sound like I made a backstreet deal with some loan shark, Mom."

"I was thinking more like the devil," Astrid quipped. "I can't understand why you'd choose to have anything to do with him after he disowned my nephew...your cousin, Saffron's brother." Astrid grumbled beneath her breath.

"I have a master plan," Kady confessed.

There was a brief silence around the table as everyone digested the uncomfortable new information about Walter Devington, the husband of Sean Malone's sister, Colleen.

Astrid's late husband, Sean, was a firefighter who died in the line of duty when their children were small, leaving Astrid a single mom raising six children. While Colleen Malone Devington was once a pleasant, down to earth woman, according to Astrid, her main interest was in social climbing, and marrying someone with money so she'd never have to work again and could afford to buy whatever she wanted. She'd succeeded on all counts, leaving her former friends and family in the dust since she now perceived them as being beneath her.

Astrid said Colleen Devington was nearly unrecognizable now as the friendly, agreeable woman she first knew as Sean Malone's sister years ago.

"When I met with Uncle Walter," Kady told them, "he was endlessly blabbing as I asked him question after question, doing my best to make him feel important. By the time I was finished he was so puffed up with self-importance, I swear, he looked like a blowfish." Bugging her eyes, Kady filled her cheeks with air, making Astrid laugh.

"That's my father all right." Saffron laughed too.

"I told him I want to learn from him because he's so wise and knowledgeable and has so much wonderful information to share, blah, blah, blah. Before I knew it, he'd suggested I come stay with him, Aunt Colleen, and Lorraine until my apartment over the bookshop is ready."

"What?! Oh good grief!" Astrid covered her forehead with her hand. "Kathleen, you can't possibly be serious."

"Uh-oh, better watch out if Mom's calling you *Kathleen*." Reen failed to hold back her rising laughter.

"Your sister Lorraine is still living there?" Astrid barreled ahead with a pointed look at Saffron. "Red's very own sister who turned her back on your poor brother when he came out to them?"

"Yes," Saffron nodded, "Lorraine—"

"She treated Redmond no better than her parents did," Astrid added. "And—" She stopped suddenly, her head tilting to the side as she glanced at the guys watching football. "Does Red know you've been talking with his father?"

"No," Kady answered swiftly. "When he and Lonan arrived for their visit, Red looked so happy and content, I didn't want to spoil that."

"I still can't believe Aunt Colleen and Uncle Walter gave Red the heave-ho via text message." Reen's eyebrow lifted. "And while Red was in Ireland on vacation, no less." With the mug halfway to her mouth, the coffee in it sloshed as Reen shuddered. "Ugh, so cold and calculating. Can you imagine treating your own flesh and blood that way? They wiped poor Red clear off their slate," her hand flew off to the right, "like he was nothing but a bothersome chalk mark."

"Um, Mom," Kady started, "what's that evil grin for?"

"I was just thinking about how my nephew's elitist mother and father will react when they learn the son they disowned is now an immortal minor god living on Mount Olympus—along with an accomplished and revered god...who also happens to be gay." Astrid's wicked grin turned joyful. "I can picture Colleen ordering her staff to get out the good china, silverware, and crystal for Red's visit."

Polite laughter erupted around the table.

"Red was incredibly kind and helpful to me when I arrived here in Glassfloat Bay," Aladee said, licking whipped cream from her upper lip after sipping from her gently spiked coffee. "He's wonderfully funny, always doing his best to keep people smiling. I don't understand why his family rejected him."

"Here on Earth," Astrid said, "people can be unfairly judgmental regarding," her hands shot up and out, "basically *anything* that may make them different from the accepted norm."

"My father is also angry because Red left what Dad considers an excellent position at the bank to pursue his dream of being a florist," Saffron explained.

"Sadly, our cousin, Lorraine, mimics her parents' views," Reen added. "With the exception of Saffron," she extended a broad smile her cousin's way, "who happens to be one of Red's biggest supporters, the stuffy, snooty, ridiculously wealthy Devingtons feel they're superior. Better than everyone else."

Nodding, Aladee said, "I do have an understanding of prejudice and bigotry. On Mount Olympus there's often bickering among the gods regarding the acceptance of this creature or that and—" She stopped and smiled. "I should clarify...the residents of Olympus are not only humans. All manner of creatures reside there. Some are more readily accepted than others. So, such narrow thinking isn't exclusive to Earth."

"That makes sense." Astrid nodded before returning her attention to her daughter. "Kady, I can't believe you'll actually be accepting a bank loan from your uncle and living in that mansion with those awful people. For heaven's sake, you'll—"

"Mom..."

"...be eaten alive by the Devingtons. They'll—"

"Mom..."

"...destroy your wonderful, kind spirit, they'll—"

"Mom!"

Astrid started. "What!?"

"I didn't say I was taking the loan or staying with them," Kady said with a smile. "I just said we talked, that's all."

"You stinker," Astrid said, expelling a sigh of relief. "You had me going there."

"Well," Kady continued, "as I manifested my psychic self talk, vibes, both positive and toxic, became nearly palpable. Achieving a state of cosmic consciousness I realized Uncle Walter is most likely working through his karma. That, of course, causes him to exist on a different spiritual plane, which tells me the universe clearly has other intentions, so—"

"Kady," Astrid interrupted her daughter. "Speak English, honey," she said with a kind smile and the others chuckled.

"Oh...sorry." With a thoughtful smile, Kady explained, "I mean I never really had any intention of taking out a loan from Uncle Walter's bank, and it wasn't necessary for me to move into Devington Manor because Hud and his crew did an amazing job completing needed repairs and bringing things up to code in my apartment over the bookshop. I never expected them to finish so quickly."

"Ohhhh...so *that's* what you said," Reen teased, with Kady accepting it good-naturedly.

"Hud made Kady's apartment a priority," his wife, Monica, said with a smile.

"I appreciate it so much, Monica. Just as I was about to call Uncle Walter to accept his offer, I got Hudson's text, telling me the apartment was ready. Coincidence? I think not. It was the universe effectively communicating not to temporarily move into Devington Manor because I might face obstacles threatening to tamper with my positivity if I tried to manifest—" Kady stopped short at the sound of Izzy's extended yawn, which got everyone laughing.

"Okay, okay, I get it," Kady said through laughter of her own. "I'm even making my own dog zone out."

"Well thank goodness you won't be staying with your aunt and uncle, or taking a business loan from Walter's bank," Astrid said, relaxing against the back of her chair. "I can't tell you how relieved I am."

"See? You had a conniption fit for nothing, Mom—*and* you called me *Kathleen* for no good reason."

Everyone laughed at Kady's words, although it took Astrid a little longer to get in the spirit of her daughter's humor.

"I'd say I had ample reason," Astrid claimed, tongue-in-cheek.

"My reasoning for this is to do what I can to bring Red's family back together and have them accept him," Kady explained.

"Oh, honey," Astrid looked sympathetic, "that's a tall order."

"I realize that now," Kady admitted. "Uncle Walter and Aunt Colleen have been this way longer than I've been alive so me trying to change them would be difficult. Now, Lorraine, on the other hand—"

"Kathleen, you're a glutton for punishment," Astrid said through a resigned sigh.

"Just hear me out," Kady said. "You heard Lorraine got engaged, right?"

Half the people at the table knew, the other half didn't.

"Well, instead of staying at Devington Manor and working on the Devingtons there, I decided to start on a smaller scale by inviting Lorraine and her fiancé to an engagement celebration dinner at my apartment. Lorraine, uh, accepted, advising me it would have to be after the holidays because her social calendar is full."

Laughing at that, Reen nearly spit out what was left of her champagne.

"It's actually good," Kady said. "That'll give me time to fix up my apartment and to plan my family-fixing strategy, as well as give me and Saffron a chance to get our bookshop operational."

"Will, um, you be doing the cooking, Kady?" Delaney asked tentatively.

Kady caught the others exchanging furtive glances. With a reconciled expression, she chuckled.

"Hey guys, I'm not completely oblivious to my lack of expertise in the kitchen. I get that none of you really like my healthy vegan options, only tolerating them so you don't hurt my feelings, which I appreciate." She offered a sincere smile. "So I've asked Saffron to prepare a selection of her vegan and vegetarian specialties for that evening."

"Mmm, they're so good," Monica said. "Even Hud, who's a serious meat lover, really enjoys Saffron's cooking."

"I didn't know you were a vegan, Saffron," Annalise said.

"I'm not, but I do enjoy vegan food now and then. I make a mean falafel sandwich and the best garlicky hummus too." She grinned.

Sabrina raised her hand. "I can attest to that."

"So, with a whole heaping bunch of love and patience, just like you've always shown all of your children, Mom," Kady gave Astrid's hand a squeeze, "I hope to start with Lorraine in my quest to help heal the Devingtons. At least to the point that they'll remember how dearly they love their only son...their gay, non-banker, florist son who grew into a fine, admirable man they *should* be proud of."

Making sure to modulate her voice so it didn't carry to the guys in the family room, Kady put a finger to her lips, indicating she wanted to keep this quiet.

"My plan is to bring Aunt Colleen, Uncle Walter, and Lorraine to a point of loving acceptance *before* they find out Red is now living a charmed life, with an amazing partner who cherishes him. More than anything, I want Red to know his parents and sister love him for who he is, rather than what he's achieved or what he has now—which is a rich, charmed, happy life that's unlike anything the Devingtons can ever hope to aspire to, regardless of how much money they have."

"They'll never be gods, that's for sure," Laila said with a smile.

"My sweet Kady, why am I not surprised? You've always been loving, bighearted and far too naïve and trusting. I'm just worried you'll be hurt." Astrid wiped a tear from her eye. "You always believe the best in everyone, even when they're determined to show you their most unkind side. But Lorraine—" Astrid stopped abruptly.

Kady slanted her mother a questioning look. "What about Lorraine?"

Hesitating, Astrid looked at Saffron, who gave a near imperceptible nod.

"It's okay, Aunt Astrid," Saffron said. "Go ahead. It's important that Kady is alert to any possible problems on the horizon."

"I didn't want to reveal anything Saffron and I spoke privately about regarding her sister without her consent first." Astrid clutched her niece's hand and smiled. "I just want you to be aware, Kady, that Lorraine has some...issues."

"Aunt Astrid is trying to find a nice way to say major personality disorder," Saffron clarified with a resigned shrug.

"She's my niece and I love her," Astrid continued, "but I would advise caution. I've always felt Lorraine isn't necessarily who she seems to be. Even as a young child she could be quite calculating, so be...aware."

"Mom's right, Kady," Delaney added. "None of us want to see you get hurt. Mom's way too nice to say her niece can be a real bitch."

"Oh dear, no." Astrid let out a little gasp. "I would never say that."

"Right, which is why Delaney said it for you," Reen quipped.

"No one knows Lorraine better than I do," Saffron said. "I'll do everything in my power not to let Kady get hurt."

"Guys, I'm not a baby!" Kady reminded everyone. "I'm a grown woman who's traveled all over the world—totally on her own, I might add—and knows how to take care of herself."

"You'll always be my baby," Astrid told the youngest of her six children, blowing her a kiss.

"I know, Mom." Kady gave a reconciled laugh. "Look everyone, I'll be careful. I promise. I'm well aware of Lorraine's antagonistic personality. Did you ever think that maybe she just needs some love and kindness to change her ways?"

Groaning and grumbling sounded around the table.

"Don't be so negative." With a sigh of frustration, Kady told them, "The power of kindness is amazing. It's my plan to reunite our family, to help the Devingtons rediscover their more loving and caring side. I wholeheartedly believe they still have that good side. It's just been buried beneath years of prejudice and bigotry."

"If anyone can do it," Reen said, "you can, Kady."

At Reen's comment, Izzy spoke up, offering a supportive little bark.

"Izzy says she wholeheartedly agrees," Aladee told everyone. "But she also urges caution when it comes to dealing with the Devingtons, especially Lorraine. She senses Lorraine could pose a serious problem."

"Sheesh, even my dog is worried about me." Sensing all the support and encouragement emanating from friends, family, and her adorable little psychic dog, Kady closed her eyes, hoping and praying she'd succeed in making a positive difference.

# Chapter 4

### *Four Months Later*

~<>~

MORE THAN EIGHT hundred years after Hildegard von Bingen's death, the mystic's serene music gently reverberated throughout Kady's apartment. While the soothing ambience of the playlist she'd selected was painstakingly orchestrated to promote relaxation and a positive vibe, an air of tension and conflict intruded. Breathing in a calming medley of lavender scented incense, candles, and essential oil, Kady tried to ignore the encroaching negativity by humming along with Hildegard's serene chants.

It wasn't working.

Unfortunately, no amount of esoteric healing influences could keep the space from prickling with Kady's indignation—even at eight o'clock in the morning.

"My own cousin, Reen. How could Lorraine do this?" Pacing furiously from living room to kitchen, she waved the printed email clutched in her fist as she FaceTimed with her sister on the phone. Showing concern, Izzy followed at Kady's heels. "I woke up to discover she had the audacity to email me an itemized list of do's and don'ts—on the morning of my dinner party, no less."

"Oh boy..."

"I'm starting to think Mom and everyone else was right about Lorraine," she grudgingly admitted while rearranging the ceramic Isis salt and pepper shakers for the umpteenth time. "The woman seems impervious to the positive effects of kindness. I've tried and tried, but haven't made any progress. None. I'm sorry I ever invited her and her egghead fiancé for dinner. I should have waited to meet him at the wedding like she suggested."

"It's not like you didn't know Lorraine was a bitch before you invited her, so it shouldn't come as a big surprise," Reen countered. "I mean, we all warned you, Kady."

"And I was too stubborn to listen. Lorraine's made it clear she thinks I'm a monumental embarrassment."

"Join the club." Reen chuckled. "None of us Malones are worthy."

"Well then I'm in good company." Attempting a lighthearted chuckle, Kady blinked back tears while her chin trembled along with the salt and pepper shakers beneath her fingertips. She was angry with herself for not having more control over her emotions. It was exceedingly rare for her to give in to negativity.

"I need to remind myself I'm on a mission and must adhere to my objective," Kady told her sister, "regardless of how asinine or belittling Lorraine might be. It takes a lot to yank me out of my positive mindset, or instill me with pessimism or unkind thoughts but—"

"But these aren't normal circumstances," Reen finished for her. "If it makes you feel any better, it's her...not you."

It was gratifying to speak to someone who truly understood. "Lorraine gets under my skin. She has a particular way about her that frustrates me, Reen. The nicer I am toward her, the more annoying she becomes. That's crazy. I don't know how Saffron managed to put up with her snooty holier than thou sister all these years."

"Yeah, I used to think Saffron was bad," Reen agreed, "but even at her worst, Saffy was never that asinine. Lorraine would make a perfect sovereign, taking unbridled joy in ordering one head-lopping after another if her subjects displeased her."

Compelling herself to tune in to the melodic chants surrounding her, Kady drew in a deep breath, exhaling it slowly. After the third such set, she smiled. "There. That's much better."

"What?"

"I took some cleansing breaths."

"Oh...yeah...okay..."

That made Kady smile. She didn't mind that her friends and family found her somewhat peculiar and didn't really get what she was talking about much of the time. As long as she knew they loved her, she was fine with it. And one thing Kathleen Doolan Malone never doubted was the powerful sensation of unconditional love surrounding her.

"Namaste," Kady offered in return, stifling a giggle at the silence on the other end of the line.

"Um...and also with you," Reen finally said, repeating the reply they'd learned to give the pastor in church during the liturgy while growing up. A moment later the sisters were giggling.

"That's actually a good response to namaste," Kady told her as her fingers settled on the covered butter dish. "I unpacked those unusual kitchen ceramics you and I found at that phenomenal Beauregard Hill estate sale last year."

"Ooh, awesome sale. It was the last day and everything was marked down, which is the only reason we could afford anything there."

"We were in seventh heaven. You found all those knitting supplies and I found this." Kady turned the phone screen toward the object. "Remember? It's the gilt-edged replica of an Egyptian sarcophagus."

"Right! So cool! And you got it cheap too."

"Marked down from fifty dollars to five," Kady recalled. "Probably because no one else wanted it. Their loss." Shrugging, she studied the items she'd placed together on the table. A devilish smile took hold. "Lorraine's going to hate this. Which is why I'm putting it at the center of the table, right along with the sugar bowl and creamer."

"The ones I said look like burial urns?" Reen asked.

"Yup. Should I mention to Lorraine they're museum replicas of canopic jars?" Kady picked up the creamer, pretending to pour. "A little mummified heart and spleen with your coffee, cousin dear?"

Reen cracked up with laughter. "I'd love to see that."

Kady indulged in some snickering before returning her attention to Lorraine's email. "Listen to this one, Reen." Her silver bangle bracelets clattered as she jiggled the paper at the phone. "Rule number three, no palm reading or tarot cards. Then another of Lorraine's endless regulations prohibits any inane babbling about the merits of romance novels. Babbling? I do *not* babble."

Kady's lip curled into a semi smile as she and Reen locked gazes.

Looking down at the dog who'd let out an odd huff, Kady told Reen, "Okay, Izzy's looking at me the same way you are. I guess I don't have to communicate with animals telepathically to know what she's trying to tell me." She chuckled. "So maybe I do babble occasionally, but it certainly isn't inane." Mumbling, she skimmed Lorraine's list with her fingertip, tapping a glittery violet fingernail against the paper when she'd caught the next source of irritation.

"Here, Lorraine states she doesn't want any ridiculous psychic displays from my dog." Giving Izzy a wide-eyed expression, Kady said, "Ridiculous? Seriously, how can she possibly call Izzy's unique gift ridiculous?"

"Uh...you might want to give Lorraine a pass on that one, Kady. The idea of a psychic dog is kind of far out, you know?"

Grumbling an inaudible reply, Kady scanned the paper, poking at the next offensive tidbit. "Avoid overzealous discussion about the ridiculous plotlines of any romance novels I'm forever championing. *Ridiculous*. There's that word again. Just because Lorraine chooses not to read romance is no reason for her to insist on labeling the entire genre ridiculous."

"Lorraine's never been a book lover," Reen said. "The last book she probably read was Dr. Seuss."

Kady headed for her bedroom, where she smoothed the fringed silk throw at the foot of her bed. A curious combination of regal and eccentric in its purple paisley design, it was one of her favorite estate sale finds.

"Love that! So pretty," Reen said when Kady showed her.

Noticing her slippers peeking out beneath the bed, Kady nudged them with her toe, sliding them a little further, out of sight.

"For Lorraine to say that about romance books, knowing full well I co-own a shop offering new and used romance novels, is unkind. And rude." She kicked at a slipper too vigorously, banging her ankle on the bed frame in return. "Honestly," she winced, rubbing her ankle, "what would Cherished Pages Bookshop be without romance books, or our popular palm readings or tarot card sessions? Customers love that."

"I totally agree. You put on a really interesting, unique show for your customers."

Shoulders slumped, Kady sat on the edge of her bed, feeling uncustomarily defeated hours before Lorraine and her fiancé were due to arrive. Izzy leapt into her lap, licking Kady's cheek as Kady bent to cuddle her dog. Izzy always knew how to make her feel better. One of Kady's favorite parts of the week was meeting with Aladee over coffee and listening with rapt attention to the uplifting and understanding messages Izzy provided through her sister-in-law's telepathic abilities.

"What the hell does Lorraine expect me to talk about, the weather?" Kady's fingertip absently trailed the paisley design through the silk.

"Probably," Reen said. "It's a safe enough discussion. *They say rain is predicted for tomorrow. Goodness me, rain? Here at the Oregon coast? My, my, how utterly fascinating.*"

"While that may be an exaggeration," Kady said, "I imagine Lorraine would prefer such banter to a stimulating conversation involving anything even remotely out of the ordinary."

"You could talk about her dear friends Muffy and Bunny and the rest of her tiresome social circle with their silly Mother Goose names, homogenized lifestyles and substantial mansions."

Kady smiled at that. "I don't know how I'll survive if I have to sit through a tedious discussion about tennis scores, the distressing shortage of good domestic help, or how damned difficult it is for Lorraine and her friends to find the latest designer dresses in a size zero."

Cradling Izzy's head with her hands, Kady looked into her dog's big brown eyes. "Did you hear that, Izzy? Zero." Shifting her attention back to her sister, Kady said, "How can anyone fit into a dress size that isn't even a number? No wonder Lorraine shudders at the mere mention of Laila's scones, or anything else with more than a dozen calories. I can't help but wonder if there's anything for her fiancé to grab onto."

That had Reen dissolving into laughter.

Kady's emotions were all over the place because a moment later her eyes stung and her cheeks heated. She wasn't sure if she was more angry than hurt concerning Lorraine's cautionary email, but she was fairly certain if she had steam vents, they'd be discharging now.

Izzy moved from Kady's lap to sit next to her on the bed, focusing her soulful eyes and full attention on her best friend. She knew better than to speak when Kady got like this. Her sweet rescue dog was incredibly intuitive.

Kady rose from the bed, neatly smoothing the throw. The lavender and indigo-blue far-eastern style rug couldn't mask the creaking of old tongue and groove floorboards as Kady paced from her bedroom to the living room.

Moving the tall Kuan Yin statue from one table to another and back again, Kady took a step back to study it.

"Which is better?"

"It looks fine wherever you decide to put it," Reen answered.

"She's the Buddhist goddess of mercy and compassion," Kady mused. "Do you think I'd still be able to consider myself a peace lover if I tried to knock some sense into Lorraine by hitting her over the head with this?" The utterly juvenile idea made her laugh.

"I'm telling Mom," Reen teased, making Kady laugh harder.

"I don't care if my cousin thinks I'm a loony oddball, to use her expression. I'm used to that, Reen. But for her to think I'd purposely do anything to jeopardize her relationship with her fiancé really hurts. If she hadn't sent me this cold, dictatorial list of rules and regulations," she waved the email yet again, "I would have been the model cousin tonight. I would have catered to her prim and proper conventional whims and done everything I could to be as pleasant and...*average* as possible."

Kady's smile turned wicked. "But that's all changed now, and Lorraine has no one to blame but herself."

"If you're waiting for me to disagree, you'll have a long wait," Reen told her.

Kady studied Izzy's wide-eyed expression and showed it to Reen. "See that look on Izzy's furry little face? That's genuine concern. She has every right to be concerned. Lorraine's worried her oddball, palm-reading, tarot card-deciphering, romance novel-loving cousin's going to scare the stuffing right out of her straight-laced stuffed-shirt fiancé."

"Well, tonight you'll see exactly what the guy's made of when they come for dinner," Reen offered.

"It'll be interesting to see if he meets the visual I'm imagining. If Lorraine thinks I'm a kook *now*, just wait until this night is over." She frowned at the placement of the tall Kuan Yin statue and switched it with the shorter Buddha figurine. "Much better. Oops, look at the time. I've got to run, Reen. Thanks for listening to me whine so early in the morning. Izzy and I have to get dressed." She glanced again at the clock in Buddha's belly. "It's almost time to head downstairs to the bookshop. We've got a full roster of psychic readings scheduled."

"I've got a beginners knitting class at String Me Along this morning, so I need to get going too. Hang in there, okay? Do *not* let our jerky cousin ruin your evening. Call me if there's anything you need...or if you just need to talk after the shindig, okay?"

Blowing her sister a kiss, Kady nodded. "Thanks, Reen." They ended their call.

Stuffing the offensive missive into her pocket, Kady whipped aside the floor length curtain of lavender glass beads that hung from the doorjamb separating her bedroom from the living room, and Izzy followed close behind. Obsessing over her cousin's email had not only spoiled her usual morning mediation, it also caused Kady to lose track of time. She was entirely off kilter today.

Twenty minutes later, she gazed at her reflection in the full-length mirror, her fingers smoothing her soft, flowing purple silk vestment. It covered her from neck to toe, concealing figure flaws while enhancing her curves. Purple was her color. Its various shades flattered her pale complexion and auburn hair while calming her.

The final touch was the large amethyst pendant she'd purchased from an old woman at an estate sale—or, rather, had *tried* to purchase. The woman took a liking to Kady, insisting on giving it to her as a gift, simply because Kady had taken the time to listen to her reminisces about her beloved, departed husband.

"The world might be a crazy place, Izzy, but it's full of kind, wonderful people." She slipped the pendant over her head, admiring the way it hung from a rope of sterling silver and amethyst beads around her neck. She'd always remember the old woman's faded blue eyes, and her wrinkled smile along with her sweet, interesting stories, especially whenever she wore the pendant.

Turning her attention to Izzy, Kady gave her dog an approving appraisal.

"You look incredible, Izzy. Absolutely perfect." Grabbing her phone she took a few pictures after smoothing her hand over Izzy's purple and gold turban and matching tunic. She'd have to thank Sabrina again for finding this shimmery material with the moon and stars design. Her brother Gard marrying an artist was a real benefit.

"You look perfect for the bookshop's paranormal romance theme today." She adjusted Izzy's askew turban so it sat straight on the dog's head. Customers seemed to love seeing Kady and Izzy presenting a bohemian flare, with flowing vestments and eye-catching jewelry when they gave their joint psychic readings.

Giving Izzy a big smile as she knelt to secure the straps on the dog's black satin slippers. Pursing her lips, she spoke baby talk. "We don't mind a little theatrics and playing dress up, do we, sweetie pie?"

Clearly sensing by Kady's more tranquil tone that it was the right time to speak, Izzy barked and licked her best friend's hand.

# Chapter 5

~<>~

"LOOK AT YOU TWO, you're mesmerizing." Taking Kady's hands in hers Saffron Devington greeted her and Izzy enthusiastically as they entered the bookshop's backroom from Kady's upstairs apartment. "I hope you're ready because we're packing them in. You've already got six unscheduled customers in line hoping you can fit them in for readings."

"Seriously?" The interest in her readings surprised and delighted Kady.

"Yup. Some are locals but we've got tourists too."

"Excellent! I need that good news today because of what'll be going on tonight." She rolled her eyes, grumbling beneath her breath.

"Hey, I told you not to worry," Saffron assured. "I'll be there with you as your sous chef, your server and, most importantly, your friend who has your back. Don't forget, I know my sister. If you look up the term *resting bitch face*, you'll see a picture of Lorraine." Saffron and Kady shared a laugh.

"She does have a permanent puckered look, like she just sucked on a lemon," Kady noted, mimicking Lorraine's usual expression.

Saffron gave Kady and Izzy a head to toe appraisal, ending with a genuine smile. "I love the outfits. Very avant-garde. You look just like you stepped off the cover of a paranormal romance novel. You even managed to get that wild, springy hair of yours into a neat little bun."

"Thank you. Yup, I finally managed to tame this unruly mop." Kady patted her hair. "I feel guilty about it though." She sank her teeth into her bottom lip.

Saffron scrunched her face. "Why?"

"Well you know how concerned I am about the environment and—"

"And recycling, and nurturing Mother Earth, and honoring animals by being vegan, and global warming, and—"

"Okay, granted, I can be a bit much." Kady laughed. "I'm feeling guilty because my neatened hairdo is thanks to half a bottle of mousse and enough damn hairspray to destroy the ozone layer." Placing a finger to her lips, she said, "Shhhh...don't tell anyone it was me."

"Why Kathleen Doolan Malone, shame on you for singlehandedly destroying our ozone," Saffron teased.

Kady offered a crooked smile. "What can I say? Vanity can be a dangerous thing." Checking out her business partner's clothing, she said, "I love the retro feel of your outfit. It's so striking and very unlike the real estate Saffron with that dull, stiff and starchy buttoned down suit look you always wore." She stiffened her posture in demonstration.

"Ouch."

"Oh!" Stunned at her unintentional thoughtlessness, Kady's hand flew to her lips. "I am *so* sorry, Saffron, I didn't mean for that to come out quite so...so..."

"Blunt? Truthful?" Saffron snickered.

"I can't believe I said that." Kady winced. "I blame my nerves. I've got such anxiety about tonight that I haven't slept well. I'm overtired, overstressed, and—"

"Kady," Saffron clasped Kady's shoulder, "it's okay, it's not a problem. I purposely strived to be businesslike, professional, and *starchy*," she made air quotes around the word, "for years. It worked fine for selling houses, but not anymore. I'm tired of looking like a mortician, as your sister, Reen, once told me."

Kady's eyes popped wide. "She didn't!"

"She did," Saffron chuckled. "Reen was the first one to clue me in about my boring clothing. She helped me take baby steps to get out of my fashion rut. Since leaving real estate I've been having a blast throwing caution to the wind and playing with my wardrobe."

"With wonderful results," Kady said honestly. "Reen, by the way, listened to me whine on the phone early this morning. She helped calm me down." The oversized scarf draped over Saffron's shoulder caught her attention. "Tie-Dye. Love this. Where did you find something like that? It looks familiar."

"Is this not the ultimate in mystic hippie-dom, or what?" Saffron did a slow pirouette. "It looks familiar because your mom gave it to me. Aunt Astrid said she used to wear it when she was a teen. She also gave me some other cool retro clothing."

"Right," Kady nodded with recollection, "I remember seeing photos of Mom wearing this." Kady smiled at the memory.

"After mentioning that I wanted to free up my lackluster corporate look, she went and dug a bunch of stuff out of her closet for me." Saffron twirled around again. "The floor-length midnight-blue maxi-skirt was your mom's too. I've never had so much fun with clothing. I was always so afraid of looking unprofessional or silly."

"You look smart and fashionable, Saffron." Pulling her cousin into a gentle hug, Kady assured, "*Silly* is the last thing that comes to mind when I look at you. You've made the retro clothing look modern and contemporary—perfect for the unconventional vibe we're going for with our bookshop."

"I thought so too." Holding Kady at arm's length, she said, "That's why I like having you around, Kady. You're kind, a little kooky, exceedingly diplomatic and, unlike me, you're creative as hell. So, are you and Izzy ready to take center stage, *Katarina*?"

Kady looked at Izzy. "Ready to charm our customers this morning, Madame Izidora?" Izzy gave a small yip in return. "Good," Kady said, "let's do it."

~<>~

Throughout the day, patrons perused the eclectic mix of modern and vintage romance novels and other genre books, scented candles, incense, and mystic-themed accessories as they relaxed at a variety of cozy tables and chairs throughout the popular bookshop.

Sipping on espressos, cappuccinos, and flavored teas while munching on flavorful scones from Laila's bakery, they eagerly awaited their turn to sit at the small purple and gold silk covered round table tucked into a corner of the bookshop to have their fortunes told.

Patrons were clearly charmed as Saffron greeted them, often recommending a book to them and pouring complimentary samples of Sumatra coffee, or ginger-peach tea, the day's specials.

As always, the adorably garbed Izzy was the center of attention, eliciting oohs and aahs. Customers were awestruck as Kady read their palms, gazed into her crystal ball, and followed up with tarot card readings. The highlight of each reading was Izzy selecting a tarot card especially meaningful for the customer. It just bowled them over.

As they departed, customers each received a business card that read, *Cherished Pages Bookshop Presents Readings by Katarina and her Psychic Dog, Madame Izidora.*

At the end of the day, Kady brought the heavy crystal ball and its silver clawfoot stand into the bookshop's backroom where Saffron was sorting through the day's receipts.

Removing her reading glasses, Saffron tapped them against the computer monitor displaying an article she'd been reading. "We should think about setting up more book signings. It says here that top romance authors, as well as cover models, draw huge crowds wherever they appear. Just think what that could do for Cherished Pages." She wiggled excitedly in her chair.

The small backroom rang with Kady's laughter. "I doubt the remote little coastal town of Glassfloat Bay, Oregon is on the must visit lists of bestselling romance authors or cover models during their book tours."

"Can you imagine the university co-eds, teachers, and this town's whole damn female community jammed in here just so they can grab a peek some hot, muscle-bound hunks?"

Kady's eyebrow lifted. "That's not all they'd want to grab." She and Saffron dissolved into girlish giggles. "I like your promotional ideas, Saffron."

"After watching what Monica went through, almost losing her life to cancer, I've decided life's too short to spend it being all straitlaced and priggish."

"I love your positive thinking," Kady said.

Returning her attention to the day's receipts, Saffron smiled. "The best damn move I ever made was going into partnership with you, Kady. As you like to say, it was karma, pure and simple."

"I knew we'd be great business partners. I could feel it in my bones."

Saffron's expression twisted. "I can't imagine why, after the way I treated you and your sisters in the past. I'd clearly been infected with the Devington snootiness and superiority complex, and lorded it over the rest of you. It makes me cringe every time I think about how insufferable I must have been."

Her eyes glistened with tears as she reached out to grasp Kady's hand. "I have no idea why on earth you'd consider going into business with me after my past behavior, but I couldn't be happier about it."

Seeing the pain in her cousin's eyes, Kady wrapped an arm around Saffron's shoulder. "I made the choice because you're my cousin, my friend, and I love you—also, because you're an avid reader who loves books. On top of that, you possess all the essential qualities I don't have but need in order to make my dream of owning a successful bookshop a viable reality."

"You're just saying that to make me feel better. You're the one with the innovation, the creativity, the clever ideas, and that wonderfully infectious spirit of positivity. *That*, Kady is what's going to make our bookshop a success."

"Ah, but *you*, Saffron, are an absolute whiz at business. You're dedicated," Kady counted on her fingers, "a tireless worker, you love research, understand how to make and read spreadsheets, you excel at tech stuff, and you ooze the professionalism I sorely lack. You, cousin, are one sharp cookie when it comes to making money."

Izzy chose that moment to offer a bark, before pawing at both Saffron and Kady.

"See?" Kady said. "My psychic dog agrees."

"I think Izzy's telling us she recognizes a mutual admiration society here." Saffron smiled. "It's going to take me a good while to get acclimated to the idea of a psychic dog, or crystal balls, tarot cards, past lives, and whatever else resides in that neo-hippie brain of yours." Chuckling, Saffron tapped Kady's temple. "But the two of us together, as a team, possess all the necessary qualities and ingredients to make this the most unique and best damn bookshop in the Pacific Northwest."

"Amen to that. Probably because we've known each other during previous lifetimes. I'm convinced we're connected by past lives and were destined to become partners in this one. One of these days we'll have to hypnotize you to regress you to some of your former lives. Wouldn't that be cool?"

"Oh boy," Saffron muttered through muffled laughter. Focusing on the crystal ball Kady set in front of the computer, Saffron gazed into its depths. "Ah yes...it's coming into view...I see pyramids and hieroglyphs and, oh look, there's an asp. I was Cleopatra and you were a lowly but loyal and humble servant who'd peel grapes for me." She braced as Kady gave her a lively whap.

"Go ahead and joke about it, Miss Smarty Pants," Kady wagged a finger, "but, like I told you, I feel it in my bones."

"I don't know about sharing past lives," Saffron said, "but I *do* know the three of us make a dynamite team in this life." Saffron reached down to pat Izzy's back. Basking in the attention, Izzy's whole backside shook as her stubby tail whipped back and forth.

"You know what I was thinking about as you gave your tarot card readings earlier?" Saffron asked. "Your Ph.D. I was still operating from my holier than thou personality when I first heard one of your sisters talking about it. I never told you how impressed I was by what you did—the way you turned yourself inside out working on that dissertation. Talk about stress!" Saffron smacked the table. "I'm surprised you survived that whole episode intact...Doctor Malone." Saffron's smile spread across her cheeks

"Who says I did?" It was an episode Kady couldn't possibly forget. "I was sooo nervous when I gave that oration. I was terrified the faculty would expel me or run out of the room aghast."

"No doubt." Saffron nodded in understanding. "If I were giving a dissertation on the historical, literary, and cultural significance of fiction's romance genre to a bunch of stuffed shirts, I'd be scared shitless about their reaction too. But," she slapped the table again, causing Izzy to start, "from what I hear, you bowled them over."

"Thanks. I must admit I was proud of myself."

"Because of you and your compelling thesis, we've got a whole slew of Wisdom Harbor University's faculty as diehard customers."

Smiling at that, Kady noted, "Even though some of WHU's finest still aren't comfortable being seen in here unless they're incognito."

"True, you can't help noticing all the trench coats, hats and sunglasses. It's like we're peddling porn instead of genre fiction." Saffron lifted a shoulder. "Hey, that's okay by me. They can dress any way they want, as long as they keep buying our romance novels, right?"

"Absolutely." Izzy let out a gargantuan yawn at Kady's feet. "Of course you realize," Kady thumbed toward the dog, "we'd only be fooling ourselves if we thought for one minute that it was our brilliant business acumen filling the till."

"I'm fully aware of who the real luminary is around here." Saffron bent to shake Izzy's paw. "That adorable little rescue puppy of yours is a veritable gold mine. Every time *Madame Izidora* hobbles through here in one of her endearing little get-ups, business flourishes." Izzy's ears perked and Saffron scratched behind them.

"Izzy's got them eating out of her...paw." Kady laughed.

"Just look at our receipts." Saffron motioned toward them. "People bought little burlap bags of Sumatra coffee beans, tins of chai spice, and mini-scone samplers after we doled out free samples with Izzy tagging along at our heels."

"I'm so happy they've been buying the dog treats Laila created," Kady said. "The labels with Izzy's photo are so darned cute. And we've already got repeat customers for those."

"You said Izzy really likes the treats too, right?"

"Loves them," Kady confirmed. "Customers also snapped up the lavender and calendula scented candles and incense we had lit throughout the store today too."

"Yup, I've got the candles on reorder already," Saffron told her. "Those scents you chose have such a calming effect."

"They do." A sigh escaped Kady's lips. "I wanted to have them on hand for today. I felt the need for something soothing after working myself up into a lather over Lorraine this morning." She tried in vain to hide a sneer. "Oh my God, I have to stop that."

Saffron's eyebrows scrunched. "Stop what?"

"This." She made the sneer face again. "If I'm not careful I'll end up with a resting sneer face." She made it again, more exaggerated this time.

Saffron cracked up with laughter. "Not gonna happen. Don't worry about it. Hey, I can't wait to check out my sister's fiancé. Any guy fool enough to want to marry Lorraine must have stir fried noodles," she tapped her temple, "instead of brains. Hey, speaking of stir fry, want to do Chinese for a late lunch?"

"I'd love to, but..." Kady resisted the urge to sigh for the umpteenth time. "I've got a million things to do before Miss Resting Bitch Face and her snooty professor fiancé grace us with their presence tonight."

"Maybe the guy's okay," Saffron said with little confidence. "Maybe he hasn't known Lorraine long enough for the inevitable fight or flight response to kick in." After Kady nodded in agreement, Saffron changed her tune. "On the other hand, this is *Lorraine's* fiancé we're talking about. Any man meeting her rigid criterion would *have* to be a pompous ass."

"We're on the same wavelength." Kady removed Izzy's turban and robe, getting a big, sloppy thank you lick on her cheek. She gently scratched the lovable bocker behind the ears before rising and snatching Lorraine's email from her pocket. Waving it at Saffron, she said, "Did you see this?"

Saffron gave a resigned laugh. "Only a dozen times so far today. Come on, Kady, did you really expect anything else from the pampered little mistress of Devington Manor?"

"I did, actually. At least I had hoped. You asked the same question Reen asked me this morning. If anyone should be dispensing rules and warnings, it should be me, not Lorraine." She held the offending email beneath Saffron's nose. "No incense or candles, no hippie clothing, no weird unconventional music..." Kady looked up from the paper long enough to utter another sigh.

"No bohemian vegan or vegetarian food, no—"

Saffron laughed. "Well she'll just love our all-veggie fare then tonight."

Kady smiled before returning to the email. "No silly romance books on display, no nonconformist attire. Can you believe that?" Looking up from the list, she narrowed her eyes. "Your sister detests the way we get into the spirit of things in the bookshop by dressing up. Says it's positively gauche. *Gauche*, in case you hadn't noticed, is one of Lorraine's favorite words."

"Oh, believe me," Saffron looked skyward, "I've definitely noticed over the past thirty-odd years."

"She also says no clothing on Izzy. The don'ts just go on and on. Did I read you the list of things I'm allowed to do?"

"At least seventy times, but let's make seventy-one the charm if makes you feel better." Saffron chuckled.

"That's another of your positive traits," she told her cousin with a smile. "Patience." After reading Lorraine's list aloud, Kady pulled her hair out of the bun at the nape of her neck. "Notice that the do's are just don'ts in disguise?" She raked her fingers from front to back, releasing wild curls. "Me mentioning your brother is on her don't list. Apparently Lorraine hasn't said anything to her fiancé about Red being gay."

"Or that he even exists, probably," Saffron guessed. "No surprise."

"Remind me again why I'm doing this tonight," Kady groused.

"Because you, my hellbent, dewy-eyed cousin, are a hopeful, determined woman intent on changing the way my family feels about the way they shunned Red."

Her shoulders sinking like they were tied down by weights, Kady said, "I'm not making much headway, am I? Maybe it really is a lost cause." She tsked. "Aw, Saffron, I was so sure I could make a difference. Shame on me for not being able to practice what I preach."

"I don't want to hear you blaming yourself, Kady. You're not used to unforgiving people like my parents and sister."

Kady knew Saffron was right. "Lorraine has me so stressed and angsty, I can barely think straight. My nice, calm demeanor has left the building, replaced by an angry, frustrated fool." She sincerely doubted she'd make any positive progress with Lorraine tonight. Spotting movement, she glanced down to see Izzy busy spinning in a circle, screwing herself into a reclining position on the floor. Kady's expression softened. Her darling dog had such a calming effect on her.

"Keep calm, we're clean out of lavender and calendula, remember?" Winking, Saffron nudged Kady with her elbow. "You're not a fool. You're a free spirit and independent thinker. My rich, stuffy family can't relate. They're mired in material wealth and believing everyone should live their lives according to what their upper crust friends think. I know this firsthand because it's how I was raised."

"I'm disappointed in myself. I'm usually such an optimistic person." Kady tsked. "Since Lorraine's email arrived though, I can feel myself slowly morphing into someone else entirely." She looked into her cousin's eyes. "I don't want that to happen to me, Saffron. I don't want to turn into someone jaded and cynical."

Offering a warm, understanding smile, Saffron clasped both of Kady's shoulders. "You won't. You can't. I believe in you. You have to believe in yourself. Don't allow my family to drag you down, you hear?"

Kady nodded. "Thanks, Saffron."

"What's his name again?" Saffron asked. "The fiancé. My sister and I haven't had much communication since the incident with Red, so I'm not up to snuff with her love life."

"Professor Rylan Kilpatrick. Some big shot science professor at WHU. Environmental science or earth science, something like that. He has all sorts of academic awards. She told me they met when he gave a lecture at her women's club."

Saffron's expression skewed. "Since when do her empty-headed former sorority sisters invite scientists to speak at their inane meetings?"

"Probably their token educational meeting of the year," Kady offered with a shrug.

"Promise me you'll be yourself tonight, Kady. Don't let either of them intimidate you into putting on airs or hiding your own wonderful personality, okay?"

"Oh don't worry." Kady was surprised by the deliciously wicked sound of her own laughter. "I'm simply going to be the Kady Malone your sister expects me to be."

Saffron let loose with a little of her own wicked laughter. "Fortunately, I already know about the fabulously evil scheme you're hatching, since you twisted my arm...er...I mean *recruited me* to take part in it."

Kady grew serious. "Listen, Saffron, the last thing I want is to make things worse between you and your sister." She worried her bottom lip. "Maybe it would be best if you didn't come."

"I doubt it's possible to make things worse." Saffron gave a dismissive wave. "I wouldn't miss tonight for the world. Besides, I promised your mom I'd watch out for you where Lorraine is concerned. There's no way in hell I'd leave you at the mercy of my sharp-tongued, twisted sister without backup. Having me there with you will throw her off guard because she won't expect it to see me. Maybe she won't go for the jugular the way she would if you were on your own."

Saffron cocked her head, giving Kady a curious look. "Damn, Kady, that smile looks positively sinister."

"Hmm, I didn't realize I had a devilish smile going on," Kady said, "but it fits. Welcome to my new resting sinister face." She laughed. "Much preferred over a resting bitch face, right? I guarantee you, this will be a night Lorraine and her egghead will never forget."

# Chapter 6

~<>~

"I DO WISH YOU would have agreed to let Forester drive us in Daddy's limo for our day trip to Seattle." Lorraine Devington arched one perfectly penciled dark blonde eyebrow. "It's such an ungodly long ride back to Glassfloat Bay." Sometimes her fiancé could be so obtuse. However, since the man looked like a Greek god, she could excuse it. The thought made her chuckle.

"We should have left earlier so I'd have time to fix myself up. I'll be completely crumpled by the time we get there."

"It's not such a bad drive," Rylan said with his trademark charming smile. "Only a couple hours, depending on traffic. And great scenery."

"Wouldn't you rather live in a more cosmopolitan city like Seattle after we're married? Glassfloat Bay should only be a stepping stone for us, Rylan, not the place where we make plans to set down roots."

He gave her a quick glance and another smile. "Nope."

That was it. That's all he had to say on the subject. That's all he ever had to say when she suggested they relocate after the wedding.

Lorraine indulged in a lengthy sigh. "As a former Chicagoan, like me, I'd think you'd be craving the luxuries of big city life, Rylan." For as much as they had in common, sometimes she simply couldn't understand the man.

"My brother and I grew up in a working class family, Lorraine." Rylan patted her hand. "Try not to cringe at that, sweetheart." He laughed. She failed to see the humor.

Gesturing to the endless frosty green landscape as he drove, he said, "All this wide open space reminds me of the trips to Wisconsin my parents took us on each summer when I was a kid. How about you? Did your mom and dad take you to Wisconsin?"

Folding her arms across her chest, Lorraine turned toward him. "I loathe Wisconsin." She felt sure she'd told him that before.

"Oh yeah, I forgot. Any place whose residents refer to themselves with pride as cheeseheads is...what was it you said?"

"Devoid of culture and refinement." She gave a resolute nod.

"I love your sense of humor, Lorraine."

She returned his quip with an icy glare. Humor indeed.

"I didn't want to spend two hours in the back seat of a limo with Forester sneaking peeks at us through his rear view mirror. I don't know how you can relax with that stuffy chauffeur around. I like it much better when it's just the two of us." Placing his hand over hers, he added, "And stop worrying about your clothes getting wrinkled. You look great, you always do. Just try to relax and enjoy the ride. After all, it's just your cousin. I'm sure she won't mind if you have a hair or two out of place."

Straightening in her seat, Lorraine flipped down the passenger visor for a mirror check. Fussing with her hair, she said, "My hair's out of place? Where? Show me." As one of Glassfloat Bay's fashion icons, she had a reputation to maintain, even if she'd be spending the evening with her atrociously garbed cousin who didn't know a designer label from a soup can label. The woman always looked like she was auditioning for the circus.

"Every pretty strand of blonde is exactly where it should be." He switched the radio from his favorite jazz station to a classical one. "Here you go, your favorite music. A little Beethoven should help you relax."

*Oh good grief.* Sighing, Lorraine shook her head. "That's Mozart, Rylan, not Beethoven." She'd have to school him before their wedding in the fall. She couldn't have her friends thinking she'd married a musical moron.

"Mozart, Beethoven," Rylan laughed and shrugged, "it's all the same to me. What's the difference as long as you enjoy it and it helps you relax?"

Lorraine twisted in her seat to face Rylan. "How can you expect me to relax when we're in for an evening of vexation at the hands of my loony oddball cousin? The thought of spending time in that decrepit, old apartment over her bookshop makes me feel claustrophobic. I've no doubt Kathleen has managed to..." her hands fluttered as she searched for the right descriptive phrase, "*junk up*, the place with all sorts of hippie paraphernalia."

Shuddering, Lorraine shifted her attention to the limitless acres of frost-covered farmlands whizzing by her window. Once Rylan met Kathleen he'd understand her angst. He'd appreciate why her stomach had been in knots over this farce of a dinner.

"I'm sure your cousin's place isn't all that bad. Didn't you say it was recently updated?"

"Yes, by the local handyman." She shuddered. "I expect it will look like something out of a bad B-movie with Kathleen's inclination for hippie decorating."

"You've mentioned hippie a few times in relation to your cousin. How old is she? Elderly?"

That caused Lorraine to titter light laughter. "She's somewhere in her early to mid-thirties but it's like she's channeling an old sixties hippie." She winced. "So disconcerting."

"You're just spoiled, Lorraine, used to living in that rambling museum full of gold and marble that you call home."

"I get that you're attempting to be humorous, Rylan, but I do wish you wouldn't insist on referring to Devington Manor as a museum." Lorraine tried to hide her smile as she gave his arm a slap. Admittedly beguiling, the man could be positively incorrigible. "And, I am *not* spoiled."

"*Au contraire*, my sweet, anyone who lives in a place full of antiquities and art treasures, *and*," he arched an eyebrow, "has to take an elevator from their fourth floor bedroom to the main floor of their house, *A* lives in a museum and *B* is spoiled, with a capital *S*, as far as I'm concerned."

"*Au contraire*," she repeated his words with a sigh, temporarily ignoring the rest of what he'd said. "I love it when you speak French, darling. It's such a turn on." Lorraine kissed her fingertips, then tapped them against her fiancé's cheek.

"Ooh la la...crêpes suzette...*merci beaucoup...bonjour...au revoir*—"

"Oh dear God, stop!" Grabbing a tissue from her purse, Lorraine dabbed tears of laughter.

"Not a problem." Rylan laughed. "That's about all the French I know."

"Oh Rylan, I do love the way you can make me laugh. It looks like you need some brushing up on your French though."

Rylan clapped his chest. "*Moi*?"

Lorraine nodded, still laughing. "You really must stop. You'll make me ruin my eye makeup. Don't worry, I have an excellent French tutor. We can set up lessons for you."

"Whoa...*excusez-moi*? I don't think so, Lor."

Addressing her fiancé as sweetly as possible, Lorraine said, "I've asked you repeatedly not to call me that, Rylan." It grated that she had to keep reminding him to avoid using nicknames she hadn't approved. *Lor* sounded common...lower socioeconomic, whereas *Lorraine* was a fine, dignified name.

"Sorry, I forgot," he said. "Don't get your heart set on me signing up for any lessons. I'm not spending the little free time I have learning how to speak French when the only place I'll be able to use what I learn is in a French restaurant."

"Or elsewhere." Lorraine made her eyebrows dance suggestively. "As for me supposedly being spoiled," she decided it was time to return to the topic, "you make it sound like there's something wrong with having money. You'll get used to it soon enough." She patted his knee. "You'll see."

Rylan shook his head. "Lor...Lorraine, there's money, and then there's *Money*—with a capital *M*." He released the black leather wrapped steering wheel to make a grand gesture with his arms. "The Devingtons are in the second category. Filthy, indecently, obscenely rich. And no, that's something I'll never get used to."

"So I'm spoiled with a capital *S* and moneyed with a capital *M*, am I?" She broadcast a good-natured smile. One of her favorite things about their relationship was the easy give and take banter between them...well, as long as Rylan didn't become too contrary. But she had plenty of time to train him.

"You're my capital woman." Rylan winked. "You know, you're awfully lucky I still keep you around."

"Oh really? And why is that?"

"Because if I would have known you were one of *those* Devingtons when I made my energy conservation presentation to your women's club last year, I never would have gotten this involved."

"Too much for you, am I?"

His expression grew more serious. "I can't help wishing you were just an average woman sometimes. All that pomp and circumstance that you call your daily life is a bit much for an average guy like me to get used to."

"That guileless, unimpressed attitude of yours is one of the reasons I find you so attractive. Are you saying you're sorry you met me?" Pouting, Lorraine tiptoed her fingers along Rylan's thigh.

"If you like, I can pull off the road and show you just how *not* sorry I am." He jiggled his eyebrows, offering a smile full of promise.

"Later...after the dinner debacle." Lorraine folded her arms across her chest. "I care for Kathleen. I mean, I have to, she's my cousin. But she's a rebel, a bohemian, and, *ugh*," she trembled, "a hawker of cheap bodice rippers." She rubbed the goose bumps rising on her arms.

"Your neo-hippie cousin is in the business of selling sex, huh?" Rylan freely gave into laughter. "This evening might turn out to be a lot more interesting than I thought."

Tsking, Lorraine chastised, "Please, Rylan, this really isn't a laughing matter." She let out a long sigh born of exasperation. "The woman is an embarrassment to the family." After grumbling beneath her breath, she added, "All I have to say is Kathleen had better adhere to that list I sent her. If she dares bring out her grisly, gauche, fortunetelling cards, we're leaving. Immediately."

"List?" Rylan's eyebrows furrowed. "What list?"

Her hand flitting through the air, Lorraine explained, "It was necessary for me to compose a detailed email imploring my cousin to handle this evening with decorum. Since she obviously doesn't know any better, my list of helpful guidelines will hopefully save us from experiencing too much torment."

"Wait a minute..." A stunned expression shot across her fiancé's face. "You sent your cousin a set of rules to follow while we're dinner guests in her home?"

"Exactly." Lorraine returned his surprised expression with a patronizing smile. Poor Rylan, he was sorely in need of coaching. She'd make a point to find the time. The professor simply didn't understand. It wasn't his fault. He had his nose buried so deep in his science books that he apparently never learned about human nature and what's acceptable and what isn't. With his many fine qualities, she could overlook his shortcomings. She'd have Rylan properly schooled in no time.

"Whoa..." Huffing a laugh, Rylan noted, "Your cousin's probably ticked off as hell. I know *I* would be if someone sent me a list telling me how to behave in front of my guests."

"Nonsense. You're making too much of this. I'm sure my aunt raised Kathleen to practice proper decorum and conduct herself with propriety. Regrettably, it appears my cousin's tutelage has fallen by the wayside." Lorraine gave him a tolerant smile. "I'm sure Kathleen appreciates my direction." She rolled the cultured pearl bracelet at her wrist, hoping she'd worded her missive with enough impact.

Bewilderment was evident across Rylan's face. Heaving a sigh, Lorraine enlightened him. "I only agreed to this dinner because you thought it would be rude to decline Kathleen's invitation. If it were up to me, I never would have accepted and we'd have our evening free to enjoy each other while sipping wine, speaking French, and engaging in...other pleasures."

"Kathleen may not be your favorite person but she's still your cousin, Lorraine, no matter what. That means she'll be my cousin-in-law. If it's important to her to host a little dinner in honor of our engagement, what's the harm? Let her have her special night. We can muddle through it. It's only one evening."

"One wasted evening." Lorraine closed her eyes in a long blink. "There's no need for a lecture, Rylan. I agreed, didn't I?"

"I didn't intend to lecture. Not my fault—that's what professor's do." As usual, his smile charmed her. "Anyway, after the buildup you've given Kathleen, I've got to meet her. She can't possibly be as bad as you say."

~<>~

Kady and Saffron painstakingly festooned Kady's apartment with a conglomeration of eclectic oddities until it resembled an intensely peculiar secondhand shop. Among the curiosities and candles were a profusion of romance novels, and posters with brazenly seductive covers from publishing houses. Every nook and cranny was full.

The women stood back, judging the motley fruits of their labor.

"This place looks like a French whorehouse inhabited by drugged-out Satanists." Wide-eyed, Saffron gave an involuntary shudder.

"Then our job is done," Kady said and they laughed together.

Wincing, Saffron said, "Lorraine's not going to be happy."

"But we will, and that's all that counts." A satisfied grin spread across Kady's face, igniting a wicked twinkle in her eyes. "It's bizarre, outlandish, and absolutely perfect." She glanced at the clock in Buddha's belly. "Come on, we need to get into our costumes so we look like we belong in this crazy, jazzed-up place." Something between a laugh and a cackle escaped Kady Malone's lips as she gave their *creative decorating* a final appraisal.

~<>~

The doorbell rang shortly after six. Kady and Saffron exchanged apprehensive smiles before Kady slipped into her bedroom, according to plan, allowing Saffron to greet her guests.

"Welcome to this humble abode." Saffron stepped aside, ushering Lorraine and Rylan inside with a broad thespian gesture as she clinked the finger cymbals on her left hand and sprinkled silk rose petals in the couple's path with the other hand.

Rylan watched his fiancé's jaw drop as she stood there silently gaping for what seemed a small eternity.

"Well, since my fiancée seems to be at a loss for words," he extended his hand, "I'm Rylan Kilpatrick. I've heard a lot about you, Kathleen." He flashed a smile. "Glad we finally have a chance to meet." He presented a bottle of expensive pinot noir. "This is for you. Lorraine picked it out."

"Saffron!" Lorraine burst out, clearly discomfited. "I didn't expect to see you here."

"Always expect the unexpected, sister dear." Saffron offered a serene smile.

"This is your sister?" The attractive brunette bore a strong resemblance to Lorraine. He'd been told the sisters weren't on the best of terms because of something or other Lorraine had declined to explain.

A look of astonishment crossed Lorraine's features as she crossed the threshold. Observing the dramatically ornamented scene and her sister's eccentric clothing, she shot Saffron an accusatory look.

"What on earth is that hideous costume you're wearing? You're a little early for Halloween, aren't you, Saffron?"

Rylan struggled not to laugh when Saffron responded with an innocent smile, batting her eyelashes.

The woman before him was costumed like a hippie. Her earrings were oversized peace symbols. She wore a long-sleeved tie-dye T-shirt, apple seed and nut shell necklaces, and sizeable peace-symbol pendants. She must have raided some old hippie's eclectic closet, right down to the 1960s style leather sandals with toe rings.

Saffron's bell bottom jeans boasted innumerable patches of rainbows and sayings. While Lorraine huffed and blustered at her sister, Rylan read as many as he could: *make love not war*; *don't trust anyone over 30*; *power to the people*; *peace & love*; *groovy*; *far out, man*; *dig it*; *flower power*...and too many more to read in a short time.

For a guy who didn't pay much attention to fashion, he couldn't help noticing all the oddities Saffron presented, including a set of brass finger cymbals. Her hair hung in a loose braid, interwoven with ribbons and flowers, that reached the middle of her back. Far removed from Lorraine's sophisticated sense of style, she was a sight to behold.

"Yes, she's my sister," Lorraine finally replied to him, "and I have no idea what she's doing here—or why she's dressed like a kook. Where's Kathleen, Saffron?"

"Happy to meet you, Rylan." Saffron clasped his hand, pumping enthusiastically. "I'm Saffron Devington, Kady's cousin, friend, and business partner."

"I take it Kady is short for Kathleen?" Rylan surmised.

Saffron nodded. "It's from the initials of her first and middle name, Kathleen Doolan Malone." Looking him up and down in the most peculiar way, she asked, "Sooo...you're the egghead, huh?"

Rylan broke into laughter. "Yup, that would be me."

"Well, I'll be damned." Raising her eyebrows, Saffron smiled.

From her demeanor, Rylan felt sure this wasn't Saffron's normal attire or manner. He speculated she was probably playing dress up in response to Lorraine's inane list of rules.

Heading for the kitchen, Saffron tossed a final handful of rose petals over her shoulder while clinking her finger cymbals three times.

"This is so annoying." Pressing her fingers to her temples, Lorraine muttered, "I feel a migraine coming on." It seemed his fiancée was particularly prone to bad headaches.

"Just as I told you, see?" she said. "A monumental bungled mess. Saffron and Kathleen co-own the creepy, occultish bookshop I told you about."

Feeling it best not to comment, Rylan placed his arm around Lorraine's shoulder, giving her a reassuring squeeze as his fiancée continued to huff and puff.

After a period of relative silence, broken only by Lorraine's piqued grumbling, while Rylan and Lorraine stood at the center of the room, a floor length curtain of lavender glass beads parted and an ethereal creature entered the room.

~<>~

Kady paused for dramatic effect before stepping into the living room. With arms outstretched, she held back the beads, giving her guests an eyeful of her carefully chosen attire—a purposely bizarre co-mingling of garish fortuneteller and debutante socialite garb.

A lavender satin ballgown trailed into lush gathers across her bottom while Kady's arms were covered by formal over-the-elbow gloves, festooned with a kitschy mixture of rings, clanking metal bangles, and bejeweled bracelets.

"Lorraine dear," Kady said, speaking above the rustle of satin and crinoline, and the clatter of jangling metal as she gathered the voluminous gown and walked, barefoot, toward her cousin. "I'm delighted to have you honor me with your presence." She offered polite air-kisses to Lorraine's cheeks, all the while swaying to the sounds of her Hildegard von Bingen chants playlist. She knew Lorraine would abhor the music.

Arms folded across her chest, Lorraine glared at her cousin. True to Kady's expectations, Lorraine was crisply attired in a conservative beige megabucks designer suit with gold and cultured pearl accessories. Her hair perfectly coifed and pulled into a smooth knot, the beautiful hazel-eyed blonde ice princess reeked of some gazillion dollar an ounce perfume.

"And Rylan, how nice to meet you." Kady extended her hand. In her mind's eye, she imagined her cartoon eyeballs boinging out of their sockets as her tongue unrolled along the floor like a red carpet. The science professor was *that* hot.

He seemed unsure as to whether he should kiss Kady's gloved hand or shake it. "Kathleen?" He sounded surprised as they shook hands.

"Yes, the loony oddball of the family...but I'm sure you already know that." She smiled before glancing toward her cousin and receiving a vacant stare. "Please, call me Kady. All my friends do."

The fiancé wasn't at all what she'd expected. He stood over six-feet tall, had wavy coal-black hair, deep cobalt blue eyes, a strong jaw, and full sensuous lips. The tweed sports coat and open collared white oxford shirt he wore over a great fitting pair of jeans added to his appeal. Suddenly aware of the inviting warmth through her gloved palms, Kady realized she still had Rylan's large hand in hers. Releasing it, she felt a blush rise to her cheeks.

Apparently there were some things her straightlaced cousin was good at selecting besides pricey wine and designer duds.

She caught Rylan glancing at her bare feet. She'd adorned them with toe-rings and jewelry that began at her toes and crisscrossed around her ankles, the perfect finishing touch to her hippie prom queen fortunetelling ensemble.

Rylan's lip curved into an appreciative half-smile as his gaze traveled from her feet to her head where her wild auburn curls were liberally sprinkled with silver glitter, and peeking out of a purple paisley scarf tied bohemian-style over her head.

While Rylan looked amused, Lorraine shot daggers at Kady.

"Forget to pay the electric bill, Kathleen?" Lorraine slapped her hand against the wall, flicking the light switch on. "There, that's better. Now I can see your masquerade costume more clearly." Narrowing one eye, Lorraine shook her head in disgust as she gave her cousin yet another once-over.

Holding the billowy skirt of the gown out to the sides, Kady twirled around, offering a wry smile. "Elegant, isn't it? You're welcome to borrow the ensemble any time, Lorraine. I found the gown at the Salvation Army thrift store and pieced the rest together from garage sale finds. All in honor of this very special celebration of your engagement."

Kady returned Lorraine's scowl with a wide-eyed look of surprise. "Don't you like it, Lorraine? I'm merely trying to live up to your expectations, and the expressive picture I'm sure you've painted of me for your fiancé." Kady looked toward Rylan, smiling. "My cousin did tell you I make my living hawking romance novels and reading palms didn't she, Professor Kilpatrick?"

There was a gleam in Rylan's eye as he offered her a twisted smile. "She may have mentioned it." Unlike Lorraine, he seemed to be on board with the stunt she and Saffron were pulling.

As for Lorraine, if her eyes grew any narrower they'd be slits in need of propping open. "At least now Rylan knows I wasn't exaggerating. He can see firsthand what a bona fide kook my cousin is."

Kady slapped her hand against the wall, turning the lights out. "We're having dinner by candlelight, cousin dear."

Glancing at her surroundings, Lorraine snickered. "After getting a better look at this shrine to bad taste that you've cobbled together, I agree, the less light the better."

"Kady and I are conserving energy in honor of the professor's environmental interests," Saffron chimed in. "We have more than three-dozen candles lit, which should be plenty of illumination for our dinner celebration, wouldn't you agree Professor Kilpatrick?"

"Fine with me," Rylan answered Saffron, stuffing his hands into his pockets and rocking on his heels. "I'm all for energy conservation, right, Lorraine?" He seemed oblivious to the icy look Lorraine transmitted his way.

"Let's proceed into the dining room, shall we?" Kady said. "Dinner is almost ready. Your sister is such a sweet soul, Lorraine. When she heard I'd invited you for dinner in honor of your romantic union, she insisted on preparing a few of her tantalizing specialties."

Squinty-eyed Lorraine shot her sister a look that could kill. "Since when do you cook, Saffron, other than microwaving frozen dinners?"

"I'm a woman of many talents and surprises," Saffron replied. "I started cooking for myself after moving out of Devington Manor. I enjoy it and have become quite the accomplished cook, as you'll see for yourself shortly."

"You're in for a true gastronomic treat," Kady assured, leading Rylan and Lorraine through her apartment's round-robin layout to the dining room while still swaying to the churchy sounds of female chants.

Aglow with candlelight, the dining room had framed dust jackets from vintage romance novels hung along the walls. The table was covered with a lavender crushed-velvet throw, bordered in deep purple fringe, and set with an eclectic mix of dishes, goblets and silverware that Kady had gathered from thrift stores and garage sales. Her Egyptian canopic replica ware sat at the center.

Presenting a flaccid smile, Lorraine gingerly brushed off her chair before taking a seat across from Rylan. "Good gawd!" she blurted once situated.

"Something wrong, Lorraine?" Kady said nonchalantly as Rylan looked up with a start. Clearly aghast, Lorraine motioned to the wall behind Rylan. "Ahhh, yes." Kady said with a reverent smile. "It takes your breath away, doesn't it?"

Spinning around to see what all the ruckus was about, Rylan chuckled as he spied the object of Lorraine's ire. Behind him Kady had mounted a huge poster of a sultan. The bare-chested, musclebound figure stood, hands on hips, his silky, Arabian vestments blowing in the wind as he modeled a proud scowl. A woman sprawled at his feet, hugged his leg while gazing up at him with a hungry, pleading expression of adoration. THE SULTAN'S SECRET shouted across the top of the poster in bold red letters.

Lorraine pushed back in her chair so fast the chair legs squealed against the floor. Shooting to a standing position, she pointed a rigid finger at the offending poster. "Please remove that obscene picture of a naked man at once, Kathleen."

"He's only three-quarters naked," Kady countered with an apathetic wave. Resting her elbows against the table and perching her chin on her folded hands, she expelled a purposefully loud, dreamy sigh. "Magnificent specimen of manhood isn't he? He's one of the cover-art models scheduled to appear at our store for a book signing soon." She'd stretched the truth on that one. She and Saffron had contacted the model via social media, but they hadn't received a response yet.

"He really packs them in." Kady steepled her fingers. "I'd be happy to send you a postcard when he's making his next appearance in our bookshop. Naturally, Professor, you're welcome to accompany my cousin to the event."

Motioning behind his shoulder with his thumb, he said, "Excuse me if I don't tag along on this one. Not exactly my cup of tea."

"If I must sit here across from that atrocious poster, Kathleen, can't we at least listen to something other than your annoying nun music?" Lorraine massaged her temples as she spoke. "It's giving me a gargantuan headache. How about something classical?"

"Classics?" Kady rubbed her chin. "I have just the right music for our dinner celebration." With a sparkle in her eye, she looked through the playlists on her phone.

"Something tells me I would have been better off staying with the chanting," Lorraine said.

"Kady's a riot, Lorraine. Why didn't you tell me your cousin was so funny?"

Snapping her head toward Rylan, Lorraine blurted, "There's nothing even remotely funny about this absurd farce. Honestly, Rylan, sometimes I just don't understand you at all."

Happily swaying in her chair to a new tune, Kady watched Lorraine's face fall.

"What *is* that?" Her cousin looked bewildered, and none too happy.

"A true classic," Kady said. "An old one...all the way from 1969. It's "The Age of Aquarius" by The 5th Dimension, from the musical *Hair*."

Rylan said, "Now that's my kind of classical music."

"This is hippie music," Lorraine stated the obvious.

"Perhaps you'd prefer something older," Kady suggested.

"Please." She nodded.

"My older classics include Elvis, Little Richard, Fats Domino, Chuck Berry, or—"

"Ha-ha. Very funny. You know what?" Lorraine's expression twisted as she caressed her temples. "I don't even care anymore. I really don't."

"Wonderful. Then "The Age of Aquarius" it is. Perfect mood music for our dinner." Heaving a dramatic sigh, Kady added, "I feel just terrible. I never should have selected those Hildegard von Bingen chants. It's such...*weird, unconventional music*." Placing emphasis on the words Lorraine had used in her list of don'ts, Kady gave Lorraine a lingering smile, to which Lorraine responded with a brittle glare.

Out of the corner of her eye, Kady caught Rylan bowing his head, covering his eyes and temples with one hand in an obvious attempt to stifle rising laughter. What a pleasant surprise he was.

Straightening against the back of her chair, Lorraine announced, "Kathleen, I think we've had quite enough of your—"

"Shall we partake in some fruit of the vine, dear guests?" Kady interrupted the expected admonishment from her cousin. "A little something to warm your insides on this chilly evening?"

"Yes!" Lorraine jumped at the suggestion. "Wine would be good. Why don't you open the lovely pinot noir we brought and give it a chance to breathe?"

"There's no need. Saffron, would you mind bringing the wine from the kitchen?" Kady called to her cousin. "It's been breathing for about a week and a half now," she told Rylan and Lorraine. A moment later, Saffron appeared with a gallon jug of red table wine, filling four large, mismatched water glasses. She took a sniff before passing them around.

"Ahhh, it's aged beautifully," Saffron noted before disappearing into the kitchen again.

Lifting her glass high, Kady toasted, "Here's to Lorraine and Rylan. May your life together be filled with love, frivolity, and happiness." She downed a hearty sip.

"Hear, hear," Rylan seconded, swilling a gulp of wine.

"Lorraine, aren't you drinking?" Kady asked.

"Firstly, one never drinks when the toast is in their honor." Lorraine shot a glance at Rylan who gave an apologetic shrug. "Secondly, I couldn't possibly drink *jug wine*," she said as if speaking of bottled snake venom. Lorraine pushed her glass away and slouched back against her chair with her arms crossed over her chest.

"Wine's not to your liking?" Kady asked. "No problem. I've also got a box of white zinfandel, and a box of Chablis. What'll it be?"

Lorraine went pale. "Wine in a box?" Kady nodded enthusiastically. "Never mind, this is just fine." Giving a weak smile, she leaned forward and sipped from the jug wine, curling her features into a sour expression.

"So, Rylan," Kady peered over the rim of her glass, "it appears you've survived the grilling my aunt and uncle must have put you through. What do you think of your future in-laws?"

"Well..." Rylan rubbed his chin, "I think Walter and Colleen Devington are the nicest of all the museum dwellers I've ever been grilled by."

Kady burst out laughing. "You don't think Devington Manor is cozy?"

"Four stories, marble columns, and elevators is not my idea of cozy."

"Oh, now that's not true at all," Lorraine said, delicately sipping her wine. "I find Devington Manor quite comfortable. My every need is attended to by our domestic staff, and I'm surrounded by every luxury and necessity I want. The library and music rooms are especially cozy, perfect for a small wine and cheese soiree or ladies luncheon."

At that moment, Kady felt especially sorry for her cousin, who seemed to have no appreciation or concept of the simple pleasantries in life.

"I'm glad you're happy there, Lorraine," she said with sincerity.

Looking surprised, Lorraine paused a moment before displaying the barest whisper of a smile and offering a gracious, "Thank you, Kathleen."

"Lorraine tells me you're a brainy, award winning, bigshot science professor at Wisdom Harbor University, Rylan."

Taking it all in stride, Rylan met Kady's mischievous gaze, swallowing an emerging chuckle. "That's correct. I'm known around campus as the undisputed science king of WHU."

Raising his glass of wine, Rylan studied it. "Watch and be amazed as Professor Egghead demonstrates the systematic process of osmosis." He took a couple swigs and placed the half-empty glass on the table, making an exaggerated wipe of his mouth with the back of his hand. "Digestive assimilation demonstration complete," he said, giving a robust *ahhhh* of satisfaction.

Laughing, Kady reached over to pat her cousin's arm. "Oh, Lorraine, your fiancé is wonderful. A real breath of fresh air." Turning to Rylan she said, "I like you, Professor. I was afraid you were going to be one of those stuffy, self-important, academic types, but you're not at all like that." Cupping her hand to her mouth in a conspirator's manner, she added, "I think you'll do wonders for my cousin, who's thirty-something going on fifty. Welcome to the family."

Raising his hand as if giving an oath, he replied, "On my honor, I promise to do everything in my power to keep a steady intravenous drip of love, laughter, and happiness flowing in your cousin's blue-blooded veins." He saluted, and Kady returned the salute.

Surprising Kady, Lorraine laughed warmly after draining the last of the wine from her glass and finally allowing herself to get into the spirit of the gentle frivolity. "I intend to wed this charming creature and turn him into a bona fide museum dweller." Kady and Rylan laughed. "Kady, when I'm finished implanting new data into Professor Egghead's brain, I promise you he'll be craving Dom Perignon and beluga caviar every morning for breakfast."

Cringing, Rylan made a sour expression. "I don't think so."

Lorraine laughed again...and Kady smiled. Lorraine hadn't called her *Kady* in ages. It reminded her of years gone by when they'd had such fun together before Lorraine realized she was *to the manner born* and embarked upon a different life-path than Kady. She wasn't sure if it was the wine or the relaxed atmosphere, but whatever it was, it was good to see Lorraine let her guard down a bit and enjoy herself for a change.

When Saffron called out, "Ready, Kady," from the kitchen, Kady removed her over-the-elbow gloves, along with the myriad junk jewelry that adorned them, and rose from her chair, heading for a shelf that held a ten-inch brass gong suspended between the mouths of twin dragons. As soon as she hit the gong with the little mallet, Izzy barked in the kitchen.

"Dinner is served, dear guests," Kady said.

Lorraine's animated demeanor disappeared. "Please don't tell me that *creature* is in the kitchen, Kathleen. It'll get dog hair all over our food."

Kady bristled. "Izzy is a *she*, not an *it*. And, while she's highly intelligent, I can assure you she wasn't involved in any of the food preparation."

Following three chimes from her finger cymbals, Saffron emerged from the kitchen, her hippie regalia now sporting a few scorched areas and a smattering of food stains. She carried two large platters holding an appetizing assortment of food.

"In harmony with our planet, we give thanks for the bountiful offerings Mother Nature has provided." Saffron bowed, clanging her finger cymbals. "With your forthcoming nuptials in mind," she directed her comments to Rylan, "I place before you a selection of vegan and vegetarian delights fit for a sultan...and," now she motioned to Lorraine, "the woman at his feet." She ignored her sister's infuriated gasp.

Before taking her seat, Saffron dramatically sprinkled the aromatic offerings with sugared rose petals.

Wrinkling her nose, Lorraine said, "My email specifically stated that Rylan is a meat and potatoes man. As in beef, Kady, b-e-e-f. You can't expect an esteemed science professor to nibble on strange vegetarian concoctions."

"I consider myself somewhat of an adventurous eater," Rylan said.

"Really? Since when, darling?" Lorraine challenged.

"Well, since uh..." Catching the quizzical look Lorraine transmitted, Rylan cleared his throat. "Well, since your sister has gone to a lot of work preparing all this," his hand waved across the platter, "in our honor. The least I can do is give it a try."

"Thank you, Professor," Saffron said. "Kady and I consider this fare food of the gods."

"Please describe each dish, Saffron," Lorraine addressed her sister civilly for the first time that evening.

After hearing the descriptions, Lorraine smiled at Rylan. "Don't worry, I'll have Cook fix you a nice big steak later this evening."

"That won't be necessary. And we're not bothering your family's cook after hours either. You know how I feel about that, Lorraine."

Swallowing a bite of toasted pita bread, Kady turned to Lorraine. "Isn't one of your favorite playwrights George Bernard Shaw?"

Lorraine nodded. "I've always admired him for his writing skills, as well as his values."

"Which," Kady continued, "I find somewhat contradictory, considering Shaw was known for satirizing the English upper class, ala Pygmalion and such." Kady's hand flitted through the air. "Did you know your literary idol was a devout vegetarian from the age of twenty-five?"

Lorraine smirked. "Probably because he lived in poverty as a young man and couldn't afford meat."

"Perhaps," Kady acknowledged. "He was fond of telling his carnivorous acquaintances that, and I quote, *a man of my spiritual intensity does not eat corpses.* Falafel, Lorraine?" She presented the platter to her cousin with an innocent smile. Rylan laughed out loud while Lorraine's scorching gaze had the intensity to set the falafel patties aflame.

# Chapter 7

~<>~

AFTER PARTAKING in a dessert of Turkish coffee, pine nut cookies, brandied winter fruits, baklava, and marbled halva, Kady ushered Lorraine and Rylan into the living room.

"That was an amazing dinner, Saffron," Rylan said. "I'm frankly surprised that everything was so delicious." Turning to his fiancée, he added, "Lorraine, you even seemed to be digging in and enjoying it."

"While I never *dig in,*" Lorraine said the words with a distinct haughtiness, "I must admit I found Saffron's dishes surprisingly flavorsome." She finished by offering her sister a smile.

"I'm glad," Saffron said. "Now that we've finished dinner, I'll be going. I have things to take care of before we open for business tomorrow morning."

"Saffron..." Lorraine began, tentatively placing her hand over her sister's. "It was nice spending time with you this evening. It's...been a long time."

Offering Lorraine a warm smile in return, Saffron patted Lorraine's hand. "Too long. I enjoyed it too. Let's consider this a first step." Lorraine smiled and nodded. After exchanging goodbyes, Saffron left.

Their brief conversation gave Kady hope that the Devingtons might be on their way to healing as a family.

"It's time for you to meet my adorable little rescue dog, Izzy," Kady told Lorraine and Rylan. "I guarantee you'll love her. Be right back."

A moment later, Izzy happily hobbled into the room at Kady's heels, dressed in her purple and gold Lurex turban and matching tunic with the moon and stars motif. As soon as Rylan laid eyes on the little bocker, he threw his head back in laughter.

Kady found his deep, genuine laugh as appealing as his appearance. She watched as Izzy made a beeline for him. After a tentative sniff, she jumped in his lap and licked his face, shaking her little stub of a tale all the while.

"Meet Izzy, also known as Madame Izidora Meszaros, the psychic dog," Kady said.

Rylan gathered Izzy in his arms. When Kady found herself considering how nice it would be to have Rylan gather *her* in his strong arms like that, she shook the forbidden idea from her head and took a deep breath. *What on earth was she thinking?*

"Kady, what on earth were you thinking?" Vaulting from the couch Lorraine looked outraged...again.

Kady's eyes went saucer-wide at Lorraine's question. She couldn't possibly know what Kady had just been thinking about Rylan, could she? *Oh. My. God!*

"Get that hairy little beast away from Rylan before she hurts him or snags his tweed sport coat," Lorraine finished, and Kady was actually relieved. Looking in Lorraine's direction, Izzy let out a lady-like growl.

"Aw, this little cutie wouldn't hurt a fly," Rylan said. "Would you, Izzy?" Relishing the masculine attention, Izzy responded by wriggling her backside and plying Rylan with another face lick. Holding Izzy at arm's length, he studied her tiny satin outfit and shifted the lopsided turban back into position. "That's about the cutest damn thing I've ever seen."

Izzy jumped from Rylan's grasp, positioning herself next to him on the couch in the spot vacated by Lorraine when she leapt to her feet in anger. Izzy rested her head in Rylan's lap while Lorraine took a seat in nearby armchair, telegraphing a glare in the dog's direction.

"Okay, I'm hooked." Rylan cuddled the little dog. "What's the scoop on Madame Izidora Whatzername? I noticed she was limping, did she injure her leg?"

"No, one of her back legs is shorter than the other, so she limps and hobbles around, but she does just fine."

"Why would you adopt a crippled dog?" Lorraine asked, making Kady count to ten before answering.

"Because it was love at first sight," was her truthful answer. "She must sense something about you, Rylan. It's unusual for Izzy to take to anyone so quickly."

"While we're on the subject of the dog, didn't you read the list I sent to you? It seems obvious you've chosen to ignore it."

"On the contrary, Lorraine, I've given your rigid list of rules and regulations serious deliberation. Gee, I said to myself, since Lorraine is fully aware that I positively abhor pretense and pomposity, she must have sent me this ridiculous list as a joke. Knowing Lorraine's rollicking sense of humor," Kady rolled her eyes skyward, "she must have wanted me to play a game with it. So that's exactly what I've done."

"Game?" Lorraine's eyebrows pinched together.

"Indeed. I decided to do the direct opposite of everything you proposed." Kady rose from her seat, heading for a bookshelf where the wrinkled printout sat folded between two books. She returned with the list and a highlighter pen.

"Let's check the no section," she shook the list open, "candles, incense, music, romance paperbacks, vegetarian food, clothing on Izzy...check, check, check." She ran the highlighter through each item. "Let's see...what's left? Oh that's right, no palm reading, tarot cards, *ridiculous* psychic displays from Izzy, or *ridiculous* conversations about romance novels." Smiling, she rose from her chair. "Be right back."

"Kathleen!"

She returned shortly with a stack of romance paperbacks in one arm, and a crystal ball and black lacquered box in the other. Depositing everything on the coffee table, she sat, cross-legged on the floor, her ballgown poofing around her.

"Here's the scoop on Izzy." Kady told them about her trip to Hungary, about Aladee's telepathic connection with animals, and all the rest, including the fact that Izzy informed them her name was Madame Izidora Meszaros, who lived a former life as a gypsy fortune teller in Hungary during the early 1900s.

Lorraine scoffed, muttering beneath her breath. It was when Kady told them about the tragic love affair Izzy had when she was human, that Lorraine cut in again.

"Kathleen...dear..." she began, looking genuinely concerned, "I think you may be unwell. Have you considered talking to a therapist? Mine is really excellent."

Kady chuckled at that. "Thanks but I'm okay. Really. I know it all sounds off the wall, and I completely understand your reservations but," her shoulders hiked in a shrug, "that's what happened."

"So..." Rylan said hesitantly, "Izzy's lover was named *Wolfgang Von Ludwig?*" He was clearly trying to squelch rising laughter.

"He was a German soldier, killed in World War I." Kady nodded. "Madame Izidora pined for him until the day she died." She looked toward Izzy in a wistful manner, while the dog let out a forlorn moan. "Isn't that the saddest, thing you've ever heard?"

"Oh...absolutely," Rylan said, clearly tongue-in-cheek. Kady understood his reservations.

"Kady..." Lorraine said kindly, "can't you see these thoughts are unhealthy? None of that is real."

"I understand why you might feel that way, and I appreciate your concern. You might change your mind though once you see that Izzy, Madame Izidora, can select tarot cards that are highly significant to each individual's needs."

"She can *what*?" Now it was Rylan's turn to look uneasy. "You're joking, right?"

"Nope. Izzy and I will give you a demonstration a little later."

"Rylan," Lorraine said, "don't encourage the poor girl's wild notions or we'll be here all night."

Ignoring his fiancée's comment, Rylan mused, "A tarot card reading by a psychic dog...yeah, I want to see that."

Lorraine groaned.

"As for these," Kady gestured to the stack of romance books on the coffee table, "reading is one of my greatest passions. This genre, written almost exclusively by women, about women and for women, is underrated and unappreciated, even by the higher echelons within the publishing industry. I have no doubt plenty elitist bluebloods enjoy curling up with a good steamy romance novel every so often."

Lorraine chuckled. "Really, Kady, can you honestly imagine any of *my* circle reading one of those bawdy excuses for real writing?"

"Trust me, you'd be surprised, Lorraine."

"I seriously doubt that. You're simply employing wishful thinking to stress your point. There's a good reason why intelligent people turn up their noses at romance novels."

"Why don't you enlighten us, Lorraine." Kady folded her arms over her chest.

"Gladly. Because they're poorly written drivel, designed to titillate and make a quick buck off uneducated, lonely, middleclass housewives, whose dull, uneventful lives leave them seeking an escape from their doldrums."

Lorraine held up a finger in protest when Kady opened her mouth. "And these undiscerning women only end up feeding their frustrations by escaping into unrealistic sexual fantasies and bodice ripping gibberish."

"Aside from developing a sense of self within a male dominated society," Kady responded, "romance novels endorse the female need for emotional and sexual gratification. It's because this genre touches on subjects still considered taboo that it's so often held in contempt by nonreaders."

One eyebrow arrowed up as Lorraine smiled. "I recognize all that mumbo-jumbo from your often lauded college dissertation."

"Dissertation?" Rylan looked perplexed.

"For her Ph.D. Kathleen defended a dissertation on the merits of romance novels—in front of the WHU faculty." Lorraine gave a throaty chuckle. "Can you imagine?"

"Wait..." A look of recognition crossed Rylan's features. "You're the Doctor Malone I've heard about on campus?" Kady nodded. "Well I'll be darned. You're the first doctor of romance I've ever met. I'm duly impressed."

"I majored in English, not romance, but since you're a professor, you already knew that." Kady wagged a chastising finger in his direction. "It's something I chose to do for my own personal fulfillment."

"And what happened? My cousin wasted her doctorate on becoming a," Lorraine shuddered, "just saying it makes my skin crawl...a fortunetelling saleswoman. You'd think with all her education she would have taken a different path rather than advocating dirty, hedonistic books."

"I'm disappointed in your lack of open-mindedness," Kady told her. "You sound like a throwback to our parents' unenlightened generation."

"I'll take that as a compliment."

"You would." Chuckling, Kady removed the paisley scarf from her head, setting it on an end table. With eyes half-closed, she raked her fingers through her hair. "Lorraine, have you ever read an entire romance novel?"

"No."

"Ever had a tarot card reading or had your palm read?"

"Certainly not."

"I've made it my mission to bring more romance into people's lives," Kady said. "I'm proud to say Cherished Pages Bookshop already boasts one of the largest selections of romance novels and tarot card sets on the Oregon coast." She offered them more coffee and cookies which they accepted. "I believe the depressing effect of the tragic news all over the headlines needs to be balanced by something lighter and more positive."

"That's actually a fair point," Lorraine agreed, surprising Kady.

"People need healthy, temporary escapism for the body, mind and soul," Kady continued, sipping from her coffee. "That's where Saffron's and my concept of romance novels combined with a little fortunetelling comes in."

Lorraine's nugget of interest dissolved.

"Saffron and I strive to provide the right mix of fantasy, love and happiness to help offset the negative news we're bombarded daily."

"Well...it sounds like your heart's in the right place," Lorraine grudgingly admitted, bringing another smile to Kady's lips. She was making progress!

"So, what's next, Kady?" Rylan asked. "You going to give us a crash course on the merits and cultural importance of romance novels?"

"No." Kady smiled. "I'm simply asking you to commit to reading one in its entirety." She selected a paperback from the stack she'd brought to the table. "The bookmark doubles as my business card." Removing the long narrow card from between the pages, she handed it to Rylan.

"Cherished Pages Bookshop," he read. "Where you can be whisked away to romantic adventures while relaxing over a fine cup of coffee." He flipped the bookmark over. "Readings by Katarina and her Psychic Dog, Madame Izidora." He glanced up. "Katarina?"

Kady shrugged. "I thought Katarina had a more exotic, mystic sound to it than Kady or Kathleen."

"So you encourage customers to use your bookshop like a combination library, coffee shop, fortunetelling tea-room?" Rylan asked.

"Exactly." Kady beamed a smile. "By providing a comfortable, welcoming atmosphere, we encourage reading. Customers enjoy having their fortunes told too. Each day we feature a different romance novel at a discount or, if they prefer, they can select a book from another genre. Customers can read their selections while sipping their tea or coffee, and then purchase the book if they want to finish it."

Rylan skimmed his fingers along his jaw. "What if they decide they don't want to buy the books? Aren't you stuck with a lot of freeloaders who just come in for the coffee and use your place like a library?"

"Bingo!" the mostly silent Lorraine chimed in. "Kathleen and my sister certainly didn't garner their business acumen from my father. How they manage to eke out a living with such a lackadaisical policy is beyond me."

"We do have a few regulars who don't purchase, but they're down on their luck for the most part," Kady explained.

"The word you're looking for is *indigents*," Lorraine said.

"The label isn't important. They enjoy reading and chatting over a good cup of coffee, because we don't pressure or rush them. We also give them free tarot card readings, highlighting the positive points to give them hope about the future."

Kady ignored her cousin's drawn out groan. "Most patrons end up purchasing several books, and we have a healthy repeat business. So..." she smiled at Lorraine, "Saffron and I do manage to eke out a pretty fair living. While money is important, it's not the most important aspect for me or Saffron."

"Sounds like you and Saffron have given your business model plenty of thought, and know exactly what you're doing," Rylan said.

"Thank you, Professor. We've also devoted a segment of our shop to used and out of print books. We'd like Cherished Pages to offer something for everyone's reading needs." Kady handed him the romance novel she held. "This one is brand new. It's an excellent science fiction romance. Read it and tell me if you don't agree the story and the author's writing style are excellent."

"*Immortal Among the Stars*," Rylan read. Taking the book, he studied the cover featuring a handsome, muscular male dressed in tight-fitting futuristic attire of lustrous emerald green with light and dark speckles. An attractive female in similar garb, purple instead of green, was at his side, her hand on his broad chest. Her outfit sported a shimmery cape to match.

Rylan's expression was curious. "Interesting." His head tilted. "Why did you pick science fiction for me?"

"I followed my instincts. I had a feeling it would be right for you."

"Huh...I enjoy science fiction, but I'm not too sure about the romance angle. Not really my thing."

"I think you might be surprised," Kady said.

"Rylan's only trying to be polite," Lorraine interrupted. "You shouldn't impose on him like this. What makes you think a respected science professor could possibly be interested in a trashy romance novel?"

"If you'd agree to read one," Kady waved a paperback in Lorraine's direction, "instead of criticizing something you know nothing about, we wouldn't even be having this conversation because you'd be a convert."

Arching an eyebrow, Lorraine let out an amused chortle. "Bodice-ripping antics hold no interest for me."

"Actually, *bodice ripper* is an antiquated and dismissive term," Kady said, "which was generally reserved for historical or gothic romances that included some semblance of violence."

Shrugging, Lorraine said, "Potato, potahto."

"I believe you're an open-minded woman, Lorraine," Kady lied, "so why not agree to give one of these books a chance? If you don't like it, I'll never bring up the subject of romance novels with you again."

Lorraine gave Kady a lengthy look. "You're my witness, Rylan, you heard her. If I read one of these books she'll never bother me about them again." She gave a smug smile. "Go ahead and choose one for me."

"I've got a better idea," Kady said. "Izzy, come." She patted her lap and the dog quickly leapt from the couch, joining her. "Pick out the best romance novel for Lorraine to read." She spread the paperbacks across the table.

Lorraine covered her mouth and laughed in spite of herself when the little bocker eagerly sat at Kady's side, looking as if she was on a mission.

The elastic band on the turban Izzy wore had slipped and the headpiece hung at the dog's chin. Kady righted the turban and tapped the top of the coffee table. Izzy propped her front paws on the edge of the table, appearing to study the books.

Looking at the books in front of her and then at Lorraine, she used her nose to nudge a paperback from the spread toward Lorraine, giving a soft bark. She then pushed a separate book toward Kady, barking again, which puzzled Kady. Her task completed, Izzy returned to the couch, resting her head in Rylan's lap.

"She actually did it." Rylan laughed, removing Izzy's headpiece and petting the dog's head. "She picked one for each of you."

Picking up the book Izzy had nudged toward her, Lorraine studied the cover. "*The Ice Maiden*. How amusing."

"Well, my little ice maiden," Rylan told Lorraine, "don't worry. Once I've finished reading my sci-fi romance, I'm sure I'll discover a broad spectrum of ways to warm you up."

Tsking, Lorraine offered a capitulating laugh.

Rylan picked up the paperback Izzy had pushed toward Kady. He studied the cover and a small smile crossed his lips. Without saying a word, he held the book out to Kady. As she took the book from his hand, their fingers brushed and Kady immediately felt her heart stutter.

*Get a grip, girl. This is your cousin's future husband you're palpitating over.* A quick study of the book's cover brought a shot of heat to Kady's cheeks and she shot an inquisitive look toward Izzy, who was too busy licking her paws to notice Kady's glance.

Just above the sensuous picture of a man and woman embracing in a bookshop, the title read, *Her Cousin's Man*. Beneath that, in smaller print were the words, *Her cousin had his promise, but she had his heart.* Kady noticed the couple on the cover bore an uncanny likeness to herself and Rylan.

She chanced a quick, furtive glance toward Rylan who was watching her reaction to the book with calculated amusement.

Caught up in a chain of yawns, Lorraine said, "So let's see what the furry little critter chose for you, Kady." She curled her fingers in a beckoning motion.

While a dumbfounded Kady remained motionless, Rylan grabbed the book from her hand and took a step toward Lorraine, purposely dropping the book onto the tabletop where the other books remained spread out. "Butterfingers," he said, giving an apologetic smile. He picked up a book, handing it to Lorraine, who laughed after reading the title.

"*Sandcastle Dreams*, that's Kady all right. Always with her head in the clouds. Looks like you have a very perceptive dog there, Kady."

Breathing a sigh of relief and flashing a quick, embarrassed, smile of thanks in Rylan's direction, Kady laughed and stroked Izzy behind the ears.

Lorraine yawned twice. "We should call it a night, Rylan. You have a class early tomorrow, don't you?"

"Not until eleven."

Since Lorraine seemed to be warming to her, Kady hoped they'd stay longer, giving her a chance at a breakthrough. "I'd love to hear all about your wedding and honeymoon plans," Kady told her cousin. She felt sure it was a topic Lorraine would embrace.

"Oh," Lorraine offered a sleepy smile, "all right, but just for a little while. I'm really tired." She looked at Rylan. "Must be that long drive back from Seattle." With another yawn, she settled against the back of the chair.

In less than five minutes, Kady heard snoring coming from Lorraine's direction. Her sophisticated cousin was blissfully sawing logs, loud enough that it could have been mistaken for Izzy snoring. Kady and Rylan shared a muffled laugh.

Returning her attention to Izzy, she wondered about the book Izzy had chosen for her. It wasn't even one of the books Kady had selected for this evening. She knew Izzy was smart and psychic, but the dog couldn't possibly have gone through her books and managed to add it to her pile. *Could she*?

"Saffron! Of course!" Kady mistakenly blurted aloud, drawing Rylan's attention.

"I'm sorry...what?"

*Oops.* "Oh, nothing. Sorry, I was just thinking out loud."

Saffron must have stuck the book in there as a joke, knowing it would grab Kady's attention. But then...why did Izzy choose it for her? She'd definitely have to talk to Saffron about it tomorrow.

As Rylan rough-housed with the dog, Kady found herself imagining what it would be like if Rylan was *her* fiancé instead of Lorraine's. How would it feel to be crushed against that enticing, imposing musculature of his? Was his chest as hard and sculpted as it appeared? And those lips, offering such tantalizing promise, did they deliver a sensation of passion beneath their fullness?

Kady's lip curled into a subtle smile as her thoughts gleefully tiptoed through the lush, fertile field of her imagination. With a quick glance Rylan's way, she found him studying her, smiling and looking away once she'd looked up.

Her fertile field of imagination promptly morphed into a clanging fire alarm, warning her to keep her forbidden, illicit imaginings far, far away from her cousin's man.

# Chapter 8

"READY FOR Izzy to give you that tarot card reading I promised?" Kady asked as nonchalantly as possible, doing her damnedest to speak to Rylan like a pal, a buddy, a man who was entirely off limits.

"Sure, why not?"

She retrieved the deck of tarot cards from the black lacquered box she'd brought in earlier, placing them on the table. While Rylan remained on the couch, she sat across from him on the floor. No way was she about to sit next to him on the cushy sofa.

As she clacked the deck of cards against the tabletop, she hoped Lorraine would quit snoring and wake up. Apparently her cousin wasn't kidding when she said she was tired.

"I've never been to a psychic," Rylan admitted. "So, what happens? You concentrate on me and read my thoughts?"

"No." Kady laughed. "I don't read minds, but my intuition has always been sharp and I've had many occasions of ESP over my lifetime."

"Interesting."

"It is. Actually, anyone can learn the intricacies of the tarot to give a fairly predictable reading if they're willing to invest the time. Same goes for reading palms."

Rylan picked up the deck of cards, studying it. "So even a stodgy science professor like me could learn to do this?"

He was far more open to curious ideas than his fiancée. "It helps if you keep an open mind and let your imagination run free," she explained. "Being a science professor, you might tend toward being analytical, exact, skeptical, and cynical." She flashed an apologetic grin.

"Gee," Rylan slapped a hand against his chest, "can't we just say I'm a realist?" Kady laughed and nodded.

"Tarot cards have been used for centuries. The deck's divided in two parts." She spread some of the cards across the worn old dark-oak coffee table and proceeded to give him a basic description of the cards and their meanings, showing him samples of each as she spoke.

"I hope I'm not boring you to tears, Rylan."

"No, it's interesting."

"The major arcana are usually considered to be more powerful, but the minor arcana are important too."

"Of course." He smirked.

Shaking her head, Kady chuckled...while Lorraine continued to snore. When she looked up and smiled, her heart somersaulted as their gazes met. Swallowing the lump in her throat, she instructed, "Shuffle the cards. When it feels right, stop, then cut the deck in three piles from left to right." Once Rylan complied, Kady arranged the cards in a spread and proceeded to do his reading.

"What's this mean?" Rylan pointed to the seven of cups card.

Kady raised her eyebrows. "It can signify confusion about a decision. Often the heart urges one direction, while the head says to go in another." She looked up at Rylan. "There are many ways to interpret the cards. They're not always what they appear to be," she told him, fingering the card. "It's natural that this card would pop up. It probably means you've got premarital jitters. You wouldn't be human if you didn't." She laughed and he followed suit.

"Let's face it," Rylan glanced at his sleeping fiancée, "when you've made it to almost forty without getting married, there's bound to be some nervousness. But I'm ready." He issued a confident smile.

Kady patted her lap and Izzy quickly leapt from the couch to join her. "Madame Izidora, the psychic dog, will now choose a significant card for you, Rylan. Place your hand on the table next to Izzy's paw and concentrate on thoughts of your future."

Rylan did as he was instructed and Izzy placed her paw over his hand, wagging her tail. With her nose, she pushed a card from the spread deck toward Rylan and gave a soft bark. She then pushed the same card toward Kady and barked again.

"What a smart pup you are," Rylan said, petting the dog's head and laughing when Izzy bolted up onto the sofa to lick his face. "What does the card mean, Kady?"

"This is so apropos." Kady smiled at him. "The ace of cups signifies new love. It usually means the person is entering into a new relationship and will be blessed with love, happiness, and a long union." She wondered why Izzy had pushed the card toward her after Rylan. Izzy had never done anything like that before. Maybe Izzy was tired, like sleeping beauty snoring away in the chair.

Rylan held his palm out to Kady. "So, what do you see on this big old paw of mine, *Katarina*?"

A quick study of Rylan's palm showed he tended to be open minded, openhearted and considerate. The upward curve of his heart line revealed he leaned toward a physical, earthy attitude to sex. She gave him a brief explanatory reading, skipping over the sex part.

"Pretty cool," he said. "I bet Lorraine would enjoy this if she let herself relax."

"I think she would too."

Motioning toward the crystal ball with his thumb, Rylan asked, "Do I get a crystal ball reading, too?"

"May as well go for the whole enchilada." Kady laughed. Moving the heavy crystal ball that rested on brass talons in front of her, she smiled to herself. People always wanted her to gaze into the crystal ball. It took an incredible amount of energy to focus her attention and concentrate strongly enough to visualize anything more than a few vague, indistinguishable images in the sphere. She was always elated when a tangible image appeared and she could decipher it for her clients.

In rare instances, a handful of her clients had even seen images in the orb themselves. Kady attributed that to the fact that some people were more in touch with their psychic feelings than others. She hoped she'd be able to see a semi-clear image tonight for Rylan.

"Focus on the center of the sphere, Rylan. Concentrate and visualize. Think about your future." Leaning toward the crystal ball, she moved her hands over it. Scooting toward the end of his seat, Rylan leaned in closer too, which didn't help Kady's concentration. She squinted as a blurry image began coming into focus.

Rylan leaned even closer, straining to see something, anything. "Whoa!" Impulsively, he grabbed Kady's wrist. "You're not going to believe this, hell, *I* don't believe this, but I'm starting to see something, Kady. It's all fuzzy. I can't make it out. Looks like shelves of books. Maybe people too. Are you seeing the same thing?"

Struggling to ignore the jolt she felt from Rylan's touch, Kady gazed with more intensity. "Yes, I see it...it's getting clearer."

"I can see something green," Rylan said.

"Me too. It's—" Then she saw it. Right there, smack dab in the center of the crystal ball, as clear as day, she saw an image of herself and Rylan locked in a passionate embrace. They were in the middle of a crowded store that looked very much like Cherished Pages Bookshop. It looked almost as if they'd stepped off the cover of *Immortal Among the Stars*, the novel she'd given Rylan to read.

Gasping in disbelief, she slapped her hands over the ball, drawing it to her chest.

"What?" Rylan asked. "What did you see?"

"Nothing!" Her heart raced so fast it was like one continuous beat. "Absolutely nothing."

"Here, let me see," Rylan said, reaching for the ball.

"No! Don't touch it!"

Clearly stunned, Rylan looked at Kady as if she'd lost her mind. Which was probably accurate.

"What about the green I saw? There was definitely something there."

"It was nothing!" He was talking about the costume of the cover model because she saw it herself, plain as day. "All you saw was a reflection from that book." Kady pointed to *Immortal Among the Stars*, sitting on the table near Rylan.

Kady's phone jangled. It was her mom's ringtone.

*Now? Really?*

Since Astrid rarely called in the evening, Kady hesitated to let it go to voicemail in case something was wrong. Still clutching the crystal ball close, Kady tried to sound as normal as possible to avoid alarming her mother.

"Hi Mom, this isn't a good time to talk. Is it important?"

"How's everything going, sweetheart? I can't wait to hear all about it. Are they still there?" Astrid asked and Kady fought the urge to laugh hysterically.

"Fine, fine. Yes, they're still here." Like Gollum and its precious, Kady maintained body-hugging possession of her crystal ball during their conversation. No doubt Rylan assumed she was insane.

"Tell my niece I said hello."

Glancing up, Kady tried to form a smile as she watched a groggy Lorraine wake from her nap. "Mom says hello, Lorraine." Returning her attention to the call, Kady said, "I'll call you later, okay?"

"Your sister's been trying to reach you, honey."

Kady couldn't help tsking at her mother's chattiness. "Which one...I've got three?"

"Reen. She said she texted and called. Didn't you see it?"

"My phone's been in the other room most of the evening. Is something wrong?" Kady hoped not because she only had about an ounce of normalcy operating in her brain right now.

"No, not wrong...but you need to call her as soon as you can. She needs to talk to you."

"I spent close to an hour talking to Reen this morning. Everything okay with her, Drake and the twins?"

"Yes, no need to worry. Just call her. Bye sweetie, love you!" Ending the call, Kady quickly glanced at the phone to see a series of missed calls and text messages.

"What happened?" Lorraine asked, covering a yawn. "Did I hear you yelling at Rylan a few minutes ago, or was I dreaming?"

"I, um, may have elevated my voice briefly," Kady admitted.

"Why? What happened? What's wrong?" Lorraine looked as confused as Kady felt.

"Nothing." Still clutching the heavy glass sphere tight to her chest, she swallowed the giant lump in her throat, and took a few deep breaths to slow her galloping heartbeat. Gazing into the ball once more, she saw only clear glass. Thankfully, the image had disintegrated. This was unreal...like being in the midst of a nightmare.

She'd never seen such a vivid image before and couldn't understand what happened, or why. All she knew is that her inappropriate attraction to Rylan had to cease. Immediately.

As Kady relaxed her grip on the glass ball, Rylan gently took it from her, setting it back in its stand.

"Oh Rylan, the poor thing looks like she's seen a ghost," Lorraine said. "You-you don't think that's possible do you?" Heading to the kitchen, Lorraine called over her shoulder, "I mean, you know, with all the hocus-pocus stuff Kady's involved in." She was back in a minute with a glass of water. Digging through her little designer purse, she drew out a small gold case, opening it and plucking out a pill. "Here, Kady, take this...it's just ibuprofen. I keep them on hand for my headaches."

Apparently Kady had managed not only to scare the hell out of herself, but out of her dinner guests as well. Although she was a medication minimalist who didn't like taking anything unnecessary, she decided this was a bad time to object. Thanking Lorraine, she swallowed the pill with water.

She must have looked a wreck because she heard Lorraine whisper to Rylan, "Do you think she's all right? Should we get her some medical attention?"

"What happened, Kady?" Rylan asked. "Did you see something upsetting in the crystal ball? Like...did it show you I'm going to die or something?"

"Oh my goodness, no!" Her hand flew to her chest. "No!" Calming her voice, she said, "I'm sorry, I didn't mean to screech. I promise, there was nothing like that, Rylan. I saw nothing about you, or anything else for that matter. Nothing materialized after you and I saw the initial blurry image. That's what made me upset. I apologize, I must be more exhausted than I realized, getting everything ready for tonight." Her hands feathered out to the sides. Gesturing to the conglomeration of bizarre stuff around them.

"I foolishly overreacted when nothing appeared. I-I was upset and disappointed."

"You were sheet-white and now your face is all flushed." Lorraine's voice was tinged with concern as she clapped her hand to Kady's forehead checking for a fever. "Are you all right?"

Every fiber of her being wanted to scream, *No! No, I'm not all right. I'm seeing deliciously forbidden images and having indecent thoughts about my cousin's hotter than hell fiancé.* Instead, Kady said, "Yes, absolutely. I'm fine, just fine. Everything is fine. There's nothing to worry about." For some godforsaken reason, she followed that up by blurting out, "Wine!"

"Wine?" Rylan and Lorraine chorused, bewilderment coloring their expressions.

"Right." Kady nodded vigorously, imagining she looked like a bobblehead on steroids. "I must have had too much wine and it made me woozy while gazing intently into the crystal ball." She prayed they'd buy her flimsy story.

Surprising the heck out of Kady, Lorraine came to her side again, wrapping an arm around Kady's shoulder in a caring embrace. It was an exceedingly un-Lorraine-like gesture.

"That cheap jug wine is full of additives and God knows what else. Oh, Kady, I'm so sorry."

"Sorry?" Kady couldn't remember hearing those words spill from her cousin's lips before. "For what, Lorraine? We drank my wine, not yours, remember?" Her attempt at laughter sounded anemic.

Expelling a heavy sigh, Lorraine replied, "It's my fault for stressing you so much that you felt the need to resort to all..." shuddering, she waved her hand at their surroundings, "all this. I-I know you've just been trying to teach me a lesson because I sent you that list of rules." She rested her cheek against Kady's for a moment. "And I deserve it. Forgive me?"

Shellshocked, Kady nodded and took her cousin's hand. "Of course I do, Lorraine. Thank you." It was an absolute joy to see her cousin come down off her pedestal and show genuine compassion. It had been a long time—if ever.

"Are you sure you're going to be okay, Kady?" Lorraine added.

Feeling as if she'd just fallen down the rabbit hole after experiencing Lorraine's out of the ordinary kindness and concern, Kady wasn't sure. That must have been one heck of a restorative nap her cousin had.

"Yes." Kady nodded. "I'm fine. My apologies for alarming you. I-I really appreciate your concern, Lorraine."

"We may have our differences, Kady, but we're cousins and I care about you. Is there anything we can do for you before we go? Oh! I know!" She turned to Rylan. "We'll call one of the housekeepers to come over to do all the dishes and clean everything up for Kady."

Rylan's laughter was contagious as he took off his sport coat and unbuttoned his shirt cuffs while Kady rejected any notion about how damned deliciously appealing he looked.

"No, my rich, spoiled fiancée, we'll do nothing of the kind. You and I will roll up our sleeves, get in the kitchen, and do the cleanup ourselves."

Poor Lorraine looked like she'd just been informed a giant asteroid was heading for Devington Manor. Her hand flying to her throat, she sputtered, "Oh, but Rylan, I-I couldn't possibly—"

"Thank you so very much but absolutely not," Kady insisted. "I never allow my guests to do cleanup." She chuckled at the ludicrous thought of Lorraine engaging in any manner of housework. "You're very kind to want to help but, honestly, I'm feeling better and don't mind cleaning up the rest of the mess. Saffron already took care of most of it."

"Huh...my sister washing dishes..." Lorraine offered a clueless shrug. "Definitely not the same Saffron I grew up with."

"No, definitely not." Kady smiled and glanced at the Buddha belly clock. "It's still early. I, um, had hoped we could have a nice chat about...things," she said carefully. "Actually, Lorraine, I was wondering if Rylan has had an opportunity to meet Red yet. I think they'd get along great." Kady already knew the answer. Lorraine and Red hadn't spoken since she, along with her parents, had rebuffed Red, but Kady thought it might be a good excuse to open a dialog about the situation.

Boy was she wrong.

Lorraine stiffened. Her expression blank, she turned to Rylan. "We should go and let Kady rest. Let's get our coats and—"

"Who's Red?" he asked.

"My cousin, Redmond Devington." Kady said with a smile that Lorraine answered with a narrow-eyed scowl. "Lorraine and Saffron's brother."

In slow motion, Rylan turned to Lorraine. "You have a brother?"

Closing her eyes, Lorraine took her time filling her lungs with air and expelling it.

Kady hadn't meant to ambush her cousin, but she couldn't let them leave without at least trying to make some headway regarding what happened with Red.

"I do. But this isn't a conversation I wish to have at the moment. I want to leave now, Rylan. Please."

"Okay...sure." Bafflement obvious, Rylan offered a clueless shrug as Lorraine went to get their coats from Kady's bedroom.

*Stupid, stupid, stupid.* Closing her hands tight, Kady dug her fingernails into her palms. She'd spoiled everything, virtually destroying any progress she'd made. "I had to go open my big fat mouth," she muttered nearly inaudibly beneath her breath.

"Sorry, what was that?"

"Nothing." Her hand flit through her air.

"Hey," Rylan chucked Kady's chin, "you take care of yourself, okay? I think you, um..." he glanced around the apartment, "overdid your dinner preparations." He winked at her and she smiled, trying in vain to ignore the electrical charge she felt when his knuckle grazed her chin.

After exchanging pleasant, polite goodbyes, he and Lorraine were gone, allowing Kady to collapse onto the sofa, pulling Izzy close.

"Ohhh, Izzy, did you see that image of me and Rylan in the crystal ball?" The bocker let out a soft bark and licked Kady's face. "I made such a fool of myself tonight. I've convinced them both I'm more of a screwball than Lorraine initially thought. What am I going to do, Izzy? Only a horrible, awful, evil person would fall for her cousin's fiancé." She let out a pained groan.

Breaking free from Kady's arms, Izzy leaped to the floor, making Kady miss her warmth. Placing her paw on a paperback, she pushed it toward Kady, then pushed a tarot card toward her with a soulful little howl that made it seem she was trying to talk—to really communicate.

Kady picked up the book. *Her Cousin's Man* again. And the tarot card was the ace of cups again. Slanting Izzy an incredulous look, she said, "Izzy, are you saying you really *were* trying to tell me something earlier?"

Tapping the book with her paw, Izzy barked.

Transmitting a skeptical glance toward the complacent little canine, Kady shook her head in disbelief. "You-you're actually trying to communicate with me about my attraction to Rylan?"

Izzy barked again.

No...it was too far-fetched. "I'm sorry, Izzy," she kissed the top of the dog's head, "but that's simply not possible." Ruffling the dog's fur, she said, "Just my overactive imagination after a long, tough day."

With her paw, Izzy nudged the book and tarot card until they fell off the table, landing on the floor next to Kady. Looking quite pleased with herself, Izzy cocked her head, gazing up at her mistress.

Giving Izzy's actions more credence, Kady slanted her head, making eye contact with her dog. "Me and Rylan? Together?" Izzy offered another soft bark. "No way, Izzy." Resolutely shaking her head from side to side, she vowed, "I would never allow anything to happen between me and Rylan."

Izzy let out a determined little moan, picked up the paperback and the tarot card in her teeth, and deposited them in Kady's lap before giving her mistress the same tongue-lolling gaze she had before.

With a ponderous groan, Kady gave Izzy a forlorn look. "I may be quirky and naïve and, well, I know everyone thinks I'm odd," she rolled her eyes, "but one thing I'm definitely *not* is a shameless brazen hussy...a fiancé stealer."

Kady's phone rang. It was Reen's ring.

"Hi, sorry I missed your calls. I was just about to call you back. Lorraine and Rylan just left. Mom told me you've been trying to reach me. Everything okay?"

"Couldn't be better. You?"

"Aside from my life spinning down into a blackhole, you mean? Yeah, sure. Peachy."

"Uh-oh. That negativity sounds very un-Kady like. Must have been a really bad night with our cousin, hmm?"

"It was...interesting. Terrible, wonderful, and shocking. A veritable roller coaster of emotions. Can I give you a call tomorrow to tell you about it? I'm absolutely beat, Reen. I need to clean up this mess and go to bed. I've got to be at the bookshop early again tomorrow and—"

"Nope."

Ready to end the call, she frowned at the phone. "What do you mean, nope?"

"I'm coming over. I'll be there in ten to fifteen minutes. Mom's coming with me. We'll help you clean everything up."

Looking around her, Kady laughed. "Better bring a bulldozer. Seriously, Reen, I appreciate the offer but it's not necessary to—"

"Make a pot of coffee and have some Kahlua ready."

"Now?" Kady looked at Buddha's belly. "It's after nine-thirty."

"You'll need it. See you soon." Reen ended the call.

~<>~

"Holy hell! It looks like a dump truck full of stuff nobody in their right mind would ever want spewed their cargo all over your apartment!" Reen said, eyes wide. "Where did you get all this junk...and why? And, oh my God, what the hell are you wearing? You look like Cinderella got stuck in somebody's nightmare."

"Um, hello Pot, meet Kettle," Kady teased. "You're the last one who should be doling out organizational advice, Reen." She laughed, stepping aside to let her sister and mother enter the apartment.

"Your sister has a point, dear," Astrid told Reen.

"Well hell," Reen said, snapping her fingers. "And here I got all excited hoping maybe I wasn't the worst one anymore."

"No such luck, Reenie." Astrid wrapped her arm around her daughter, giving her a squeeze.

"I may have gone ever so slightly overboard in my quest to get under Lorraine's skin," Kady admitted.

"Maybe just a tad." Considering it, Reen offered a wide smile. "Did it work?"

"Yes and no." Kady laughed again. It felt good to be able to relax and laugh now that much of the angst was over. "I'll tell you all about it tomorrow."

"Well, not all of it looks like junk," Astrid noted as she walked around, fingering one object after another. "There are some interesting things here. Actually, some of it's mine already," she said with a shrug. "I loaned a number of items here to Kady for tonight's dinner, so it goes back with me...unless you'd like to keep any of it, Kady."

"Well," Kady grinned, "I've become attached to the Buddha with the clock in its belly."

"It's yours."

"Come back with your own car then, Mom," Reen jokingly warned, still taking everything in, "because none of this shall enter my vehicle."

Since Reen was an avid thrift shopper whose car often housed her own latest finds, Kady knew she didn't mean a word of that.

"I'm detecting elder abuse here," Astrid teased.

"Okay, you two, you're very amusing but I'm exhausted and need to get some sleep. Big day tomorrow for me and Madame Izidora." Kady thumbed toward the sleeping dog. "So what's up?"

"Did you make the coffee?" Reen asked.

"And get the Kahlua?" Astrid asked.

"Yes and yes." Getting an exciting notion in her head, Kady eyeballed Reen. "Wait a minute...don't tell me. Are you pregnant?"

Reen glanced down, patting her fairly flat belly. "That," she patted the slight protrusion, "is the result of our sister's scones, not any magic orchestrated by my husband."

"Okay so," lifting her arms in the air, Kady let them fall, slapping at her sides, "why are you here at," she checked Buddha again, "almost ten o'clock, after I've had a grueling Lorraine day?"

Reen glanced around the apartment again. The dining room table was one of the only clear spots. "Let's sit here." She took a chair. "Coffee please." She clapped twice, making Kady and Astrid chuckle.

"Such a taskmaster," Kady teased, bringing her ornate Turkish coffee set to the table.

"Ooh, I love that," Astrid said, rubbing her hands together.

Kady filled the espresso-like cups and set the bottle of Kahlua on the tray next to the little copper pot after pouring a small amount into each cup.

"A toast to my little sister," Reen said, holding her cup aloft to clink with the others. She and Astrid drank, but Kady held back. "How come you didn't drink?" Reen asked.

Kady shrugged. "Lorraine says the person being toasted is never supposed to drink to themselves."

"Bullshit," Astrid said and her daughters' heads swiveled toward her as they laughed.

"Mom!" Kady chastised. "Language!"

"Who cares what prissy Miss Manners says?" Astrid went on. "I'm your mother and I say drink up!"

"Yes ma'am!" Kady and Reen chorused, laughing harder before they both polished off the coffee in their cups.

"So tell me, why am I being toasted?" Kady asked.

Reen held out her hand, wiggling her fingers toward Kady in invitation. "Take my hand and hold tight." Once Kady clasped it, Reen slipped her hand away, leaving her heartwish ring in Kady's hand.

With an audible gasp, Kady said, "Oh my gosh, the heartwish ring! With everything that happened today, the idea of this being the reason for your visit tonight never even crossed my mind."

"That special knowing feeling came over me probably about the time you were sitting down to dinner with Lorraine and her fiancé. It's just like everyone else who's had the ring described. I felt it here," Reen covered her heart, "deep inside. I knew, without a doubt, that it was time to pass my ring on to you, Kady. For the first time since I put the ring on, I was able to remove it. Exciting, huh?"

"Yes! Extremely."

"You look a lot more awake now than you did when we first got here." Astrid laughed. "I can't wait to see what your heartwish will be. Knowing my Kady, you're going to try to find a way to save the world and everyone in it." Astrid's smile was warm and kind as she took her daughter's hand. "Go ahead, put it on your finger, honey."

Kady scrunched her features. "Is it weird that I'm kind of, sort of afraid?"

"Nope, I get it," Reen said. "I felt the same way. I think you were still traveling overseas when the rest of us had the rings passed to us, so you haven't really had a chance to hear about everyone's experiences."

"Most people receiving the ring," Astrid said, "seem to feel somewhat uncertain. And they worry about making the right wish."

"Exactly." Kady gingerly slipped the ring onto her finger, immediately feeling the band grow pleasantly warm. An almost imperceptible bluish glow from the stone followed. Blazing a bright smile, she said, "Oh I have so much to think about!"

"Cool how the ring fits each recipient perfectly, isn't it?" Reen asked. "My fingers are bigger than yours," she wiggled them in demonstration, "but the ring fits you as if it was handcrafted just for you."

"Truly amazing." She looked up at Reen and Astrid. "I'm glad I didn't know about this until after Lorraine and Rylan left. I was such a nervous wreck earlier. It would have been worse if I'd just learned about getting the heartwish ring."

"With all your eclectic interests," Reen said, "I'm dying of curiosity about the wish you'll make. Any thoughts crossing your mind yet?"

"Only about a million," Kady joked. "I imagined that one day I'd probably receive the ring so, yes, I've given it some thought. It will be one of the most difficult and important decisions I've ever made."

"One of the best things," Reen told her, "is that, as confused as you might feel about choosing the right wish and not making some awful mistake, you'll discover that when the time is right, your heart basically makes the wish known to you. It's like waking from a fuzzy dream where, all of a sudden, there's amazing clarity and you know, you really know, what you must wish for."

"It feels like a big responsibility. I'll spend some time talking to everyone who's had the ring so I can pick their brains and see what experiences they had."

"Good idea," Astrid said.

"I've got something to tell you about tonight," Kady said, feeling edgy. "It's really bothering me and I'm sorely in need of good advice." She proceeded to tell her mother and sister everything, including the crystal ball, and Kady's inappropriate feelings toward Rylan. By the time they'd finished talking it was nearing midnight. Kady felt immensely better getting their input, and assurance that she hadn't turned into a terrible, awful person.

The best part, Kady told them, is she wouldn't have to see Rylan again until the wedding because Kady sure as hell wasn't about to invite them over again.

"Okay," Astrid rubbed her hands together briskly, "time for us to get cracking and clean up this mess so you can get some rest and Reen and I can head on home." She rose from the table with Reen and Kady following her lead.

The kitchen was already pretty cleaned up and Astrid and Reen told Kady they'd be happy to stop by tomorrow to help Kady take down all the garish decorating she'd installed all over the apartment.

As for getting rest tonight, Kady strongly doubted she'd even be able to go to sleep with everything on her mind.

# Chapter 9

## *Two Weeks Later*

~<>~

A PERFECT practitioner of Miss Manners' rules of etiquette, Lorraine sent a note of thanks and a bouquet of flowers to Kady after the dinner. She included an invitation to come to Devington Manor for dinner with her family the following weekend. Kady politely declined, blaming her busy schedule at the bookshop. The real reason was her need to avoid the electrifying professor.

As pompous as her social butterfly cousin could be, Kady cared for Lorraine too much to risk getting too close to Rylan.

"The shop's been so busy lately," Kady said to Saffron while stacking books on the shelves. "Which is great. I'm certainly not complaining. But it's good to have some downtime so we can get caught up on all these boxes of books we've received, isn't it?"

"You had a good idea about giving yourself at least one day a week where you aren't committed to doing your fortunetelling shtick," Saffron said. "Customers can't get enough of you and Madame Izidora. You needed a break."

"I agree. I've had so much on my mind, with getting the heartwish ring and all, that I haven't been able to give my tarot card or palm readings the attention they deserve." A lively smile took hold. "I absolutely love what you're doing with the customers' children, by the way. The parents and kids love it. It's the perfect addition to Cherished Pages."

Kady was talking about Storytime with Aunt Saffy. The original name the two of them came up with was Aunt Saffy's Storytime but, thankfully, they realized the acronym would be ASS so they shelved that bright idea. *Saffy* was a nickname Saffron used to hate, or at least claimed she did, when Reen called her that to get under her skin before the cousins mended their fences and became good friends. The new Saffron had embraced the nickname and made good use of it.

"You would have made a great children's librarian. The kids love it when you use different voices for each character, and add the bit of extra action too."

"I'd enjoy being a children's librarian," Saffron said. "I'd looked into it as a career option when I was in college but Mom, Dad, and Lorraine ridiculed me, saying the idea was stupid." Shrugging, she said, "It's funny, I never thought I liked kids much, and didn't want any of my own, until I moved away from Devington Manor and my family. The atmosphere there was so..."

Kady saw her cousin struggling to come up with the right word. "Oppressive?" she offered.

Wide-eyed, Saffron pointed at her with a resounding, "Yes! Exactly. Getting out of there was like a weight lifted from my soul, Kady."

"I understand." She really did. Each time she visited Devington Manor, Kady came away feeling uncharacteristically downhearted, as if she'd been sucked deep into its bottomless pit of negativity. It wasn't a happy place. No wonder Lorraine was such a curmudgeon.

"And now?" Kady prodded.

"Now?" Hugging herself, Saffron engaged in joyful chuckling. "I can't wait to have children of my own. The joy I get from reading to them is a great mood elevator. Seeing the animated smiles on their little faces when I do my silly character shtick is so rewarding. I think I'd be a good mom too. I'd just put them first, the way I used to put my real estate business first. If I can be salesperson of the month for ten months straight, then I can be mom of the month for at least three."

"Months?" Kady asked.

"Nope." Offering the most heartwarming smile, Saffron said, "Kids. At least three kids."

It made Kady's heart glad to witness Saffron's transformation from a starchy, all-business and no-play woman, to a warm, spontaneous, child-loving free spirit.

"All you need now is to find the right guy for you," Kady said.

"She says as if it's as easy as a walk in the park." Saffron huffed a humorless chuckle. "If I haven't found someone by now, I doubt it'll happen. But no problem. I'm perfectly fine with adopting. I'll just have to..." making her voice sound like a man's, she finished, "create a dad character for the kids." They laughed at her dad voice and the idea.

"Now listen, Missy," Saffron said, planting her hands on her hips while staring Kady down. Grinning, she added, "That was my mom voice, by the way."

"Very effective," Kady told her. "You had me quaking in my boots."

"Good, that's what I want to hear. Anyway," Saffron went on while unpacking a new shipment of paranormal romance paperbacks, "I want you to know I'm well aware the heartwish ring isn't all you've had on your mind lately. You can't avoid Rylan Kilpatrick forever, Kady. What, are you afraid you're going to jump the guy's bones the next time you see him because he's got you mesmerized?" One eyebrow vaulted.

"There, you see? It's rubbing off on you." Kady slit open another new box of books.

Tilting her head in confusion, Saffron asked, "What is?"

"My psychic abilities." Once it sank in, Kady joined Saffron in laughter. "It's best if I steer clear of him, Saffron. It's not like Lorraine and I are bosom buddies who do lunch, you know. There's no reason for me to see her, or her fiancé, until they're walking down the aisle in October. It's just a silly crush. I'll be over it by then."

She'd be lying if she said Rylan hadn't been on her mind the past two weeks. The most mundane things often reminded her of him. While watching an old movie on TCM she wondered how a man with his matinee idol looks and raw animal magnetism could end up teaching science at a university. He belonged in the movies, or on stage, or between the covers of a magazine, or...between her sheets.

With an audible grumble of self-reproach, Kady asked herself for the thousandth time what in the world was the matter with her. Why did she continue having ribald thoughts about her cousin's fiancé?

"Somewhere along life's journey I must have taken a wrong turn without realizing it and headed down *Harlot Lane*," Kady muttered aloud with a distinct shudder. She hadn't meant to verbalize it...it just popped out.

"What the hell are you grumbling about now? You've been doing that ever since the night you had him and Lorraine over for dinner."

Kady wanted to laugh Saffron's lighthearted comment off with a cheerful response, but she couldn't. For some crazy reason thoughts of Rylan sometimes made her want to cry and this was one of those times.

When Kady remained silent, continuing to stack new paperbacks on the bookshelves, Saffron came over, draping her arm over her shoulder. "Aw, you poor thing. You've been coveting your cousin's prize catch ever since you laid eyes on him."

Saffron's words stunned her. "*Coveting my*..." Slapping her hands over her face, Kady said, "Ugh! Do you have to make it sound so lecherous?"

"I was semi-teasing." She gave Kady a supportive squeeze. "I'm simply an impartial observer who speaks the truth as she sees it. Listen, Kady, there's nothing wrong with inappropriate sexual attraction, as long as you don't act on it. And we both know you—"

Kady gasped. "Never! I would never, ever do that." She slammed the next stack of books onto the shelf with more emphasis than necessary. "*Ever*."

"You know..." Saffron began, a devilish glint in her eye, "I wouldn't be at all surprised if the professor's been having second thoughts about Lorraine since he met you."

"No, no, no..." Turning, Kady pointed at her. "Don't go there, Saffron. I mean it."

The bell on the door bing-bonged, alerting them someone had come into the bookshop.

"We're putting new books on the shelves," Saffron called out. "Let us know if you need any help." Returning her attention to her cousin she said, "Seriously, I saw how Rylan looked at you that night. There was definitely mutual attraction. Since then he's probably been thinking he picked the wrong cousin."

"Oh good grief." Kady scrunched her face. "That's not helping. Do you honestly believe that will make me feel better? Because it doesn't. Not by a longshot." Shaking her head, she brought a finger to her lips in a shushing motion before grabbing another handful of paperbacks. "And keep your voice down. We've got customers and don't want them tuning in to my soap opera problems." Smiling, Kady rolled her eyes. "Getting back to my, um, situation...your sister may be a little haughty and arrogant but—"

"A little?" Saffron barked a laugh. "That's like saying rice may be a little white."

Kady tsked. "I'm trying to be serious, Saffron. I could never do anything to come between my cousin and the man she loves. That would be atrocious, heinous, reprehensible and—"

"You've been studying new vocabulary words, haven't you?" Saffron teased.

"Saffron!" Kady tsked again, only to have Saffron put a shushing finger to her lips. Wagging a chastising finger at Saffron, Kady quietly said, "Rylan is in love with your sister. Whatever fanciful scene you thought you saw during dinner is wrong. Just your imagination working overtime."

Taking a stack of books from Kady and placing them on the shelf, Saffron gave her a warm smile while speaking softly to her cousin. "It would be inconceivably tragic to find your one true soul mate and give him up to the wrong woman."

For some ridiculous reason Saffron's words brought tears to her eyes It was the last thing Kady needed to hear. Letting out a protracted groan, she said, "Saffron I—"

"Hey, the rumors *aren't* true. You haven't fallen off the face of the earth after all."

Jolted by the rich, masculine voice behind her, Kady turned abruptly, knocking the half-full box of books to the floor.

No...*no*!

Kady and Saffron exchanged stunned expressions. Kady knew her cousin must be thinking the same thing she was—that they hoped to hell Rylan hadn't heard them.

"Rylan! What-what are you doing here?" Both bending to recover the books, they clacked heads. Kady prayed he couldn't hear the rapid thumpity-thump of her heartbeat.

"Is that how you welcome all your potential new customers?" Laughing, he kneaded his head while stuffing books back into the box. "I promised Lorraine I'd check up on my future cousin-in-law and sister-in-law." Tsking, he shook a reprimanding finger at them. "She said neither of you have returned her emails."

"Oh, sorry..." Kady said, wincing. "I haven't checked my email in days."

"Same here," Saffron agreed. "I've told Lorraine she needs to start sending texts instead of emails so people will be sure to see them."

"You know your sister." Rylan shrugged. "She can be a little...old fashioned about things. It took her forever to get used to email instead of snail mail. I'm still working on her about texting."

Awestruck yet again, Kady did her best to smile naturally, rather than like a lovestruck hyena. Her pounding heartbeat made it hard to hear what Rylan was saying as he told them he'd just been looking around their bookshop and thought it was really nice.

"Lorraine suggested I take you two lovely ladies to lunch. She would have joined us but she's got some," Rylan twirled his hand as he searched for the right words, "woman's club thing to attend."

Swallowing hard, Kady was aware her hot cheeks must be blushing peppermint pink. "Lunch? What a shame. I couldn't possibly. We're shorthanded, plus I've got to be here to give some scheduled tarot card readings, isn't that right Saffron?" She telegraphed a pleading look.

This was terrible. Rylan looked even better than she'd remembered. That glorious thatch of wavy black hair, butter-soft black leather bomber-style jacket, black turtle-neck and tight jeans hugging his butt... Those penetrating blue eyes and adorable dimpled smile were pure overkill.

"Don't be silly," Saffron the traitor said, giving an indifferent wave. "It's been slow all morning. You've got to eat lunch sometime, Kady. Besides," she telegraphed a guiltless smile, "you must have forgotten, you don't have any readings scheduled for today. No worries, I'll watch the shop while you're gone."

Kady shot her a toxic look as the shop's door bing-bonged again.

"Hey Kady, Saffron," their parttime clerk, Anna, called from the front of the shop. "My late morning literature class was canceled so I came early to help you guys out." Once she found them she started. "Oh, sorry, I didn't realize you were helping a customer."

"He's not a customer." Thumbing toward Rylan, Saffron told Anna, "He's my future brother-in-law."

Rubbing his hands together briskly, Rylan said, "Perfect. Now you can join us, Saffron. My brother, Quinn, is outside waiting in the car. We'll make it a foursome."

Saffron's face fell.

"Yes, Saffron," Kady said emphatically through clenched teeth while discreetly pinching her cousin's elbow. "That means you can join us."

Good. Safety in numbers.

"Perfect timing then," Anna said. "You two go ahead and enjoy your lunch. I'll handle everything here." She looked at the books on the floor. "Starting with shelving those."

"I should probably stay," Saffron said, "I'd hate for you to be alone here if it gets busy, Anna."

"Erin's scheduled to be here any minute," Kady reminded Saffron, who already knew it. "Remember?"

"Hey, are you slowpokes ready or what?" The question emanated from a man who looked enough like Rylan to be his brother. He'd just sidled up to Rylan, draping an arm around his shoulder. "I'm starving, bro. Come on already, let's go get some lunch."

"Kady, Saffron, this is Quinn, my always hungry brother."

"Pleasure to meet you, Quinn." Kady extended her hand. Glancing at Saffron, she could swear she saw stars in her cousin's eyes. As Saffron gawked at Quinn, her jaw dropped. She followed that up with a giggle. Saffron Devington almost never giggled.

"Hi," Saffron said, sort of shifting left and right as she stood in place. Holy cow, Saffron was blushing!

"Nice to meet you both." Quinn nodded. "Let's go. I've got to fill this gaping hole in my gut. I'll wait for you guys in the car," Quinn said, heading for the door. "Thai okay?" he called, pulling the door open, and the other three nodded in agreement.

"I didn't know you had a brother," Saffron mused, watching Quinn make his exit.

"Well then we have something in common," Rylan replied through a half-smile. "I didn't know you and Lorraine had one either."

Saffron and Kady exchanged apprehensive glances before Saffron said, "I'll get our coats," and disappeared around the corner into the back room.

Although it was only for a moment, Kady didn't like the feeling of being alone with Rylan—well, actually, she *did* like it. Far too much.

~<>~

"I'll have pad Thai with shrimp and chicken, a double order of chicken satay with extra peanut sauce, and a couple spring rolls on the side." Quinn told the server.

"My goodness," Kady addressed the lean, muscular Quinn. "Where do you put all that food?"

Winking, Quinn smiled. "Hollow leg."

Saffron giggled before placing an order for fried bean curd satay.

"This guy," Rylan thumbed toward his brother, "never outgrew his hyperactive-kid stage. He's got the appetite and metabolism of a starving elephant."

After ordering the laad naa with beef, Rylan took off his leather jacket, draping it over the back of his chair, As he pushed up the sleeves of his black turtleneck, Kady gave an inadvertent sigh. Nothing on the menu looked half as tempting as Rylan. The simple act of watching the rhythmic rise and fall of his chest as he breathed sent a tingle down the back of her neck.

Shaking herself out of her indulgent trance, she told the server, "I'll have the Lorraine jungle vegetable curry, please," while trying to avert her eyes from Rylan's impressive physique.

"Gee, I must have missed that one on the menu," Rylan teased while the young server covered her mouth and tittered.

Realizing what she'd said, Kady laughed. "Sorry. Guess I had Lorraine on my mind. Make that the *green* jungle vegetable curry. That's vegan, right?" The server assured her it was.

"Saffron, you a vegan?" Quinn asked once their meals had been brought to the table.

"No but I enjoy vegan food and eat a mostly plant-based diet." Cupping her hand at the side of her mouth, she added, "Bacon is my Achilles' heel."

"Who doesn't love bacon?" Quinn said with a grin. "I was vegan for about a year, back in college." Leaning toward Saffron, he adopted a serious expression. "But then one day I asked myself...self, if God didn't want us to eat animals, why'd he make them out of meat?" His eyebrow rose pensively.

"That's pretty cute," Saffron said after yet another giggle.

In the past, Saffron would have scoffed at such silly humor. It was impossible not to notice she was clearly smitten with the very handsome Quinn Kilpatrick.

"My brother tells me you're the one responsible for that scandalous romance dissertation at WHU," Quinn said to Kady. Aiming an outstretched finger at her, he added, "The infamous *Doctor Romance*."

Rolling her eyes, Kady laughed. "Guilty as charged."

"I pal around with a few of the professors there and remember hearing how your dissertation shook up the old fogies. You're a woman who's not afraid to defend the principles she believes in.

I like that." Quinn flashed a smile. "So you're the fiancée's cousin, huh?"

"None other."

Quinn gave Rylan a hearty slap on the back. "If Lorraine's anything like her cousin, you've got yourself one terrific woman."

"What a nice thing to say, Quinn," Kady said over the roar of her heartbeat. "Thank you."

"Lorraine's terrific, but she and Kady aren't really anything alike," Rylan said. "They're each special in their own right."

Kady liked that Rylan knew how to be diplomatic, rather than telling Quinn that Kady was a kook with a fortunetelling dog. She looked across the table at Saffron, whose gaze was glued to Quinn. "Saffron is Lorraine's sister, Quinn, She used to be in real estate and now she and I are business partners in the bookshop."

"You're the one who made the all-veggie dinner my brother's been raving about?" Quinn asked and Saffron gave a shy nod. "I'd love to try some of your vegetarian specialties sometime, Saffron."

"Sure. I'd be happy to have you over for dinner, or lunch, or, you know," Saffron's hand fluttered as she tried to compose herself, "just a snack, or whatever."

"Sounds like a plan." Quinn gifted Saffron with a charming smile.

*Boom.* Saffron was in seventh heaven.

"Are you a professor at WHU too?" Saffron asked Quinn.

"No, I'm a neurosurgeon."

Saffron laughed before telling him, "Oh really? Well I'm an astrophysicist when I'm not working in real estate or minding the bookshop." Her laughter continued while Quinn just smiled at her.

"Saffron..." Rylan began. She unglued her gaze from Quinn long enough to glance in Rylan's direction. "My brother is a neurosurgeon."

Kady watched all the color drain from Saffron's face. "Oh my God, I'm so sorry, Quinn. I thought you were joking. I mean, it's not every day you meet a neurosurgeon, you know?"

"No problem at all." Quinn's smile was genuine. "When you have me over for that vegetarian dinner you can fill me in on astrophysics."

Dropping her head into her hands, Saffron groaned and Quinn and Rylan laughed.

Kady's intuition told her Quinn was interested in Saffron. The looks they exchanged confirmed it. Nothing would make her happier than Saffron finding someone she cared about. It had been a long time since she'd been in a relationship.

At least there was some good coming out of Kady's angst about seeing Rylan again.

"Are you a vegan because of principle, Kady," Rylan asked, "or because you don't like meat?"

"Mostly principle but partly because I don't like a lot of meat. As a kid I was served a steak so rare it nearly mooed." Kady shuddered. "And it had this inch-thick ring of fat all around it." She demonstrated with her fingers. "I've embraced vegetables ever since...although sometimes I give in to the urge for some seafood."

Clearly feeling somewhat more comfortable around Quinn, Saffron leaned toward him, placing her hand alongside her mouth in a conspirator's manner. "Better keep an eye on your food, Quinn. Kady's been known to pirate an occasional shrimp from someone's plate."

Covering her hand with her mouth, Kady broke into laughter. "Shhh, no one's supposed to know, Saffron."

"Uh-oh...looks like your vegan cover has been blown," Rylan noted with a laugh. "Quote, *a man of my spiritual intensity does not eat corpses*, unquote," he said, doing his best impression of Kady's voice. "Sound familiar?"

Kady felt the color rise in her cheeks. "Oh, *that*." She slunk down in her chair.

"Yeah, that." Rylan grinned while Kady squirmed.

Straightening in her chair, Kady boasted a proud smile. "I believe the atrocious email list of dos and don'ts Lorraine sent absolves me of spouting that George Bernard Shaw quote."

Quiet for a moment, Rylan smiled at her. "I'd have to agree with you there. I think Lorraine feels bad about it." Seeming distracted, he moved the food around on his plate with his fork. "I, uh, have a confession to make."

Kady's fork stopped midway to her mouth. "Oh?"

"There's another reason I wanted us to have lunch together today." He looked into Kady's eyes with a cobalt gaze so intense she got lost in it.

*Thud-boom-thud-boom...*

It was the sound of Kady's heart lodged in her throat.

"Oh?" she said again, amazed she was able to speak.

"Yeah, I wanted to ask you..."

Kady was tempted to scream, *What for God's sake? What?!*

"Yes?" she calmly asked instead.

"About Lorraine's brother," Rylan finally finished, and Kady breathed a massive sigh of relief. Yes, addressing the situation with Red would be sticky and problematic, but a million times less worrisome than what she feared Rylan might say.

"I've asked Lorraine about it several times but she won't talk about it. She said it's a private family matter and can't go into it. We, um," his shoulders hiked in a shrug, "got in an argument about it. I told her I was about to be part of her family too and felt I should know whatever it is she's hiding. But..."

Trailing off, Rylan went back to moving the food around his plate for a lengthy stretch, before asking Kady, "Can you tell me about Red and what happened?"

"Oh, well, I..." Kady wanted more than anything to mend family fences but going behind Lorraine's back to discuss Red with her fiancé didn't seem like the right way to go about it.

"I hesitate to discuss it with you, Rylan," Kady began, "only because I don't want Lorraine to—"

"My brother Red is gay," Saffron said.

Rylan and Quinn exchanged surprised glances. "That's all?" Rylan asked. "That's the big mystery?"

Taking in an extended breath and expelling it, Saffron explained, "My sister and parents aren't happy about it and haven't spoken to Red since he came out. There's a lot more to it, Rylan, but it's probably best if you get the rest from your fiancée."

His head bobbed slowly as he took in what Saffron shared. "I understand. Thanks for telling me." He shifted his attention to Kady, resting his hand over hers. "I apologize for putting you on the spot like that. I didn't realize."

"It's okay." She slipped her hand from beneath his. "I hope Lorraine will decide to talk to you about it. I want nothing more than for Red and his family to heal together over this. Maybe you'll be the one who succeeds in orchestrating that, Rylan. Lord knows I haven't had much luck."

"Same here," Saffron agreed.

"On a different note," Rylan sat back in his chair with a smile, "Lorraine wants me to make sure you haven't succumbed to some horrible, crippling disease that's prevented you from picking up the phone and calling her. Aside from her recent emails, she said she's called a few times and left voicemails but you haven't returned any of her calls. She's convinced you've been avoiding her the past two weeks."

"Uh-oh..." Kady curled her lip. "I'll have to give her a call later."

"*Have* you been avoiding her," Rylan asked with a dimpled smirk.

Why, why, why did he have to be so damned charming and adorable?

"Yes," Kady said absently. Rylan lifted his eyebrows in surprise. "I mean no! No, of course not." Nervously clearing her throat, she added, "I've just been tied up, that's all. Immersed in the bookshop and my scheduled readings, and, um—"

"I can vouch for that," Saffron said, coming to Kady's aid. "We've been busy because we took out a new ad for our featured romance paperback of the day, as well as Kady's fortunetelling. It's given us lots of foot traffic. Kady and Madame Izidora have developed quite a following."

Saffron reached over to pat Kady's hand. "If that weren't enough, Ms. Workaholic here stays up all hours whipping up all sorts of healing balms and tinctures and such that she gives away without charge to people she believes would benefit." Adding a warm smile, she said, "That's one of the areas where Kady's psychic abilities come into play."

"Sounds like you two have a lot going on there. Good for you!" Rylan flashed his dazzling smile. "So, where's Madame Izidora today? I didn't see her at the bookshop."

Doing her best to keep a straight face, Kady said, "Izzy's back in the apartment, lapping up chai lattes while researching reincarnation and past-life regression therapy so she can educate me."

Rylan and Quinn telegraphed clueless looks of bewilderment before realizing Kady was teasing. Crossing his arms over his chest, Rylan nodded slowly. "Very funny, *Katarina.*"

"I want to meet this psychic wonder dog." Quinn scooped a hefty portion of the complimentary marinated cucumber slices into his mouth.

"You can usually find Izzy prancing around the shop, charming the customers," Saffron said. "Stop by any time."

"I definitely will." He and Saffron locked gazes for a moment. "Kady, I heard how you had Izzy all dolled up and had her pick out paperbacks and tarot cards. You've really got her trained well."

"Believe it or not, there was very little training. Izzy simply knows what needs to be done." Kady beamed a smile. "She's surprising intelligent and has great intuition."

She cringed when she recalled the way Izzy nudged *Her Cousin's Man* toward her. "Too intelligent, sometimes," she muttered beneath her breath. Before the words even left her lips, Kady had a brief sense of knowing journey through her mind. It was a fleeting but unmistakable premonition about Saffron and Quinn—together, as a couple.

"Well I'll be darned," she said, absolutely delighted at the prospect.

"What are you being darned about, Kady?" Saffron asked with a teasing smile, reaching for a spring roll the same time as Quinn. When their fingers touched Kady could almost see the spark.

"Oh...nothing. Don't mind me. I'm just thinking out loud...you know, about bookshop stuff."

"Speaking about your shop," Rylan said, "it's got a great combination coffeehouse bookstore vibe. Has Lorraine seen it yet?"

Kady and Saffron exchanged glances. "Once," Kady said. "I don't think it was her cup of tea, exactly."

With a knowing grin, Rylan guessed, "Not classical or cultural enough, hmm?"

Looking down at her food, Kady stabbed a forkful of black mushrooms and bok choy. "Something like that." In reality, Lorraine pretty much detested everything about the shop.

"Rylan tells me both your families moved to Oregon from Chicago," Quinn said. "Same for me and Rylan."

"I still miss Chicago's deep dish pizza and Italian beef sandwiches," Saffron said with a chuckle.

"I heard about a place a couple towns up the coast that supposedly makes great Chicago style pizza," Quinn said reaching for another skewer of chicken satay.

"I'd only believe it if the owners are former Chicagoans," Saffron said. "I've been disappointed too many times by promises of authentic Chicago-style foods."

"Well there's only one way to find out. If you're not busy Saturday night, why don't we give it a try and see for ourselves?" With a wink, Quinn added, "Rylan can attest that I'm relatively trustworthy."

Kady watched as Saffron's cheeks colored peppermint pink. Cutest thing ever.

"Oh, well, I..." Saffron began, obviously a bundle of nerves. Kady had rarely seen the former real estate salesperson without her usual bold, self-confident demeanor.

"Oh, she's free," Kady said. "Saffron told me she was just planning to start a new series on Netflix Saturday night. Isn't that right, Saffron?" Kady gave her cousin an innocent smile.

"Right," Saffron said, her eyes on her lap. Glancing up, she smiled. "I'd, um, sure...I'd be happy to do some pizza testing with you Saturday, Quinn."

Quinn said, "Great!" And Kady and Rylan exchanged amused smiles.

"By the way, Kady," Rylan said, a teasing gleam dancing in his eyes, "I couldn't help notice you aren't wearing any toe jewelry today."

"It's under my socks," Kady told him.

Rylan's smile turned baffled. "Really?"

"Gottcha." Kady gave his arm a playful punch.

"Don't forget to tell them about Lorraine's whatever it is she called it," Quinn said.

"Oh, right," Rylan nodded, "her *soiree*." Rylan chuckled. "I've been instructed to invite you both and not take no for an answer. It's three weeks from Saturday, at Devington Manor."

"Devington Manor." Quinn snickered. "Sounds like a restaurant."

"Think museum, Quinn," Rylan answered. "Four stories, with an elevator." He snatched a plump shrimp from his brother's plate with his fork, popping it into his mouth.

"Sheesh." Quinn slumped back in his chair. "You grew up in that place?" he asked Saffron.

She nodded. "Since my early teens. It became stifling as I got older. I couldn't wait to get my own place, which my sister can't understand." Saffron laughed.

"She loves that place," Rylan said.

"I go back to visit," Saffron continued, "when my guilt barometer tells me it's time to see my parents." She asked Quinn, "Have you seen Devington Manor yet?" He shook his head, no. "Well when you do, you'll know what I mean." Saffron let out a lengthy sigh. "This invitation you're talking about, Rylan, is for Lorraine's annual spring bash. It's usually a big to-do, full of all her blue-blooded friends."

"Lorraine is Miss Organization," Rylan said.

"That's her staff you're thinking of," Saffron said with a laugh. "She has a personal secretary who handles all these things for her."

"Really?" Rylan's eyebrows arrowed down. "I didn't realize that." After a moment, he said, "Hey, Kady, you can wear your fancy purple prom dress to the soiree." He broke into laughter.

"I'm sure Lorraine and her friends would love that." Kady laughed. "I don't know if I'd be comfortable attending, to be honest. I'm not really very good at mingling with those upper crust types. I never know what to say."

"That makes two of us," Quinn said, yanking a grilled strip of chicken from its wooden skewer and dragging it through the peanut satay sauce.

"Come on now," Rylan pleaded, "you guys can't bail on me. I need backup. Besides, if the three of you don't say yes I'll never hear the end of it from Lorraine. You don't want to be responsible for me disappointing my fiancée, do you?"

"We can't have Lorraine thinking her fiancé is a failure," Saffron said. "Don't worry, Kady and I will be there."

"But Saffron, I—" Kady stopped short. What could she say? *But Saffron, you know I've got the hots for Rylan and want to be around him as little as possible or I'm afraid I'll shapeshift into the family slut?* No...probably best if she just agreed to attend. She could make a showing and leave early.

Swallowing a forkful of curry, Saffron said, "Just to prepare you for Lorraine's *little* soiree, Rylan, my sister doesn't know the meaning of the word *little*. It'll be black-tie with formal engraved invitations. Everyone who's anyone will be there, including the Mayor of Glassfloat Bay."

Kady had come to love Rylan's perplexed expression.

"No," he shook his head back and forth, "not this time. I've already talked to Lorraine about her guest list. She knows how I feel about fancy-shmancy affairs. She gave me her solemn promise that she'll limit the guests to only a few close friends, her parents, and the four of us. No black-tie, no stuffy formality, and no engraved invitations." He held out his hands, palms upturned, and shrugged. "Problem solved."

Kady knew better and so, of course, did Saffron. Poor Rylan was in for an unpleasant surprise.

"So we have to spend time with your parents?" Quinn asked Saffron. "Rylan says they're—ow!" He bent to rub his shin. "Hey! What the hell. Ry?"

"Oops, sorry," Rylan said. "I didn't mean to kick you while you were putting your foot in your mouth. Lorraine's parents are, uh...well, they're not really so bad."

Without realizing it, Kady shot Rylan a genuine look of stupefaction, and Rylan laughed.

"I'm sure we'll all have a good time at Lorraine's little soiree," he assured with an emphatic smile."

Expelling a collective groan, Kady and Saffron exchanged knowing smiles.

Patting Rylan's hand, Saffron said, "You poor, dear, naive man."

"On the contrary, you, future sister-in-law, will discover that Lorraine has become more agreeable lately."

Resting an elbow on the table, Saffron propped her chin on her fist. With a challenging gleam in her eye, she said, "You don't say?"

Rylan chuckled. "Scoff if you must but, as a for instance, Lorraine is very open to my suggestion that we consider moving into a nice little U-shaped ranch on half an acre of land where we can have a big vegetable garden."

"Where will the servants' quarters be?" Saffron asked. "Over the garage?"

Kady couldn't resist laughing, covering her mouth as she did.

Rylan dismissed them with a wave of his hand. "I'm telling you, Lorraine has mellowed."

"I dunno, buddy," Quinn chimed in, "from what you've told me, your fiancée's pretty enamored of that mansion she lives in. Why would she chuck it all for a little house on the prairie?"

His expression was so full of belief in Lorraine, it hurt Kady's heart. Her psychic intuition told her they'd be facing some heated arguments ahead. Hopefully she was wrong. Lorraine couldn't possibly be foolish enough to risk losing a man like him. Could she?

"You guys just don't get it." Rylan chuffed a laugh. "Lorraine will be on board for one reason—because she loves me." He rapped his clawed fingers against his chest. "Me, the man she wants to spend her life with. That's what she really cares about. She's told me that in so many words. She knows I want us to have a real home in the country, not some marble-columned museum up on Nob Hill."

Lifting a finger, Saffron corrected, "It's Beauregard Hill."

"Whatever." Rylan shrugged. "I want us to have the whole enchilada. A dog, a house full of kids and—"

"You're such an idealist," Saffron said.

"My little brother's always been that way," Quinn said.

With a genuine look of concern, Saffron placed her hand on Rylan's sleeve. "That's just not Lorraine, Rylan. I love my sister. She's a good woman with wonderful qualities. And I'm sure she loves you very much but..." Her eyebrows pinched. "I'm sorry, Rylan, but my sister would wither and die if she were cut off from her social circle and the lifestyle she's accustomed to."

"Maybe you should listen, bro," Quinn said. "Saffron's her sister, so she should know, right? Are you sure you told Lorraine exactly what you want—with all the trimmings and specifics?"

Kady hated to see Rylan's eyes so filled with trust, hope, and expectation. She sent up a silent plea to the universe to keep him from being hurt...or to have Lorraine actually change her stagnant thinking.

"Lorraine and I talked about it at length," Rylan answered Quinn. "She told me she found the whole idea positively charming. Those were her exact words."

Kady took in a deep breath. *Charming.* It was one of Lorraine's words for something tolerable but for the little people, not for her. Other words in that category included *quaint*, *sweet*, and *enchanting*.

Steepling her fingers, Saffron asked Rylan, "Has my father talked to you about your plans yet?"

"Your father? No, why?"

"Be prepared. I can guarantee you he will."

Seizing a saucy cube of bean curd from Saffron's plate and popping it into his mouth, Quinn said, "I think Saffron means she doubts her father's going to let you whisk his pampered princess away from the Devington opulence to muss her pretty manicure doing all those housewifey things you have in mind, Ry, much less planting vegetables in your backyard garden."

"If there's any vegetable growing to be done after you two are married," Saffron said, "set your mind to the fact that it will have to be on the rooftop of Devington Manor, in a neat little row of planters, with your delicate bride directing the gardener."

Wisely keeping her mouth shut, Kady was glad Saffron and Quinn were saying what she wished she could, and trying to get Rylan to see the light before he let himself in for some major disappointment.

Rylan chuckled. "Go ahead and be doomsayers. I," he thumbed his chest, "have complete faith in Lorraine. She wouldn't lie about something this important to me. You should have seen the excitement on her face when we shared our hopes and dreams for the future. Lorraine wants the same things I do."

Quinn, Saffron and Kady looked at each, silently for a long moment. With a compassionate smile, Saffron clasped Rylan's hand.

"You're a good guy, Rylan. I'll be proud and happy to have you as my brother-in-law." But Saffron wasn't finished. Repeating the same words she had earlier, she finished with, "You poor, dear, naive man."

# Chapter 10

*Early in March*

~<>~

KADY WASN'T AT all surprised when the formal engraved invitation for Lorraine's *Spring Soiree* arrived in the mail. She was even less surprised to see the words *black-tie optional* at the bottom of the invitation. The addition of the word *optional* no doubt being Lorraine's concession to Rylan's wishes to keep her party simple.

Kady breathed a deep sigh. She knew there'd be a house full of stuffed shirts. Rylan would get a crash course in what it means to marry a Devington—at least *that* Devington. He'd learn quickly that social rules, regulations, and obligations were a necessary part of his future as Lorraine's husband. For Rylan, tonight's soiree could be titled *Marrying a Devington 101.*

But there was some very good news that had Kady smiling, while reinforcing the usual accuracy of her premonitions. Saffron and Quinn had become all but inseparable since their date at the Chicago-style pizzeria, where the duo discovered the owners, indeed former Chicagoans, knew exactly how to create a mean deep dish pizza.

~<>~

"It's strange," Saffron said, as Quinn's car started up the long, winding driveway. "Although Devington Manor is my family home and I've been to more than my fair share of hoity-toity gatherings here, I still feel awkward attending these things. That's it just up ahead on your right." She pointed to a huge white marble building. "You can just pull up in front. My father always hires a team of valets for these events."

"Holy shit, Saffron," Quinn said in utter amazement. "*This* is your family's house?"

Saffron laughed at his drop-jawed reaction. "I tried to prepare you."

"Yeah but...when you said Devington Manor was up on Beauregard hill, I knew it had to be ritzy but this place is a-a—"

"Museum?" Kady offered.

"Yeah...now I understand what Ry meant," a staggered Quinn noted through laughter.

As Quinn maneuvered into the valet parking queue he glanced at Saffron. "Just what *does* your father do for a living, if you don't mind me asking."

"Walter Devington is the president of Wisdom Harbor Bank."

"I probably should have worn a monkey suit after all," Quinn mumbled in a barely audible voice, while fiddling with his tie and eyeballing the mansion.

While opting against black tie, Quinn wore a sharp looking dark suit and tie that should pass Devington scrutiny. Quinn told them that Rylan, on the other hand, was wearing black tie to make Lorraine happy—and hating every minute of it. He'd arrived in his own car earlier.

"You look wonderful," Saffron told Quinn honestly.

"And you..." Quinn gave his date in the passenger a loving smile, "are truly radiant, Saffron. I'll be proud to have you at my side." Lifting her hand to his lips, he kissed it.

Kady's eyes brimmed with happy tears. These two were so obviously in love already...like a match made in heaven.

"Oh, Quinn," Saffron said, "that was so sweet and romantic. But..."

"But?" he asked with a concerned expression.

"But you shouldn't keep telling me such beautiful things because you're going to make me cry—again." She laughed. "And I don't have any makeup with me to cover the blotchy red nose I get when I cry."

Quinn gave her another appraisal. "Sorry. I meant to say you look like hell, Saffron. It'll be damn tough admitting to anyone that we're here together."

The three of them burst out laughing and the taut lines of tension etched in Quinn's face melted away.

"Okay," Quinn said, "let's go, I'm ready to party—and I'm dying to see how my poor brother is faring."

~<>~

Rylan slipped two fingers between his shirt and bow tie, tugging the shirt away from his neck. "Damn rented monkey suit," he grumbled under his breath.

"What was that, darling?" Lorraine handed him a glass of champagne from the server's tray.

"Nothing." Giving Lorraine an appreciative once-over, he smiled. She looked elegant as usual. The short-sleeved beige sequined top over a long, flowing beige chiffon skirt made her look like she just stepped out of some fashion magazine.

As they stood on the second floor landing, Rylan looked down, up, and to each side. People. Nothing but people everywhere he looked. *Small soiree my ass.* "Saffron was right." He gulped back half the champagne in his glass.

"Rylan, what *are* you mumbling about?" Lorraine laughed.

"Lorraine, you promised you'd keep this gathering intimate." He tugged at his shirt collar again. "There are hundreds of people here for chrissakes."

Laughing, Lorraine leaned close to Rylan and patted his cheek as she whispered, "Only the best ones." She pushed his hand from his neck. "Do stop fussing with your collar, Rylan, it's gauche."

Finishing his champagne, he set the empty glass on the marble railing. "What happened to the small party you said you were planning? This..." he threw his arms out to his sides, "this is monstrous, Lorraine." A twisted laugh caught in his throat.

"There you go exaggerating again." Lorraine smoothed her finger down the lapel of his dinner jacket. Taking a step closer, she pouted as she looked up into her fiancé's eyes. "It's not really so bad, is it?"

"The only party I've ever been to that could begin to compare in size and magnitude is the university's annual charity ball. The only difference is that I didn't have to buy a ticket to get into this shindig." Rylan hailed a passing server, helping himself to another glass of bubbly.

"Don't be silly, Rylan. How could you possibly compare my spring soiree with its carefully chosen guest list to some public philanthropic event where just *anybody* who has the price of a ticket can gain admittance?"

Lorraine clearly didn't realize Rylan was just an *anybody*. In her mind, him being a professor somehow elevated his status from an anybody to a somebody.

"You'll get used to it soon enough, darling. Remember, with whom you socialize is all-important. One's career or fortune can be irreparably damaged because of social faux-pas." She waved and blew a kiss to the mayor and his wife as they caught Lorraine's eye. "By the time we get married this autumn, you'll consider these people your close friends. We'll make a Devington out of you yet." She winked.

Taking a step back, Rylan slanted Lorraine a befuddled grin. "Funny, I was under the impression that we were going to turn *you* into a *Kilpatrick*."

"Of course, Rylan." Lorraine flittered her hand through the air. "You know what I meant. And, do be careful with all that champagne. You wouldn't want to make a poor first impression on our guests." Lorraine straightened his tie and brushed invisible crumbs from his dinner jacket.

"Speaking of champagne," Rylan snaked his arm around Lorraine's waist, tugging her close, "what say we grab a bottle of bubbly and steal away to some private, uninhabited corner of this museum? We'll escape from all these stuffed shirts and all your social obligations and have an intimate little party of our own." Breaking into a devilish grin, he leaned in to kiss his fiancée.

Jerking back from his advance as if he had a disease, Lorraine gaped at him in astonishment.

"Rylan, what *are* you doing?" She looked to her left and right. "This is neither the time nor the place for a public display of affection."

She must have noticed his startled, angry expression, because she gave a nervous laugh and toyed with the neckline of her sequined top. Rylan wanted to tell her to stop fussing with her collar because it was *gauche*, but choked back the impulse.

"Can you imagine the hubbub if I were to carelessly prance off for a rendezvous with my fiancé in the middle of my hostess duties?" Lorraine shook a chastising finger beneath Rylan's nose, as if he were a naughty, mischievous child. "You must learn to be patient. Don't forget, darling, we have our whole lives to spend together."

"In our little vine-covered cottage in the country." Rylan slipped his arm around Lorraine's waist again. "Just you and me, our friendly pooch, and some little Kilpatricks running around, getting into mischief. We should start looking at properties. Maybe sometime this week."

Lorraine stood wordlessly, with a blank expression for a moment. "That all sounds charming. Positively quaint. We have plenty of time to talk about our living arrangements, Rylan. You, me...and Dad." She offered a honeyed smile and touched his cheek before floating off to greet a guest.

"Dad?" Rylan mouthed quizzically as Lorraine left his side to mingle with the upper crust. "What the hell have I gotten myself into?" he whispered beneath his breath. Downing his champagne, he turned and groaned as he spied the perpetually angry looking Walter Devington walking toward him.

*Damn*... He half considered taking a leap from the second floor landing but thought better of it and mumbled an expletive instead.

"Professor Kilpatrick," Walter Devington said through his frown. "If you have a moment, I'd like a word with you in the library." He turned and headed down the stairs without waiting for Rylan's answer.

"Certainly," Rylan said to the back of the man's silver-gray head, aware that he probably didn't hear him. Devington's overbearing, authoritarian manner made Rylan feel like an awkward adolescent being confronted by the school principal. And this is the man who'd be his father-in-law.

Once Rylan entered the library, Walter closed the enormous, elaborately carved double doors and took a seat in the oversized, high-back burgundy leather chair behind an imposing, mahogany desk. He motioned for Rylan to sit in one of the smaller chairs opposite him, which he did, feeling dwarfed and insignificant as he sank into in the low chair. Choosing two Cuban cigars from his humidor, Walter looked to Rylan and raised one of his wild, wiry gray eyebrows.

"No thank you," Rylan held up a hand, "but please go ahead."

"I fully intend to," the older man said with what Rylan thought might be some semblance of a laugh. After clipping the end of the cigar and lighting it, Walter took a few puffs and sat back, in a somewhat relaxed pose. "Don't you indulge in the enjoyment of a truly fine cigar now and then, Professor?"

"Well, I—"

"Ever had a Cohiba?"

"No, I can't say that I have."

"Well there's no time like the present." Devington thrust a cigar, lighter and the cigar cutter toward Rylan, who looked at it all in bewilderment. Glancing up at Lorraine's father, Rylan noted the man's smug smile, giving Rylan the distinct impression that this was some sort of highbrow test he was being put through.

Although he'd never smoked a cigar, he'd seen his brother do it occasionally. Taking the cigar from Walter, Rylan clipped off the end of the cigar, lit it, drew in a mouthful of smoke and expelled it without coughing. So far so good.

"So, what do you think, my boy?" Walter said through a cloud of smoke.

"Excellent, Mr. Devington." He just couldn't bring himself to call the guy Walter. "Very robust." Robust sounded like a good cigar word.

Devington nodded in approval. "Kilpatrick, have you given any thought to our little discussion the other day?"

"You mean about accepting a position with Pacific Northwest University?"

"Precisely. Cognac?"

"Thank you." Rylan nervously cleared his throat as he watched Devington pour them each a jigger of aged cognac. "Actually, I've given it a lot of thought." He took a deep breath and tried, without much success, to sit taller in the low chair. "I realize Pacific Northwest is a prestigious private university, and I certainly appreciate your offer to use your connections to intercede on my behalf, but I'm happy where I am." He took another draw on his cigar, waiting for the retort.

"Happy at a public college?" Devington chuckled. "Nonsense, my boy. I don't think you understand what you'd be giving up by not letting me arrange this for you." He held his glass of cognac up to the light, silently studying it. "You like that cognac you're drinking?"

Rylan nodded affirmatively, even though he hadn't tasted it yet.

"That cognac is 140 years old. Over ten thousand dollars a bottle."

Rylan's eyeballs nearly bounced out on springs.

"It's just one of the many simple pleasures in life you can't afford on a professor's salary at a public university, Kilpatrick." As he sipped from his cognac, Devington's eyebrows knitted into a deeply creviced vee. Reaching for a pad of notepaper and pen, he scribbled something, tore the sheet from the pad and held it out to Rylan. Before releasing the paper, he pulled it back. "You *do* want to make my little girl happy, don't you, Professor Kilpatrick?"

"Yes, of course, but—"

"Good." He thrust the paper into Rylan's hand. "Then you'll call this man first thing Monday morning and make an appointment to see him. Just mention my name, he's expecting your call." He took another series of puffs from the long, fat cigar, tapping the ash into a marble ashtray. This family sure did like their marble.

"You have to remember, son. The Devingtons have an image to uphold, and you're going to be a part of this family. It's important you let me guide you in these matters. I know what's best."

Opening his mouth to protest, Rylan thought better of it. "Thank you." His broad shoulders slumped. If he had a mirror he was sure he'd spy a look of abject defeat across his features.

"My daughter tells me you've thought about moving away from Glassfloat Bay after you're married." The man's words were fraught with the same disapproval glaring in his eyes.

Rylan sipped the aged cognac, wincing as the potent, pricey liquid glided down his throat like molten lava. Trying to stifle a coughing jag, he gasped for air. "Yes, Lorraine's enthused about the idea. Probably somewhere between Glassfloat Bay and Portland. Rainspring Grove is nice. Ever been there?"

"Hmmm." Ignoring Rylan's question, Devington's eyebrows were knitting together again. "I suppose it wouldn't be a problem to find a quaint little weekend house for you and Lorraine out in the country. My brother has a small estate just outside of Glassfloat Bay. I'll talk to him about setting up a lease for you. It's only a few hundred acres, but there are adequate servant quarters and a riding stable on the property."

"That's very kind of you, Mr. Devington, but Lorraine and I will find a place on our own. Something I can afford on my salary." Downing another sip of cognac, which went down smoother this time, Rylan had the distinct sensation of shrinking...growing smaller and less significant with each word Devington spoke, as if the little chair threatened to swallow him whole. He straightened his back in a failed attempt to add enough height so that he could look Lorraine's father straight in the eye, rather than having to look up at him.

"I have a little savings set aside. I'll be able to provide very well for your daughter, if that's what you're worried about, sir." At this point, even his own voice sounded insignificant to Rylan. As if he were mouthing the words, but a cartoon character's voice was coming out. He puffed again from his cigar, failing to keep from coughing this time.

As if he hadn't heard a word Rylan uttered, Devington said, "Colleen and I have decided to turn over the entire west wing of Devington Manor to you and Lorraine."

Rylan cocked his head with a quizzical expression. "For what?"

Looking at Rylan like he was crazy, Devington told him, "For your home, of course, what else?"

"But, Mr. Devington, I just told you, Lorraine and I want—"

"Lorraine was elated when her mother and I told her of our decision last month." Devington sucked on his cigar, letting out a chortle. "She and her mother have been running back and forth to decorators ever since she found out she'd be able to re-do the west wing to her own liking."

After downing the rest of the cognac, Rylan rubbed his fingers against his throbbing temples. "Lorraine's known about this for a month?" He found himself growing livid at the idea Lorraine had let him make a fool of himself, going on about his dreams for their future, all the while knowing and planning. His jaw muscle twitched as he clenched his teeth.

"Well of course she has." Walter huffed a semi-laugh. "And with my brother's estate outside of town, you'll be able to satisfy your yearnings for the country life when you and Lorraine want to get away for a weekend now and then."

He drew a deep drag from his cigar, casting a sideways glance at his future son-in-law. "My little girl's happiness is very important to me, Kilpatrick. I intend to ensure she lives a life she deserves. If you love Lorraine as much as you profess, I'm sure you feel the same way and will agree to whatever is necessary to make her happy."

He raised an eyebrow in question. When Rylan's only response was a vacant stare, Devington continued. "You need to stop all this nonsense about some little tract house in the country and spending your life working for pennies at a public college. With my help, you'll achieve things you never dreamed possible, son. I guarantee you, it will be a good life."

With a wave of his hand, Devington cracked a half smile and dismissed Rylan by saying, "Off with you now. Go find my daughter. I'm sure she's eager to introduce you to her friends."

Having been brutally cut down to size by Lorraine's father, Rylan rose from what felt like a child-sized chair. He couldn't ever remember feeling this inconsequential. He snuffed out his cigar and headed for the great double doors.

Devington turned in his chair to face the doors Rylan was about to open. "Kilpatrick," he said, "there are many important, influential people here this evening. It would do you well to court their favor. Do you understand?" He turned back in his chair, puffing on his cigar.

"Yes...I understand," Rylan said through clenched teeth as he exited the library. He'd never felt so furious, crushed, and deflated in all his life.

~<>~

"This place is crawling with the cream of Pacific Northwest society," Quinn said, seizing a handful of hors d'oeuvres from a passing silver tray. "Saffron, you hit the nail on the head when you described what this *little soiree*," he hung air quotes around the words, "would be like tonight." He popped a smoked salmon and cream cheese topped cracker into his mouth.

Saffron sighed. "Believe me, I know how persuasive my sister and my parents can be. Poor Rylan never had a chance."

Taking in her surroundings and the massive throng of well-known personalities in attendance, Kady smoothed her strapless, floor length, purple brushed-silk gown and adjusted the amethyst and marcasite choker at her neck. The straight, form-fitting gown was a far cry from the Salvation Army ball gown she wore the first time she met Rylan.

"I don't see Rylan or Lorraine anywhere, do either of you?" Kady asked.

"Yup, my sister is coming toward us at three o'clock." Saffron nodded to her right.

"Arm-in-arm with your mom," Kady noted, sucking in a deep breath. Admittedly nervous, she was determined to wiggle Red into the conversation at some point this evening with Aunt

Colleen and Uncle Walter. She hoped it would be possible without any angst. Knowing the last thing Lorraine and her parents wanted was any sort of public spectacle was definitely to Kady's benefit. They'd have to be civil to her if she brought up the conflict regarding Redmond.

"Okay you two," Saffron warned, "prepare yourselves to be skewered, roasted, sliced, diced, chewed and spit out."

As Colleen and her daughter came closer, Kady flashed her best smile. "Aunt Colleen, Lorraine, it's so good to see you both."

"It's been far too long, dear." Colleen extended her thin, wrinkled, bejeweled hands toward Kady. As her niece took hold of them, Colleen brushed both of Kady's cheeks with her own. "I'm glad you agreed to join us this evening. It was the right thing to do, dear."

Although she had no idea what her aunt meant, Kady smiled and nodded.

Giving Quinn a withering glance, Colleen said, "You must be the brother."

"That would be me." Quinn offered a broad grin as he extended his hand.

Lightly clasping his fingers, Colleen said, "Charmed," while giving him an unfavorable appraisal. "Pity you weren't advised about the dress code for my daughter's soiree."

"For heaven's sake, Mother," Saffron said, "Doctor Kilpatrick looks just fine. The invitation said black tie optional, remember?"

"Doctor?" Colleen's interest was stirred.

"Yes, Quinn is a neurosurgeon," Saffron explained, giving birth to a whole renewed interest on her mother's part. Kady wasn't at all surprised.

"Doctor Kilpatrick, it's a pleasure to have you join us." There was no mistaking how impressed Colleen was at the prospect of her daughter in the company of a neurosurgeon. "Then you must know Doctor Chesney."

"I do." Quinn gave an affirmative nod. "I studied under him. Brilliant man. I'd heard so much about Devington Manor and," he glanced all around him, "I can say it certainly lives up to its reputation." Kady bit her tongue to keep from laughing. Knowing Quinn's true feelings about the colossal dwelling, it was the smoothest, most elegant putdown, she'd ever heard.

Colleen's hand flew to the pearls at her neck as she made a sound reminiscent of a giggle. "Why thank you, Doctor. So you practice here in Glassfloat Bay along with Doctor Chesney?"

"I've been at Wisdom Harbor Hospital for several years but I'm taking a leave of absence at the end of the month to teach doctors in Nigeria."

At the surprising news, Kady watched Saffron's head whip in Quinn's direction.

"Nigeria." Colleen's expression mimicked one after drinking sour milk. "Why would you go there when there are so many places here in America where you could teach?"

"Because they have a great need," Quinn replied. "Nigeria's healthcare system currently ranks among the lowest in the world, so they can clearly use the assistance."

"How long will you be gone?" Saffron asked, disappointment etched across her features, although Kady could tell she tried to hide it.

"I've committed to a three year term." His gaze quickly flicking to Saffron, Quinn looked regretful. "Longer if I'm needed." Their eyes met and held for a moment before Saffron smiled, nodded, and looked away.

The poor thing looked lost. Kady surreptitiously reached for her cousin's fingers, giving them a supportive squeeze, feeling Saffron's near-crushing clasp in return. She knew what a disappointment it must be for Saffron so soon after finding a man she really cared about—one who'd really connected with her. It had been so long.

"So is the hospital paying your salary to teach the Blacks how to operate on each other's brains?" Colleen asked. "Or will this be coming out of our taxes?"

Both Saffron and Kady winced. Kady knew the Devingtons weren't open-minded. They had narrow views and were unashamedly status conscious, but Colleen's questions and distinct uppity attitude still managed to startle her.

"I'm going there to teach Nigerian physicians on a volunteer basis, with Medicine Without Boundaries, a charitable organization funded almost entirely by donations," Quinn explained, his manner still polite but noticeably cooler. "Brain surgery is just a small part of what neurosurgeons do, Mrs. Devington. Most of my cases have been spinal surgery, in fact. Neurosurgeons deal with the entire nervous system."

"Volunteering." The word spilling from Colleen's lips sounded the same as someone else saying *rodent infestation*. With her chin elevated, Colleen said, "You said funded by donations. From where? This organization you're traveling with, are they political or religion based? There must be some agenda. There usually is."

"I carefully vetted the Medicine Without Boundaries organization before joining. Their mission, and mine, is based solely on providing help where it's needed, anywhere in the world," Quinn said diplomatically. "This international organization, based in the U.S., has neither political nor religious affiliations. Donations come from the public. I'd be happy to provide information for you and Mr. Devington if you'd like to consider becoming benefactors...like Doctor Chesney."

"Oh!" Colleen's eyebrows shot up. "No thank you. We have a long list of charitable organizations here in America that we already support. Doctor Kilpatrick, please tell me your brother isn't planning to cast aside his professorship to join you in your charity endeavor."

"Rylan?" Lorraine huffed an incredulous laugh at her mother's comment. She'd been chatting with others here and there but her ears didn't miss talk of her fiancé. "Of course he isn't, Mother. He's not a physician, he's a professor."

"My brother plans to stick it out at WHU until his books really take off," Quinn informed them.

"Books? What books?" Wide-eyed, Colleen and Lorraine said in unison.

Quinn's expression brightened. "Writing's always been Rylan's first love," he replied as Lorraine and her mother gave him blank stares. "He's really good too. Rylan's been working on a series in his spare time. He lets me read his manuscripts along the way so I can give him feedback before they get sent to his editor."

"Is this a series of instructive textbooks?" Lorraine asked. "Or do you mean a series of educational science books such as Cosmos by Carl Sagan?"

"Or Neil deGrasse Tyson?" Kady asked. "He's one of my favorites. I follow him on social media."

"Who?" Colleen asked with a clueless expression.

"He's an astrophysicist, author, and science communicator," Saffron explained. "Brilliant while humorous and entertaining at the same time."

Leaning close to Colleen, Lorraine advised her with a hushed whisper, "He's Black, Mother."

"Oh." Colleen clutched her pearls again, while Kady and Saffron exchanged a fleeting knowing glance.

Kady had always suspected her aunt, uncle, and cousin might be racist. Now she no longer had to wonder.

"Nothing like that." Quinn shook his head. "While both Rylan and I enjoy the late Sagan's work, as well as deGrasse Tyson's, my brother is a science fiction novelist."

"Oh dear..." Straightening to her full height, Colleen cleared her throat before addressing Lorraine. "Clearly you need to have a talk with your fiancé."

"Obviously," Lorraine agreed. "I mean, if Rylan were penning significant nonfiction books, I could understand...but a genre fiction writer?" She chortled a laugh. "Oh no...no, that won't do at all."

"Well...okay then." Quinn rubbed his hands together. The man had obviously reached his limit of diplomacy. "I've got to find that guy with the tray of appetizers. The salmon ones are really good." He turned to Saffron. "Back in a few."

"Take your time," she said, clearly aware of Quinn's need to escape.

At the same time, catching sight of one of her friends, Lorraine headed in the opposite direction.

Kady wished she could have subtly recorded reaction videos of her aunt and her cousin each time they heard something that differed from their narrow ideology. Poor Rylan. He'd be getting a talking to for sure. Kady found it fascinating that he wrote science fiction...or that he was a writer at all. No wonder Kady's instincts led her to recommend the science fiction romance novel to Rylan the night they met. She hoped Lorraine would appreciate his love of the arts, rather than belittle his dream of being a published author.

Placing her hand at the long peach colored chiffon scarf draped strategically over the pearls at her crinkly throat, Colleen Devington looked left to right. Kady was struck by how much older her aunt looked than her mom, since the women were about the same age.

Speaking in hushed tones, Colleen leaned her slender body close. "You being here, Kathleen, is a sign of solidarity regarding that..." she clasped her throat tighter, "unfortunate matter with Redmond." Succumbing to a slight shudder, Colleen continued, "Do be sure to mingle about, telling everyone how delighted you are about Lorraine's engagement, won't you dear? It will help dissolve any gossip of a family rift."

Now Kady understood her aunt's earlier comment about her doing the right thing by attending Lorraine's soiree. Glancing around the room, she let a polite, affected laugh escape her lips before responding in a hushed tone matching her aunt's. "You're no doubt referring to the *unfortunate matter*," she parroted her aunt's words, "of you, Uncle Walter, and Lorraine rejecting your son, Redmond."

"Certainly. We can't have people making improper assumptions," Colleen replied. "Can we? Regrettably, a number of them already know about our son's..." her voice became a near whisper, "*unnatural proclivity*. I'm sorry to say your mother and the rest of your family have made it quite evident they're neither sympathetic nor supportive of our difficult decision to excise Redmond from the family. Believe me, Kathleen, the choice was not made lightly. Your uncle and I are so pleased to have your understanding and support."

*Whoa...*

With a brief glance in her daughter, Saffron's, direction, Colleen offered a more anemic smile. "Your attendance is noted and appreciated as well, Saffron." It was an icy reception at best. The only reason she was this receptive was probably because Saffron brought a neurosurgeon to the party.

Kady was blown away by the notion that her appearance at Lorraine's party indicated to her aunt that she was taking sides, specifically her aunt and uncle's side, regarding the abominable way they'd treated Red. While she hated confrontation, Kady needed to set her aunt straight.

"I'm sorry, Aunt Colleen, but I'm afraid you've misinterpreted my—"

"Oh, there you are, Doctor Chesney," Colleen cut in, her arm flitting high like a flamenco dancer as she spotted the Chair of Neurosurgery at Wisdom Harbor Hospital. "I've just been chatting with Doctor Kilpatrick about his upcoming volunteer trip to Nigeria."

"Quinton? He's a fine, devoted young man," Chesney said to Colleen. "Passionate about helping others."

"My thoughts exactly," Colleen agreed, which was nothing short of hilarious. She scurried off to mingle before Kady had a chance to say more. Depending on who was in the vicinity, the woman's manner changed as fast as a breath blowing out a match.

Lorraine had returned in time to watch her mother dart off to greet the high profile doctor. Smiling, she said, "After tonight Mother will be regaling everyone with her coup at getting the renowned Anton Chesney as a guest in her home. Exciting, isn't it?"

Kady offered a simple smile in return because answering, *Not really*, wouldn't be polite. Interesting. If Kady's mother were to host a bigshot doctor in her home, Astrid's biggest concern would be making the doctor feel comfortable and at home among the other guests, rather than what it might do for her social status.

Returning to their circle after Colleen left, Quinn smiled at Lorraine. "So I finally get to meet the woman who succeeded in putting a ring through my brother's nose." He extended his hand. "I'm Quinn. Good to meet you."

Instead of clasping her future brother-in-law's hand to shake it, Lorraine rested her fingers against his palm, looking almost as if she was waiting for Quinn to kiss her hand. "My pleasure," Lorraine said. "Rylan speaks about you often." One eyebrow arrowed up. "Although I had no idea you were a doctor."

"I'm sure it would have come up sooner or later," Quinn said.

"As for me putting a ring through Rylan's nose, while you speak metaphorically, it wasn't my intention to, *trap*," Lorraine used air quotes, "your brother. The two of us enjoy a reciprocal relationship."

After pausing for a beat, Quinn shrugged. "Sure."

Turning her attention to Kady and Saffron, Lorraine said, "I echo Mother's pleased response at your attendance. It's good to see cohesiveness in our family after our inopportune issue with my brother. Thank you for showing your support. I know it means a lot to Mother."

"About that," Kady said, only to be interrupted yet again by Colleen calling to Lorraine, asking her to join the circle with Dr. Chesney. Kady fought to keep herself from growling out of frustration.

"Excuse me." Lorraine patted Kady's arm before she sped off.

Chuffing mild laughter, Saffron draped her arm over Kady's shoulder. "Can't get a word in edgewise, hmm?" Kady nodded in accord. "Welcome to my world."

"And there goes the hostess with the mostess." Quinn chuckled. "Your mom and sister are a pair, Saffron. Seems there's a lot of intolerance masquerading under the guise of savoir-faire and finesse."

Saffron winced when Quinn so aptly described her mother and sister. "Sorry. My family isn't exactly known for embracing causes unless they directly benefit them."

"I kind of gathered that. I'm sorry, Saffron," he said, watching Lorraine rejoin her friends, "but your sister's got a stick up her ass."

Quinn's unexpected words managed to ease some of the tension Kady felt. Obviously Saffron felt the same way because the two of them dissolved into laughter—albeit quiet, reserved laughter. God forbid anyone attending Lorraine Devington's soiree might witness her sister and cousin behaving like normal human beings having fun at a supposed party.

"I'll bet you wanted to include my mother in your little stick realization," Saffron noted through her laughter.

"Hey," Quinn lifted his hands in surrender, "I'm a gentleman and gentlemen do not diss the mothers of women they care about." He leaned toward Saffron, giving her a kiss on the cheek.

Kady could almost see the joyous sparkles, rainbows, and unicorns emanating from Saffron's elated aura. Kady was both thrilled and heartbroken for her deserving cousin who was about to lose a wonderful man it had taken her years to discover.

As she looked around, Kady spotted Rylan up on the second floor landing, leaning forward, resting his elbows on the white marble railing. He looked as lost as Saffron. Kady couldn't help noticing that Rylan looked good. Damn good. As in Superman in a tux good.

# Chapter 11

~<>~

RYLAN HAD REACHED his limit dealing with Lorraine's *intimate* army of pretentious friends, not to mention that arrogant ass destined to be his father-in-law. He debated about bailing from the party, telling himself Lorraine was so busy fulfilling her precious social obligations she'd probably never even notice he was gone.

And then Rylan spotted Kady

Gazing at her from the second floor landing, Rylan was taken aback by the sensual vision of luxurious curves appealingly packaged in the alluring lavender gown. She stood out amid the monotonous sea of beige, off-white, and pastel designer finery around her.

He watched as Lorraine and her mother parted company with Kady, Saffron, and Quinn. When Kady looked his way, he momentarily wondered if she was having the same sort of licentious thoughts about him as he was about her.

Was she thinking of the two of them, skipping out of this stuffy affair to go somewhere private, where they'd slip out of their soiree finery and enjoy exploring each other, skin to skin? Was she thinking about him lovingly torturing her sweet spot until she trembled all over, begging for more? Was she thinking about caressing him with her soft hands while he lavishly licked every luscious inch of her body?

No. Of course not. He was engaged to the woman's cousin for chrissakes. And yet...there were those few, brief, unguarded moments when he could swear he saw something more than friendly interest in those liquid violet eyes of hers.

Rylan returned Kady's friendly wave as she pointed him out to Quinn and Saffron. He watched as they crossed the room, noting he wasn't the only male eyeing the exquisite vision in purple silk. He had no right to be jealous as other men approached her, stopping to talk. No right at all. So why did he burn with envy each time Kady touched one of their sleeves, accepted a friendly hug, or a kiss on the cheek?

As the trio ascended the stairs, Rylan forced inappropriate thoughts of his fiancée's cousin from his thoughts. He refused to be some selfish, thoughtless bastard who planned to marry one woman while lusting after her cousin.

*But, shit...isn't that exactly what he'd been doing since he first set eyes on Kady Malone?*

Damn. He was in trouble.

"Hey, buddy." Quinn gave his brother a sportive whack. "Where the hell have you been? We've been looking for you all over this rambling maze of marble and mahogany."

"I've been busy courting the favor of the important and influential." Rylan's laughter was brief and humorless. "Just as I was instructed."

"My father?" Saffron asked, wincing when Rylan nodded.

"Oh boy," Kady said.

"Sorry, Rylan. Father can be a bit of a bear."

"Uh, *a bit of a bear* isn't among the more descriptive terms that come to mind," Rylan muttered.

"You think *you* had trouble?" Quinn asked in a teasing manner. "We had to deal with your fiancée's mother down there." He thumbed toward the first floor. "Believe me, I can think of a few descriptive terms myself when it comes to your future mother-in-law. Of course," blowing on his fingernails, Quinn polished them on his lapel, "I managed to suitably impress her."

Rylan wasn't surprised in the least. "No doubt Colleen got wind that you're a neurosurgeon," he surmised with a chuckle.

"One with a close connection to Anton Chesney," Saffron said. "In case you hadn't noticed...my parents can be a touch pompous." She held her thumb and forefinger an inch apart. "Just a smidgen."

"Are you kidding?" Turning back to his brother, Quinn clapped Rylan's back. "You poor bastard. That woman is the epitome of the mother-in-law from hell." As soon as the words left his mouth he shifted his attention to Saffron, looking guilty and apologetic. "Whoa, I'm sorry, Saffron. I forgot for a minute that she's your mother. I didn't mean for it to come out quite so...uh..." He scratched his head.

"Quite so accurate?" Saffron laughed. "It's okay, Quinn, I'm not offended or upset. I love my parents. And my sister," she quickly added, "but I've got more than my share of problems with them, with pomposity toward the top of my list."

Rylan worked to keep his mouth shut, rather than blurt out his thoughts, primarily that Saffron's father was a bloated, arrogant, selfish old bastard obviously accustomed to getting his own way. Rylan could imagine himself slowly morphing into someone like that if he agreed to the life Walter Devington and his daughter were mapping out for him. The chilling thought made him shudder.

"Just before we came up here, I spotted you looking awfully forlorn and maybe a little lost or bewildered," Kady told Rylan. "Everything okay? I assume my cousin's *intimate little soiree* has you feeling somewhat overwhelmed."

"An accurate, though minimized, assumption." Rylan returned Kady's smile. "I feel like a naughty child who's been reprimanded and made to stay after school to be lectured by the principal."

It bothered Rylan that the mere sound of Kady's voice turned him on. Logically, he told himself, it had to be misplaced lust because Kady reminded him of Lorraine—the woman he loved and planned to marry. Memories of his disturbing conversation with Lorraine's father flitted across his mind, reminding him his fiancée hadn't been honest with him for who knew how long. Once he and Lorraine had a talk, clearing the air, things would be better and he'd stop fixating on Kady.

"I should have listened to you two," Rylan gestured between Kady and Saffron, "about Lorraine's idea of a small gathering." He raked his fingers through his hair. "This whole thing is too much. I feel like I'm suffocating." He tugged at his shirt collar.

"Monkey suit's not the most comfortable, huh?" Quinn asked, watching Rylan fidget.

"There's no way I can express my innermost feelings without offending the ladies' delicate ears." Rylan engaged in a meager laugh.

"Uh...since we're on the subject of discomfort," Quinn said to his brother, "this might be a good time to warn you that I inadvertently let the cat out of the bag."

Frowning, Rylan wasn't even sure he wanted to ask. "Okay, I'll bite, what are you talking about?"

"I didn't realize you hadn't told your fiancée about your writing goals and, um," Quinn shrugged, "well, now she and Colleen know you write science fiction."

Pressing his hand to his forehead, Rylan gave in to resigned laughter. "You don't need to tell me their reaction. I think I can be just as psychic as Kady on this one." He glanced at her, catching the look of pity across her features. "They both hated it, right?"

"Detested it," Quinn confirmed. "Loathed and despised the very idea of you writing genre fiction, much less one day planning to give up being a professor to write fulltime."

"You told them that too, huh?" Rylan hit the heel of his hand against the marble railing.

"Sorry." Quinn shrugged. "I didn't know it was supposed to be a secret. I figured you'd already told your fiancée about it."

"I should have. I was just waiting for the right time." Right time? With Lorraine? What a joke. "Don't worry about it, Quinn. I'll talk to Lorraine about it. I'm sure she'll understand."

"You just keep up that cheerful, upbeat, positive attitude, Ry." Quinn punched the air for emphasis. "I'm sure that'll make all the difference."

Knowing his brother well enough to know he sure as hell wasn't serious, Rylan whapped Quinn on the arm.

"Ow!" Laughing, Quinn made an exaggerated motion of nursing his arm.

"Oh hell," Saffron said. "Here come Antoinette and Jocelyn and their husbands. They're my cousins on my father's side. They're insufferable, nosey and gossipy. Aaand...they're zeroing in on you, Rylan. They're dying to corner and interrogate Lorraine's fiancé."

Rylan didn't intend for his groan to come out quite as low and growly as it did. "I don't think I can take another round of interrogation today," he admitted honestly. He had no patience or courtesy left.

"They can be awfully prying and meddlesome," Kady agreed. "Saffron, can we get Rylan out of here before they confront him?"

Glancing over the railing down to the main level, Quinn mused, "Think you can jump without breaking a leg?"

"Don't think it hasn't already crossed my mind." One eyebrow shot up as Rylan answered his brother. "But since you're only a neurosurgeon instead of an orthopedist, I'm not willing to give it a try."

"If you land right and break your spine I can help." Quinn offered, causing them all to laugh at his dark humor.

"There must be someplace in this gilt-glorified warehouse that's not crawling with people." Rylan said hopefully.

"Follow me." Saffron led them to an elevator at the end of the floor. Once they entered, she pressed the fourth floor button.

Scurrying past the smattering of people milling about the fourth floor, she opened a set of gilded double-doors and hustled them into the room, closing the doors behind them.

Switching on the light, Saffron gazed around the room and smiled. "We'll be safe here, at least for a while. This is my brother Red's room—well, it used to be." She shrugged and breathed a sigh.

Turning slowly to take in his surroundings, Rylan mirrored Saffron's smile. "I like it. It's the only room in this place with any warmth or character."

"Without even meeting the guy," Quinn said, glancing about him, "I can already tell he's got a great sense of humor."

"Oh, Red's a riot," Saffron said, chuckling. "He's also a trickster who loves playing practical jokes. I remember the year my parents gave Red a G.I. Joe for Christmas. My father was intent on *masculinizing*," she made air quotes, "his son. So that year they also gave him a toy knife, a gun, and a construction set, complete with a little tool belt. It was hilarious because all poor Red really wanted was a Barbie. Of course he could never let my parents know." She laughed at the memory.

"I remember hearing about that from my brother, Nevan," Kady said. "Nevan ended up with Red's G.I. Joe soldier doll." Laughing, Kady amended that. "Oops, I forgot. Nevan insists it's an action figure, not a doll." They all laughed. "Anyway, Red promised Saffron, who detested math—"

"I still do."

"Says the Cherished Pages bookkeeper." Kady laughed, as Saffron offered an *oops* smile along with a shrug. "Red promised he'd do all your math homework for the next semester in exchange for your Barbie. Right?"

"Yup. Red literally begged me," Saffron said. "It was while he was wearing his tool belt and he looked so forlorn and silly that I had to give in. Once I gave him my Barbie he had to keep it in my bedroom so our parents wouldn't get wise. Nevan, who was disappointed because he didn't get the G.I. Joe he wanted for Christmas, got Red's in exchange for teaching Red enough about football and baseball so Red could fool our father when he asked what games Red was playing outside with the other boys."

Kady glanced around the pizazzy room again. "Red's always had a flair for interior design, as well as a sparkling wit," she noted. "I'm surprised Aunt Colleen and Uncle Walter haven't had this room cleared."

"When we were removing his items to deliver them to Bekka House," Saffron said, "I made sure to be the last one to leave. I told them the room was cleaned out because I was relatively certain my parents and sister would steer clear of Red's room after everything that transpired." She sucked in a deep breath. "I wanted him to feel at home if things changed and he came back, even for a visit."

Rylan watched Kady's expression bloom with a genuine smile as she looked around the room done in shades of pink and off-white with gold accents. He was sure there must be an interesting story behind Red being able to pull off a color scheme like this without his parents insisting he change it. Maybe they avoided Red's room and weren't even aware it was such a festive space. He'd have to ask Kady about it.

*Kady*...smiling seemed to come so natural to her...and often. It was rare that he'd seen her look sullen. While she was quite clearly a full grown woman, Kady possessed a wonderful childlike quality. She wasn't afraid to let herself fall into unguarded laughter and enjoy herself, while Lorraine was stiff and overly concerned with what others might think if they caught her expressing joy.

Rylan hoped Lorraine would eventually feel comfortable enough with him so she could let her hair down, laughing out loud when the mood struck her.

It hadn't so far.

"This is wonderful, Saffron," Kady said. "You managed to keep Red's essence and sense of style along with his wittiness. I always loved this room."

"When we were younger," Saffron fiddled with some of the little toys lining a bookshelf, "I remember you telling Red that coming into his room reminded you of walking into a combination candy and toy shop."

Laughing, Kady admitted, "I still feel the same way. It's just a feel-good space where you can't help but smile." She turned to Rylan and Quinn, broadcasting her beautiful smile. "Can you feel it? The happy vibe?"

"I can," Rylan said honestly. There was so much to look at, with much of it being vintage, retro, and probably quite valuable. But, unlike items of value throughout the rest of Devington Manor, everything in Red's room was left out in the open, free to be admired and touched, rather than locked behind glass.

"Look at that stack of comics." Rylan flipped through the clear-cover-protected comic books. "Whoa, he's got some number ones here. Lots of real gems. I'll bet he's got a fortune in vintage comics here."

"Probably," Kady agreed. "Red's always had a good eye for collecting. He chooses things for the joy they bring him, not for the monetary value."

"He's the one who got me started on going to estate sales," Saffron told them. "Before that, the very idea of me looking through other people's discards was positively ghastly." Saffron chuckled. "Red and I had to sneak around because we knew there'd be fireworks if our parents discovered we were rifling through people's rejects. I was nervous about getting caught but Red loved fooling them. He was fearless. He'd make up all these elaborate lies...like us going to the library to study and do homework, etcetera."

"Looks like your brother's really into Broadway shows and old movies too." Quinn studied the framed posters on the walls, many of which were signed by celebrities. "This one's signed by Danny Kaye, there's a Julie Andrews, and, wow, here's Hugh Jackman. Cool."

"You name a musical," Kady said, "and Red can probably sing every song, and really well too."

"Lorraine and my parents never liked this room," Saffron said. "According to them, it suffers from the three G's—too gauche, gaudy, and garish. I suppose now they'd tack on *gay* as the fourth G." She gave a long blink and sighed. "So they steer clear of it, which is why we're less likely to be bothered in here."

"Come on, sit down," Kady said, casting herself onto the bed and patting it after kicking off her shoes.

The room's furnishings were sparse, without enough chairs for everyone to sit. Rylan imagined it was probably because the rest of the furniture had been moved out or trashed. Without even meeting Red, it made him feel sad for the guy.

"Make yourselves comfortable. Kick off your shoes, take off your ties, and let down your hair," Kady added. "You don't have to worry about putting on any airs here. I have no doubt Red would wholeheartedly agree."

"Absolutely." Removing her heels, Saffron and joined Kady.

Rylan found himself mesmerized by the free-spirited woman who'd splatted herself across the bed in her fancy silk gown. Lorraine wouldn't do that in a million years. She'd be far too uptight about wrinkling her dress and, heaven forbid, mussing her hair.

*Nope—bad idea to make comparisons.*

Rylan reminded himself that he and Lorraine would get their differences sorted out soon. Until then, he needed to keep his wandering, and wondering, thoughts in check.

"You still look troubled," Kady told him, watching him sit on the window seat while Quinn cozied up next to Saffron on the pink-satin-quilted king-size bed. "You've had quite an indoctrination to all things Devington today." She smiled. "It'll be better by tomorrow. You'll see."

Rylan chuckled. He certainly couldn't share with her one of the main reasons why he looked troubled. Lust, with a capital L, plain and simple.

"I'm just stressed," he claimed honestly. "Your uncle is making plans for me to transfer to Pacific Northwest University." He scraped his hand through his hair. "After I told him explicitly that I wasn't interested. After I expressed to him that I'm quite happy at WHU." Rylan shrugged. "It seems Walter Devington doesn't take no for an answer."

"No, he doesn't," Saffron said. "I figured it was probably something like that. I have a feeling the last thing you'd want is to teach in a stuffy, stodgy, prestigious setting."

"Did you hear that, Kady?" Rylan asked in teasing fashion. "Your cousin's a psychic too."

Kady scrunched her face into an expression that should make her look unattractive, but...

"Uncle Walter can be quite, um...persuasive," Kady said, carefully measuring her words. "He has a reputation for rushing in and taking the bull by the horns."

"Whether the bull wants to participate or not," Quinn added with a laugh.

"So...does that make me the bull?" Rylan laughed along with his brother.

"I'm afraid so. You're the bull calf that Daddy Dearest wants to nurture and shape into a proper Devington," Saffron said. "He means well. I know it's hard to believe, but he really does. Good grief, he can be unrelenting though."

"So the old man's got your career all mapped out for you, does he?" Quinn continued.

"Only for the next thirty years or so," Rylan said, feeling a familiar throbbing at the base of his skull that came on only when he was utterly exhausted, or thoroughly stressed. Straining his neck, Rylan tugged at his collar before loosening his tie and opening the studs at the top of his fancy-shmancy tuxedo shirt. Feeling somewhat more comfortable, he breathed a prolonged sigh.

"He summoned me to the library earlier, plying me with some old, powerful, heinously expensive cognac, and a huge honker of a cigar."

"Since when do you smoke cigars?" Quinn asked.

"Since Lorraine's daddy made me." Rylan couldn't help laughing, and the others joined in. "Between my stomach getting queasy from the cigar and—"

"Did you inhale?" Quinn asked.

"Yeah." Rylan shrugged. "Damn thing made me buzzed."

"No wonder. You're not supposed to inhale. That's why you got a widdle tummy ache," Quinn razzed him.

Rylan rolled his eyes at his brother. "With the cigar, the burning down my throat from the cognac, and the unnerving conversation, I felt green at the gills by the time I got out of there."

"I don't know why you let him bother you, Ry," Quinn said. "Just tell the guy no, that you already have plans for your future. Period."

Saffron and Kady's laughter caught the brothers' attention.

"I know exactly why they're laughing," Rylan told Quinn. "You don't just say no to a man like Walter Devington. I tried, believe me. But he made me feel like," he shrugged, "I don't know, like—"

"An insignificant child," Saffron finished for him, "sitting in a tiny chair opposite him at his massive desk."

"Spot on." Rylan nodded. "I stood my ground. I told him, with all due respect, that I flat out wasn't interested. Told him I'm happy where I am."

Wide-eyed, Saffron gasped. "*At a public college?*" She'd imitated her father's blustery voice to a tee.

Pointing at her, Rylan said, "His words and temperament to a T. He didn't care what I had to say. He's got it all planned out for me. Even right down to where Lorraine and I are going to live."

"Uh-oh...don't tell me," Saffron said, "the west wing?"

Rylan offered a slow affirmative nod. "The guy seriously thinks we're going to live with them—get that? Me, living here with my bride's parents, in this swanky museum they call a house." His head bobbed slowly as he let the repulsive idea sink for them. "Lorraine's apparently thrilled at the prospect." He moved his hands in an excited fashion. "Walter said she and her mother have been making plans and shopping for weeks." The muscle in his jaw twitched.

"Ouch," Saffron muttered.

"Ouch is right. Between that morsel of news, and this shindig she promised would be small and intimate, I'm not exactly happy with my fiancée at the moment."

"I'm sure once you and Lorraine talk," Kady, the ever positive, said, "and she understands how you feel, everything will be fine."

Throwing up his hands in frustration, Rylan said, "I don't know what the hell I'm going to do. Walter has me wedged into a corner, where any decision I make, that differs from his, is going to have negative consequences. Anything I do that remotely veers from his grand plan demonstrates my callous lack of affection for his daughter. I'm screwed." He choked out a laugh.

After a couple minutes of silence, Kady said, "I know what we need to get you out of those doldrums, Professor." She reached for the handset of the gold-trimmed ivory-colored French provincial phone on the nightstand.

"Hi, this is Kady...yes, that's right, Miss Kathleen." She rolled her eyes and shrugged. "Please bring a few bottles of champagne and something to eat up to Mister Redmond's room. Thank you." She hung up and turned back to the others. "Everything looks better after a little champagne, I always say."

"Or a little jug wine." Rylan tossed a good-humored wink.

"Indubitably." Kady's lighthearted laughter lifted his dark mood. "Any fruit of the vine will do in a pinch. The food and drink should be here shortly. In the meantime, I know what we can do." Her smile was incredibly inviting, sending Rylan's imagination cruising down a course where it definitely didn't belong.

"You do, do you?" he said, almost afraid to hear her idea.

"Mmm-hmm." Kady's sweet smile spread across her face. "We can talk about Lorraine."

Sitting back in his chair, Rylan studied Kady for a moment. Maybe she really was psychic after all because that was probably a very good idea.

A short while later, the four of them sipped champagne while feasting on cold leftover terrine of pork, lobster medallions, oven roasted vegetables and baguettes of French bread.

"Right now you might find this hard to believe, Rylan," Kady speared a roasted wedge of zucchini, "but your future in-laws are good people." The pin-drop silence following her comment didn't deter her. "I know they can be overbearing and pretentious—"

"Haughty and pompous." Quinn stuffed his mouth with buttered bread.

"Arrogant," Rylan added, cutting a slice of the layered terrine.

"Pampered and spoiled." Saffron nibbled on a slab of roasted eggplant. "However, they've donated a small fortune to philanthropic causes, and my mother has given of herself tirelessly through her volunteer work. They're not all bad. Really."

Rylan and his brother responded with unimpressed groans.

"Aunt Colleen and Uncle Walter just want what's best for you and Lorraine, Rylan."

He sat back in his seat, arms folded across his chest, determined to let Kady finish, no matter how fiercely he disagreed. He loved listening to her talk, even if it differed greatly from his viewpoint.

Kady held up her hand. "Okay, *their* idea of what's best." She gave in to a little shrug. "They truly mean well. I just think they don't know any better. This is the only way they've done things, for decades. It's what works for them."

"Is that why they jettisoned their son from their family?" Quinn asked without a trace of his usual humor.

"I'm afraid that's one area where I can't make any excuses for them." Kady expelled a lengthy sigh. "Saffron and I are working on fixing that terrible situation."

Rylan had no clue what she meant, only that she seemed incredibly sincere, naïve and trusting. This was a woman who truly seemed to care about people wholeheartedly. Who loved openly and unabashedly, putting the interests of others ahead of her own. She was so unlike Lorraine the differences were unfathomable. While Kady was all hearts, rainbows, and flying unicorns, Lorraine was square pegs, round holes, and blood sucking bats.

"It's going to take some time and effort," Kady went on. "but I'm optimistic they'll come around and the rift in the Devington family will be repaired...slowly but surely."

"Isn't my cousin the sweetest thing?" Saffron asked the brothers with a smile. "I'll have you know none of that is put on either. She's the real deal."

"Saffron..." Kady's cheeks blushed deep pink. "Pay no attention to her, guys. That's just the champagne talking. In all actuality, I have a resting sinister face. Isn't that right, Saffron?" Kady made what Rylan supposed was her idea of a sinister expression before she cracked up with laughter and Saffron joined in.

With a purposely dramatic shudder, Rylan teased, "So sinister I can barely look at you." He covered his eyes and laughed along with the others.

Getting up from his seat next to Saffron on the bed, Quinn filled his plate and poured more champagne all around. "When you get married, Ry, you should just change your name to Devington. You may as well make it easy on yourself."

"Lorraine's probably already working on that one," Rylan answered with a twisted smile. "She told me they'd change me into a Devington in no time."

Making a raspberry sound, Kady gave a dismissive wave. "Oh she was just kidding, Rylan."

"Kidding?" Quinn's eyebrows shot up in surprise. "You mean Lorraine has a sense of humor?"

That hit Rylan's funny bone. "I didn't think much about it at the time, but after my conversation with her insistent father, I suspect Lorraine's comment was more than just idle talk or humor." He gulped back some champagne. "She'd love for me to be Rylan Kilpatrick Devington." He huffed ironic laughter. "And that's exactly who I'd be if I live in this massive mausoleum—with my in-laws."

His eyebrows pinched. "Somewhere along the line I lost control of my life." He couldn't keep from laughing at the situation. It was either that or cry, and he sure as hell wasn't about to do that in front of his future sister-in-law, cousin-in-law, or, worst of all, his brother.

"It'll be weird," Quinn said. "My kid brother from the south side of Chicago...a guy who worked hard as hell for everything he got, living in..." he spread his arms wide, "this."

"Just call me little Lord Fauntleroy." Rylan curtsied.

"All joking aside," Quinn continued, "I think it'll be cool. You deserve to finally live a pampered life after working two jobs to put yourself through school and everything else you did to get where you are today. I just feel bad because I won't be here for the wedding, or to visit you in your fancy digs, for a long time."

Something sounding like a forlorn sigh came from Saffron, who glanced up, obviously embarrassed she'd let that slip.

Rylan appreciated his brother trying to put a positive spin on things, even though he knew Quinn hated the idea of being under anyone's thumb as much as Rylan did.

Kady stopped at Rylan's side on her way to the table with the food and champagne. Resting her hand on his shoulder, she said, "I'm sorry all this has happened, Rylan. I understand how you must be feeling. My aunt and uncle are kind of in a different stratosphere from the rest of us everyday folks." She gave a gentle laugh. "Would you like me to try talking to Lorraine and my uncle to try to help them understand your viewpoint?" Rylan missed the warm sensation of her hand when she removed it. "I think I might be able to get through to them."

Seeing Kady's genuine expression of concern, Rylan smiled. Sometimes she seemed too good to be true, making him wonder if she was genuinely this sweet and kind, or if it was just an act she put on around people. His gut told him she was one hundred percent authentic.

Closing his eyes, he took a deep breath, clearing away all notions of holding her in his arms. "I appreciate the offer but it wouldn't be fair to put you in the middle of this, Kady. Your uncle's got a serious case of tunnel vision where Lorraine's future is concerned. I doubt he'd listen or even give a damn about my viewpoint, much less understand it at all."

Taking a seat on the edge of the bed, Kady had a look of resolve etched across her features. "But I already *am* in the middle. I'm your future cousin-in-law. I want to do whatever I can to ensure that you and my cousin get off to a good start." She cocked her head to the side and smiled. "I think Uncle Walter has a bit of a soft spot for me, so I might be able to break through his crusty exterior. Please say you'll let me help."

Unable to keep from smiling at Kady's earnest expression, Rylan shelved his disappointment over the situation with Lorraine. "Sure, go ahead if that's what you really want to do." She looked so pleased at his positive response. "You know," he told her, "I wonder if Lorraine realizes what a terrific cousin she has."

The timing of his words was impeccable. The double doors to Red's room opened and Lorraine walked in with rubbernecked cousins, Antoinette and Jocelyn, and their husbands in tow. Looking from her fiancé's open collar, untied bowtie, and stockinged feet to the other three in the room with him, Lorraine displayed a chilly mask of indignation.

"I've looked high and low for you, Rylan. You seem to have forgotten you have guests."

This was the proverbial straw for Rylan. He didn't take well to being publicly reprimanded. Slapping his linen napkin on the end table next to him, he rose from his chair.

"*I* don't have guests. They're *your* guests, Lorraine." He couldn't be much more specific than that.

Bristling before regaining her composure, Lorraine turned her scorching gaze on Kady and Saffron. "I should have known you two were behind Rylan's disappearing act. Hiding my fiancé when there's a houseful of guests is thoughtless and irresponsible." She turned her ire on Rylan. "Your place is downstairs with me."

"Whoa-ho-ho," Quinn let out, looking at Lorraine as if she were nuts.

"Hold on, Lorraine." Rylan crossed the room, slipping into his shoes. "Don't blame Kady or Saffron. We all needed a break from your *intimate soiree*." He failed to conceal his emerging sneer, in fact he didn't even bother trying to hide it. "Your sister was kind enough to give us a little temporary respite from the swarm of people out there who I don't know from Adam." He felt his jaw twitch as he ground his back teeth.

"This *swarm*, as you so deftly put it, are the people who will be part of our social circle," Lorraine informed him. "Which is why you need to mill about and interact with them."

"Lorraine..." Rylan began, distracted by the sound of Antoinette and Jocelyn mumbling in the background. His tone, stiffened stance, as well as the look of annoyance on his face, must have registered with Lorraine because her attitude shifted in the blink of an eye.

It caught Rylan off guard until he remembered, *ah yes...God forbid she make a scene, or come off looking any less than Princess of the Manor to her nosey cousins.* It was evident she was making a concerted effort to maintain her poise.

With a hasty glance at those present, Lorraine flashed a plastic smile. Her smiles never reached her eyes the way Kady's did. Lorraine had told him that breaking into a full smile created crow's feet at the corners of the eyes, and deep lines around the mouth—and she couldn't possibly allow smiling to age her prematurely.

"You're right of course, darling," she said to Rylan, causing Quinn's jaw to drop. Rylan had to stop looking at his brother because Quinn's exaggerated facial expressions were making it hard as hell to keep a straight face.

"I understand completely," Lorraine added with what she must have thought was a cute little pout. "Do forgive my overreaction. I'm exhausted and afraid I'm dealing with the onset of one of my migraines." Walking over to Rylan, she fastened his shirt studs and fixed his tie, which Rylan suddenly likened to a noose around his neck.

"I'm just so glad we found you, Rylan, because my cousins have been so eager to meet you after I've gushed about my wonderful fiancé." When she finished fussing with his apparel, she turned to her cousins. Looping her arm through Rylan's, Lorraine said, "Well, here he is. The magnificent man I've been telling you about. See how patient he is with me? I don't deserve him at all." Getting on her toes, she kissed Rylan's cheek.

Rather than feel any emotion, Rylan felt like a mannequin in the store...just a handy prop used for staging.

It was becoming obvious to Rylan that everything Lorraine did was calculated, designed to elevate her status in the eyes of others. Nothing was left to chance. Her every word and expression was for the benefit of anyone in the vicinity. While most people deal with self-esteem issues at some point, Lorraine's incessant concern over what others thought of her bordered on being obsessive.

Eyeing Rylan as if he were a succulent prime rib of beef, Antoinette and Jocelyn continued trading whispers and smiles of appreciation while their husbands made introductions and exchanged small talk with Rylan and Quinn. After ten minutes of mindless prattle, an invasive grilling, and the cousins' juicy gossip about those who were part of the *swarm* downstairs, the foursome bid adieu and left the room—leaving Lorraine and her icy glare behind.

"Thank you all for embarrassing me in front of my guests." A caustic tone replaced any previous sweetness in Lorraine's voice.

Rylan reveled in sardonic laughter. "Lorraine, you never cease to amaze me. You switch moods faster than a chameleon changes colors."

"We can't have my cousins thinking there's a rift between us, Rylan, then spreading it around. Gossip travels fast."

"Stop being so dramatic, Lorraine," Saffron said. "It was only Antoinette and Jocelyn. You dislike that insipid twosome and their geeky husbands as much as I do."

"Regardless, they're gossips and I don't want to supply fodder for their hearsay," Lorraine countered. "What about the rest of my guests? They've all been asking where my fiancé is hiding. Utterly embarrassing."

Rylan realized the more he objected, the harder Lorraine would come down on Kady and Saffron for bringing them to Red's room.

He'd never seen Lorraine this angsty or out of sorts before so he decided to give her the benefit of the doubt. Maybe she was only acting like a damn shrew because she was overly stressed about this soiree thing of hers. It seemed extremely important to her, and if she believed he'd messed it up for her, that could explain her antagonist attitude. While patience wasn't one of his virtues, Rylan decided to try for all their sakes.

Positioning his arm around Lorraine's shoulder, which felt as cold and unyielding as one of Devington Manor's marble columns, Rylan chose to bite the bullet and give her the apology she believed she deserved. Hopefully she'd be satisfied and drop the matter, as well as her bitchy attitude.

"You're right." The words stuck in his throat. "I shouldn't have wandered off. It was thoughtless. I apologize." Damn, that was harder to get out than he'd expected. "But you shouldn't care so much about what everyone else thinks, Lorraine. We've talked about that before. As long as we're happy together, that's all that counts, isn't it?"

Rylan's words sounded hollow to his own ears. *Happy?* Something gnawed deep in his gut. He was engaged to a beautiful woman and should be feeling over the moon excited...shouldn't he?

Smiling up at Rylan, Lorraine made her little pout face again as fingers crept up the placket of his tux shirt. "Oh but, I *do* care what others think, darling. That's just the point. And you should too." While there wasn't any recrimination in her words, they came out sounding like baby talk as she patted his arm in a condescending way.

As calm, logical, and understanding as he tried to be, something about Lorraine's manner rubbed him the wrong way. He felt...manipulated. That was a huge negative in his book.

His posture instinctively stiffened. "Did your father tell you he spoke to me earlier?" He caught a fleeting glint of nervousness in Lorraine's eyes.

"Why no, I, uh...did you two have a nice chat?" Averting her gaze, she smoothed the unwrinkled skirt of her dress.

"We got real chummy over some ancient cognac and Cuban cigars." Lorraine eyed him with cautious interest but didn't say a word. "So tell me, Lorraine, how are the decorating plans coming for the west wing?" Crossing his arms over his chest, Rylan couldn't keep from glaring at his fiancée.

It took a beat or two before she sidled up to Rylan, looping her arm through his. "Isn't it wonderful, darling?" She rested her head against his arm. "I knew we could expect something special from Mother and Dad for a wedding gift, but I never imagined they'd be *this* generous." She gave his arm an affectionate squeeze. "It must be because they're so fond of their future son-in-law." Lorraine's tone couldn't be any more honeyed.

"We'll have the entire west wing of Devington Manor all to ourselves. Isn't that splendid news?" Lorraine swiftly looked away after noticing his narrowed gaze. "I was keeping it a surprise, darling. I-I knew you'd be just delighted."

"You're kidding, right?" Rylan took a step back. "You can't possibly be that insensitive, Lorraine." He didn't believe that for a minute. Of course she could.

"You mean as insensitive as you were, not sharing your writing goals with me?" Lorraine countered. "About you entertaining the foolish notion of leaving your professorship to pursue writing science fiction? Really, Rylan," she chuffed a laugh, "how absurd."

"Which is exactly why I didn't mention it," he retorted, "to avoid the inevitable criticism."

Clearly unwilling to meet Rylan's stern gaze, Lorraine turned her back to him, fidgeting with the decorative items atop Red's dresser. Glancing into the dresser's mirror, she addressed Rylan's reflection.

Flipping back to the original topic, Lorraine said, "You'll fully embrace the idea of occupying the west wing once you get used to it, you'll see. It's the best of both worlds. You won't be giving up your plan of us having a little place in the country because we'll have my uncle's cottage whenever we need to get away."

Rylan became aware of the silence surrounding them. Even his wisecracking brother avoided adding anything to the conversation which, at this point, was for the best.

"Between my career and our living arrangements," Rylan started pacing, "it seems you and your parents have planned my whole damn life out for me."

A quick glance at Kady, Saffron and Quinn nearly made him laugh aloud. The silent threesome were the involuntary audience for a very badly produced, completely absurd reality show. *Welcome to The Shit Show, ladies and gentlemen, where a pissed off man and his highfalutin fiancée make total asses of themselves for the sake of your entertainment.*

"You mustn't look at it that way," Lorraine insisted. "Let's not exaggerate." She glanced at the mirror to Kady, Saffron and Quinn who'd kept their eyes open and mouths shut. Turning to face Rylan, Lorraine swept a light touch across his arm. "We'll talk all about this later, Rylan," she said in a near whisper, "when we don't have an audience."

"It's a little late for that now, isn't it?" Rylan muttered.

Clearly intent on changing the subject, Lorraine looked around Red's room as if she hadn't realized where she was. "I haven't been in here for eons. I don't remember it being pink the last time I saw it. All this conglomeration of toys and posters fit for a teen's room makes my head hurt." She rubbed her temples while Rylan wondered if there was ever a time Lorraine's head didn't hurt. Maybe it was contagious because he had a whopper of a headache now too.

Frowning at Saffron, Lorraine said, "I thought you told mother, daddy and me that you bagged up all of...all of his...of this stuff.

"Did his name get caught in the back of your throat?" Saffron asked. "His name is Red, Lorraine. Our brother's name is Red. And I kept what I damn well felt like keeping of our brother's belongings because I love him and what he picked out for his sanctuary away from the rest of stuffy Devington Manor. I'd seriously caution you not to make an issue of it, or have any of it removed or discarded."

Lorraine cleared her voice. "Oh for heaven's sake, look at you two." She'd changed the subject so lightning fast Rylan wondered what he'd missed. Giving Saffron and Kady a once-over, Lorraine used a teasing tone, chuckling as she said, "You're both wrinkled and your hair is a tousled mess, springing out every which way. Please be sure to make yourselves presentable before rejoining the party. We have an image to maintain."

Her semi-smile seemed forced, but it was better than the bitch mask she'd worn since entering Red's room.

Addressing Quinn, Lorraine added, "You'll need to tuck in your shirt, fix your collar, and put your tie back on." With a long blink, she tacked on that odd smile that looked like she'd forgotten how to do it. "Please," she added as if unfamiliar with the word. "Appearances mean everything."

After saluting Lorraine, Quinn did one hell of a job holding his tongue. A true accomplishment for him. Fumbling with their clothing and hair until each button, snap and shoe would pass inspection, Kady and Saffron were similarly quiet.

Seemingly satisfied with their response to her request to spiff themselves up, Lorraine turned her attention to her fiancé, pasting on the phoniest smile he'd ever seen on her.

"Come along now, Rylan. It's time for us to rejoin our guests. There are important people I want you to meet." Spinning on her heel, she headed for the double doors, opening them. When Rylan made no move to follow her, she turned back to him. Arching one perfectly penciled eyebrow, she said, "Rylan?"

"I'll be along in a while, Lorraine."

"You've played hooky long enough, Rylan." Her smile was robotic now. "I'd like you to come with me now...please."

The muscle in his jaw flexing, Rylan projected a steely glare. Henpecked before he was even married. He couldn't even manage a semi-smile before replying, "I *said* I'll be along in a while."

With a quick, glacial gaze at the four of them, Lorraine's chin jutted high. Without another word, she turned and left the room. Once the doors closed, a chorused whoosh of sighs practically echoed off the walls.

"I don't know about you, Quinn," Saffron said, "but I couldn't be more ready to get the hell out of here."

"Good." Returning to the table, Quinn stuffed the last of the lobster medallions in his mouth. "You can't get me out of this place fast enough." Before going any further, he looked at his brother.

"Unless you need me to stick around, Ry. I'd hate for you to have to face the Devington's wrath all by yourself."

Rylan's chuckle sounded old and tired, just the way he felt at the moment. "No, you go ahead, I'll be fine. Don't worry, I remember those boxing moves you taught me as a kid, Quinn. If things go south, I can knock 'em all out. And on the off chance I get beat up and they break my back, you can operate on my spine to fix it."

"Deal." Laughing, Quinn responded with two thumbs up.

"Um...before we go," Saffron said, "I want to apologize."

Kady and Quinn looked as confused as Rylan felt. "For what?" Kady asked.

"I've known Lorraine all my life." Saffron's eyebrows lifted as she sighed. "I should have known better than to bring you all up here. She's always been prone to hissy fits when she hosts one of her *little*," she hung air quotes, "get togethers. Her nerves get the best of her because it's so important to her that everything, and *everyone*," she glanced at Rylan, "is absolutely perfect. So," her shoulders hiked in a shrug, "sorry for ruining your evening."

"You don't owe anyone an apology," Rylan told her. "Coming up here to your brother's room is the only real enjoyment I've had all evening. It's the only room in this house I've ever felt comfortable in. Saffron, if it weren't for you and your escape plan, especially after I'd been cornered by your father, I probably would have bailed on this ridiculous excuse for a party hours ago."

"Ry's right, Saffron." Quinn cupped her face, brushing a kiss across her lips. "Zero apology necessary, you hear?" Saffron smiled and nodded. "This is the only space in the house I wasn't afraid I'd back into some priceless antique and break it. Everywhere I turn in this place the words, *you break it, you buy it*, ring in my ears." They all laughed along with him.

"They're both absolutely right," Kady assured her cousin. "I really enjoyed the time we spent here this evening...or afternoon...or whatever the heck it is now." She laughed. "And I know how pleased Red will be to learn you managed to keep his room decorated with things that have meaning for him."

Rylan decided Lorraine's atrocious behavior was more of a help than a hindrance because it brought him to this point—the point where he knew exactly what he needed to do now. Gathering his courage, he stepped in front of Kady, placing a hand on her shoulder.

His voice a gentile whisper, Rylan told her, "I've got my car. Let me drive you home, Kady. I-I really need to talk to you."

# Chapter 12

~<>~

POOR RYLAN looked wounded and confused. His gaze was so penetrating, Kady could almost feel it pierce clear through to her heart. She wanted more than anything to reach out and comfort him, hold him, kiss him until all the hurt was gone—but she knew better. Being alone with Rylan for the drive, no matter how short, was asking for trouble.

Taking his hand, she covered it with her own. "Thanks, but I've got a ride with Quinn and Saffron." Aware the enticing warmth of his skin was melting her resolve, Kady pried herself from his magnetic hold.

"Besides," she said softly, smiling up into his eyes, "I don't think Lorraine would like it. And I doubt you want to give her any more reason to be upset." She made an O-face, causing him to smile. "You two need to clear the air tonight. We can talk for a few minutes until you rejoin Lorraine and her party." She walked toward the window seat. God, she needed some air.

"I'm not going back to that party." Rylan followed her. "I've had it."

"I think you know that would be a very bad idea," Kady said kindly, watching the realization dawn on Rylan as she spoke.

"Kady, Quinn and I are going to go get his car now," Saffron said, elbowing Quinn and giving him the high sign. "We'll text you when we're ready to go, okay?"

Kady nodded. "Perfect, thanks." And then Quinn and Saffron were gone. Kady knew Saffron understood why she didn't want to be alone with Rylan for long, especially after everything Lorraine had put him through tonight. No doubt he was feeling lost, as well as angry. That combination was dangerous because he might misunderstand Kady's caring or sympathy for something more. It would be horrific if he sensed she had feelings for him.

God knew it was hard enough for Kady to keep her emotions in line where Rylan was concerned. With him feeling vulnerable, her instinctive nurturing gene kicked into high gear, telling her she needed to offer support and comfort.

Kneeling on the window-seat, Kady lifted the window's latch, opening the French casement outswing windows. Resting her elbows on the ledge, the cool March breeze whisked through her hair, causing more of her wild curls to break free, but it didn't matter. She'd be leaving soon and could sneak out the kitchen entrance to avoid running into Lorraine.

Aware of Rylan's close proximity behind her, she said, "I'll have a talk with Lorraine and Uncle Walter tomorrow." She turned to face him. "Everything will be all right, Rylan, you'll see. I know my cousin loves you. She's...well," she sucked in and expelled a deep breath, trying to decide how best to phrase it, "Lorraine's just had so much on her mind with her party and your October wedding. I'm afraid it's taken a toll on her, causing her to act out of character."

"Is that what you call it?" Rylan huffed a laugh. "That's putting a great spin on it."

"Once you two sit down," Kady continued, in her most reassuring voice, "and have a good, healthy talk, you'll both feel better. Just think of this as a blip. Somewhere along the line you two got your wires crossed, that's all." As she smiled, she noted he was studying her face. "As they always say, good communication is the key to any successful relationship," she tacked on.

Arching an eyebrow, he got a teasing gleam in his eye. "Is that something you read in those romance novels you love so much?"

"Well, that," Kady laughed, "and a bit of wisdom I've picked up from self-help books. Hey," she gave Rylan a lighthearted poke in the ribs, "speaking of romance novels, did you ever read *Immortal*

*Among the Stars*, the book I gave you when you came for dinner? Seeing that it's March already, I'm sure you have." She flashed a kidding smile.

A sheepish grin curling his lip, Rylan admitted, "Not exactly. I keep meaning to though. And I will. Real soon. So you enjoy reading bawdy, sex-filled romance books where everyone shucks off their manly sultan gear and sexy slave girl clothes before they do the deed, hmm?"

Kady rolled her eyes at his silly description. "Romance novels fall into many categories and subgenres," she said. "The ones you're talking about would be considered spicy, or at least mildly spicy. There are also sweet or clean romances where most of the intimate moments happen behind closed doors. There are so many different tropes and—"

"I suppose as a writer, I should know this but...what's a trope?"

"Basically character traits and plot devices that work like building blocks for stories. Like ideas within the romance...friends to lovers, fake relationships, secret babies, time travel, one night stands, billionaires...know what I mean?"

"Who doesn't? They all sound positively fascinating," he joshed.

"I wouldn't laugh, Mister Sci-fi Writer in the Making. You'll be facing tropes yourself as you write your books."

"Right, like the secret alien baby trope, or the robot and alien friends to lovers trope, or the evil alternative universe lovers trope, or the—"

"Okay, okay." Holding up her hand, Kady laughed. "I'm sure your books will be positively fascinating."

"What's your favorite trope?" he asked her. "Do you like the spicy getting naked stuff?" Rylan had the most charming, mischievous smile.

"I suspect you're trying to bait me, Professor." Kady jabbed his chest with a pointed finger. The last thing she needed was to get any deeper into a conversation about romance and sex when she'd been curbing forbidden thoughts of how delicious it would be to rip open Rylan's shirt and run her fingers over his well-defined chest...before exploring further. Moving closer to the open window, she welcomed the cool breeze across her flushed cheeks.

"The bookshop owner is evading the question." Rylan wagged a finger. "If you're so passionate about the merits of romance novels, you should welcome the opportunity to defend them."

"I thought we were having a conversation about you and Lorraine," Kady reminded him, watching as Rylan's teasing expression transformed to sullen and contrite. "You two need to have a good heart to heart, preferably tonight, before any of the problems have a chance to fester."

"Are you speaking as the notorious Doctor Romance now, or as Katarina the fortune teller?"

"Neither, Professor Smarty Pants." Kady smirked at him, struggling to ignore how appealing he was. "Just plain old me, Lorraine's cousin and your future cousin-in-law."

"Plain old me indeed," Rylan muttered, catching Kady's surprised attention. The raw emotion she saw in his eyes frightened her—and excited her. Definitely time to extricate herself from the risky direction this conversation had taken.

"You said you wanted to talk to me," Kady said. "Saffron will be texting me soon, so we still have a few minutes to talk about you and Lorraine."

"Right." Rylan indulged in a prolonged noise that was part sigh, part groan. "Sorry, I guess it's obvious I've been avoiding the issue." Nodding, Kady offered a sympathetic smile. "I don't know about this engagement anymore, Kady." Leaning forward, he rested his arms across his knees while gazing at the floor. "I don't know if I can go through with it."

Instinctively, Kady reached out to smooth her fingers through Rylan's mussed hair, stopping and jerking her hand away the instant her fingers made contact and she realized what she was doing. This wasn't the time for her compassionate side to take over.

"Rylan, you love my cousin, don't you?"

"Yes, I..." He was silent for a moment. A long moment. "I don't know. I'm not too sure of anything anymore." He looked up at Kady.

How quickly she could get lost in the depths of his deep blue eyes. For the sake of her sanity, she had to look away.

"Of course you love her, and she loves you." She ran a finger across the windowsill to avoid meeting his gaze. "By tomorrow Lorraine will have come to her senses and will be begging you to forgive her for her behavior today." She patted his shoulder. "You'll see."

"Lorraine and her parents are trying to make me into something I'm not. I don't want to live that way." The crease between his eyebrows burrowed deep. "Money, prestige, power, position, they're all so vitally important to the Devingtons. That's not me. Not the way I think." Taking her hand, he gave it a gentle squeeze. "You understand, don't you, Kady?"

Working valiantly to keep her composure as she enjoyed the warmth of his hand clasping hers, she sucked in a deep breath and nodded. "Yes, I understand." She slipped her hand from his grasp. "You're fun-loving and spirited, Rylan. That's why you're perfect for Lorraine. She needs a man like you in her life, and you need *her*, too."

Studying Kady's face, as if memorizing her features, he clasped her shoulders, drawing her close, until they were mere inches apart.

He brushed an errant curl from her forehead, then cupped her chin.

Kady's pulsed raced with a drumming beat so forceful, she worried he might be able to hear it.

"You're so very sweet," he said in a near whisper, trailing his fingers through her hair, unleashing random, bouncy wisps. "Full of fire and passion," his voice grew husky, "yet so caring and concerned. You're an amazing anomaly, Kady Malone."

As Rylan gathered her closer, Kady's hand immediately flew up between them, pressing hard against his chest, resisting his advance. It was one of the most difficult things she'd ever had to do.

A blue light flashed from her fingers, surprising them both. It took a while for Kady to comprehend that the light came from her heartwish ring. She had no clue what message the ring was trying to impart, only that she knew it was dead wrong if it saw Kady and Rylan as a couple.

As the light dissipated, his gaze locked on her hand, while his clasp tightened on her shoulders. "Did you see that? What was that?"

"Oh...my, um, the stone in my ring sometimes glows when it picks up the light." Spreading her fingers as she held her hand outside the window, she tried to smile. This wasn't the time to go into an explanation about the magic of heartwish rings, and Odin, and family lore, and miracles and—

"There's no light," Rylan noted. "It's dark out."

Kady's laughter sounded forced and nervous. "Ah...so it is. Well, sometimes the stone, um, it reflects light like," she gazed out the window, "like the landscaping lights around the long driveway." She thought her quick thinking was quite clever.

"Very...weird," Rylan said, losing interest and returning his attention to her. The weirdness of the occurrence didn't stop him from inching closer to her lips. "Kady," he whispered, lowering his lips to hers.

With the faint brush of skin on skin, she said, "Oh my God, Rylan, stop. Please." She worried her thudding heart had just popped out of her throat, landing on the floor of Red's room.

He did as Kady asked without hesitation, gazing into her eyes with a look she'd remember forever. Oh how easily she could give her heart and soul to this man—this man who'd just told her he loved her cousin.

"Rylan, listen to me," Kady said softly, aware her heart hadn't absconded after all because she could barely hear her own voice over its hammering in her ears. "You're," she cleared her throat, searching for the right words, "you're confused right now and acting on a mistaken impulse due to stress. I'm just the one who happened to be here when you needed someone." She projected a kind smile.

"No, Kady, that's not it. It's you...it's the way you make me feel, I—"

"Rylan!" Cognizant by his stunned expression that she'd just all but barked at the poor man, Kady was tempted to slap her hands over her ears, singling la-la-la to drown out any sweet words Rylan might say. "Rylan," she repeated, her tone softer and more in control, "we're going to forget that almost-kiss ever happened, okay? Remember, we'll be cousins-in-law soon."

She had no idea what that had to do with anything, but it was the best she could come up with under the circumstances of her brain having turned to mush. Rylan was a good man. If she appealed to his sense of honor, Kady felt sure that would work.

"I love my cousin, Rylan, and you just confirmed to me that you love your fiancée."

"But I—"

"Please understand this can't happen again. Ever. It wouldn't be fair to me." With those words, she spotted the realization in his eyes. "There'd be guilt, awkwardness and regret between us. If Lorraine ever suspected there was something between us, it would crush her, and forever ruin my relationship with my cousin. That means we both need to be responsible adults and keep our emotions in check."

Kady concluded by patting his hand. "I think it's time for you to go now, Rylan...back to your fiancée's party and her guests. Don't you?" His gaze didn't budge for a small eternity. If he kept looking at her like this she was going to cry.

"Yeah," Rylan nodded, "yeah. You're right." He breathed an extended sigh while straightening his collar and tie. "Professor Rylan Kilpatrick has responsibilities." He offered Kady a semi-smile. "I'm sorry I made you uncomfortable, Kady. I didn't stop to think—"

"There's no need for apologies." She smiled. "I understand."

As he got to his feet, Kady's phone gave a text alert—Saffron telling her they were in Quinn's car waiting for her at the kitchen's entrance. The timing of the text couldn't have been better because Kady's resolve had taken a wicked beating and she didn't have much left.

~<>~

"So the blue glow really caught me off-guard," Kady told her mother who was busy absently straightening books on the bookshop's shelves. "How in the world do you explain a heartwish ring to someone who knows absolutely nothing about them? I just made something up that must have sounded ridiculous about light reflecting off the stone."

"You say this happened when Rylan was closing in for a kiss?" Astrid asked.

Nodding, Kady insisted, "Only because he was upset and confused. Otherwise it never would have happened...because he loves Lorraine."

"Oh sweetheart..." Astrid's expression turned sympathetic. "You have feelings for this man."

"No I don't." Looking away from her mom, Kady shook her head. Her mom was far too perceptive.

Izzy offered a series of soft barks, as if talking to them.

"There, you see? Even your dog agrees with me." Astrid bent low. "Don't you, sweetie?" Tail wagging, Izzy replied with more bark-talk sounds.

"You don't do dog-speak, Mom, that's Aladee." Kady chuckled.

"Listen here, Kathleen Doolan Malone," Astrid said with a kind tone, "you might be the psychic one in the family, but I'm your mother, and mothers have their own psychic abilities concerning their children. I just worry about you getting your heart broken."

Kady's shoulders slumped. "I won't, Mom. I'm well aware Rylan Kilpatrick and my cousin are getting married in a several months. I simply found him attractive, that's all. You'll understand when you meet him."

"Mmm-hmm...I'm sure you're right, dear."

"I have an important goal. I want to patch up the family." Kady gave in to a sigh of frustration. "So far I haven't had any success." Probably because thoughts of Rylan had disrupted her concentration. She felt ashamed thinking about her lack of focus on the issue of the Devington's treatment of Red. She had no business finding her cousin's fiancé attractive, or charming, or witty, or... Her head suddenly pounding, she groaned.

"Lorraine is still young enough that you might be able to change her views about her brother...even though I doubt it." Astrid breathed a sigh. "But for decades, Colleen and Walter have been...well, sadly, the only word that comes to mind is *bigots*. It's so deeply ingrained it might be impossible to change their thinking."

"I understand your reasoning, Mom, but I still believe I can help make a positive difference so they'll realize and regret how they've treated Red. I need to try, at least."

"You're in danger of getting in too deep, Kady. The money-focused Devingtons aren't like us, and certainly not like you with your open, trusting, believing spirit. Your penchant for always trying to help people could come back to bite you in the...butt." Astrid smiled at her near slip. "As for Rylan and Lorraine, let them iron things out for themselves." Her head angled to the side. "Why do you think the heartwish ring glowed when it did?"

"No idea. I don't know the first thing about this thing," she waved her hand, "or how it works. I'm sure it's nothing important." That's what Kady had been telling herself since it happened. She wasn't convinced.

"I think it was a sign about you and Rylan."

"Feel free to help yourself to some coffee, Mom." Kady said. "Today's blend is a combo of French roast and Sumatra."

Astrid laughed. "You're trying to change the subject."

"No...I'm just ignoring you," Kady admitted, and mother and daughter shared a laugh.

Izzy sidled up to Astrid, sitting at her feet and looking up at her adoringly.

"Your granddog loves you," Kady said.

"The feeling's mutual." Squatting to get down to the little dog's height, Astrid massaged around Izzy's ears...and baby talk commenced. "Izzy knows her grandma loves her and thinks she's absolutely adorable, isn't that right, Izzy?" Izzy replied with a little yip before licking Astrid's hand.

Returning her attention to her daughter, Astrid asked, "So why am I here bookshop sitting this morning? Not that I mind. I love the vibe you and Saffron have created here. I'm just curious."

Kady collected her purse and the keys to her twenty-year-old used car, that must be as magical as the heartwish rings because it just kept on running long after it had every right to give up the auto-ghost. "Because Saffron has to be at a closing this morning. She still has a few real estate transactions she needs to get off the books before she's free of all her Realtor commitments."

"Are you leaving Izzy with me? I'd be glad to watch the little cutie pie for you."

"No, thanks. I'm bringing her to my meeting with Uncle Walter so she can work her puppy charms on him."

"On Walter?" Astrid made a raspberry sound. "Oh, honey, Walter and Colleen aren't dog people. They're hardly even *people* people." She and Kady shared a laugh. "I doubt crusty Walter will be moved by our Izzy's adorableness. He'll just consider her an intrusive annoyance, that's all."

"My instincts tell me he'll feel different about Izzy," Kady assured Astrid.

"Well," Astrid shrugged, "what do I know? Since Izzy is a reincarnated fortunetelling psychic, she probably has plenty of tricks up her sleeve," she tugged at the sleeve of Izzy's sparkly lavender sweatshirt, "than I can begin to imagine."

"Aladee had one of her telepathic talks with Izzy," Kady said. "Izzy communicated to her that she'll do her best to help bring the Devingtons around. Using her psychic abilities, she'll see what she can sense. Afterwards, she'll let Aladee know, then—"

"And then Aladee will let *us* know," Astrid finished for her daughter.

"Don't you absolutely love it, Mom?"

"I do." Astrid chuckled. "What a wonderfully strange family we have."

~<>~

"Your uncle is in the library, Miss Kathleen. He's expecting you."

"Thank you, Williams. Is Miss Lorraine at home?" Kady addressed the family's very proper British butler as she fastened a leash to Izzy's collar, gave her a kiss on the top of her head, and placed her on the marble floor of the foyer, holding the leash out to Williams.

Reluctantly taking the leash, Williams bristled as the little bocker sniffed while circling at his feet. "Miss Lorraine and your aunt are engaged in a repose with a pot of tea in the solarium. Eh...what shall I do with the, uh, canine while you're visiting with Mr. Devington? You know how your uncle feels about...furry creatures."

"Why don't you give Izzy the grand tour, Williams. I'm sure she'd love to check out what you have in that mammoth kitchen. Then you can bring her to me in Uncle Walter's library."

"Oh, I don't believe Mr. Devington will approve of—"

"It'll be okay," Kady assured him. "I'll take full responsibility." Cocking her head, she smiled to see the usually unflappable butler squirming with discomfort. "Don't worry, Williams, Izzy won't bite."

"Thank you, Miss Kathleen." Holding the leash as far from his starched body as possible, as if it were a live wire with a mountain lion at the end, Williams cleared his throat. "Come along now, little pooch." When, instead of following him, Izzy planted herself in a sitting position and proceeded to lick her private parts, Williams turned to Kady in horror.

Muffling her laughter as best she could, Kady told him, "If you want her to follow you, just give the leash a gentle tug and say, *Izzy come*. Go ahead, try it."

"If you say so, Miss Kathleen." After clearing his throat again, Williams weakly tugged on the leash. "Izzy come." The little dog rose and hobbled along, making little tickety-tack sounds on the marble floor with her nails as the butler led her from the foyer.

Kady crossed the foyer, approaching the library. She gave herself a discreet once-over in the enormous fancily-framed mirror, chuckling when she barely recognized herself. She'd dressed in the most conservative clothing she owned, a purple linen blazer with cream-colored top beneath it, a lavender and cream silk scarf softly draped at her neck, and lavender linen slacks. While the linen was too summery for the weather, it was the best she could do without going clothes shopping at *Dull Duds R Us*.

Knocking first, as her uncle preferred, she announced herself before opening the great wood doors at the sound of his gruff "Enter."

Sitting behind his massive desk, wearing an indigo-blue satin smoking jacket, puffing on a fat cigar, and reading the Wall Street Journal—he and Colleen still embraced paper rather than digital—he gave Kady a quick nod of acknowledgment.

"Good morning, Uncle Walter." Closing the doors behind her, she crossed the room and planted a soft kiss on his cheek. To her uncle's surprise and apparent discomfit, she pulled a chair next to him, rather than sit across the desk from him, where she'd most likely sink from view.

"Well, Kathleen," her uncle said, expelling a stream of smoke before giving his niece a peck on the cheek, "it's not often we see you here at Devington Manor two days in a row. Coffee?" She nodded and he poured them each a cup from the silver and glass carafe positioned over a small canned heat flame. He motioned for her to help herself to the extravagant assortment of rolls in the silver mesh basket. There were enough rolls and pastries to feed twenty people.

"What brings you here so early this morning?"

"Uncle Walter, it's nearly noon." Adding sugar to her coffee, Kady laughed.

Walter let out a half-laugh as he checked his pocket watch. "Why so it is." His silvery eyebrows knitted in a look of concern and he leaned toward his niece. "So what's going on, Kady? Are you having financial problems? Do you need money?"

"No, I'm fine." Smiling warmly she placed her hand on the sleeve of her uncle's smoking jacket. "But thanks for asking."

"Well then," he sat back in his chair, gnawing on his cigar, "is this merely a chitchat visit?" Looking down, he flicked a heavy ash into the marble ashtray. "Which is fine with me. We don't see enough of you here at Devington Manor."

"Actually, I wanted to talk to you about Lorraine. Well, Lorraine and her fiancé...as well as a few other things." Walter's ostracized son, Red, topped the *other things*, on Kady's list, but she was wise enough to know it was too early to bring up the sensitive topic. "Williams mentioned Lorraine and Aunt Colleen are out in the solarium. I'd love to have them join us so we can all visit together."

His brows merging into a tight, silvery vee, Walter told her, "Lorraine's nursing one of her prodigious headaches. Apparently she and Kilpatrick had words last night." He grumbled while puffing on his cigar. "Bullheaded young man. Never met anyone so adverse to taking sound advice and accepting a helping hand."

"I'm sure you're pleased to know Professor Kilpatrick isn't a fortune hunter, or the kind of man who intends to live off your money," Kady said, sipping from her coffee—which was too weak and insipid for her taste. "He's independent, self-sufficient, and determined to provide for Lorraine on his own."

Walter looked pensive. "Point taken. However," he gave a dismissive wave, "bahhh. Do you honestly think my Lorraine would be happy living on the salary of a professor teaching in a public college?"

"Well I believe—" before Kady could finish, there was a knock. Looking up, she saw Aunt Colleen and Lorraine entering the library.

"It's just me and Mother," Lorraine said, stepping across the threshold. She sat on one of the burgundy leather loveseats with brass nail-head trim. "Kady," she coolly acknowledged her cousin.

"Good Morning, Kathleen, dear." Colleen Devington touched cheeks with her niece before taking a seat. "What brings you here so bright and early?"

Kady laughed. "It's noon, Aunt Colleen."

"Apparently, she's here to champion Professor Kilpatrick." Walter poured himself another cup of coffee.

"What?!" Lorraine jerked toward her cousin.

With a warm smile, Kady told her, "I was just telling your dad how fortunate he is to be getting Rylan for a son-in-law."

Kady heard the air deflate from her cousin's lungs.

"I'm not sure that's something Daddy needs to concern himself with. I'm perturbed about Rylan this morning." She crossed to her father's desk, helping herself to coffee while bypassing the tempting assortment of carbs. "He's being unreasonable and stubborn about us living here, and at Uncle Chauncey's property in the country. Then there's the prestigious position Daddy's worked hard to secure for him at Pacific Northwest University." Closing her eyes, Lorraine took a deep breath. "Rylan just turned up his nose at it. So ungrateful..."

"You're engaged to a man intent on making it on his own," Kady said, "rather than someone after the Devington money."

As if she hadn't heard anything Kady said, Lorraine complained, "I don't understand him. Rylan's misplaced idea of bliss is living a pastoral life out in the country with dogs, pigs and horses. How a brilliant man of science can have so little ambition or appreciation of class and culture is beyond me. Can you imagine me as the-the apron-wearing wife of a...a farmer?"

Keeping herself from laughing at Lorraine's silly description of Rylan wasn't easy. Facing her cousin, Kady said, "Rylan loves you, Lorraine. Have you considered how it made him feel when he discovered you knew all about taking over the west wing and didn't tell him? You led him to believe you shared his dream about living in a little house in the country with a dog and children."

Lorraine gave an ironic blip of laughter. "Me, isolated in some common little frame house with a pride of sniveling rugrats tugging at my hem and a furry beast dirtying my home?" Wincing, she sipped from her coffee. "Surely you realize I was merely placating Rylan until Mother, Daddy, and I could work out more acceptable living arrangements."

Frustrated and carefully measuring her next words, Kady scraped her fingers through her hair, inadvertently loosening a cluster of curls from the neat bun her mother had helped her create at the nape of her neck. Brushing the hair behind her ear, she blew out a sigh.

"I think Rylan might feel betrayed because the woman he loves wasn't open and honest with him."

Narrowing her gaze, Lorraine asked, "Did Rylan put you up to coming here today—to defend him?"

"Not at all," Kady answered. "I just saw how upset you both were last night. You and Rylan are good together, Lorraine. He's a good man. You don't want to lose him, do you?"

"The young man is a fool," Colleen Devington said before Lorraine could reply, "if he thinks he can marry into this family without making some changes. Letting go of that dreadful commonality he finds so endearing is at the top of the list. I fail to see the supposed sacrifice he's making. He wanted a house in the country, and we've arranged it so he can have Chauncey's country cottage What more does the man want?"

"How do you think I felt learning that my fiancé plans to leave his professorship to write science fiction books for a living instead?" Lorraine glared at Kady. "Which, by the way, he kept from me."

"That would be impossible," Walter blustered. "Inexcusable."

The conversation was headed for the toilet and a good flushing. Kady felt she might as well be talking to three granite statues.

"Kady," Lorraine said, her voice unexpectedly tinged with kindness, "I know you're an idealist, a romanticist who always sees the best in people and who believes there's always a pot of gold at the end of every rainbow. That's what makes you special. But..." smiling, she offered an elegant shrug, "I don't see why I should give up everything I know to satisfy my future husband's unrealistic dreams of a utopian existence. I'm sorry but that's something you would do—not me."

Lorraine was spot on. Kady would move heaven and earth to have a man like Rylan Kilpatrick love her. If she were Lorraine, she'd do everything possible to hold their relationship together. She'd even read every environmental science book she could get her hands on, just so she knew what was important to Rylan.

"I don't dislike the young man." Walter selected another Cuban from his humidor, clipping it before lighting. "He's respectful and has a lot of gumption. The potential is definitely there." He savored a satisfying drag from his cigar, expelling a stream of smoke. "Once he understands the responsibilities and expectations that come with marrying my daughter, I think he'll come around and fall into place."

Kady was at a rare loss for words. Her uncle spoke about Rylan as if he were a dog or a puppet, not an independent man with hopes and dreams of his own.

"Something I don't quite understand," Lorraine said to Kady. "Why are you so concerned about my relationship with my fiancé?"

"Because you're my cousin and I care about you. And because I truly believe you and Rylan are good for each other. It would be a shame to see you two go your separate ways because of a minor disagreement. I think some compromise might help." Kady waited for Lorraine's response as she watched her cousin silently, and languidly, sip from her coffee. As the silence dragged on, Kady finally asked, "Did that answer your question, Lorraine?"

Lorraine smoothed her blonde hair, although, as usual, there wasn't a hair out of place. Looking at Kady coolly, she said, "I'm just considering what you said."

Kady breathed a sigh of relief. Maybe she was finally getting through to Lorraine.

"I think I may have made a mistake," Lorraine continued. "It's becoming increasingly clear Rylan and I have little in common."

Kady's sigh of relief had clearly come too soon.

"He's certainly no Reginald Von Austerly," Walter touted, tapping his cigar ash.

"Who's that?" Kady asked. The name was familiar but she couldn't place it.

"Lorraine's former fiancé," Colleen said, surprising Kady. She didn't know about Lorraine's prior engagement. "A real catch. Sadly, Lorraine broke things off."

"Perhaps an unfortunate mistake," Lorraine said. "Rylan and I had a heated discussion last night after you, Saffron, and Quinn left. I'd entered the kitchen to check with staff on our champagne supply and caught Rylan about to sneak out the back door." Lorraine huffed an incredulous laugh. "My own fiancé. Like a thief in the night. Can you imagine?"

*Oh...not a good move, Rylan.* There wasn't much Kady could say in his defense after that. She'd warned him it would be best to return to Lorraine's party and talk to her.

"He shouldn't have done that," Kady agreed. "All I can say is I know he loves you. He told me so. I think you still love him too, Lorraine."

The agonizing silence enveloping the room was broken by the drumming of Walter's fingers on the leather-topped desk as he puffed on his cigar. Colleen silently fingered the society pages of the newspaper, and Lorraine quietly sipped her coffee.

"I suppose you have a point, Kady," Lorraine said, finally breaking the tension and causing Kady to chance another sigh of relief. "I may have been unfair not telling Rylan about my decision for us to live here in the west wing." A slow smile spread across Lorraine's lips. "He *is* an incredibly handsome creature. Isn't he, Kady?"

Nope. No way was Kady responding to that. Instead, she said, "You two make such an attractive couple, Lorraine."

Lorraine's smile broadened as she looked skyward, arching her eyebrows, as though visualizing Rylan's finer physical points. "Yes. I suppose he deserves another chance."

Kady produced the most supportive smile she could. She half wanted her cousin to live happily ever after with Rylan, while the other half wished Lorraine would toss him aside so he was free for Kady to pursue.

Her fantasy bubble burst when she remembered Rylan had professed his love for Lorraine last night—even if it wasn't necessarily wholehearted. The man was upset with Lorraine, that's all. At least Kady would always have the memory of the all too brief taste of his lips on hers before she shoved him away.

Oh how easily Kady could have succumbed. If she wasn't so principled, so loyal to her pompous cousin, Kady would have surrendered to the enticing promise of Rylan's kiss. She imagined ripping open his shirt, popping off the studs and letting them fly every which way, before the two of them—

"Lorraine, dear," Colleen said without looking up from the society page, snapping Kady out of her *never-should-have-gone-there* trance state, "don't make the mistake of marrying a man because of his physical attributes alone. There are hordes of striking men from moneyed families who'd love to be in Rylan's shoes."

"Your mother's right, Lorraine," Walter said. "Look at your mother and me. The perfect union. Looks, money, class."

Rising from the loveseat, Lorraine walked to the French doors that opened to the library's patio. Parting the velvet drapes and sheer curtains, she watched the bright sunlight dancing across the perfectly manicured topiary.

"Kady is right." Lorraine turned back to face her parents. "Her surprisingly passionate defense of my fiancé made me realize I owe it to myself to make every effort to cultivate our relationship."

Lorraine walked to her cousin, resting a hand on Kady's shoulder. "I'm glad you stuck your nose where it doesn't belong." She laughed lightly and, after the initial surprise, Kady joined her. "Thank you for helping to open my eyes about Rylan, Kady."

As Lorraine headed back to the loveseat, Kady rose from her chair to stand behind her uncle's chair, loosely wrapping her arms around his neck. Resting her cheek against his, she said, "Uncle Walter, promise you'll try to be a little more understanding regarding Rylan, okay?" She coiled his silver hair around her finger.

"All he wants," Kady continued, "is an opportunity to make his own choices and not have his entire life mapped out for him by someone else. You're a good, fair man, Uncle Walter. I know you'd never sit in judgment of anyone before they've had an opportunity to prove themselves."

Fidgeting in his chair, Walter grumbled a bit. Patting Kady's hand, he said, "Well, I like to think I'm fair-minded. All right, I'll talk to him again and see if we can come to an agreeable compromise."

"Thanks, Uncle Walter." Kady planted a kiss on his cheek. Swallowing hard before broaching the far more difficult subject, Kady remained standing, moving to the center of the room so she could face everyone at the same time.

"I'm particularly happy to hear you say you're glad I stuck my nose where it doesn't belong, Lorraine...because I'm about to do it again."

# Chapter 13

~<>~

WILLIAMS CHOSE that moment to knock, entering the library with Izzy in tow. "I've given the animal a tour as you requested, Miss Kathleen."

"What on earth?" Walter growled.

"You brought your dog?" Lorraine said, stating the obvious.

"Oh dear...the hair, the dander, the odor," Colleen said, her hand flying to her throat, looking as if she'd spotted a convoy of rodents.

*Boy they're a tough crowd.* Apparently picking up on Kady's thoughts, Izzy replied with a soft yap as she hobbled to her side.

"Izzy was bathed early this morning with the special perfumed doggy-friendly soap I created for her, so she's clean and smells good too. She sheds very little and whatever hair you may find can be easily vacuumed up." Bending, she picked Izzy up. "Isn't she adorable? She loves people, so she's very friendly." She walked over to her uncle who stiffened against the back of his chair.

"Say hello to Uncle Walter, Izzy." Allowing Izzy to turn on her charm, Kady watched as her little dog gently tapped Walter's arm three times.

"Oh...well..." Walter's features relaxed and he even succumbed to a chuckle. "She's a cute little thing." Once he lifted his hand to stroke behind Izzy's ears, Kady knew she had him.

Next, Kady headed for her aunt, who was clearly not only unenthused, but downright antagonistic about having a dog in Devington Manor.

"Aunt Colleen, I remember you telling my mother some years ago that your favorite designer was Coco Chanel, and you loved her iconic suit jackets." Looking as if Izzy might pull a knife from her outfit and plunge it into her, Colleen offered a hesitant nod. "Take a good look at what Izzy's wearing."

Kady had asked her sister-in-law, Sabrina, if she could duplicate the look of the classic Chanel boxy jacket with its contrasting braid and small pockets at chest and waist as a costume for Izzy. Using the sparkly lavender sweatshirt material she found, and bordering it with deep purple braiding around the edges and pockets, Sabrina had created an absolute winner.

Once Colleen allowed herself to look at the dog, really look, and then study what she wore, an amazed smile took hold. "Oh this is marvelous. Wherever did you find a Chanel-style outfit for a dog? How clever and inventive."

"My brother Gard's wife, Sabrina, made it for Izzy," Kady said, delighted at her aunt's interest and praise. "She's an accomplished artist."

Izzy lifted her paw and cocked her head, looking at Colleen.

"Oh, does she want something?" Colleen asked, slanting her head at the same angle as Izzy.

"Mmm-hmm, she wants to shake your hand. Go ahead and take her paw." Colleen did and within thirty seconds she was making little cooing noises at Izzy. Kady was so proud of her little dog. Breaking through those Devington walls was *not* an easy task!

Lorraine buffed her fingernails against her beige cotton-knit sweater while watching her mother fuss over Izzy. "I must admit, Kady was right about Izzy. She certainly is a charmer."

Convinced Izzy had worked her magic, softening up the three of them as much as possible, now it was Kady's turn to see if she could preserve their elevated moods.

"It made me happy to hear you refer to yourself as fair-minded, Uncle Walter." Kady tossed him a smile that he returned. Pausing, she swallowed the sizeable lump in her throat. "So I thought perhaps now might be a good time for us to start a nice family conversation about Red."

Although Kady had done her best to begin with a lighthearted approach, she was amazed to witness the immediacy of the Devington walls of iron slamming into place before she'd even finished speaking. All three became inflexible where they sat, smiles eradicated, leaving the trio looking like kids who'd just been told there's no Santa.

In essence, she guessed that's how they felt about Red. He was as nonexistent to them now as Santa Claus.

Their joint reaction was so unsettling, so chilled, Kady couldn't help shuddering.

"As I expressed last night, Kathleen," her aunt began, "I appreciate your show of support regarding Redmond. It's comforting to know there's at least one Malone who understands and agrees with our stance about his...his choice of living a perverted lifestyle." Colleen appeared to rub goosebumps from her arms.

"Definitely," Walter concurred. "It was beneficial for our guests to see someone from Colleen's side of the family stepping up in the vein of support and solidarity."

*Oh dear...*

"I tried talking to you about this yesterday, Aunt Colleen, but you were understandably preoccupied with the guests, so we didn't have a chance to talk. I'd wanted to tell you that," Kady sucked in a deep breath, letting it out with a shudder, "my presence at Lorraine's soiree wasn't meant to indicate my agreement regarding what transpired with Red. In fact, I wholeheartedly support him."

She saw her aunt's gaze grow saucer-wide, but continued talking. "It was my intent to hopefully help patch the terrible rift between you and your son so our family can be happy and whole again."

Following a lengthy, awkward silence, Colleen lifted her wrist, looking at her watch. "I didn't realize it was so late. I have an important call to make."

As she rose from her seat, Kady quickly said, "Aunt Colleen, please don't be angry with me. It breaks my heart to see my family torn apart this way. I know you love Red. He's your son. You gave birth to him and held him close when he was a newborn. Remember? You nurtured him and loved him and—"

"You were entirely accurate about sticking your nose where it doesn't belong, Kathleen." Colleen's eyes were watery and her voice wobbly, but her stiff, unrelenting posture was unmistakable. "I have no intention of discussing our decision about Redmond with you, or any of your family who have turned their backs on us in this difficult time. I'd greatly appreciate it if you didn't press the matter."

"No one in my family has turned their backs on you, Aunt Colleen. They tried communicating with you about your son but once you realized they supported Red, you basically shut the door on any further discussion."

One eyebrow hiking at the same time her chin shot up, Colleen replied to Kady, "That's what doors are for."

Frustrated, Kady turned her attention to her uncle, in an attempt to soften him by raising happy memories. "Remember, Uncle Walter, how you and Red would stroll through the beautiful gardens surrounding Devington Manor and you were so amazed and proud when he was able to not only name all the foliage but tell you about the properties of each as well?" She caught a spark of recollection in his eyes.

"I remember you praising Red and having him demonstrate his acumen about flowers and weeds and such for the family when we were all together and—"

"Your aunt is right, Kathleen." Walter's face had colored a purplish-red, the veins in his neck and forehead bulging. "This issue isn't open for discussion. I'm asking you to respect that."

Desperate, Kady turned her attention to Lorraine. "Did you know your brother was back in town just a few months ago? It was shortly after we all learned you were engaged. Red was elated to hear you were so happy, Lorraine. He said you deserve nothing but the best."

Curiosity obviously getting the best of her, Lorraine said, "What do you mean back in town? Red isn't living in Glassfloat Bay anymore?"

Kady sure as hell wasn't about to lead with, *Oh, haven't you heard? Your brother lives up on Mount Olympus now, fraternizing with all the gods and goddesses.* But before Kady could reply, her aunt pressed herself into the conversation.

"It doesn't matter where he lives, Lorraine," she chastised her daughter. "It's no longer any of our concern."

"He moved quite far away last year," Kady hurriedly told her cousin. "He and his partner came to brunch at Bekka House a few months ago. You should have seen Red, he looked so—"

"Don't do this, Kady...please." Lorraine looked as though she might be on the verge of tears. Kady wondered how much of Lorraine's attitude toward Red was her own, and how much might be merely a show of support for her parents. Of the three of them, Kady thought she'd have the best chance making any headway with Lorraine.

"I love the three of you so much," Kady told them. "Between yesterday and today, we've enjoyed such a nice visit, along with some healthy conversation. Can't we put our differences aside and continue having a nice, calm, reasonable discussion about the elephant in the room?"

"Kathleen," her aunt looked as though she felt ill, "you clearly have no conception how painful this is for us. Redmond chose to leave a fine job at the bank to open a flower shop and become a homosexual. It's something we won't tolerate, which is exactly what we expressed to him. If Redmond chooses to reconsider his abnormal choices and leave this humiliating foolishness behind him, we're willing to reopen the discussion with him. Until then, please respect our decision to let it be."

There was so much that needed addressing in her aunt's words that Kady didn't even know where to begin. She hadn't grasped the full extent of their feelings, or their confusion and lack of knowledge about what it means to be gay. She wasn't qualified to be a counselor or therapist, making this discussion far outside her realm of expertise. The last thing she wanted was to make things worse by saying the wrong thing, so, regrettably, Kady decided to honor their request and drop the subject. For now.

"Dealing with the realization Redmond is not only abnormal," her uncle said, "but is prancing around, entirely happy about it, isn't something we choose to discuss or debate. The knowledge that the boy we raised now has a *partner*," Walter used finger quotes as he spat the word, "doesn't help. I find the idea utterly appalling."

Apparently, Astrid was right, in trying to warn Kady she was too naïve, inexperienced, and Pollyannaish to tackle something of this magnitude. Her aunt and uncle's misconceptions were deeply ingrained from years of intolerance. Kady's attempt to have a healthy, positive discussion about Red had failed miserably, leaving her feeling incredibly sad. And like an utter failure.

The sound of Izzy whimpering mixed with soft howling distracted Kady from her inner reflections.

"What's wrong with your dog?" Lorraine asked with an expression of concern.

"She's crying," Kady said, aware how easily Izzy could zero in on people's vibes. "And I'm afraid if I don't leave now I'll be doing the same." Addressing her aunt and uncle, she said, "Thank you for meeting with me today. I'm sorry I upset you." She received no response from either of them.

"I'll see you out." Lorraine rose from the loveseat. Without Colleen or Walter uttering another word, Kady, Lorraine and Izzy exited the library, closing the doors behind them. It was one heck of a long walk leaving that chilly, cadaverously-quiet room.

As she and her cousin walked together, with Izzy's nails tack-tack-tacking along the marble floor, Kady glanced down at the heartwish ring on her finger. Since she clearly wasn't able to heal the situation on her own, at least she could use her heartwish to fix things for Red and his family. Her mother told her the ring somehow knows the right wish for the bearer's heart to make, glowing to confirm it, so Kady expected her ring to show off some radiance or something as it realized her wish decision, but it remained still.

"I know that was rough for you with my parents," Lorraine acknowledged. "I'm sorry, Kady. I know you meant well."

Lorraine's expression of kindness left Kady stunned as they walked through the long art-filled corridor toward the huge marble-walled vestibule which would take them to the front door.

"Thank you. I appreciate that, Lorraine. It seems I'm not quite as adept at making peace as I thought I was. I really botched that up, didn't I?" Her chuckle was anemic at best.

"No, you didn't," Lorraine assured. "It's not you my parents are angry with, it's the entire situation. They don't understand and are at a loss as to how to cope...or act. You think *I'm* overly concerned with what others think? Ha!"

Listening to her cousin laugh at herself, again surprised Kady.

"For Mother and Father, the fear of them being judged and possibly excluded from their social circle because their son is gay is something they're not equipped to deal with."

Amazed and pleased to hear Lorraine's take on the situation, Kady said, "I had a feeling you might be hesitant to accept Red being gay because your parents might see it as a betrayal."

"Something like that." Lorraine nodded, then glanced at the floor when Izzy growled. Kady couldn't help notice that Izzy didn't seem to care for Lorraine. She'd have to ask Aladee about it.

"Lord knows," Lorraine continued, sidestepping the dog, "I have my own issues to work through." She gave another smile, reminding Kady of how attractive her cousin was when she did away with that awful resting bitch face. "I'm aware I can be...opinionated at times. I was upset with Red when I first heard he was gay, mostly because my parents were devastated. I was angry at him for hurting them."

"But Red didn't mean—" Kady began, stopping when Lorraine held up her hand.

"I know. It was irrational reasoning on my part but," her shoulders hiked in a modest shrug, "so be it. That's what happened. I don't know how to approach them about forgiving and, eventually accepting, Red, for something he certainly didn't choose. But, as you heard, Kady, that's their belief."

Kady nodded. "I had no idea your parents were so..." About to comment on their views, Kady stopped. What could she say? Intolerant? Ignorant? Bigoted? Homophobic? Racist? All of the above? Better to keep her conclusions to herself. They were Lorraine's parents after all.

"I'm disappointed," Kady said instead, "that I couldn't be of some help but, honestly, Lorraine, I'm at a loss."

She didn't want to mention making her heartwish to fix everything because, what if something went wrong and she ended up disappointing her cousin? She doubted Lorraine even believed in the magic of the heartwish rings anyway.

Although Kady had spent most of her life immersed in what her family termed her *quirky alternative beliefs*, even she had difficulty accepting that a stone, supposedly from Odin, great chief of the Norse gods, could hold such immense power. The magnificent results of her siblings' wishes were undeniable though.

As Lorraine continued talking about her parents and their narrow views, Kady's thoughts drifted to the night before, when she got back to her apartment after the soiree. She got ready for bed, lighting her favorite incense and playing one of her favorite meditative playlists softly in the background. While sitting cross-legged on the mattress, Izzy centered at her lap, nuzzling against her.

She had hoped her twice-daily ritual of meditating might help clear her mind after what happened with Rylan and the almost-kiss, and reveal the best path for her to take.

"...and of course Mother and Daddy have strong opinions about racial issues..." Lorraine's words interrupted Kady's thoughts. "You'll notice they've never had Blacks on their household staff payroll because, well, they're concerned about cleanliness..." And Lorraine just kept going. While Kady felt somewhat guilty tuning out all of her cousin's reporting about her parents' thoroughly dogmatic views, she could only take so much ugly rhetoric.

Kady usually began her nighttime tradition by talking to her beloved, departed grandma, Bekka. She'd often get positive signals from Grandma Bekka, like the inviting fragrance of her gingery pepperkaker cookies baking, or the tinkling sound of Bekka's wonderful laughter, or even the sound of her grandmother's sweet, whispered assurances in Kady's ear. But last night Kady was unable to sense a connection, causing her to wonder if it was because Kady was on the wrong track.

Or, worse, perhaps because of Kady's improper attraction to Rylan.

Was she inadvertently giving off some sort of come-hither signals Rylan picked up on, leading him to try kissing her while he was confused and upset with Lorraine? The idea made Kady feel queasy.

"What about your psychic feelings," Lorraine asked, snapping Kady out of her reverie. "Don't they give you some sign about how you could reach my parents?"

Giving her cousin a curious look, Kady said, "I thought you didn't believe in any of that psychic stuff?"

Lifting her hands in surrender, Lorraine said, "I more or less have to act like I don't believe because none of my friends buy into any of that. And I can't be—"

"Different or independent of their belief system," Kady finished for her cousin and Lorraine nodded in agreement. "As for my psychic intuition," Kady sighed, "unfortunately I get nothing when I focus on your parents regarding any of this. No feelings or specific vibes. Maybe it's too close to home. I'm afraid of making Uncle Walter and Aunt Colleen so angry they'll decide never to speak to me again. Then what good will I be to them, or to Red?"

"You don't have to worry. They both love you very much. In fact, I'm sure Daddy has a soft spot for you."

"I'm glad." Kady suspected as much, so it was good getting confirmation. "But I worry they'll isolate themselves from the family, perhaps causing irreparable damage to our joint family dynamics." Lorraine's head bobbed in acknowledgement.

"It's easier—well it was, up to now, anyway—to just let my parents think I'm on their side. It-it really..."

When Lorraine paused, they'd almost reached the front doors and Kady glanced at her cousin, noting she was fighting back tears. It surprised Kady and broke her heart. She'd rarely seen Lorraine close to tears. Guilt and shame washed over Kady like hot spilled soup. As the one in the family known for being empathetic and compassionate, what did she do? She sat in judgment of her cousin, thinking the absolute worst, never considering Lorraine's feelings.

"Come here, you." Kady pulled Lorraine into a hug as her cousin sniffled. "I love you Lorraine. I owe you an apology. I never stopped to think about how difficult all this is for you." Breaking their embrace, Kady reached into her tote bag, pulling out her pack of travel tissues, handing one to Lorraine, who dabbed her eyes and nose. She seemed to be crying, although Kady hadn't detected any actual tears.

"Thank you. I love you too, Kady. You have nothing to apologize for. All this, including the idea of my brother not being at my wedding in October, has had me so upset that I've been taking my angst out on everyone else, including you and Rylan. I'm aware of how I must sound when I'm upset, but it's like I have no control. I just keep going, digging that hole deeper and deeper until I fear I'll lose Rylan who'll probably willingly jump into that hole to get away from me."

"I know he wasn't happy about yesterday," Kady told her honestly, "but relationships have survived and thrived after far worse. You two can fix this as long as you keep the lines of communication open."

"I'm not so sure." Sniffling, Lorraine appeared full of self-doubt. Poor thing.

Izzy delivered a disagreeable growl.

"Why does she keep doing that to me?" Lorraine asked, narrowing her gaze at the dog.

"I don't know." Kady didn't have a clue, but Izzy had made her dislike of Lorraine clear. "Maybe too much hobbling around Devington Manor has her leg sore. Anyway, Lorraine, just tell Rylan exactly what you told me. Be honest with him. He's a good man. His heart isn't made of stone. Once he realizes what's caused you to be, uh..."

"A bitch?" Lorraine offered helpfully.

"Well," Kady's smile mirrored Lorraine's, "once he realizes, he'll understand and forgive you. All couples have disagreements. Consider this one your first and move on from there."

"How did you get to be so wise?" Lorraine asked. "You know, I screwed things up with my sister too. When Saffron became vocal in her support of Red, challenging our parents to stop being so bigoted, she included me in her wrath, which made me dig in my heels, determined to side with my parents. Again, completely illogical. I know my attitude has hurt our relationship. Saffron and I always got along well. I miss being able to talk to her."

"You're sisters, Lorraine. You love each other. This is just a bump in the road on your life's journey. The good news is you can repair that roadblock with a little bit of work." She wrapped her arm around Lorraine, jiggling a buddy-hug.

"I was aware of how grueling my sister's work schedule had been the last two years. I wondered why she felt it necessary to work around the clock. I wasn't sympathetic, and ridiculed her for being power hungry." With a sigh, Lorraine shook her head back and forth. "I had no idea Saffron was handling Monica Sharp's workload as well as her own. I didn't even know Monica had cancer."

"None of us knew," Kady said. "She'd pledged Saffron to secrecy. The chemo left her too weak to work. Your sister stepped in to make sure Monica didn't lose her job or any pay, because Saffron knew Monica was supporting her mother."

Lorraine's eyebrows pinched. "I was so focused on me, myself and I that I never thought to see if Saffron was okay. I naturally assumed the worst about my sister."

Izzy barked once at Lorraine, causing her to start, while surprising Kady as well. She followed the bark with yet another growl.

"Oh my goodness, Izzy." Kady squatted, getting down to her dog's height. Cupping Izzy's face, she said, "That wasn't very polite," ending with a kiss to the top of Izzy's head. Rising, after Izzy licked her hand, she said, "I'm sorry, Lorraine. That's not at all like Izzy. She must have heard something." Kady wondered if perhaps it was a sign of Izzy having some sort of psychic awareness. She'd definitely have to give Aladee a call, asking her to communicate with Izzy so she knew what the heck the menacing growls and barking were all about.

"Maybe you should put a muzzle on her when you take her out," Lorraine said, only to be met with another growl. This time Kady fought back the urge to laugh. Her cousin's suggestion obviously didn't sit too well with Izzy.

"Anyway," Lorraine went on, "as I was saying about my sister, Saffron's had the worst luck and experiences with men. I hope she finds a man who'll treat her with kindness and respect, and love her as much as she loves him. Have you...have you received any insight about perhaps a match between Saffron and Doctor Kilpatrick? They seemed pretty cozy."

"No...I haven't," Kady said, twisting the truth. Although she and Lorraine seemed to have developed a new bond, Lorraine and Saffron were still at odds. Kady didn't feel it was her place to reveal anything personal about Saffron and Quinn. She'd leave it up to Saffron to talk to Lorraine if she chose to. Besides, with the new development of Quinn soon leaving for Nigeria to teach, it's possible the two of them might never see each other again.

What a pity. All Kady's instincts told her they were an ideal match. Poor Saffron. She was so lovestruck.

"I've made such a horrific mess of things with my sister...and Rylan. Tell me, Kady, have you sensed any psychic vibes about me and Rylan?"

"Sorry, I haven't," Kady replied.

"Nothing at all?"

"Not a thing." Lorraine looked so disappointed Kady was half-tempted to lie to make her cousin feel better. She decided being honest was the wisest choice. "Don't feel bad." She offered her suddenly melancholy cousin an encouraging smile. "I don't often see things about romantic relationships. The psychic feelings and sensations come and go, hitting me when I'm not expecting it, or thinking about anyone in particular."

"If I ask you a question will you answer me honestly?"

"I'll do my best," Kady replied, her insides prickling with uncertainty.

They'd reached the house's enormous entryway and both stepped outside into the sunshine. Lorraine opened a small hidden panel, picked up an intercom phone, and asked to have Kady's car brought around.

"If you saw or felt something about someone," Lorraine began, "take me for example, and what you saw was negative, would you tell the person? Would you tell...*me*?"

Studying her cousin's pretty face, Kady generated her warmest smile. Not wanting to jeopardize their breakthrough by lying to her cousin, she told her the truth.

"It depends. Most of the time, no, I wouldn't tell the person, unless it was something like a clear and present danger, like an impending accident, or an attack that could be avoided by my warning. As long as it's something I sense the person has the power and ability to change, I'll tell them. You know, like...don't get on that flight today, or don't travel by car on Tuesday, or make sure someone walks you to your car in the parking garage after work tomorrow."

Lorraine's expression grew solemn. "Have you had to do any of those?"

"Many times throughout my life, even as a child." Giving a slow nod, she recalled how often she'd been in such a situation. "I believe I have this gift for a reason so I do my best to use it wisely, to help people in any way I can."

"It sounds like this gift, as you call it, comes with carrying tremendous responsibility on your shoulders," Lorraine noted.

"It all comes down to balance," Kady said with a long blink. "Joy and sorrow...anticipation and fear. Always praying I make the right decision so I don't inadvertently hurt anyone. If I sense someone is suicidal I'll stay with them, even if I don't know them, talking to them while offering my support. I share the contact information for crisis counselors that I always carry with me. Sometimes it backfires with people warning me to mind my own business. But I won't leave them if I sense the reason I'm there is to help keep them from taking their life."

"My God, Kady...I had no idea. That could be dangerous."

"One black eye," Kady's hand covered her right eye, "a cracked rib, a broken wrist, and a big swollen jaw worth of dangerous." She chuckled.

Looking befuddled, Lorraine asked, "That's funny?"

"While the memory of the incidents and pain aren't amusing, I'm laughing from joy because I kept those four individuals from leaving the planet before their time."

"But how did you know it wasn't their time?" Lorraine asked.

"I don't know how, Lorraine." Shrugging, Kady smiled again. "I just knew." Kady balled a fist just below her sternum. "Deep in here. They all still keep in touch with me too. They were people I met on my overseas backpacking trips."

"Other American travelers?"

"No. Each was from a different country I'd visited."

"Different ethnicities then?" A frown creased Lorraine's brow.

Kady nodded. "Right." She glimpsed what she perceived to be a note of disapproval in Lorraine's temperament.

Eyebrows raised in surprise, Lorraine smiled. "They weren't even people like us and yet and you still risked your life to help them from committing suicide."

*People like us.* It was an odd, uncomfortable statement...a bit too close to Aunt Colleen's earlier assertions while speaking with Quinn about his trip to Nigeria.

"Well of course I did." Kady couldn't help the light laughter escaping her lips. "I don't make a habit of asking people their nationality, race, color, creed or political leanings before helping them."

She wondered how Lorraine might react if she told her one of those people was Black, one Asian, a Pakistani, and the fourth a gay Jew. Sadly, the nugget of insight Kady had wasn't positive because she envisioned Lorraine with a repulsed expression. Hopefully her intuition was wrong on this one.

"How magnanimous of you," Lorraine said, with an unreadable expression. Izzy clearly wasn't happy with Lorraine today because she offered another throaty snarl. "Stop that!" Lorraine snarled back at the dog before clearing her throat and regaining her composure, presenting a tranquil smile. "So what are some things you see in your psychic visions that you *won't* tell people about?"

"They're more thoughts or insights than visions," Kady explained. "That's a tough question. Difficult decisions." Kady drew in a deep breath. "If I sense my words would create a problem rather than help, I'll keep quiet. If my intention is to soothe and calm, but I feel I'd only create angst and grief, I stay quiet."

"What about romantic relationships, or family problems? If you sensed problems between me and Rylan, would you say something?"

Lorraine's questioning was making Kady uncomfortable. She wondered why the sudden interest in her psychic abilities—and why all the questions regarding Lorraine and Rylan's relationship.

"Most often, no. I don't believe it's my place to interfere in the natural course of things, the natural cycle of life, the ups and downs we all experience. People can become terribly stressed if I tell them about a problem I've sensed. They might become convinced it means things are hopeless and nothing can be done, so they don't even bother trying. My feelings are just that, Lorraine, feelings, sensations, emotions I've tuned into."

"Not necessarily absolutes," Lorraine surmised.

"Correct." Remembering so many psychic messages she'd received over the years, Kady added, "I'm not infallible. Sometimes I'm wrong. So it's wise for me to know when to keep my mouth shut." Her features twisted into a humorous *yikes!* expression. "What I've sensed is often nothing more than a temporary minor problem that will iron itself out in time."

"I've never bothered to give your psychic abilities any credence, Kady. I had no idea it was so interesting or involved. And I, well, I ridiculed you behind your back too."

Lifting one eyebrow while offering her cousin a knowing smile, Kady winked. "I know." She gave Lorraine a hug before getting into her car. Through the car's open window, she said, "And I forgive you."

Before taking off, after adjusting Izzy's seatbelt harness and buckling her own seatbelt, Kady looked in the rearview mirror at Lorraine, who hadn't yet gone inside. Izzy had positioned herself so she could look too. She and her dog exchanged glances when Kady noticed her cousin's peculiar expression. It was hard to tell from the small mirror image but Lorraine seemed to be smirking, enjoying a tongue-in-cheek smile.

"She must have found something I said funny," Kady told Izzy, who replied with a low growl. All this growly business was so unlike her. The poor little dog must be tired. She'd had a full couple of days.

Kady drove off feeling much better than she had after leaving her aunt and uncle in the library. Salvaging her relationship with Lorraine, and learning Lorraine didn't bear any ill will toward her brother, Red, made Kady's trip to Devington Manor today worthwhile and at least a partial success.

Kady couldn't recall ever having such an open discussion with her cousin. Lorraine's new, mostly kind and surprisingly honest, demeanor was a pleasant change. Kady hoped it was lasting.

It was gratifying to know Lorraine truly cared about Rylan and regretted her behavior at the soiree. Armed with that knowledge, though she had mixed feelings, Kady would make certain her feelings of happiness for her cousin and Rylan overruled her feelings of melancholy.

# Chapter 14

~<>~

"I THOUGHT WE'D do Thai for lunch again today," Quinn told his brother. "Okay with you?" Staring off into space, Rylan slipped his phone into his pocket. "Hello? Anybody home?" Quinn teased, turning into the restaurant's small parking lot. "So was that the little princess texting you again?"

"Huh? Oh, yeah...none other. Sorry, I've got my mind on all this stuff with her." It was only partially true. Ever since he and Kady shared that semblance of a kiss the night before, the main focus of his thoughts had been Kady. He couldn't get her off his mind, whether wide awake or asleep.

"Lorraine wants us to have a talk," he told Quinn. "Again." Rylan rolled his eyes. "She suggested we go to dinner at..." His hand twirled through the air as he tried to remember the name of the showy French restaurant she'd chosen. "Chez something or other. I put the kibosh on that, telling her if she wants to talk, it can be over breakfast tomorrow morning at a restaurant of my choosing."

"Why do I have a feeling you have something up your sleeve?" Quinn asked with a half-smile as he parked and unfastened his seatbelt. "What restaurant are you talking about?"

"Your favorite breakfast place and mine." Rylan grinned.

Giving his brother an incredulous look, Quinn asked, "Annalise's place?" He laughed when Rylan nodded. "Aw man, she'll hate Griffin's Café, Ry. Why take the princess there?"

"Because I," he thumbed his chest, "feel comfortable there. I'm not a *Chez Whatever* guy, and she knows it, but she's determined to make me into one. I have other reasons for taking her there as well."

"Don't try being cryptic with me." Quinn snickered. "You're taking her there to see how Lorraine acts in a diner...how she'll treat the staff."

221

"As if I didn't already know." Rylan chuckled as he massaged his temples. "I still have a headache after last night's *lovely* chat, with Lorraine hammering her points home repeatedly. So, yeah, I want to see how she behaves with average people. It'll tell me a lot."

"Your lovely chat...could you be referring to the heart-to-heart you and Lorraine had, right after that shit show soiree of hers? You know, after your sweet-tempered fiancée caught you sneaking out of her super fun party?"

Cringing at the recollection, Rylan admitted, "Yup. Sneaking out like the yellow-bellied coward I am." He was trying to be funny while his mind felt more scrambled than the eggs he'd picked at over breakfast. "I barely made it out of Devington Manor alive. After Lorraine found me heading for the kitchen's back door, she was pissed as hell. Told me she's having second thoughts about our blissful union."

"I'll bet she's not the only one," Quinn said.

"You'd win that bet. Kady also texted me a few minutes ago, right after talking to Lorraine, who supposedly feels terrible about her behavior yesterday and wants to apologize." He squeezed his eyes shut. "Damn, I don't know, Quinn. I saw a whole new side to Lorraine yesterday. A side I wouldn't want to wake up to each morning."

"Did you happen to catch sight of her pointy black hat and the broom in back of her closet while you two talked?" Quinn snickered.

Removing his seatbelt, Rylan laughed. "She was so different when I first met her."

"You sure it's the same woman? Because I can't figure out what the hell you saw in her in the first place. I mean, yeah, she's a looker but...whew." He whipped his head back and forth.

Rylan's shoulders hefted into a clueless shrug. "The first time I met her, when I gave a lecture on energy conservation to her women's club, she was sweet, pleasant and graceful, like someone you'd see in one of those paintings rich people have over their fireplace mantels."

Giving his brother a poke in the ribs, Quinn said, "I saw the oil portrait of your sweet, graceful fiancée hanging in one of those rooms with the fancy names at her *little* house."

"The drawing room," Rylan said sheepishly. He couldn't believe it when he first spotted that painting. Who the hell had a gargantuan painting of themselves hanging in their house—especially one big enough to extend from nearly floor to ceiling? The huge, ornate frame alone probably cost as much as a month of his salary.

He and Quinn got out of the car, heading for the restaurant.

"When I first met Lorraine," Rylan said, "I was struck by the fragile quality about her. I thought she was elegant and beautiful."

"You know what Mom always taught us about beauty, Ry."

"It's only skin deep," they chorused together, leaving Rylan huffing a lackluster laugh. "It was more than just looks. She was smart, witty, and had a quiet, refined air of royalty about her."

"We've all had ample opportunity to experience her air of royalty." Quinn rolled his eyes.

"I actually thought that uppity little air of hers was cute at first," Rylan admitted when they were a few steps from the restaurant's door. "You don't like Lorraine much, do you Quinn?"

"Nope. She's an arrogant bitch."

Giving his brother a hearty clap on the back, Rylan said, "That's what I like about you, buddy. I can always count on you to give it to me straight, no beating around the bush." Unfortunately, his description was all too precise. "It's almost like a Jekyll and Hyde thing going on with Lorraine, you know?"

"Hello PMS." Quinn opened the door and the two of them walked in, cheerfully greeted by the owner who recognized Quinn as a regular.

"For someone so refined and genteel," Rylan scooted into the black vinyl booth, "she sure as hell can come on strong when she feels she's been wronged."

"I noticed." Quinn snort-laughed. "You'd better be careful. I'm not kidding...she's one scary dame, Ry."

"By the end of the argument," Rylan scrubbed his chin, "she almost had me believing I was the bad guy. She even had me apologizing."

"What the fuck for?"

"Damned if I know." A slow grin spread across his Rylan's face. "Okay, that's not entirely true. It's because I never told her about my plan to leave the university one day so I can write fulltime."

"That was an omission, not a lie," Quinn pointed out. "There's a difference."

"I think I'm going to call off the engagement, Quinn. I can't see hitching myself forever to someone who makes me feel more like a disobedient child than the man she's going to marry."

"Maybe she's into BDSM." Quinn laughed. "Never know, it could be fun." Catching his brother's unamused expression, Quinn grew more serious. "No, seriously, Ry, I'd do the same if it were me—call it off, I mean." He suddenly looked concerned. "Actually...I've got an issue of my own going on, Ry."

"Saffron." Rylan sipped from the jasmine tea brought to the table.

Surprise was evident across Quinn's features. "How did you know?"

"Because you're my brother."

Gulping back all the tea in his small ceramic cup, Quinn smiled. "Saffron Devington is the best thing that's ever happened to me. Why did this have to happen now...when I'm signed up and committed to being away for three years?"

"Don't go." Rylan shrugged.

"I can't do that and you know it. All the arrangements have been made and Doctor Chesney, as well as the rest of my team, are depending on me. We've got the entire itinerary planned out, traveling to each different location, each medical facility. When I signed up I didn't hesitate choosing one of the longer terms because I'm unmarried without any kids. Nothing to keep me here."

"I feel slighted."

Reaching across the table, Quinn whapped Rylan's arm. "You know what I mean." He laughed. "I'll come back to visit my bestie bro every six months or so."

"Bestie?"

"I dunno..." he shrugged, "I saw it online. Just trying to stay relevant."

"Quinn?"

"Yeah?"

"Don't call me that again."

"Okay, Professor Cranky Pants. That better?"

"Much." Rylan chuckled at their easy exchange. It had always been that way between them. He was going to miss Quinn like hell. "Getting back to Saffron, you've known her for like, what? Two minutes?" The two of them made room on the table for the several platters the server brought. Taking all the food in, including a few different appetizers, noodle dishes and meat and seafood offerings, Rylan smirked at his brother.

"It looks like being in love hasn't dulled your appetite any."

"Who said anything about the L-word?" Digging in to the spring rolls, Quinn tried looking nonchalant as hell.

"Don't be blasé with me, Quinton. You can't fool me. You're besotted."

"Only a professor would use a word like *besotted*." Locking gazes with his brother, Quinn's expression morphed into a frown. "I'm crazy about her, which is why I asked you to lunch today...well, that and also so you could fill me in on how your love life took a dive into the toilet last night."

"Flushed, right down the drain." Rylan grinned, making a twirling motion with his finger. "I like Saffron. She seems genuine, has a great sense of humor, which I know is important to you, and she's—"

"Hot," Quinn finished with a wicked grin. "I know more about Saffron's likes, dislikes, happy life moments, and sad life events than I've ever known, or *wanted* to know, about anyone. Including Sylvia. For most of my life, I've done what everyone else, including Mom, Dad, and my ex-wife, thought I should do. I wasn't happy. What I wanted always took a back seat. I knuckled under and fit my square-peg self into a round-hole world to make Sylvia happy. Did everything she asked and expected. Then she dumped me."

Rylan watched his brother's expression shift from lighthearted to dejected while reminiscing about the significant difficulties with his ex.

"Now," Quinn continued, "I follow my instincts, go with my gut feelings. They haven't let me down yet. That's what led me to sign up with Medicine Without Boundaries. The idea of giving back made me happy, plain and simple. But..." his sigh sounded close to a growl, "that's before I met Saffron. I need to have a talk with her. I should have told her straight off that I was leaving Glassfloat Bay in a few days and wouldn't be back for a long while. But that's before I fell hard for her. It's not fair of me to ask Saffron to wait for me."

"Ask her to come with you," Rylan offered.

"To Nigeria?" Quinn's expression turned incredulous. "I don't think so. It's not like we'll be staying at some first-rate hotel.

Besides, she and Kady have their bookshop to run here. Ever notice how Saffron's eyes light up when she talks about their shop?"

"Yeah." Rylan nodded, "Kady too." He recalled the way she looked sitting at the open window in Red's room, with moonlight streaming though her hair. The feel of her cool, velvety skin as he held her shoulders. Those deep, liquid violet eyes. He pushed the ginger beef around his plate, as if studying the saucy strips of beef would bring him a revelation of some sort.

Rylan sucked in a breath. "I'm in trouble, Quinn."

Quinn looked up from his plate long enough to say. "No shit." His tone was matter of fact.

"I don't mean about Lorraine, I mean—"

"Miss Kady Malone," Quinn said. "You don't trust yourself to be alone with your fiancée's cousin." He didn't look up from his plate.

"Fuck..." Rylan winced. "Am I really that transparent?"

"You do a fairly good job of hiding it. It's just because I know you so well. You can't hide that kind of shit from your *bestie*." He grinned.

Rylan gave him the arm-swat he deserved.

"I'm engaged to one cousin and can't stop thinking of the other." Resting an elbow on the table, Rylan dropped his head into his hand, massaging his forehead. "I'm not sure how I feel about Lorraine anymore."

"That's a copout." Quinn slurped down his remaining tea and poured another cup for both of them. "You're not being honest with yourself."

"I thought I'd found the girl of my dreams with Lorraine, and then she turns out to be—"

"Arrogant? A snotty rich bitch? A controlling shrew?" Quinn helpfully interjected.

Rylan couldn't help laughing at his brother's all too perceptive crack. "I was *going* to say, she turns out to be someone entirely different from the woman I thought she was." Uttering a dejected grumble, he pushed away his half-eaten plate of food.

Dragging Rylan's plate close, Quinn devoured the rest of his ginger beef. "Look, I'm no good at dispensing advice to the lovelorn, but you can't tell me you don't already know how you feel about Kady. I knew right away with Saffron, and I'm pretty sure she's on the same page. You're stalling, Ry, and you're too chickenshit to do anything about it." With an affected cowboy drawl, he added, "That, pardner, makes you a yellowbelly."

"You're right." Rylan's lips twisted into a smirk

"About you being a yellowbelly?"

"No. About you not being any good at giving advice to the lovelorn."

"Deny it all you want." Quinn shrugged. "It's your funeral not mine when you lose Kady and find yourself stuck with that severe, unforgiving museum dweller because you," Quinn poked his finger at Rylan, "were too much of a goddamned fraidy-cat to do what you should."

As Rylan watched his brother spear a forkful of chicken and noodles from his pad Thai, depositing it in his mouth, then taking a bite of the spring roll he'd dipped in sauce before he'd even swallowed the noodles, he wondered how the hell Quinn maintained his buff physique.

"Remember what I said earlier about liking the way you give it to me straight—no beating around the bush?" Quinn nodded with a crooked smile. "Well forget it," Rylan said, "I changed my mind." He and his brother shared a laugh.

"You know how I told you Lorraine wanted us to have dinner in that fancy French restaurant?" Quinn nodded. "I neglected to mention that the call came from—get this—Lorraine's *secretary*."

Nearly choking as he laughed, Quinn slurped down water. "Don't be too hard on Lorraine, Ry. Maybe she was unable to lift her phone or press speakerphone because she broke a nail."

"That *should* sound ridiculous...but it doesn't." His brother always did have a way with sarcasm. "Our worlds and lifestyles are so far apart, I don't see myself fitting in."

"There's your problem. You shouldn't be the one worrying about that—your fiancée's the one who should be concerned about fitting in to *your* world."

"Oh she's concerned all right." Rylan chuckled. "I'm not sure how to handle this. I don't want to hurt Lorraine."

"I wouldn't worry about that," Quinn assured him. "It would take a wrecking ball to break through that rock-hard, icy exterior of hers. Hey," he angled his head, "you sure there's a heart under there?"

"Sometimes I wonder. She showed me the engraved wedding invitations the other day. You thought her little soiree was packed with stuffed shirts? You won't believe how many people the Devington's are inviting to the wedding." He rolled his eyes.

"We're talking big shots, Quinn. Senators, congressmen, mayors, governors, judges, pretty much anyone who's anybody within metropolitan Portland and its environs. The mega-bucks Lorraine's father is shelling out is probably enough to feed an entire third world country for a year. Things have progressed so far, and I feel trapped. Dammit, how the hell can I back out at this late date?"

"Late date?" Quinn looked at him like he had two heads. "For chrissakes, Rylan, the wedding's not until October. It's only March."

"According to Lorraine, everything has to be booked months in advance, complete with hefty nonrefundable deposits."

"Did you ask the Devingtons to do that?"

Rylan scoffed. "Of course not."

"If they want to throw their money around like that, it's their decision—unless you requested your wedding be turned into a three-ring circus media blitz. Did you?"

"Hardly. I tried convincing her to elope, or at least plan a small wedding with a handful of family and friends. Three guesses as to how far *that* conversation got."

"It's like everybody's a conductor," Quinn told him, "and you're just a passenger."

Aiming his finger at his brother, Rylan said, "Perfect analogy." He couldn't believe how spot on Quinn was. "I need to take back control of my life before I lose it completely."

"Before you turn it over to a pushy, overbearing woman," Quinn added. "Remember, I speak from experience." Rylan new that was damn true. Quinn's ex-wife, Sylvia, had put him through the wringer before leaving him with nothing.

With new resolve, Rylan decided it was time to extricate himself from a very bad situation.

# Chapter 15

KADY PLACED the boxes of incense cones she held in her arms on the shelf and sighed. "I'm glad you're back. I need to talk to you about a few things," she told Saffron. "Sasha's covering the floor and it's not too busy so why don't we put on a pot of ginger tea." Arm in arm, they walked to the shop's back room.

Kady set out a couple mugs while Saffron scooped the fragrant loose tea into a tea-ball, placing it into an old, crackled blue and white china teapot Kady found during her backpacking trip to England.

"How did your trip to the hospital with Reen go?" Kady asked.

Saffron, Kady, and Reen had created and packaged up a load of treats for the sick children at Wisdom Harbor Children's Hospital. Their delivery included knitted character hats and matching lap comforters from Reen, and coordinating animal and creature-shaped, hand-sized cookies from her sister Laila's bakery. The cookies were wrapped in cellophane with tiny labels noting all ingredients. Laila made the large batch of cookies gluten-free as well as nut-free so kids with sensitivities or allergies could enjoy them without concern.

As time passed, Kady had become more aware of Saffron's whimsical creative side. She'd designed the cutest six-inch-tall rag dolls for the kids. She kept them small so the children could hug them close when they went for tests or for doctor visits. She called the dolls Aunt Saffy's Friends.

Saffron and Kady had put together a number of self-care kits for the nurses too, containing Kady's herbal tea and herbed honey, two items that were a hit with family and friends, topping the miniscule list of healthful food items she prepared that didn't make others cringe. The boxes also held decadent brownie bites from

Laila's bakery, and Cherished Pages business-card-bookmarks offering one free paperback or children's book of their choice.

The small boxes were tied with satin ribbon and included little cards describing the contents. Saffron and Kady called their nurse gifts *Just Because You're Awesome*, which was printed at the top of each card.

"It was wonderful," Saffron said. "It might sound odd but the kids loved my little dolls so much it almost made me cry. I felt like a hero doing something that brought smiles to their sweet little faces."

"Not odd at all," Kady said. "I've experienced the same thing when I've made deliveries to the hospital with Reen. And I know she has too. Making those kids happy is the best, most gratifying feeling."

"Absolutely. The kids even put in special requests for imaginative new doll designs for me to create. The most frequent one I got was for—"

"For dolls that looked like them," was Kady's educated guess.

"Yes! I asked each child to tell me what yarn hair color they want and what kind of clothes they'd like to see. I took photos of the kids so I could reference them while making the dolls. So," she held out her palms, "we'll see if I'm up to the task or not."

"Of course you are." Kady drew Saffron into a hug. "You can't fail when you're acting out of love for those children. I guarantee whatever you make for them will be cherished."

"I hope so." Saffron smiled. "I think my favorite time was when I read to the children. I'm hoping to make book lovers out of each of them. Those wonderful, hardworking nurses were really pleased that we thought of them too. They especially loved the sentiment we used on the gift cards about them being awesome." Saffron smiled as she filled the teapot.

Removing the lid from the vintage ceramic container she'd brought to the shop, Kady showed Saffron the mouthwatering assortment of mini-scones from her sister, Laila's, bakery. She gestured for Saffron to help herself.

"Oh...did you make these?" Saffron asked with a limp smile before making a selection.

"Real subtle, Saffron." Rolling her eyes, Kady smacked her cousin's arm. "You don't have to worry, these aren't mine." She laughed, well aware of her baked goods' less than glowing reputation. "My baking just takes some getting used to because it's full of healthful ingredients, like," she counted on her fingers, "desiccated coconut flour, dehydrated chopped kale, hemp seeds, goji berries, collagen peptides, apple cider vinegar with the mother, and—"

"Sadly, my vinegar never had a mother," Saffron teased with a pout. "I only have orphan vinegar."

"Go ahead, cruelly mock me," Kady teased back, "just remember that those who eat my special power-foods will outlive everyone else."

"My special power-foods are chocolate and ice cream—the real kind with sugar and cream, not that fake frozen beany stuff you eat." Saffron shuddered. I'm willing to enjoy what I eat and kick the bucket five years earlier."

After sharing a laugh, Kady told her, "These scones are Laila's, from The Great Pretender, and they're scrumptious. These are blueberry with lemon icing. And those," she pointed, "are chai spice with cinnamon-nutmeg icing. Both sugar-free as well as gluten-free"

Biting into one, Saffron's eyes closed in appreciation as she *mmmmed*. "Honestly, I don't know how Laila does it. Outrageously good!"

"I wanted to ask you how things are going with Quinn," Kady asked, watching Saffron's expression sink.

"Oh Kady, what am I going to do? We connected right away. We've both been burned before. At this point in our lives, with me closing in on forty and Quinn just past it, we both know what we do and don't want."

Kady offered a sympathetic nod. "And what you want is to grow old with Quinton Kilpatrick."

"Mmm-hmm. And that's the one thing I can't have because he's going far away and chances are I'll never see him again." She scrunched her features. "Not fair."

"I told you I had a strong psychic feeling about you two. Everything tells me you're perfect for each other." Kady took Saffron's hands in her own. "In a way, it almost seems like you and Quinn have always been together. It feels natural and right."

"You've just expressed my feelings exactly, but that only makes parting all that much more bittersweet. Remember the tarot card reading you did for me shortly after Quinn and I met?" Kady nodded. "You said all the signs pointed to a new, long-lasting love. I'm sorry, but I think your psychic wires got crossed."

"Even Izzy saw it," Kady reminded Saffron. "The card she selected for you signified great happiness and security."

At the mention of her name, Izzy sidled up to Saffron's leg, nuzzling it. "Hey there, cutie." She bent to massage the dog behind her ears. "I'm afraid Izzy's psychic wires might be crossed too." Izzy whimpered at that.

When Izzy offered a small bark, Kady said, "Well there you go. Izzy says she agrees you and Quinn are meant to be together."

"I thought you couldn't read Izzy's mind."

Chuckling, Kady said, "I cant. That's Aladee's area of expertise. But I've come to know Izzy well enough that I can pretty well figure out what she means." Bending to rest her hands on her knees, Kady asked, "Right, Izzy?" Furiously wagging her tail, Izzy quickly gave a louder bark. "I think we can agree Izzy's answer is unmistakable."

"Hey, you know what?"

"What?"

"Quinn makes me feel young and beautiful."

"Um, maybe that's because you *are* young and beautiful?" Kady noted, judiciously arching her eyebrows and making her eyes go wide as she looked down at Izzy, hoping the dog would bark again, confirming Kady's words.

"Ahem, I saw you give Izzy the high sign just now, oh sly one," Saffron noted with laughter. "Apparently she hasn't picked up on all your sneaky signals yet."

"Oops! But she meant it anyway, didn't you, Izzy?" Yawning, Izzy circled in place four or five times, screwing herself into position on the floor. Glancing at the dog, and then at each other, Saffron and Kady again slipped into laughter before getting back to the topic of Quinn.

"I never saw or thought of myself as beautiful." Saffron shrugged. "I was always the stiff, starchy Realtor in undertaker garb." She wrinkled her nose, then glanced down at the bold patterned dress she wore, complete with complementary chunky jewelry. Her resulting smile was genuine. "I've come a long way from my ultraconservative duds, haven't I?"

"You finally let your freak flag fly, Saffron, and gave yourself permission to fully embrace life and love. Evidently, Quinn saw the same thing in you. I really like him. He's a great guy." *So much like his brother*, Kady thought but didn't verbalize.

"So much like his brother," Saffron said, surprising Kady, who felt her cheeks flushing. Sighing, Saffron continued. "This," she motioned to herself, "my life I mean, is like one of those sad, poignant romance books. The kind I hate to read."

Kady wasn't sure what to say to help make Saffron feel better. In fact, she realized she'd already made things worse by insisting Saffron and Quinn were meant for each other. What an idiotic dumbass thing to say to a woman on the verge of losing the man she'd fallen in love with. So what if they were perfect for each other? While she always meant well, Kady grasped that preaching about her positive vibes and instincts wasn't always what people wanted or needed to hear. She had to learn when to keep her big mouth shut.

"Those classic romance books," Saffron just kept going, "where the hero or heroine dies at the end and the survivor lives the rest of their lonely life with nothing but bittersweet memories. And they get old and lose their hair and their teeth and even their dog and sit in a rocking chair knitting or reading or peeling potatoes and crying but no tears come out because they've cried them all out over the many decades while they waited to just wither up and die."

Feeling her eyes grow wide, Kady muttered, "Holy shit." It was one of the rare times she ever used off color language.

Saffron's wide-eyed expression probably mirrored Kady's. "Holy shit, you never swear. My pathetic tale of woe must have ripped your heart out, just like it's ripped mine out, huh?"

Kady wasn't used to seeing her cousin absorbed in such a weird mix of humor and pathos. "I'm so sorry I kept talking about how you two are an ideal couple," Kady said. "The last thing I want to do is make your pain about losing Quinn worse."

After a long blink, Saffron smiled at Kady. "It's okay. I understand. I know how trusting you always are about everything working out in the end." Lifting Kady's hand, Saffron held it between her own, bringing it to her heart. "Don't feel bad about what you said. It's not your fault that my one chance at happiness is a couple days away from taking up residence in Nigeria for God knows how long and I'll never see him again."

Saffron's combination of humor and pain broke Kady's heart.

Checking the teapot, Kady noted, "I think it's steeped long enough." She poured the fragrant liquid into their cups and *ahhhed*. "I love the smell of ginger, don't you?" She attempted to keep the conversation as light and carefree as possible.

"My favorite, right next to chai lattes," Saffron agreed, scooping a spoonful of Kady's herbed honey into her tea and stirring. "Let's not talk about my depressing *Wuthering Heights* life and talk about something else instead. Like you, for instance...and Rylan."

Kady stilled, unmoving like a statue. "Rylan?" Stirring her tea furiously, some sloshed over the rim of her mug and onto the table.

"Hello?" Saffron rapped her knuckles on Kady's head. "Did you suddenly get amnesia? The handsome guy who's Quinn's brother, remember?"

"There's nothing to discuss there. He's your sister's fiancé. Period. Case closed. Speaking of your sister though, I had a good talk with her earlier today."

"I know." Saffron smiled. "Lorraine called me after you two talked, asking me to meet her for lunch tomorrow. She told me she owes me an apology." One of her eyebrows curved. "I wish to hell I'd been recording the conversation because no one will ever believe Lorraine Devington actually said that."

"She cares about you deeply," Kady assured her, "and wants to repair the rift in your relationship. She knows she's mostly to blame."

"My sister told you that?" Saffron's features scrunched into a skeptical expression. "Are you sure it was Lorraine and not a doppelganger? Seriously, I want to know exactly what you did to work your magic on her. Some kind of talisman? Maybe a magic potion? What mysterious psychic connection did you use? It was a spell, wasn't it?"

Laughing so hard she almost had tea shooting out of her nose, Kady said, "For heaven's sake, Saffron, I'm a psychic, not a witch. I don't cast spells." She shook her head slowly. "People change, Saffron. We all do. Lorraine's entering a stage of transformation, like a caterpillar to a butterfly, leaving what's unimportant or hurtful in the past and looking ahead to a new, better, more positive life journey."

"I'd like to say you helped her do that, Kady but, I'm sorry, I don't buy her supposed transformation." Izzy chose that moment to utter a low growl, similar to the one she gave when Kady caught Lorraine's smirking expression in her rearview mirror. "Ooh," Saffron noted, "that sounded kind of ominous."

"I think Izzy's just tired." Kady gave a dismissive wave. "Although she was growling quite a bit at Lorraine toward the end of our visit."

"Did you get a chance to check it out with Aladee?"

"I did. I went straight there with Izzy before coming to the shop after I left Devington Manor. Aladee said Izzy doesn't like Lorraine. Izzy communicated to Aladee that I should be careful not to trust or believe Lorraine. I don't understand why she feels that way because Lorraine and I had a great heart to heart talk. She was open and genuine."

"Well I'll be darned." Bending low, Saffron pet the little dog. "I'm becoming more of a believer in your psychic abilities all the time, Madame Izidora."

"No, really, Saffron, Lorraine told me she's been mega-stressed, with a great deal on her mind and...well, I'm going to let her tell you the rest herself. I think you'll be pleased and hopefully the holes in your relationship will start to mend as you two continue to keep the lines of communication open."

Crossing her arms over her chest, Saffron said, "You could be a psychologist. Granted, the most naïve psychologist ever," she snickered, "but..."

"Me?" Looking skyward, Kady chuckled. "Not by a longshot. I may be insightful when it comes to helping others, but I suck when it comes to getting my own stuff together."

"I think that's the definition of a good psychologist. Getting back to you and Rylan—"

With a monumental sigh, Kady said, "Again...there is no me and Rylan."

"You have feelings for him." She locked gazes with Kady. "You should let him know before things go further with him and my sister. You owe it to yourself and to Rylan."

"No, Saffron." Kady shook her head back and forth. "I could never do that to Lorraine. Your sister spent nearly an hour pouring her heart out to me, telling me how much she loves Rylan and how she wants to do everything in her power not to lose him. Talk about me being a witch...that's exactly what I'd be if I tried to break them up so I could have Rylan for myself."

"Are you aware Rylan is just as attracted to you as you are to him? Even Quinn noticed it. He said Rylan couldn't keep his eyes off you at the soiree." Her eyebrows danced with mischief as she added, "I'll bet he had quite the inner struggle keeping his hands off of you too."

"You're just being silly now, Saffron."

"Well..." with a nonchalant shrug, Saffron noted, "you two *were* in Red's room an awfully long time after Quinn and I left to get the car. Perhaps a little something transpired that you neglected to mention?"

Remembering the almost-kiss, Kady cringed before clapping her hands over her heated cheeks. "Please don't joke about something like that. Rylan doesn't have any real interest in me.

He was just upset because of his talk with your father, and his argument with Lorraine. The only reason he wanted to talk to me at the soiree was because he loves Lorraine and hoped I could help. That's all. I told him I'd talk to Lorraine and her parents, and I did. End of story."

"End of story indeed." Tapping her mauve-lacquered fingernails against the desktop before jabbing a finger toward Kady, Saffron said, "There's guilt written all over that blushing face of yours. You don't have to be honest with me, that's your choice, but don't try to tell me nothing happened because I don't buy it."

Letting her head drop back, Kady groaned. "Has anyone told you you're relentless?"

"Sure. That's what made me a dynamite real estate salesperson. So...?" She scooted to the edge of her chair, giving Kady her full attention. At the same time, Izzy crawled close to Kady's legs, resting her head on Kady's foot.

Bellowing a deeper groan, Kady admitted, "All right, we *almost* got carried away with the moment, but I pulled back before anything happened. However," Kady raised her forefinger to emphasize her point, "Rylan only moved in for a kiss because he's distraught over what happened between him and Lorraine." Her shoulders sagged. "And..." she sniveled, "I'm a mess over it all, so please, no more jokes. It's hard enough for me already. Now I know how awful you must have felt when I kept badgering you about Quinn being your ideal match."

Saffron's face crumbled and she pulled Kady into a hug. It must have been obvious that Kady was close to tears.

"I'm so sorry. Really. I was just being a jokester and here you—well I had no idea what you might be going through over this. I feel like a complete ass now."

"Not a complete one...maybe half," Kady mustered the inner strength to tease her cousin, "which would make you half-assed."

"I'll accept that." Saffron offered an apologetic smile. "Listen, Kady, regardless of how enlightened you believe my sister has become, you should pay attention to Izzy's intuition about her. Lorraine isn't necessarily who or what she seems."

Kady looked uncertain. "Isn't that describing most of us?"

"I'm trying to tell you, Kady, that I don't believe Lorraine is truly in love with Rylan. I think she's still carrying the torch for Reggie."

"Reggie?" Kady searched her memory. "Your father brought him up. Reginald van something or other, right? They used to be engaged but Lorraine dumped him?"

"Reginald Von Austerly." Saffron nodded. "Lorraine met him years ago when Reggie and I were dating. Suitably impressed, she went after him for herself...Lorraine's usual modus operandi whenever I've been interested in someone."

"Aw, Saffron, that's terrible. I'm sorry." She couldn't imagine any of her sisters doing that to another sister. The same way Kady couldn't imagine herself doing it to her cousin, Lorraine. "Were you in love with Reggie?"

"Not really, although I thought so at the time." Looking as though she was miles away for a moment, Saffron smiled. "It was my senior year of high school, so I was very young. It turned out for the best that Lorraine hooked Reggie. They went together for years. Everyone was sure they'd marry one day. My mother," she chuckled, "even helped Lorraine pick out her silver, and her china pattern."

"I can so easily imagine Aunt Colleen and Lorraine huddled together choosing items for her bridal registry. She and Reggie must have been pretty serious."

"They were. He's always been Reginald to her, never Reggie." Using a pretentious tone, Saffron added, "Lorraine abhors nicknames, you know, because it makes a person sound so *common*." She added an affected shudder.

"You do that so well," Kady said, laughing.

"That, my dear," she used the same affected tone, "is because I was raised the same way as my sister, and I used to be as much of a snob as she is." Saffron followed her self-deprecating words with light laughter. "Reggie and I make far better friends than lovers. Not that I can attest to that from experience," Kady could tell Saffron was trying not to laugh, "because Reggie never even tried to get past first base with me. I actually thought he might be gay. Guess I wasn't the femme fatale I thought I was at seventeen."

"Do you still talk to him?"

"Often. His father is one of the partners in Wotring Realtors, the real estate company I worked for. When Reggie calls or texts, it's usually about Lorraine. He fell hard for her and is devastated she's engaged to Rylan with a wedding date set. Poor Reggie is always pumping me for information about both Rylan and my sister."

"Do you know why your sister dumped Reggie?"

"Lorraine has a short attention span when it comes to men." Saffron gave a resigned sigh. "I think Rylan, the hot, handsome, hunky professor, is the interim guy whose main purpose is to make Reggie jealous enough to beg Lorraine to take him back, which she'd gobble right up. Reggie doesn't have Rylan's looks but he's got the pedigree, along with the financial portfolio and social standing to go along with it. We're talking big bucks, Kady."

Kady's eyebrows jacked up. "Not bigger than your family." The Devington's were stinking rich as far as Kady knew.

"While I can't be sure, I believe the Von Austerlys' wealth eclipses my father's. Reggie's family owns a fancy chalet just outside Paris, plus a colossal private yacht there too. They go floating on the Seine the way we go on Willamette River dinner cruises." She laughed. "Paris is my sister's favorite location in the world. She'd love to live there. Seeing as Rylan doesn't go yachting on the seine, or spend his evenings relaxing at his chateau, I believe Lorraine sees that as a huge disadvantage."

"Right. Instead of living the Parisian life, Rylan yearns to live in a cabin in the woods with a wife, kids, dog and a desk where he can write his science fiction novels." Kady shrugged. "Frankly, sounds like the ideal scenario to me." Oh what she wouldn't give to curl up in a cozy armchair, with a cup of tea and a thick knitted afghan, reading Rylan's first book release one day. The inviting scenario had her expelling a sigh.

"So tell me, Kady, which man do you think Lorraine would rather marry?"

After digesting this new information, Kady brooded for a moment. "But you should have heard Lorraine, Saf. She was so sincere. None of my psychic feelers," she made a silly gesture with her fingers at the sides of her head, "went off when she and I talked. I got no indication she wasn't being truthful."

"Probably because your psychic feelers," she mimicked Kady's gesture, "aren't keyed into skilled bullshit artists." The corner of Saffron's lip hiked into a crooked smile. "I don't doubt Lorraine was being sincere. I also don't think she was purposely lying to you. I think she believes everything she told you. For the moment. But that'll change. It always does with Lorraine. She has some serious issues, believe me."

Pressing her hand to her forehead, Kady said, "You're saying you think Lorraine played me."

"Oh, honey, like a violin," Saffron confirmed. "You need to understand how she thinks so you don't get the selfless notion in that *always-be-kind-to-everyone* brain of yours," she tapped Kady's temple, "that you should sacrifice your happiness because of an hour-long talk you had with my sister."

"I don't know what to think now. I'm so confused." Kady was so sure Lorraine was on the level. Their exchange seemed so genuine...so honest.

"Look, Lorraine and I may have our differences but she's still my sister and I love her. I love you too. I don't want to see either of you get hurt or be unhappy. But I do want you to be cognizant of what may be going on. I sincerely believe we haven't heard the last of the Lorraine and Reginald Von Austerly story, and," Saffron winked, "I don't need to be a psychic to know that."

"I'll admit I wondered why, after being so ticked off with Rylan at her party, Lorraine developed a sudden renewed interest in him."

"During your conversation, did you praise Rylan to my sister and my parents, you know, pointing out his good qualities?"

"Of course I did. I spent plenty of time on Rylan's positive points—extoling his virtues. I want Lorraine to recognize her fiancé's worth."

"Mmm-hmm." Saffron nodded slowly. "I was afraid of that."

Inclining her head, Kady said, "Okay, you lost me there. Afraid of what?"

"If my sister has even the slightest speculation that you may have an interest in Rylan, or he has an interest in you, that would bring out Lorraine's killer instinct."

Giving a dismissive wave, Kady assured Saffron, "Oh no, nothing like that. I was explaining to her why I thought she and Rylan would make a perfect couple. She'd have no reason to suspect I was interested in him." She'd be humiliated, positively horrified, if Lorraine assumed Kady was crazy about her fiancé. "Lorraine wasn't mean or bitchy when we talked either. She was really nice, and surprisingly kind. I doubt killer instinct really applies here."

"Aunt Astrid was right. You can be as naïve as a babe in the woods, Kady." Saffron chuckled to herself.

"You know," Kady, folded her arms across her chest, "I'm not very happy with everyone seeing me as some gullible, emptyheaded woman always in need of protection, or rescuing. I backpacked overseas, Saffron, all by myself, keeping away from the tourist spots and hotels, and frequenting the places locals preferred instead so I could learn about the people, their countries, customs and cultures. If I didn't have street smarts, I wouldn't be here with you today. So, please, give me a little credit for being at least somewhat savvy, okay?"

"Well," lifting her arms high, Saffron let them slap at her sides, "I was a half-ass before and it looks like I've managed to graduate to complete-ass. You're right, Kady. I apologize. We all love you because you're sweet and selfless, always caring for everyone else's needs before your own which, I guess, makes you seem more naïve and vulnerable than the rest of us. Then," she shrugged, "our protective instincts kick into high gear. I greatly admire and respect you, Kady. I don't think I'd have the nerve to travel to far off foreign countries all alone."

"Thanks, I appreciate that. Sorry I went off on you. I just hate being seen as somebody just this side of sainthood, you know? Seriously, who wants to hang out with a sickeningly sweet goody-two shoes? I never want to be that dull and boring. Sorry," she said again. Saffron's tsking caught Kady's attention.

"There." Saffron pointed at her. "See what you just did? You're apologizing when you did nothing wrong. Let me have *my* chance to apologize, okay?"

"But I—" Kady stopped when she caught the frustration in her cousin's expression. "Okay," she said with a smile, stuffing a chai-flavored mini-scone into her mouth to help keep it shut.

"Good. What I wanted to say is that Lorraine and I weren't brought up like you, your sisters, and brothers. We were raised to be arrogant, devious, pompous, and a generous list of other unsavory adjectives. We excel at manipulating people. Lorraine knows you, Kady. She knows how kind and trusting you are and...for God's sake, don't take this the wrong way..." She paused, lifting an eyebrow, seeking understanding.

"I won't," Kady promised, clueless as to what she'd just given a promise for but determined to hear what Saffron had to say without immediately jumping to her own defense again.

"Lorraine," Saffron continued, "knows how easily you can be conned, because she's aware your first instinct is to believe in people and take what they say at face value. I don't think I'd believe you if you told me you didn't experience some people trying to take advantage of you when you were traveling alone. There must have been some sketchy times that had you worried about your safety, right?"

"Well...sure. Happily, shady people were in the minority but, yes, there were some worrisome incidents. I depended on my intuition to warn me, or go for help if I needed it. I can detect negative things more easily with strangers than with people I know and love. I don't really know why." She lifted her hands in resignation. "So if Lorraine was conning me as you believe, that would explain why I didn't realize it. It's not something I'd expect or suspect from a family member."

"I'm not trying to criticize you, or ridicule what I perceive to be your naiveite either. I don't consider being somewhat naïve to be a negative, as long as you're aware of it so you can be alert to the possibility of people trying to take advantage of you."

"I understand." Kady nodded. She really did. She knew herself well enough to realize she was overly trusting, and her automatic-belief system sometimes led to trouble.

Adding hot water to the teapot, Saffron said, "As long as you don't spontaneously believe everything Lorraine tells you, you should be fine. Sadly, sometimes family can be worse than strangers when it comes to manipulating us. People we know and love sometimes use their ability to take advantage of us. I, um..." Saffron's sigh was hefty, "I speak from experience because I've done it myself." She gave a contrite smile. "You have to be careful because Lorraine can be dangerous too."

"Dangerous?" Slanting her head as she digested her cousin's words, Kady asked, "As in, *look out, she'll steal your chocolate when you're not looking*...or dangerous as in *holding a knife to your throat*?" After thinking about it a moment, she succumbed to a chuckle. "Hmm, I'm not sure which is worse."

"Well she was definitely a chocolate stealer when we were kids but then," Saffron offered a guilty shrug, "so was I."

"My chocolate stash is sacred," Kady informed her. "As long as you're over that tendency we'll be fine."

Smiling, Saffron said, "Actually, I wasn't joking about my sister being dangerous. She's especially skilled at intimidation, threats, and even blackmail."

"Oh now Saffron," scrunching her features in disbelief, Kady said, "aren't you maybe going a little bit overboard?"

"I'm not. Lorraine's an envious, jealous woman. You know how gorgeous Monica is, right?" Kady nodded without hesitation, the woman was a stunner. "Well when Lorraine caught Reggie eyeballing Monica at work, she became convinced Monica was after Reggie—which was ridiculous because Monica's always been crazy about Hud. Lorraine told me to find a way to get Monica to stop working at Wotring Realtors' Glassfloat Bay office...or she'd make Monica pay."

"No." Saffron gave a confirming nod. "Your sister wanted Monica to transfer to another office or she'd make trouble for her?"

"Mmm-hmm." Saffron nodded slowly. "Seattle preferably. Since Reggie worked out of this location, Lorraine hated that they saw each other on a frequent basis. She also warned me to keep

Monica away from Devington Manor. That's when I still lived at home, before moving in with Monica. I told my sister that since Monica and I were a dynamite sales and listing team for Wotring, besides being great friends, there's no way I'd want her to transfer. I wanted to continue working with her."

"Well sure. But that's not blackmail, Saffron."

"No, but Lorraine telling me that unless I found a way to get rid of Monica, she'd tell Reggie's father, who's one of the Wotring partners, that Monica had altered paperwork, stealing little bits of commission from other salespeople and adding it to her own proceeds—*is* blackmail."

"No!" Kady's jaw dropped. "She didn't! What did you do?"

"This wasn't the first such occurrence with my sister, so I was prepared. I told her if she did anything to hurt Monica I'd have a nice long talk with Reggie, letting him know that she lied to him about being a virgin the first time they slept together. I'd spill the beans to Reggie that, the night before she and Reggie had sex, Lorraine had slept with Stephen, Reggie's brother."

"Omigod." Kady coughed a laugh. "Did she...or was that something you just made up?"

"Oh she most certainly did. Their sister, Rochelle Von Austerly, has been a close friend of mine since school. Lorraine's done some wicked stuff to Rochelle too, so you could say Lorraine had a place of honor on Rochelle's shit list." Kady laughed. "So Lorraine knew I had her. I also did my best to convince her that Monica had zero interest in Reggie because she'd been hooked on Hudson Griffin forever. But," she offered another sigh, this time one of frustration, "Lorraine didn't believe me...still doesn't. But at least she kept her big fat mouth shut."

"Growing up with her must have been quite an experience."

"Like a bad soap opera," Saffron said. "I'll share one of the multitude of experiences so you can get an idea. We were around ten years old, fighting because she'd stolen my brand new sweater and wouldn't give it back. She warned me she'd get me grounded if I didn't let her keep it. I refused, telling her Mom and Dad wouldn't believe her because I hadn't done anything wrong. So..." She paused while shaking her head from side to side.

When she was silent a few beats too long, Kady said, "Sooooo?"

"So my sister took my hairbrush and, using the hard plastic handle, she beat herself on the arm until she'd raised welts, snickering at me the entire time. Once she'd finished she started crying, real loud, calling for my parents. When Mom got there, Lorraine showed her the swollen ridges along her arm and said I'd done it."

"Oh my God, Saffron..."

"I tried telling Mom Lorraine did it to herself to get me in trouble but she didn't believe me and, surprise, surprise, I was grounded. It always went that way. They believed Lorraine was their perfect little princess and I was the troublemaker. She did similar stuff to Red too. Now you have a better idea of why I told you she's dangerous and to watch your step."

"I don't even know what to say, Saf." Kady rubbed the goosebumps that rose on her arms just from thinking about it. "My sisters and brothers and I had typical sibling spats where we acted terrible to each other, but nothing out of the ordinary, and certainly nothing like that. Ever. That's just—" She stopped herself from saying *crazy* because she wasn't a fan of name calling.

"Crazy," Saffron said the word for her. "That's just one of dozens of incidents. Monica and I swapped stories about our homelives growing up. She told me she thinks Lorraine is a sociopath."

"Was Monica joking or serious?" It sounded like Lorraine really did have a mental health disorder. Kady recalled learning about sociopaths and psychopaths in her college Psych 101 class, finding the topic of aberrant human behavior fascinating. Sociopaths tend to be more rage-prone than psychopaths. Studies show that while treatment may help, the condition isn't curable. After thinking about it, Kady remembered the technical term for what people call sociopaths, ASPD, which stands for antisocial personality disorder. It really did seem to fit.

"Well, seeing as how her hairbrush scheme was one of Lorraine's milder stunts during our lifetime, what do you think?"

"I think I love you, Saffron." Wrapping her arms around her cousin, Kady kissed her on the cheek.

"Ditto." She returned Kady's cheek kiss, hugging her back.

"You risked hurting my feelings or making me angry by being honest, and I truly appreciate that, Saf. I think it's called tough love." They shared a laugh at that. "My heart breaks for the poor little girl who often had to pay the price for what her sister did. I'm so sorry. How awful that must have been for you growing up." She thought for a moment. "I wonder if Rylan has detected anything like that from Lorraine."

Kady hoped Lorraine wouldn't pull any of her funny business with him. It's not like Kady could go up to him and say, *Oh, by the way, Rylan, keep your eyes and ears open because you might be engaged to a sociopath.*

"I doubt it," Saffron answered. "Lorraine can be a regular Mother Theresa when she wants or needs to be. But God help Rylan if Lorraine suspects he's crossed her in any way." Saffron made a scary, wide-eyed expression.

Kady's expression pinched. "That's frightening."

"It can be." Saffron nodded. "Even now, my sister sometimes frightens me. It's been that way since we were kids. One day she's my best, most supportive friend, and the next..." She sighed. "Lorraine excels at knowing exactly how to rob me of my joy whenever I'm really happy about something. She's the last person I want near me when something especially good happens for me."

Hearing that made Kady especially glad she hadn't told Lorraine anything about Saffron and Quinn being perfect for each other.

"That's just awful. You're one of the strongest women I know. It's hard to imagine Lorraine getting the best of you like that. She must really be devious."

Saffron's laugh was devoid of humor. "Subtle, sneaky, and crazy like a fox."

Kady sent up silent thanks that she had such a wonderful relationship with her own sisters. Shifting the topic, Kady told Saffron, "Regarding Quinn, I really believe everything will be fine in time."

"Eventually..." Saffron nodded. "Once he's gone I'm going to lock my feelings for Quinn away in a special little parcel of real estate deep in my heart and throw away the key."

"We're on the same page," Kady said. "A secret cupboard is being constructed in my heart as we speak." She smiled. "All my feelings about Rylan will be locked away there. Thank you for sharing your misgivings and warnings about Lorraine with me. I promise to keep my eyes and ears open when it comes to her." She thought about what she'd just said. "And I'll keep my distance too."

# Chapter 16

~<>~

RYLAN WATCHED as Lorraine took baby sips from her silver thermos. "You have some boozy morning coffee concoction in there? You've been sipping it since I picked you up," he noted with a touch of laughter. When Lorraine didn't respond, he said, "A little rum? Brandy? Ahh, perhaps vodka, which has earned a reputation as the de facto drink of choice for those who don't like the taste of alcohol or want it readily detected on their breath, hmm?"

"Just coffee. Caffeine becomes a priority when your fiancé gets a notion to pick you up at the crack of dawn for breakfast," Lorraine answered, her tone decidedly cranky.

"It's eight-thirty, Lorraine. Hardly the crack of dawn." He couldn't help rolling his eyes. She was in one of *those* moods. "Their breakfast specials run out fast. I don't want to miss my favorites. Plus I've got a full roster of classes today, which is why we're meeting early."

Ignoring Rylan's comment, Lorraine held her thermos aloft, turning it back and forth. "It's a special blend of beans created especially for me by a small-batch coffee purveyor in Seattle. I have Cook grind the beans just before she makes the coffee so it's not stale. It's a mild, blonde blend. Would you like to try some?"

The idea of watered down mild, blonde coffee couldn't be less appealing. "No thanks. You didn't wake that poor woman up to make this for you this morning, did you?"

"I didn't wake her, she was just stepping out of the shower. I told her to get a robe on and have my coffee ready by your arrival time." Lorraine must have noticed his less than agreeable expression, because she added, "I need the caffeine to keep me alert at this early hour, Rylan. What else was I supposed to do? Besides, it's part of Cook's job."

"What's her name?"

Lorraine gave Rylan a strange look. "Whose name?"

"Your cook."

"Oh..." She gave a disinterested wave. "I'm not sure...Doris, Diane, something like that. Domestic help come and go so often it's hard to keep track of their names. It's more prudent to call them Cook. They always answer." She gave a smile that said this was a normal, everyday response regarding people in someone's employ.

"Didn't anyone ever teach you how to use a coffeepot?" Rylan asked, knowing it was a ludicrous question.

The clueless expression she gave him was priceless. "Oh Rylan," she clasped his arm, "you have such a marvelous sense of humor. Why on earth would I make a pot of coffee for myself? I suppose you think I should have ground the beans too." She laughed with exuberance. "That's what domestic staff is for, darling. Once we're married, you'll never have to do anything as mundane as making a pot of coffee for yourself again. You'll have a full staff eager to cater to your every whim."

So Lorraine still assumed they'd be living with household staff. It seemed she hadn't bothered taking any of his objections seriously. He wasn't surprised that well-meaning Kady had obviously failed to get through to Lorraine when they talked.

"I've told you before I'm not comfortable with the idea of servants hovering around me. Believe it or not, I like doing things for myself. My own way."

"Once we're married and you get a taste of the genteel life, trust me, you'll quickly become addicted."

Rylan swallowed his groan. She just didn't get it. He supposed he should give her the benefit of the doubt because, after all, this pampered lifestyle is all she'd ever known.

"But we don't want to focus on our differences this morning." Lorraine's fingers tiptoed along his forearm, up to his shoulder.

"We want to focus on all the wonderful things we have in common. And to focus on the apology I owe you for being such an overcritical grump during my soiree."

Rylan assumed she thought she looked cute when she pouted. She didn't. It just accentuated the frown lines bracketing her mouth—lines prominent because she always seemed to be pissed off about something or other.

"I'm truly sorry if I spoiled your time at the soiree because of my behavior, Rylan. You have every right to be upset with me."

*Damn right I do.* "I appreciate that, Lorraine."

Well that was a step in the right direction. He looked forward to hearing what else she had to say...unless he'd just heard all of it. It was becoming increasingly difficult for him to reconcile the differences between the woman he fell in love with, versus the woman she'd become. They were two different people. Since she was trying to make amends, he decided he owed it to Lorraine to give her the benefit of the doubt, before giving her the heave-ho at breakfast.

"Here we are." Rylan pulled into Griffin's Café's small gravel parking lot, tires crunching along the way to the spot he chose.

Lorraine gasped. "A truck stop." Neither question nor statement, it was the kind of sound someone makes when spotting a cockroach skittering along the floor.

"It's a café, Lorraine...kind of an upscale diner."

"Upscale?" By the way Lorraine coughed out the word while gawking at him, Rylan wondered if he'd suddenly sprouted horns.

"You don't really expect me to dine in a greasy spoon frequented by truckers and lowlifes, do you?" Her hand clutched her throat. When Rylan was silent, she tacked on, "I'm becoming familiar with your quirky sense of humor, Rylan. I expect this is one of your jokes. Please tell me it is."

"Look, your ladyship," Rylan gestured to the crowded parking lot, "this is the most popular breakfast and lunch spot in Glassfloat Bay. Annalise Griffin is the owner." Lorraine gave him a blank look. "She's Hudson Griffin's sister." Still no recollection. "Hud's the contractor-owner of Griffin of all Trades—he married Monica, one of your sister's best friends."

"You bandy those names around like I should know them."

"Well their sister, Sabrina, is married to your cousin, Gard Malone, Lorraine. Now," he stretched his grin, "don't tell me you don't remember your cousin either." He'd purposely used a playful tone meant to disguise his festering annoyance.

"Yes, I do remember my cousin marrying the divorcee with the slow child. What does any of that have to do with us eating breakfast here?"

Mentally counting to ten before he spoke, Rylan offered a phony smile. It was all he had left. "The food is great. I can attest to it. Why not throw caution to the wind and give it a try? How bad can it be, right?"

The agonized look on her face had him struggling like hell not to laugh.

"*How bad can it be?* What a resounding endorsement." Her shoulders slumping, Lorraine transmitted a look of vexation while rolling her eyes. "Apparently I don't have much choice." She grabbed her thermos, clutching it close.

"Their coffee is excellent," Rylan assured her. "Annalise has special proprietary blends created for the café."

Shooting Rylan a resigned look, Lorraine answered, "If I *must* eat at this establishment, at least allow me to bring my own coffee so I'll have something I know I can digest."

~<>~

"Hi, honey. What'll it be?" the middle-aged server with henna-orange hair asked between chomps on her chewing gum.

Positioning her hand at the base of her throat, Lorraine looked left and right. Arching an eyebrow, sarcasm dripped from her lips as she said, "Are you by any chance addressing me?"

Rylan wasn't sure if he wanted to cringe or laugh.

"Sure, honey. It wouldn't be polite if I asked the gent first, would it?" Winking, the server offered a friendly grin. "Roast beef hash is good. Annalise made it fresh this morning." She thumbed behind her toward the open kitchen. "That's one of your favorites, isn't it, Professor?"

"Great stuff." Rylan nodded. He watched the disbelieving *you-mean-she-knows-you?* look crossing Lorraine's face.

"We got a mess of fresh blueberries in, so Annalise is makin' blueberry flapjacks—and they're goin' like hotcakes." The server snort-laughed. "It's a joke, get it?" She elbowed Lorraine's arm, causing Lorraine's eyes to bug wide. "The flapjacks are goin' like hotcakes." Her laughter was so infectious, Rylan couldn't help joining in.

Sitting rigid in the booth seat she'd so meticulously wiped down with the antibacterial wipes she carried in her purse, Lorraine expelled an indifferent sigh. "May I order now?"

"You betcha, honey. Oh," she lifted a finger, "one more thing. In case the professor didn't tell you, Griffin's has the best darn Dutch baby pancakes on the entire Oregon coast." Smiling again, the server held her order pad and pen. "Shoot."

"I'll have two coddled eggs. I want the yolks loose, but the whites must be firm rather than gelatinous. Toast points, lightly browned, with the crusts removed. A mélange of fresh fruit—and don't substitute canned or frozen because I can easily tell the difference. With that I'll have a glass of freshly squeezed orange juice, finely strained, with only the barest hint of pulp. Devoid of seeds, of course."

"Of course." Shifting her weight to one leg, the server planted a fist against one hip. "You sure that's all?"

"Some Earl Grey tea would be nice," Lorraine said. "Served in a ceramic teapot, not a metal one. Also," she picked up her fork, showing it to the server, "you'll notice my fork is spotted and needs replacing." She managed a partial smile for the server.

The stupefied server stood in place, holding the rejected fork and eyeing Lorraine for a moment before giving in to laughter. "Oh, I get it." She looked around. "I'm on one of those hidden camera type shows, aren't I? You recording me with your phone?"

"Certainly not," Lorraine huffed, straightening her spine. "I'm at a loss as to what you found so amusing about my order."

Rylan leaned forward, propping his elbows on the table, which was a big no-no in Lorraine's book. Right now he didn't give a damn. "I'm surprised you didn't request a side of Osetra caviar with a bottle of Dom Pérignon to wash it down." Lorraine's explicit reply was simply one arched eyebrow. "Maybe you should just order something off the menu, Lorraine, hmm?"

"I believe my request was simple and straightforward." Turning her attention to the server, she asked, "Was there something about my implicit instructions you weren't able to comprehend?"

"No worries, little princess." The server's expression was unreadable but her smile was gone. "While I'm used to plain English, I think the kitchen and I can manage to decipher your implicit instructions." When her gaze shifted to Rylan, she have him a bright smile. "And for you, Professor?"

"I'll have some of Annalise's roast beef hash with a couple fried eggs on the top, fried potatoes, rye toast, and coffee. Thanks, Heidi."

"You got it, sugar."

"Say, how are those grandkids?" he asked her.

Heidi's expression brightened. "The youngest one starts kindergarten this fall. Can you believe it? She feels so grown up."

"Before you know it she'll be taking one of my classes," Rylan teased. "Time goes fast."

"Don't I know it! Thanks, Professor." With a wink, the server turned on her heel.

"Darn," Lorraine muttered.

"Something wrong?" Rylan asked.

"I should have instructed her to have the eggs cooked directly in a cup, and not plopped onto the toast. I can't eat soggy toast." She shuddered. "If the kitchen understands coddled I'll get them that way, rather than poached, which means..."

Rylan tuned her out as she went on *and on* about proper food this and proper food that, like Martha Stewart doing a show, but without the humor or charm.

"Lorraine..." Rylan began, "Kady told me you two had a good talk. She said you told her you want to change." He was graced with Lorraine's full smile, a rarity. The woman was beautiful when she smiled, but her personality was quickly tainting her allure.

"That's right, darling. I'm aware I can be persnickety at times, mostly because I'm concerned about what others think." Her laughter was short and polite. "It's what *you* think of me that matters most, Rylan. That's my top priority goal."

Rylan returned her smile, although he found it a chore. Lorraine's habitual uppity behavior left him little to smile about. "Perhaps you can start by not treating working people as if they were second class citizens," he suggested, holding her gaze.

Bewilderment etched across her face, Lorraine leaned closer. "You're not referring to the waitress, are you?" She looked staggered when Rylan nodded in confirmation. "I-I don't know what to say, Rylan, she's a common server. What did you expect me to do, ask her to do lunch?" Even her laughter sounded haughty. "Unlike you,

I have no interest in the woman's grandchildren, her views on life, or anything else a minimum wage earner might want to jabber about while I'm waiting for my breakfast."

Lorraine had acted exactly the way he'd expected. Too bad. "How about just trying to be civil for a change?" He nodded his thanks as Heidi brought their coffee and Lorraine's tea, in a metal pot, to the table.

Once she departed, Lorraine said, "Explain to me why I should waste my time and energy courting the favor of people with whom I have nothing in common...much less incompetents like your waitress friend. As you heard, I explicitly asked for a ceramic pot, and," she flipped open the top of the metal pot, "you can see what I received."

In a handful of words Lorraine had managed to voice the question prominent on Rylan's mind. Why indeed should he waste his time and energy courting the favor of a woman with whom he had nothing in common?

Their breakfasts were served. He watched as Lorraine nitpicked her way through the meal, criticizing and complaining about one thing after another while he thoroughly enjoyed the hearty, homemade fixings. Heidi had even brought a complimentary stack of blueberry flapjacks for them to share. It came as no surprise when Lorraine wrinkled her nose, refusing to try them.

Leaning forward, she quietly posed her questions to Rylan. "How do we know where those berries came from? Who picked them? Were they washed? Some indigent may have urinated on them." She shuddered. "You can never be sure with a third rate establishment like this, which is why I prefer to dine in..."

And she was off and running on yet another tangent, busy schooling him in matters he didn't give a damn about. He let her ramble on for a while before cutting in.

"You told me you had some important things to say to me," he reminded her. "It's the reason we're having breakfast together this morning, remember?" He'd made a valiant attempt to be forgiving and understanding but, by this point, Rylan was convinced he and Lorraine were like oil and water.

She was a spoiled little rich girl whose life only teetered on the rim of the real world. She'd obliterated any loving feelings he'd had toward her. He'd tried to maintain his romantic interest but she'd succeeded in abolishing it, one word and action at a time.

"...and Kady was such a dear when I told her..." Lorraine was saying, and Rylan realized he'd tuned her out again. He hadn't been listening because his thoughts were on the woman she'd just mentioned. Hearing Kady's name, Rylan remained alert.

"...that sometimes I hear myself acting like a terrible complainer, fully aware of how I must sound, but it's like I have no control." Shrugging, she drained her thermos of the rest of the prized coffee she'd brought, pouring it into the thermos cap rather than use one of the diner's cups.

Giving Rylan her best puppy-dog-eyes expression, which affected him the same as her cutesy pout, she continued, "I told Kady I just keep going, digging the hole deeper until I'm afraid I'll lose you, Rylan...because you might willingly jump into that hole just to escape from me."

*Holy shit.* He couldn't believe how spot on Lorraine was. She'd described his feelings perfectly.

"I don't want that to happen, Rylan. I love you. And I know you love me."

Unfortunately, he could no longer agree with that statement.

"So what did Kady have to say when you spoke?"

Lorraine's expression shifted. "Kady?"

Rylan nodded.

"Well, she's flighty and kooky but she means well. The woman is very childlike and immature, like a ten-year-old in an adult's body, which I'm sure you've noticed...haven't you, Rylan?"

Nope, he wasn't getting caught in that one. "Your cousin seems like a nice person," he said, keeping it as bland as possible.

"She is, the poor dear. She can't help being backward."

Rylan didn't have a clue what Lorraine meant, other than she seemed determined to belittle Kady in his eyes for some reason.

"She's so enamored of her mystic, occultish, feel-good philosophy, which is to her detriment."

"How so?"

"Kady marches to the beat of her own drummer. Her world consists of meditation, singing dolphins, herbal cures, fortunetelling, and that silly dog of hers." Lorraine engaged in a slight shudder. "Fortunetelling animal indeed. I worry about her mental health. Rylan."

Rylan had missed all the seemingly evident signs before. Maybe he didn't want to see them. He realized now he'd failed to notice his fiancée's talent for subtly tearing down people she supposedly cared about. Is that what she'd do with him after they'd been married a while and she felt the initial magic had worn off? Sure, why not? Why should he be any different?

"While I usually eschew my cousin's obsession with her spiritual-related oddities, there is one thing that brought a smile to my face. It's what she saw in her crystal ball...about us, Rylan."

Once again, Lorraine had snagged his attention. He remembered Kady acting strangely the evening they'd met after she'd gazed into her crystal ball, claiming she hadn't seen anything...which Rylan knew was untrue. The recollection brought a smile to his lips.

"Kady told you what she saw the night she had us over for dinner...when she got upset later in the evening?"

After a brief look of puzzlement, Lorraine bobbed her head. "Oh, um, right. That's what I'm talking about," Lorraine claimed unconvincingly. "Kady saw the two of us, you and me, Rylan, darling, and our beautiful happily ever after life together. She said she'd never had such powerful psychic intuition about a couple before. She also saw it in those ghastly skeleton devil cards she uses."

"Her tarot cards?" Rylan couldn't help chuckling.

"Yes, I suppose." Lorraine's hands flit through the air. "Whatever it is she and her dog use."

One minute Lorraine was busy ridiculing Kady's alternative interests, only to champion them the next, because it fit her narrative. Rylan never claimed to be an expert on women or how their minds work, but he was getting a fast tutorial here.

"Isn't that wonderful, darling? How heartwarming to have our deep love for each other confirmed by outside sources. Kady said her perceptive dog saw all the same signs, that we're destined for each other and make the perfect couple. Perhaps I've been wrong about the dog all along." She tittered an insincere laugh.

"Very...interesting." Rylan's inner radar had been triggered. He didn't readily buy what Lorraine was trying so hard to sell him. He would have seen some indication in Kady's face if what Lorraine claimed was true. Not that he actually bought into Kady's hocus-pocus stuff, but she seemed sincere and passionate about her beliefs and her real or imagined psychic abilities.

Rylan found himself entranced, not by Lorraine's dubious claims regarding their apparently idyllic pairing, but by the mere mention of Kady and what was important to her.

He had the distinct impression Lorraine was trying to manipulate him by filling his head with falsehoods about Kady. *Why*, was the question. Was she afraid of losing him—perhaps to Kady? That gave him pause. While he wanted to avoid hurting

Lorraine, Rylan realized the importance of being honest with her now, revealing his misgivings about their engagement.

Before he lost his nerve, before he got sucked in too deep to climb out again, before he could pursue Kady, Rylan had to break things off with Lorraine. He didn't believe for a minute that Kady had seen any of the lovey-dovey Rylan-Lorraine scenarios Lorraine claimed she'd visualized while crystal ball gazing.

"Kady encouraged me to talk to you, Rylan, about the tremendous stress and anxiety I've faced that ultimately turned me into someone unpleasant to be around. Kady assured me you'd understand and forgive me, because..." She paused a moment, her expression morphing into a winning smile. "Because Kady is convinced you and I are meant for each other. I sincerely regret my actions and behavior at my soiree. I'm embarrassed and ashamed and hope Kady is right about you forgiving me."

Rylan gazed at her a while before asking, "Exactly what tremendous stress and anxiety have you been dealing with, Lorraine?"

"Oh...far too much to detail here. Planning and overseeing my soiree for one thing. My personal staff turns into incompetents when I need them most and, as usual, I must step in and handle things on my own." Closing her eyes with a long blink, she uttered a dramatic sigh. "Then there's the unfortunate matter of my..." she looked left and right before whispering, "homosexual brother and the distress he's caused my family. Frightful for us to deal with, Rylan. So upsetting." Dabbing her forehead with her napkin, she offered a theatrical sigh.

"My family and I are continuously being judged. It's not easy feeling as though you're always in the spotlight, your every move being watched. That's what I've been facing. Unwarranted scrutiny from people waiting for me to fail."

If Lorraine was some bigshot celebrity with paparazzi following her everywhere, he might understand but she was nothing but a whiny, opinionated, self-important woman from a wealthy family living in a small coastal Oregon town. A big, bloated fish in a very small pond.

"I'm sorry you feel so stressed," he responded, carefully measuring his words. "As far as what happened at your soiree, I appreciate your apology and forgive you. There is, however, something important I need to discuss with you. I'm afraid—"

"Give me a moment, Rylan." Resting her Hermès bag on her lap, she dug through the purse, retrieving a bottle of pills. "I feel one of my headaches coming on. Most likely because of additives in what this diner laughingly refers to as food. We'll have the discussion another time, darling, when I'm feeling more myself," she decreed and, damn, how he hated that dismissive attitude of hers.

After checking her makeup in the purse's small mirror, powdering her nose, and freshening her lipstick, Lorraine looked up at him with a smile. "I'm ready to leave now, Rylan."

"After we have our talk," he said, signaling their server for more coffee.

"But I just told you I—" Aggravation more than evident, Lorraine narrowed one eye. "Really, Rylan?" He responded with a slow nod. Eyeing Rylan with a quizzical expression, she offered an offhand shrug. "Well, if you insist."

"I do insist." She looked concerned but Rylan bet her insides weren't churning with nerves anywhere close to what he experienced at the moment.

"I hope whatever it is will be short. I have a full social calendar today. I'll need a restorative nap and suitable meal before I can function properly and meet with people."

"You've got a tough life." It was a cheap shot but Rylan couldn't resist the sarcasm. Lorraine had managed to tilt his frustration lever from medium to high, making it difficult to maintain his usual cool, calm demeanor.

"Thank you for understanding." She covered his hand with hers, clearly thinking he was being serious. He had to keep himself from laughing, which wasn't easy.

Swallowing hard, Rylan told himself it was now or never.

"You're a beautiful woman, Lorraine. I care a great deal for you, but—"

"Well I like the direction of your discussion," she cut in, smiling and obviously missing or purposely ignoring the 'but' he'd included before she interrupted.

Heidi poured him a fresh cup of coffee before turning to Lorraine. "Anything else I can get you, princess?"

"Hardly," Lorraine replied without even glancing at Heidi, who winked at Rylan before taking off again.

"But I don't think this," Rylan motioned back and forth between them, "our relationship, is going to work," he finished, suddenly feeling like a heel as he watched Lorraine's hopeful expression crumple. "You've said it yourself, Lorraine, we have little in common. You'd be much happier with a man who fits into your upper crust social circle and understands all that comes along with it. I'm not that guy. You're a Chez fancy French restaurant woman, while I'm a Griffin's diner guy. I don't see that changing."

On Rylan's mental list of Lorraine's possible reactions, full blown laughter didn't even make the top hundred. But there it was, stupefying him.

"Is that all?" She wiped tears of laughter while Rylan remained drop-jawed. "You're just going through a phase, Rylan. I've often seen it happen to my engaged friends. Men are especially prone to having such misgivings. Reluctance and doubt are a natural part of the engagement process. Don't worry, it's not permanent. You'll soon be over your cold feet and feel more positive and confident about our relationship." She patted his hand. "You'll see."

"Lorraine, you're not listening. It's important that you—"

"Granted, our relationship's been strained of late, driving a wedge between us, but after you hear the marvelous news I have for you, everything will be different. I guarantee you'll be positively elated."

*News?* Rylan's thoughts immediately flew to the place most men's would...but he was ninety-nine point nine percent certain Lorraine wasn't pregnant. Thank God.

"You're not making this easy, Lorraine. You need to understand that it's over. Our engagement ends here and now." He'd planned to end things far more kindly but her stubborn insistence on misinterpreting his words made things particularly difficult.

"Over?" Hollow bitterness tainted her laughter now. "You have no conception of how much time and money my parents have invested in our union. Hundreds of thousands of dollars, Rylan. If you back out now, my parents will lose a fortune, and I'd face untold humiliation within my social circle. All because you have a temporary case of the jitters."

"That's not what this is." Rylan sat forward, resting his elbows on the tabletop. He sat that way, staring at the salt, pepper, and sugar containers for a long moment before speaking again. "Knowing how I feel, you're telling me you'd still want to go through with this?"

"Certainly. Just because we had a tiff the other evening doesn't mean we've stopped caring for each other." Lorraine patted his arm as if placating a child. "Initial attraction and feelings of ardor fade over time...but where love disintegrates and eventually dies, values and tradition rise to the forefront and thrive."

This sounded more like going into business rather than a marriage. Listening to Lorraine's unappealing description of the course a husband and wife's relationship takes had Rylan's stomach acid agitating, creeping up into his throat. She'd never make it as a motivational speaker, that's for sure.

"Take my parents for example," she went on. "Theirs wasn't a union of romantic love. It was a union of money, tradition, and prominence. They've been married for more than forty years and you can see how well matched they are."

"They're a real pair, all right," Rylan agreed. She was right, Walter and Colleen Devington were perfectly matched—the in-laws from hell.

"They are indeed." She offered a proud smile. "Mother and Daddy have grown comfortable with each other." Lorraine made puppy dog eyes again. "The same way it will be for us, Rylan. I hope that puts your mind at ease." Her condescending smile made him feel like a kindergartner taking direction from the teacher.

Never would he have expected breaking up with Lorraine to be so difficult. He'd been fully prepared to state his decision to end their engagement, providing his reasons, expecting she'd cry a little, and, *voila*, the end. But no...Lorraine even had to make terminating a relationship into something exceptionally problematic. He didn't even want to think what it would be like if they were married and he wanted a divorce.

Half tempted to run, screaming from the diner, he sat, plowing his hand through his hair, realizing too late he'd probably just slithered butter from his toast, and whatever else he'd touched at breakfast, through his clean hair.

"Lorraine, what if..." *Careful...if you don't handle this right it could get ugly.* "What if I told you there was someone else?"

Lorraine visibly bristled for the first time during their conversation. "That's ludicrous. A man of your moral character would never humiliate his fiancée by dallying with her cou—" She stopped abruptly, clearing her throat before the word *cousin* popped out of her mouth. "With anyone else," she quickly corrected—just not quickly enough for him to miss her meaning.

So Lorraine had figured it out. She presumed, correctly, that he was interested in Kady.

"While males are naturally given to libidinous urges," Lorraine said, "it's nothing more than lust. What you and I share, Rylan, is far deeper. Purer. I trust you implicitly, darling. You're not an uncouth womanizer, you're a gentleman. A true gentleman would never hurt or humiliate the woman who loves him."

Rylan was amazed at how she kept her practiced, polished smile in place throughout their unnerving discussion. The term *cool as a cucumber* must have derived from situations like this.

Damn.

He'd foolishly allowed himself to be railroaded, resulting in him feeling more trapped than ever, nowhere close to being cool as a cucumber. How the hell had he lost control of the discussion he initiated? It wasn't supposed to happen this way. He was supposed to drop Lorraine off at home, feeling an oppressive weight lifted from his shoulders. Instead, she'd mired him in guilt and shame, cuffing him in responsibility shackles, all but forcing him to spend the rest of his sorry days in a bleak, desolate, loveless marriage.

*Fuck.*

"I was about to tell you—" Lorraine started when Heidi approached, asking if there'd be anything else. Once Rylan declined, she left the check. "Oh good grief, I hope that's the last we see of that intrusive woman." Lorraine tsked. "Anyway, now that I've helped minimize your concerns, I want to get back to my marvelous news."

Rylan imagined his eyes must be bugging. This woman simply did *not* take no for an answer. Was she really that dense? That completely devoid of pride or self-respect?

"Last night Mother, Daddy, and I discussed our living arrangements after the wedding."

"Is that so?" Rylan huffed a humorless laugh. "And what did the three of you decide about my life this time?" Sitting back against the booth, he folded his arms across his chest.

"You'll be so pleased. Giving your feelings and concerns utmost priority, we've decided it would be more to your liking if we moved to my uncle's country property, living there for a while, rather than residing in the west wing right away."

"More to my liking? And why is that?" Rylan polished off the last of his coffee, wishing his cup held something a hell of a lot stronger.

"It was Kady's idea, actually."

Once again, her name had Rylan's ears perking. For God's sake, he was like a dog with the promise of a bone where the mere mention of Kady was concerned. For the sake of his sanity, he had to stop fixating on the sweet, auburn-haired beauty—at least until he'd gotten through this impossible breakup.

"It was obvious you felt somewhat bamboozled upon learning my parents had gifted us with Devington Manor's west wing."

"If you recall, I was *bamboozled* because you neglected to tell me about it," Rylan corrected.

"Mmm-hmm, well Kady's sage advice was for us to compromise. Actually," she tittered a counterfeit laugh, "for *me* to compromise. So I've made a concession." Smiling, she held her hands open before him. "I'm meeting you halfway, Rylan. You get your little place in the country, just as you'd wanted, and I don't have to give up the luxuries or the social circle to which I'm accustomed. It's the perfect arrangement, don't you agree?"

With a quiet laugh of resignation, Rylan thought about his brother's words. "Everybody's a conductor and I'm just a passenger," he muttered beneath his breath.

"I'm sorry, what was that, darling?"

Slowly shaking his head from side to side, Rylan answered, "Nothing. It doesn't matter. It all sounds peachy. Jim-dandy." He decided that probably came across better than telling her he thought every word she uttered was pure horseshit.

"Tell me, Lorraine, what kind of *compromise* did you and your parents decide would be appropriate concerning my career?" Because he knew damn well the Devingtons weren't about to let go of that bone before they'd gnawed, tore apart, spit on, and utterly demolished the last remaining skeletal remains of his long-range plans.

"I'm so glad you asked, because that's the other half of my fabulous news, Rylan. I know you'll be just as excited as we are about it."

"I can't wait." Rylan was too damn emotionally spent to roll his eyes.

"Daddy is aware of your standing in the scientific community, including the countless awards and accolades you've received for your tireless work in conservation and environmental safety."

Well he had to give her points for knowing how to suck up.

"Since you're intent on remaining at that public college for the time being, Daddy reached out to his connections on your behalf." She clasped his hand now, with a firm squeeze, while offering a glowing smile.

If they ever decided to do another remake of Dr. Jekyll and Mr. Hyde, Rylan would nominate Lorraine as a top contender for the role. Why should male actors have all the fun with the part when a female like Lorraine could inject so much realism?

"They've arranged a series of lectures for you to conduct for faculty and students at Pacific Northwest University. Daddy is certain once you become more familiar with PNU's offerings, you'll be on board with making the switch."

"Lucky me." Outside of making a memorable scene in Griffin's Café, what the hell else could he say? This morning's breakfast was like being in the midst of a horror movie where your life is slowly, methodically taken over by meddling aliens. He couldn't believe her old man had actually tampered with his teaching career. Scratch that—he most certainly *could* believe it. Seems his fiancée had done everything possible to ensnare Rylan so deeply he wouldn't be able to disengage.

"I knew you'd see it that way," Lorraine told him. "Your first lecture series begins after the summer break, which should give you plenty of time to prepare. Daddy will go over all the particulars with you. With his guidance you'll slowly ease your way out of WHU and into PNU until, a year from this fall's semester, you'll be teaching solely at PNU."

His head hanging, Rylan rested his elbows on his knees. "So that's the compromise, huh?" A weak attempt at laughter caught in his throat. "You and your parents get everything you want while I give up all that's important to me. Great compromise." Rylan clapped his hands slowly.

Laughing, Lorraine grabbed one of his hands, squeezing it. "There you go making jokes again. You're so witty, Rylan. Isn't it all just too wonderful? We've ironed out our differences, alleviating your minor concerns about our nuptials, adjusting our housing goals, and injecting new life into your career. And all over breakfast at your favorite, uh, truck stop. I'm positively ecstatic, aren't you, darling?"

Rylan smiled, valiantly resisting the urge to grab his deceptively beautiful fiancée by her lithe, graceful neck and squeezing until, just like in the cartoons, her pretty little eyes bulged from their sockets. "I can't begin to describe how all this makes me feel," he related honestly. Well, he could, but it probably wouldn't even register with her if he told her straight out that he felt trapped. Caught. Stuck. Wedged. Deceived. Tricked. Cornered.

Worst of all...hopeless.

"Isn't it amazing what a little compromise can do, not to mention what a difference just a few minutes makes?"

"Astonishing."

"Look at you, darling," she gestured at him with open palms, "your whole demeanor has changed. See? I told you it was just a passing phase. We'll have a wonderful marriage, Rylan. With such a handsome, esteemed professor for my husband," she actually batted her eyelashes then, "and a neurosurgeon for my brother-in-law, I'll be the envy of all my friends."

"I know how important that is to you."

"You see? You do understand after all."

"I'm sure all your hifalutin friends will be real impressed when I leave teaching to write my science fiction novels fulltime too." Hey, why not throw in that reminder so Lorraine and her parents could find a way to mangle that dream of his as well?

"I see no reason why you can't pen your little books as a sideline to your hard-earned professorial career," Lorraine assured him. "Naturally, you'll need to use a pseudonym to keep your writing hobby private."

"It's not a hobby," he informed her for the umpteenth time. "My goal is to become a bestselling author."

"That sounds like fun, darling." She gave him her kindergarten teacher smile. "I'm sure you'll enjoy writing your stories and sharing them with your professor friends."

"Yeah, we'll have fun when we talk about it after school when we're playing ball together. Then we can all go to Devington Manor for milk and cookies."

Lorraine looked confused. "Play ball...is that what you professors do after class to release tension? I've read that exercise is a good way to deal with stress. And, goodness, I'd think you'd all prefer a glass of scotch and a cigar over milk and cookies, but Cook would certainly accommodate you."

Rylan almost burst out laughing. She either actually thought he was serious, or she was being purposely obtuse. Either case was unfortunate. Yup, no doubt about it, he'd fallen down the rabbit hole.

When he remained quiet for too long to suit her, he saw her smile turn acrid.

"Look, Lorraine, I'm sorry but—"

"I just had a terrible thought." Lorraine's hand flew to her chest. "Whatever would you do if your superiors at Wisdom Harbor University were to hear," she shuddered, "it chills me just to think of it...if they were to hear an ugly, albeit untrue, rumor that you've slept with some of your students?"

*What. The. Actual. Fuck.*

Cocking his head, Rylan glared at Lorraine, finding it hard to believe, even after everything else she'd orchestrated, that she'd just openly threatened him—while broadcasting a hypocritical smile of guiltless innocence.

"Is it just me or did that sound like a veiled threat?" he asked.

"Threat? Dear God, Rylan," she looked for all the world like a sad-eyed wounded kitten, "I know your fondness for humor but that wasn't funny in the least."

"I didn't think so either, Lorraine."

"In fact," she continued, "I'm afraid you posing that question to me makes you sound like you may be paranoid delusional." She chuckled then...a rather odd reaction, he thought, but what else was new? "You certainly wouldn't want WHU to be concerned you might have psychological problems, would you?"

*Holy...*

If only he'd had the foresight to hit record on his phone. No one would believe him if he tried telling them about this conversation. It was like something out of an old movie. *Maltese Falcon,* came to mind. He'd be Bogart's Sam Spade, while Lorraine was perfect for the sneaky, lying, conniving, venomous Mary Astor's Brigid O'Shaughnessy.

Lorraine broke his train of thought with another brief chortle of laughter. "But you don't have anything like that to worry about as long as we're together, darling."

*Darling*. He'd grown to loathe that term of endearment.

"You're clearly feeling stressed. Just put all those forlorn thoughts aside and focus on us instead. You and me and the happy, prosperous life we'll build and share. Together."

Nope. There was no fucking way he'd allow this loony woman to dictate his life for the next five minutes, much less the rest of his life. He'd take his chances with her blackmail. His higher-ups had known him for years and Rylan doubted they'd readily believe the rantings of a spurned woman. And if they did believe her, or whoever she hired to spread malicious gossip, he'd demand a hearing to clear himself—and he'd win, dammit. Most likely these were empty threats Lorraine was spouting anyway.

"Go ahead, Lorraine, have a field day making your threats become a reality. Anyone who knows me would never believe it. So conjure up all the malice you can think of. I don't give a damn anymore."

To think he'd actually felt sorry for this woman. He'd spent hours crafting the best, least hurtful or traumatic way for him to approach the subject of ending their relationship to keep poor

Lorraine from being crushed. *Poor Lorraine* indeed. The woman was a viper.

"Excuse me?" She gave him a shifty-eyed look while brushing invisible crumbs from her being-on-beige top. He couldn't remember ever seeing her in anything but some shade of beige. "I have no idea what you're talking about, Rylan. I do believe our conversation somehow became derailed along the way."

"What I'm talking about, Lorraine, is being done. Finished. Through. I wanted to have a nice, civil conversation with you to let you down easy this morning after you turned into a barracuda at your soiree, but you had to go and complicate matters with threats and blackmail."

Dislodging more invisible crumbs, she offered a virtuous smile while claiming, "Again, I have no idea what you're talking about, darling. You must be unwell. Are you feeling all right?"

She had the audacity to reach across the table to place her hand against his forehead—as if she actually cared about him. Nice try.

"What's most amazing," he told her, "is that you actually believe I'd still want anything to do with you after this. So go ahead and tell my higherups whatever you damn well please. Tell them you think I'm delusional. Lie to them about me having affairs with my students. I'll take my chances. Consider our engagement terminated as of this very moment. That clear enough for you?"

He threw his napkin on the table, ready to get up and out of there before he detonated in the middle of Annalise's café.

"My goodness, Rylan, as if I would ever dream of resorting to the terrible things you're suggesting." She did a helluva job looking shocked and wounded. "Your unkind accusations hurt me deeply. It's like suggesting," her hand covered her heart, "oh, I don't know...that I'd resort to making certain Medicine Without Boundaries learned some unsavory information about your neurosurgeon brother that might nullify their professional relationship, forcing him to return from Nigeria prematurely. Never able to work in another hospital here in the U.S. again."

Rylan's eyebrows shot up. Attempting to screw up *his* life was one thing. It was a whole different story when she chose to involve someone he cared about. He was prepared to let Lorraine do her worst to him, just so he could untangle himself from her merciless clutches. But for her to suggest destroying his brother's name and career after Quinn had worked so damn long and hard to achieve his well-respected standing in the medical community?

"Do you hear yourself, Lorraine? You're threatening my brother's dreams and his livelihood, just to keep me from walking out on you. Is that what you really want? Is that the sort of relationship you want to nurture with a man you claim to love?"

Her fingers tiptoed from his hand to elbow until he snatched his arm away. "Oh now don't get so defensive, darling."

She said it so matter of fact, with such carefree nonchalance, it was uncanny. The way she sat there, with an inviting smile, looking fresh as a daisy, maintaining a cool, unruffled façade while providing a hostile list of what-ifs unnerved him. He realized he had no idea what Lorraine might be capable of.

"What an active imagination you have. I was merely providing examples of things I'd never dream of resorting to, that's all," Lorraine said. "For instance, an example involving," tapping a finger against her cheek, she looked up before returning her razor-sharp gaze on him, "oh, let's say my cousin, Kady."

Rylan saw one of Lorraine's eyes narrow as her smile transformed into something spiteful.

"Let's pretend for a moment that you and Kady were attracted to each other. Since I love you both dearly, I'd never dream of speaking to Daddy."

Hot lava churned in Rylan's gut during the prolonged silence. "About?" She'd hooked him and he bit.

"About the mortgage for Cherished Book Pages, which is held by my father's bank." Lorraine's chin elevated as she looked down her nose at him. "It would be heartbreaking if it somehow went into foreclosure and poor Kady lost the bookshop she loves so dearly, as well as her apartment upstairs from the shop."

"As long as she and Saffron pay their monthly installments on time, there's no reason for your father to foreclose." While Rylan wasn't a banker or attorney and didn't know all the legalities, it sounded right to him.

"Good point. You're such a quick thinker, Rylan." She tapped her temple. "But, getting back to my example, Daddy might hear about Kady and Saffron's lesbian relationship."

"Their what?!" His face must have screwed and scrunched every which way. He knew she was baiting him...knew he should keep his mouth shut and let her have her venomous say, but he couldn't help taking the damn bait.

"Remember, Rylan, I'm only providing examples of things that could conceivably happen." There was that sweet, innocent smile again. "We all know of my father's deep-rooted revulsion regarding homosexuals. If he believed Kady and another of his own children were engaged in whatever it is that homosexuals do together," her hand flit through the air, "I guarantee you he'd find a legal way to foreclose and poor Kady and Saffron would be out on their ears."

This woman was amazing, in the worst possible sense.

"Plus," Lorraine continued, "Saffron would be disowned and disinherited...leaving me the sole beneficiary of my parents' vast estate."

Looking at his fiancée now, Rylan had to assume he was witnessing firsthand what's known as a shit-eating-grin.

Folding her hands neatly in front of her, Lorraine eyed Rylan as if he were a special student in need of clarification. "Those are the types of examples I'm talking about, darling. Examples neither of us ever need to worry about since we're happily engaged and will be married this October. And will remain married until death...do us part."

Rylan had been aware for some time that something was definitely off with Lorraine but he'd never figured her for a sociopath. A textbook case, she lacked empathy or remorse. Although, listening to that last line of hers about *until death do us part,* where she'd paused just after *death,* holding his gaze, chilled him to his core, making him wonder if sociopath was too lenient because the term *psychopath* loomed too close for comfort.

This was unreal. What the hell had he gotten himself into? And what could he do about it, other than follow his brother to Nigeria to escape his scheming fiancée and her controlling parents? Even that wouldn't work. It was one thing for Lorraine to threaten him, but virtually blackmailing him with the intention of ruining Quinn, Saffron, and Kady was something else entirely.

"You understand now, Rylan, don't you, darling?" a sweet-smiling Lorraine asked, with the same demeanor as if asking him if he wanted jelly or preserves on his toast.

"Yes, Lorraine," Rylan said through gritted teeth. "I understand. Perfectly."

"Wonderful. I was sure you would." She patted his hand. "I'm pleased and relieved that you appreciate the far-reaching ramifications of calling off our wedding plans, Rylan. Kady felt sure you'd be on board."

"Kady again." Rylan said, somewhere between a question and a statement as he narrowed his eyes at Lorraine.

"Mmm-hmm. Kady saw a sign indicating you'd get cold feet. You see, she understands the importance of loyalty and commitment, which is why she and Ramon have such a good, solid relationship."

"Ramon?" Rylan's entire head throbbed.

"Oh dear..." Sucking in a gasp, Lorraine covered her mouth. "I shouldn't have said anything. It's supposed to be a secret. But," she tossed her hands up in a joyful motion, "at least I no longer need concern myself with my fiancé having inappropriate feelings for my cousin. Not," she reached out to grasp his forearm, "that I ever dreamed you had feelings for Kady, of course. However, with Kady happily in love, that's one worry I can cross off my list."

No doubt a list of people she deemed deserving of her threats and blackmail schemes. Rylan wondered how long the list was. Probably anyone Lorraine perceived as having ever done her wrong had a place of honor.

Rylan also wondered how many of those people had suffered because Lorraine had followed through on her thinly disguised threats. He felt like all his brain cells had taken a hike because Rylan was clueless about how to handle this—handle her. He could talk to her parents but they probably already knew what she was like. Or, because she was their precious little princess, they wouldn't believe she was capable of such malevolence.

"Her lover's full name," Lorraine surreptitiously looked left, then right before quietly saying, "is Ramon Gustavo Taramino. He's a sexy Latin lover type." With a disapproving roll of her eyes, she continued, "Disgraceful but," she shrugged, "I'm supportive because the poor lovesick girl needs someone on her side."

Rylan tried to ignore the images floating across his mind. Nope, he didn't want to picture Kady with another man, much less some sexy—

"Ramon and Kady have been hot and heavy for a while now," Lorraine said, her voice happily interrupting the unwelcome streaming video his brain had fabricated.

Getting back to finding a solution, Rylan thought hard. He certainly wouldn't burden his brother with any of this crap right before Quinn left to work in a foreign country for at least three years. And there's no way he felt comfortable speaking to Kady about it, especially now that he knew she was in a serious relationship with...*Ramon*.

Rylan's imagination invented a good looking dude wearing a shirt open to his waist, with a cartoon twinkle in his eye, a dead-sexy foreign accent, and a big, long—

Shaking the disagreeable thought from his mind, Rylan thought about Saffron. She was probably all too familiar with her sister's sinister thoughts and capabilities. But now that Lorraine was also targeting her own sister, Rylan couldn't risk talking to her about all this either. There wasn't anything Saffron could do other than worry about both Quinn and Kady.

No, Rylan would have to figure out a way to handle this problem that defied solving entirely on his own, without involving anyone else that Lorraine might hurt if she suspected Rylan had taken them into his confidence.

"They hope to marry soon," Lorraine said. "Knowing my kooky cousin, it'll probably be a silly outdoor hippie-style wedding."

Rylan's thoughts sprang to Kady wearing a crown of flowers on her gently curled auburn hair. He imagined her in a long wispy dress with angel sleeves that moved like soft, flowing veils as she stepped barefoot through the grass, to the melodious tune of chirping birds. The angelic dress concealing a body made for sin. However it wasn't Antonio Banderas waiting for her at the outdoor altar, it was Rylan himself.

He had no clue where in the hell that finely detailed image came from. He wasn't a romantic who thought up lovey-dovey stuff like that. But when he thought of Kady, he was reminded of the fairytales his mom read to him and Quinn when they were kids. Kady was ideal as the beautiful princess, loved and adored by all who knew her...except for one particularly evil cousin.

He'd just added the wicked cousin part today due to a perfect casting opportunity.

Tapping a finger to her lips, Lorraine said, "It's very hush-hush, Rylan. The Malones don't approve of Kady hooking up with the sexy Brazilian." She lifted a judgmental eyebrow. "Is Antonio Banderas Brazilian?"

"Spanish, I think."

"Same thing," Lorraine said with a flippant wave. "That's who Ramon looks like, only younger, taller and more muscular."

Having never heard anything about Kady being in a relationship, Rylan assumed she was unattached. The unwelcome revelation was like throwing a bucket of ice water over his head. Though he itched to know more, he wasn't about to let Lorraine know of his interest. He kept his mouth shut and resumed thinking about possible solutions so he could rid himself of the Wicked Witch of Glassfloat Bay once and for all.

The police? Lorraine hadn't committed a crime...at least not that he knew of. The notion she may have, gave him chills. There hadn't been any formal blackmailing he could prove either. Psychiatric doctors? She didn't appear to be a threat to herself or others, plus Lorraine was one of those ultra-composed individuals who could skate right by all their evaluation questions and come out looking saner and more clear-headed than they were.

"So," Lorraine continued her interminable chitchat about Kady and Antonio Banderas, "Kady lied to everyone...told them she wasn't seeing Ramon anymore."

His head angling to the side, Rylan struggled to take all this in. Granted, he didn't know Kady very well but this new information didn't gel, didn't feel right.

"You're talking about Kady Malone, your cousin?" As soon as the words left his lips he realized how stupid his question sounded—a truth Lorraine quickly pounced on.

She looked at him like he'd just spoken a foreign language. "Who else would I be talking about? Keep this just between us, Rylan. Kady shared it with me in confidence. She'd be upset to know I broke my promise."

"No problem." His words proved hilarious under the highly problematic circumstances.

Rylan wasn't sure Lorraine was even telling the truth though. Maybe Ramon didn't even exist. Maybe she'd made him up to—

"As you may know, Kady's been all over the world," Lorraine said, intruding on his skeptical thoughts. "Backpacking, of all things." Her pinched expression fully telegraphed her distaste. "She and Ramon met when Kady traveled to Brazil, where they enjoyed a whirlwind romance. In true Hallmark movie fashion, Ramon realized he couldn't live without Kady, so he came here to Oregon to surprise her. They've been inseparable ever since. Kady filled me in on the details when she visited Devington Manor after my soiree."

Damn...it sounded like it was legit.

The only potential solution was for him to follow through and marry Lorraine Devington...then have her committed to a psychiatric hospital. While the strategy sounded reprehensible, like something out of a bad B-movie, it was the only possible solution he had. He'd need to research it, to see if his idea to have her committed had substance. He'd do some serious Googling after his late-morning class.

Yup, there were only two clear choices. Marry Lorraine...or murder her.

It was at rare times like this Rylan wished he possessed a true killer's instinct. But as satisfying as it was imagining murderous scenarios involving his conniving fiancée, he could never do it. Although...he could picture himself spending the rest of his days in a prison cell, or frying in the electric chair, more easily than spending the rest of his life as the utterly pussy-whipped *Mister Rylan Devington.*

The big question—could he manage to play along as Lorraine's loving fiancé, and then her husband, for as long as it took to get her out of the picture? He'd need a will of iron. And by *out of the picture* he, of course, meant having her committed, not murdering her. Well...unless absolutely necessary. It probably wasn't a good thing that the thought made him smile.

With the wellbeing of his brother, Kady, Saffron, and any other unsuspecting individuals on Lorraine's payback list, at stake, Rylan decided he was capable of doing whatever necessary to protect those he loved.

Sliding across the booth seat, Lorraine stood up, Hermès bag in hand. "I want to leave now...unless you have something else on your mind, Rylan."

"Nope. My mind's a blank." That was a barefaced lie. His brain was on overload and in danger of imploding due to the breakfast date from hell.

Kady Malone having someone special in her life, who also happened to be a sexy Latin lover, was the toxic icing on the cake Lorraine had served to him this morning.

# Chapter 17

"RYLAN IS OVERCOME with joy," Lorraine told Kady over the phone. "And so am I." She'd been talking Kady's ear off for twenty minutes, endlessly effusing about her *fabulously ecstatic relationship news*, as Lorraine referred to it—multiple times.

"And why shouldn't he be?" Lorraine continued. "A house in the country, an outstanding new career opportunity, and most important of all, our relationship and love for each other is stronger than ever. I know I probably shouldn't be sharing any intimate thoughts or details but..."

Her eyes growing saucer wide, Kady's thoughts screamed, *Please don't...oh God, Lorraine, puhleez don't!*

"...but I can't help myself from sharing a few tidbits because I'm in seventh heaven."

Kady wondered why her back teeth ached so much, only to realize she'd been grinding them so hard they were probably on the verge of crumbling from the pressure.

"I can tell you," Lorraine continued, "that Professor Rylan Kilpatrick knows how to satisfy a woman. Mmmm. Do you know what his biggest problem is, according to Rylan?"

Kady was about to answer *no*, but it appeared Lorraine wasn't actually looking for a reply, she just wanted to hear herself talk, because she kept right on yakking.

"His biggest problem is trying to keep his hands off me because I'm so captivating. Which is evident by his amorous actions." She offered another *mmmm*. "Isn't that romantic?"

Kady remained silent until Lorraine repeated, "I said isn't that romantic, Kady?"

Ah, so she was expecting an answer this time.

"Very romantic. I'm really happy for you, Lorraine," she valiantly lied.

"I know you are. None of this would have been possible if you hadn't made me see the light, Kady. It's clear that your psychic powers knew how much Rylan loves me. I'm so fortunate to have you as both my cousin and my friend."

Kady struggled to corral a boatload of negative thoughts, like the one squawking inside her head saying she was a damn fool for playing relationship counselor for her cousin and the man Kady was so hopelessly in love with.

Whoa! Where had *that* come from? She had feelings for Rylan...but love? No way. It was too soon, and definitely verboten. It was just a crush, a minor case of lust, that's all. It was her own fault for keeping her nose stuck in all those romance novels she read. How could her thoughts avoid turning to love when that's all she read about?

Yeah...that's all it was.

As Lorraine kept up her inexhaustible dialogue, Kady offered supportive comments where necessary so Lorraine wouldn't suspect Kady hadn't provided her undivided attention.

"You convinced me to talk to Rylan," Lorraine was saying now, "to explain how I feel, and to apologize for my behavior at the soiree. Our talk over breakfast yesterday was nothing short of magic. Thank you for your insight and wisdom, Kady."

After her conversation with Saffron about the long-standing state of Lorraine's mental health, Kady couldn't be sure how much, if any, of what Lorraine told her was true. It must be, considering how extraordinarily pleased and happy Lorraine sounded. She and Rylan must have sorted things out and were back on track.

Instead of being thrilled for her cousin while Lorraine went on ad nauseum about all the sparkly wonderfulness in her life, Kady's thoughts sang the blues. She silently chastised herself for not being genuinely happy for Lorraine.

Fortunately, the bookshop bustled with customers. If it had been empty Kady might have succumbed to sobbing, which would have been terribly selfish. She had no right feeling sorry for herself and no business daydreaming about her cousin's fiancé. Or having him star in her dreams at night either, much less her fantasies.

She'd done the right thing by helping Lorraine mend her relationship with Rylan.

She really had. Really.

Grandma Bekka always told her, *Everything happens for a reason.* She'd say, *This was meant to be, Kady. Never fear, for all is well with your little corner of the world, sweet child. Now close your eyes and breathe deep. Fill your heart with gladness—for yourself and for those you love.*

Kady tried. She really did. But instead of gladness flooding her heart, it was waves of melancholy sloshing around in there. Still, she managed a supportive reply to Lorraine's thanks.

"My pleasure, Lorraine. I couldn't be happier for you and Rylan. I was sure everything would be better if you two talked. It's wonderful that Rylan is on board with all your plans now."

Even though she didn't know Rylan all that well, Kady was surprised and maybe a little disappointed that he'd so readily agreed to the major life-changes Lorraine and her parents had set into motion for him. It seemed to Kady that her intuition was in need of repair because she'd been off about Rylan.

The biggest surprise was how deeply Rylan must love Lorraine. Why else would a talented, intelligent man like Professor Kilpatrick give up on his hopes and dreams. And his goal of being a fulltime novelist? But, if Lorraine was to be believed, that's exactly what happened.

With a book in her hands, Sasha, one of the sales clerks, approached Kady, clearly with a question. Smiling at her, Kady made a shushing motion.

"I'm sorry, Lorraine," she said into her phone, "but the shop is full of customers and I'm on my own until Saffron gets here so I need to let you go. Again, I'm truly happy for you...and Rylan."

During their endless conversation, the shop had mostly cleared out. Sasha was covering the floor and had just finished ringing up several sales, so Kady told Lorraine a little white lie. She just couldn't listen to her cousin another minute about how perfectly matched and in love she and Rylan were.

Once off the phone, Sasha asked Kady her question, then teased her by making a shame-shame gesture. "Maybe I should blackmail you for keeping quiet next time I see your cousin." She and Kady laughed.

With a fake worried expression, Kady jokingly admitted, "I'm a terrible person," while looking up the book in question and printing out a new price sticker to replace the blurred one. She probably *was* a terrible person, because she should have been sincerely happy about Lorraine and Rylan patching things up.

Kady muttered beneath her breath as she repositioned books that had been moved to the wrong shelves by customers. There was something so satisfying about organizing books. The process helped take her mind off her problems, until she came across covers that sparked a memory, or matched one of her fantasies.

When the door bing-bonged, she looked up and smiled, giving Saffron a wave. She'd been at the hospital this morning, reading to the sick children and passing out a new batch of her adorable little rag dolls, the custom ones she'd created to match requests from the kids.

Kady's smile disintegrated when she fully caught sight of Saffron's face after her cousin removed her oversized sunglasses. It was red, blotchy and puffy.

Izzy made it to Saffron's side first, with Kady following close behind. "Aw, sweetie, what happened? Why are you cry—" Kady stopped abruptly, remembering tonight would be the last time Saffron and Quinn saw each other before he left for Nigeria in the morning.

"Ohhhh, Saffy, sweetie..." Grasping Saffron, Kady held her close, rocking her back and forth, patting her back while Saffron cried on her shoulder. Izzy engaged in a series of soft, sympathetic whimpers as she hugged Saffron's leg.

"My God that little dog of yours is sweet," Saffron said, before adding, "tissue please," as she held her fingers together, waving them. Backing out of their embrace, Kady zipped to the back room, returning with a box of tissues.

Feeling at a loss, Kady said, "I wish there was something I could do to make it easier for you." What could she do, other than suggest Saffron meditate while listening to soothing ocean wave sounds, dolphin songs, and chirping birds on one of Kady's playlists? Unfortunately none of that sounded therapeutic enough to alleviate her cousin's grief.

"Nothing could make this any easier," Saffron said, sniveling, blotting, and blowing. The poor thing was a mess. "But I need to snap myself out of this crying jag so I don't look like Rudolph the red-nosed pity-party freak when Quinn picks me up tonight. I want to look as good as possible so he'll remember me that way."

"I wish I had something stronger in our storeroom's cabinets than just my ginger tea concoction."

"You won't get an argument from me. Looks like we need to go shopping for some booze." Saffron attempted to chuckle, which came out sounding more like a goose honking. "But I love your ginger tea with your herbed honey. I'm sure it'll make me feel much better."

Even when consumed by sorrow, Saffron told the kindest, most heartening untruths.

"Come on." Kady looped arms with her and walked. "I'll make us a pot of tea, extra potent on the ginger, just the way you like it, and we'll pretend it's something stronger." Before heading for the shop's back room again, Kady called out, "Sasha, Saffron and I will be in the back if you need me."

Dragging another clump of tissues from the box as they walked, Saffron said, "Quinn told me he'd take me anywhere I wanted to go for dinner tonight. Know where I picked?"

"Of course I do." Patting Saffron's arm, Kady said, "The Thai restaurant where the four of us went the first day you met Quinn."

Saffron started blubbering all over again.

Kady led Saffron to a chair when they reached the back room. "Okay, sit." She took a couple paper towels off the roll, doused them in cold water and wrung them out before getting two ice cubes from the small, office-sized freezer, enclosing them in the damp towels.

"Blot," Kady instructed, "while I get the tea going and prepare to deaden your angst, as well as your tastebuds, with copious amounts of ginger."

"Not too copious," Saffron said, attempting another chuckle.

"Hey, I thought you were a gingerholic like me." Kady laughed, trying to keep things as cheerful as possible.

"I am...but sometimes my aging digestive system can't handle too much of a good thing."

"Same here. Weird how things change as we—"

"As we approach the autumn of our lives." Saffron's tears returned in full force. "And I'll be spending the winter of my life all alone, without Quinn in a rocking chair beside me." She said more but it was hard to decipher everything through Saffron's hiccupping sobs. Her cousin's obvious heartbreak spoke volumes though.

Kady searched through the cabinets for the right mugs, avoiding anything with hearts or sentimental sayings. The idea was to lift Saffron's spirits, not make her feel worse. She chose two cute, cartoony designs with funny dogs, hoping they'd make her smile.

"Quinn said it wasn't fair of him to ask me to wait for him, because he didn't know when he'd be back. But he said if I'm still free and unattached whenever he does return, he'll immediately swoop in and ask me to marry him on the spot."

"Oh Saffron, that's *so* romantic. It's clear Quinn loves you very much."

"I told him he doesn't have to worry about me finding anyone else, and that I'll definitely be waiting for him."

While talking, Saffron's tears subsided, so Kady did her best to keep her cousin talking.

"Did you ever think about moving to Nigeria with him?"

"Have I?" Saffron laughed. It was good, hard, cleansing laughter. "If you only knew how much time I've spent Googling about Nigeria, American expats living there, job opportunities..." She counted them off on her fingers as she spoke. "Cost of living, safety concerns, the political climate, housing, Language barriers." Saffron took a deep breath. "Etcetera, etcetera."

"Wow!" Kady smiled. "By now you must be an expert on the place, the people and the language, hmm?"

"Language!" Saffron grinned. "Good news! I learned English is the official language of Nigeria. Isn't that great?"

"It is," Kady agreed, thinking it sounded like Saffron had been talking herself into moving there. "Makes things easier for Americans moving there."

"Ooh, and what I learned about their underfunded healthcare system," Saffron continued, clearly engrossed about the idea of living in Nigeria, "explains why Quinn and the Medicine Without Boundaries team are so needed there. Some of the stuff is surprising, and pretty scary. Like polio, malaria, cholera, tetanus, HIV, and tuberculosis are still common in Nigeria, even though it's a developed country."

"Yikes." That surprised Kady. "You're right, that's really scary."

"I read their limited health facilities are well below Western standards. After lots of research, I understand why Quinn is so passionate about making a positive difference to help Nigerians."

"Getting back to my original question, have you been thinking about moving there to be with Quinn?"

"I have. But it's not a simple matter of packing a suitcase and hopping on a plane." Saffron chuckled. "There's so much to consider. Quinn said he wouldn't feel comfortable asking me to consider making such a major move without him getting some firsthand experience."

"That makes good sense."

"Then there are my commitments here, like Cherished Pages. I can't just take off and leave you here alone, Kady. That wouldn't be fair."

"Oh my God, Saffron, I would *hate* it if you turned down an opportunity to be with the man you love because you're worried about me and the bookshop. The shop and I will be just fine. Please don't let something like that keep you from going with Quinn."

"He spoke with MWB and they aren't currently allowing spouses, family, or significant others to travel with members of their organization. The teaching location is too remote, for one thing. There must be a waiting period for decisions about housing, etcetera. That's why they chose only single, unattached and unencumbered individuals to make this trip."

Saffron indulged in a lengthy sigh. "Soooo...it looks like me moving there with Quinn is a no-go."

"But there's a possibility in the future, right?"

Shrugging, Saffron said, "I'm not really sure. Quinn will look into it more once he's situated there. And he's asked Rylan to check into things for him from here. MWB told Quinn it will be at least a year before suitable housing could be constructed for spouses or family, and before everything else necessary can be achieved."

"A year. Well that's not really too bad." While Kady didn't believe that, she wanted to keep it upbeat so she wouldn't add to Saffron's angst.

"I looked for job openings there," Saffron said, "thinking perhaps I could find something I'm qualified for. Real estate agents are definitely not in demand." She laughed. "Same with bookshop owners, although they're looking for librarians and teachers. I'm not qualified for either."

"Why not? You'd make a fantastic librarian or teacher, Saffron."

"Thanks but I don't have that almighty important piece of paper," she rubbed her fingers together, "that says I'm qualified."

"A librarian or teaching degree," Kady acknowledged. "But you do have a bachelor's degree. A couple of them if I recall."

"Mmm-hmm, purely business-related degrees. I took several classes required for librarians and teachers but never went any further. If I'd made English my major instead, that might have helped but my father insisted I learn all about business. I don't know, Kady."

Saffron gave a downhearted shrug. "Maybe I can find a job there that fits my skills and their requirements. However," she raised her index finger, "there's no way I'm going to take off for parts unknown and leave you here to manage our bookshop on your own. It's already more than enough work for two people."

"Hey, didn't we already talk about that?" Kady clasped Saffron's shoulders, giving her a gentle shake. "I'll never forgive you if you put your happiness on hold because of me or our bookshop. Listen to me. I. Will. Be. Fine! Got it?"

"Got it." Saffron laughed and saluted. "I'm so glad I have you in my life, Kady."

"Ditto." Kady winked. "Hey, I have some good news about your sister," she said, determined to conceal her own sorrow while sharing Lorraine's newest update about Rylan.

"Lorraine said she and Rylan had a great talk and everything is fine. He's even agreed to all of her plans about where they live and about his job." Even as Kady said the words, they rang false.

Silent for a moment, Saffron finally offered a crooked smile. "Bullshit. I don't believe a word of it, and neither should you."

~<>~

*That Evening*

"You light my world, Saffron. I've never known anyone like you." Reaching across the Thai restaurant's table, Quinn cupped the bottom of her chin, leaning in to bring his lips to hers for a kiss.

"I've been a fortunate guy most of my life. I've never had anything handed to me but whatever I worked hard to achieve, I succeeded at. All my plans, hopes, dreams...one by one they've all come to fruition. Until now. I've had setbacks and I've lost people I love throughout the years but nothing compares to this. To us. Discovering each other only to have to say goodbye too damn soon."

Saffron was thankful Kady suggested she bring a large purse so she could include plenty of tissues because she was going through them faster than an elephant shelling peanuts.

Cautiously blotting more tears, doing her best to avoid raccoon eyes, she said, "I wanted so much to look good for you tonight...as pretty as possible, so you'd remember me that way. But look at me," Saffron's forlorn laughter was mixed with tears. "I'm a teary, snotty, red-nosed mess and this is what you'll picture from now on whenever you think of me."

Quinn rose from his booth seat and came to her side of the booth, sliding in beside Saffron and drawing her into his arms, patting her back and using a napkin to dab at her tears.

"What you just said is so ridiculous I don't even know where to start." Quinn chuckled as he smoothed her damp hair from her face. "You're a beautiful woman with a beautiful heart and soul, Saffron. That's what I'll picture. Always. This," his finger circled around her tear-stained face, "temporary mask of sadness can't distract from the inner and outer beauty I've come to know and love during the short time we've known each other."

"Funny," Saffron said, resting her head on his shoulder and caressing his arm, "Rylan's the writer in the family and yet you just spoke the most beautiful poetry to me."

"Huh...you're right, it *is* funny. I've never had a way with words before but being with you ignites something deep inside me and, *voila*, all the right words flow naturally."

"Maybe you'll decide to do some writing yourself in your spare time while you're in Nigeria." At the mere mention of his far off destination, new tears streamed silently down her cheeks.

"I already have, actually."

"Really?" That came as a surprise. "Tell me about it." Quinn being a writer was just one more reason she, as a lifelong reader and booklover, was drawn to him.

"It's a medical-themed mystery, the first in a series. The protagonist is a neurosurgeon. Original, huh?"

"Well they do say writers should write what they know, right?"

"If that was true, Stephen King would have been locked up a long time ago in a prison psych ward," Quinn pointed out. The two of them laughed at that.

"My doctor character gets involved solving unusual medical-related criminal cases the police and detectives haven't been able to crack. Rylan's been encouraging me to write more because he thinks my stuff is good." Quinn shrugged. "He thinks it'd be cool if we got published around the same time. We'd market ourselves as a brother writing duo, and maybe even write books where our characters cross over from his books to mine and vice versa."

"Ooh, I love this so much! I'd definitely read your book." She smiled, noting how animated he'd become while telling her about his writing.

"That's good because the protagonist has a main squeeze, who happens to be based on the beautiful woman sitting next to me." Quinn kissed the top of her head. "She helps me solve cases. I made the female character a real estate agent instead of a bookshop owner because I thought that would give the doc a better chance of getting into houses to search for clues. That way I can pick your brain so you can tell me what does and doesn't work, real estate-wise."

"Perfect! We can email back and forth," Saffron said, loving thoughts of communicating to keep their connection open while Quinn was gone. It could almost be like he was just in the next town for a few days.

"Afraid not," he said, bursting her tiny bubble of hope. "Most of the remote areas we'll be working in don't have wifi or internet connections."

Saffron's shoulders slumped. "Phone?" she asked, only to be let down when Quinn's head shook from side to side.

"They don't even have landlines. I think we could use satellite phones," Quinn suggested. "They're outrageously expensive but we could talk for—"

"Fifteen seconds at a time?" Saffron offered with a teasing smile. The little bit of levity was welcome and needed.

"It's an option." Quinn's smile was optimistic. "It would be the best fifteen seconds of my day. Basically, we'll have to depend on snail mail. You mind writing letters?"

"To you?" Incredulous laughter spilled from Saffron. "Are you kidding? I'll spend every spare moment jotting down everything that's going on here so you'll have your very own version of the Glassfloat Bay Gazette. And," she shook a warning finger, "you better reply," she teased.

"The only problem is—"

"Oh hell," Saffron said with a groan, collapsing even more into the booth's seat. "Don't tell me you won't have a mailing address either."

"We won't."

"I said not to tell me!" With a valiant attempt at laughter, she gave his arm a whap, but inside she was busy squelching an impending flood of tears at the thought of not being able to communicate with Quinn in any way while he was gone.

"Medicine Without Boundaries will be processing mail similar to the way they do in wartime. There will be central addresses for mailings, then every so often couriers will visit outlying locations to deliver mail and packages, and pick up outgoing mail."

"So we'll be able to communicate but we could be senior citizens by the time our letters reach each other," Saffron said, again, doing her best to keep their dialogue upbeat and lighthearted.

"You'll make a damn cute little old lady." Quinn kissed the tip of her nose.

Their conversation was interrupted by the arrival of their food order, giving Saffron time to think as the restaurant owner spoke with Quinn, who'd told him he was moving away. Saffron thought it was so cute when Quinn told the guy to make sure to treat Saffron well whenever she came there to eat because she'd be reporting back to him. Fortunately, the Thai owner laughed and nodded.

When Quinn rose from his seat next to Saffron to reclaim his spot across from her, the owner gave him a hearty clap on the back, smiling broadly as he winked and promised to take good care of *Mr. Quinn's special lady-friend*. Arching his eyebrows, he looked from Quinn to Saffron and back again before jiggling those expressive brows. The poor man probably thought she was a prostitute or a kept woman, which both tickled and embarrassed Saffron.

As they ate and talked, the evening progressed much like any other they'd spent together. Easy conversation, sharing mutual interests, and talking about their jobs—all of it sandwiched with words of love between each topic along the way. While Saffron knew this might be the last time she ever saw Quinn, somehow it hadn't fully registered because, here he was, sitting across from her as they chatted, laughed and strived to keep things positive and light.

After dinner they went back to Saffron's to spend a few more hours together before Quinn had to leave. His apartment was already vacant, with the landlord wasting no time posting a *for rent* notice.

With Kady's help and inspiration, Saffron had fixed up her rented condo, the one she'd shared with Monica before she and Hud were married last year, with colorful posters Kady had purchased from the local Medicine Without Boundaries merchandise shop in Portland. The photos of doctors, nurses, and smiling children from different localities around the world added a marvelous warm, happy vibe to the condo.

While creating her custom dolls for the sick kids at the hospital, Saffron also made two special little adult dolls representing herself and Quinn. Pleased at how adorable they'd turned out, she propped them on a stand at the center of her dining table. One was a doctor in blue scrubs with a teensy stethoscope around his neck—because everyone knows the only way to tell if someone's a genuine, bona fide doctor is by seeing that thing draped over their shoulders.

The other doll had a tiny stack of books in one arm and a *for sale* real estate sign in the other. Her choice worked especially well with what Quinn told her about the female character he'd created for his book series.

Saffron and Kady spent time the past week creating other niceties like a glittery bon voyage banner, now hanging over the French doors leading to her balcony. There were also little congratulatory cards, offering best wishes, positioned here and there. Saffron had purchased Quinn's favorite libation, Jack Daniel's Tennessee Whiskey, and baked his favorite dessert, double chocolate chip cookies, placing them at the feet of the dolls at the table's center.

Before leaving the restaurant, Saffron surreptitiously sent Kady a text saying 'leaving now' so Kady could stop by, use her spare key, and light the profusion of candles the two of them had placed around the interior of the condo...including Saffron's bedroom. Kady would also start the special romantic playlist they'd chosen for the evening.

Most of it was the very creative Kady's idea, and Saffron adored her for thinking of everything to make the last night with Quinn delightfully memorable. *Memorable* because Saffron longed to stage their last night together with a soul-deep feeling of beauty, romance, and everlasting love.

Saffron was sure she'd succeeded when she and Quinn crossed the threshold to her condo, eliciting a wide-eyed, boisterous "Wow!" from Quinn as he took in his candlelit, music-filled surroundings.

Those three beautiful words, *I love you*, were spoken countless times during the evening, along with wordless expressions of love.

While Quinn had avoided discussing the possibility of his own illness, or even untimely death, the stark reality of risk was ever present. He insisted it would be the height of pure selfishness for him to expect Saffron to put her life on hold hoping they could be together within a reasonable amount of time when he couldn't promise anything.

But of course she would wait. She'd wait for as long as it took. And in the painful event Quinn happened to meet someone else while he was overseas, Saffron would hold her head high and celebrate his happiness, rather than grieving, because Quinn Kilpatrick's joy was her joy.

Their last night together couldn't have been more perfect. It was like the best of all her favorite romantic movies and books rolled into one. And their lovemaking? It was slow, lush, rapturous, bone-deep exquisiteness.

Saffron Devington would remember and cherish this one, single, extraordinary night for the rest of her life.

# Chapter 18

~<>~

A FAMILIAR sound hauled Saffron out of a fitful sleep, interrupting another nightmare about Quinn. Focusing on the jarring noise she realized it was a text alert. She pried one eye open, picking up her phone from the night stand to check the time and the sender. It was only eight-thirty and Kady was texting her. The text read, 'Are you up?'

"Well I am now, thank you very much," Saffron muttered to herself, her voice sounding like a moose with a bad cold. It was too damn early to answer her well-meaning cousin's inevitable questions.

"No," Saffron texted back. "Only got three hours sleep. Need more. See you tomorrow."

Returning the phone to her night stand, she turned over to go back to sleep.

The text alert jingled again.

"Aw hell." She yanked the covers up over her head, trying to ignore the incessant jingle-jangle. About ten blissfully silent minutes went by before the text alert sounded again. Swearing a blue streak as she rested on an elbow in a half-sitting position, Saffron grabbed her phone, texting, "Not in the mood. Go away."

"I am going...all the way to Nigeria." A laughing emoji and a heart closed the sentence.

"Omigod, omigod, omigod!" Saffron shrieked, scrambling to fully sit up. Texting him back, she said, "Quinn!! Sorry, I thought you were Kady. Where are you?" She looked at the time again. Quinn's flight left PDX two hours ago, at six-thirty. Since it was at a nineteen-hour flight with a three-hour layover in Amsterdam, he still had to be in the air.

"Are you on the plane now?" She added six different types of hearts.

"Yes. Just wanted to tell you again that I love you. Last night together was epic. Wifi is spotty but had to try before we lose contact. Miss you already, Saffron."

"Me too!" Saffron added a few more lines before sending, only to growl in disappointment when she got the dreaded *text cannot be delivered* message. "Oh no...no!" She gave up after trying several more times only to receive the same message. Her hopes were raised when another text alert arrived, but this one was from Kady again.

Uttering a monumental sigh, Saffron texted, "I'm not in the mood to talk, Kady. Sorry. No more texting please."

"Get your butt out of bed, wash your snotty, tear-stained face, and put on some clothes. I'll be there in an hour, with breakfast and coffee."

"Seriously, Kady, I don't feel like company."

"Picture an emoji of a woman clapping her hands over her ears and singing la-la-la-la," Kady texted, "then get your ass out of bed and get ready because I'm coming over!!"

"Not answering the door!"

"No problem. I still have the key you gave me. Over and out!"

As cranky, out of sorts, and depressed as she felt, Saffron couldn't help laughing. Even on her best days she could never hope to match Kady's naturally upbeat persona. Being around someone buoyant and cheerful all day, every day, could be maddening if you were the sort of person, like Saffron, who wasn't naturally a happy-peppy people person. It was something she'd had to battle during her years in real estate—doing her duty by putting on her effervescent sales demeanor with clients and customers. It was much easier relating with readers at the bookshop.

"Stop your bellyaching," Saffron told herself as she got out of bed, dragging her fingernails through her hair, "and do whatever the hell is necessary to look and act at least halfway human by the time Kady gets here."

~<>~

"Okay, I gave her an ultimatum," Kady said, laughing into the phone as she talked to her mom. "Saffron wasn't happy about it but I'm sure she'll be ready in an hour. She thinks it's only me, so she's in for a surprise when I take her to Bekka House. We'll all either make her feel better, or we'll irritate her so much it'll take her mind off Quinn. Either way is a win-win."

"We'll do our best," Astrid said. "Poor thing. I feel so sorry for her. She finds the love of her life only to lose him."

With Rylan at the forefront of her thoughts, Kady sighed. She could relate all too well. "Sometimes life can really be unfair."

"How about you, sweetie? Are you doing okay?"

"Me?" Kady made sure to ramp up the positivity. "Oh sure, I'm great. Well, except for feeling terrible about what Saffron's going through. You know what I hate?"

"What, sweetie?"

"That unlike when we lived in Chicago, here in Oregon you can't buy alcohol, other than beer and wine, in the grocery store. What an antiquated, inconvenient law. I'm just not a fan of having to go into a liquor store to buy some Kahlua or Baileys, or the ginger brandy I need."

"I know. I feel the same way," Astrid agreed. "If you don't want to go, that's okay, honey. I can stop on the way to Bekka House and buy the stuff we need."

"As if you don't already have a ton of stuff of your own to do. No thanks, Mom, it's okay, I'll go. I was just griping." Kady chuckled. "It's silly for anyone else to go because the liquor store is on my way to Saffron's place. Anything else you need me to pick up?"

"No, I checked in with everyone else and we're good. Annalise got over there early to set up her omelet station, and Laila brought a batch of fresh-baked triple-ginger scones. All we need is the booze." Astrid's voice was tinged with humor. "See you there soon."

~<>~

Rylan had never been much of a drinker, other than maybe a beer or two while watching football, or a glass of Cabernet with dinner, but after that talk to end all talks he'd had with crazy-ass Lorraine, he decided this was as good a time as any to start imbibing—to graduate to something more potent. Quinn was a fan of Jack Daniel's and he also liked Scotch, so Rylan decided to start there. Since he didn't have anything at home...time to go shopping.

It was the first time he'd been inside Glassfloat Bay Liquors. Not being an aficionado, he was surprised by how many brands and types of Scotch there were. Single malt, single grain, blended malt, blended grain, and blended Scotch whisky. He remembered Quinn saying he preferred single malt, so Rylan picked the most expensive bottle, assuming it must be the best.

When he found himself in the aisle, or rather multiple aisles, of assorted sweet liqueurs, he spotted the two brands he'd heard Kady and Saffron mention, Kahlua, and Baileys. Noting the wide variety of flavors, some of them quite odd sounding, Rylan chuckled. They sounded more like something you'd find in a candy shop rather than a liquor store.

"The idea of mint mocha makes me laugh too."

The voice startled Rylan. It was undeniably Kady's. Turning to look at her, he smiled. Damn she was a cutie. This morning she looked like a walking, talking ad for springtime, with a quirky outfit of bright florals, plaids and prints, none of which should go together, but on her it looked like something out of Vogue. The best way to describe the way she dressed was...happy. Her interesting, appealing outfits always made him smile, which was something for a guy who was generally indifferent to clothing or fashion.

About to reply with something light and humorous, he remembered Ramon, and the smile abruptly vanished from his face. He also thought about his impossible to predict fiancée. Immediately, he glanced around to make sure she hadn't magically materialized in the next aisle, or sent a spy to keep an eye on his every move. The last thing she'd want to hear is that Rylan and Kady were clandestinely meeting in a liquor store so they could secretly be together. That's how her possessive, distrustful brain seemed to work.

It would take a small eternity for him to adjust to Lorraine's insane thought process. If he ever did. She said he sounded like a paranoid delusional. Rylan wasn't sure about the delusional part, but thanks to Lorraine's berserk set of *what-if* examples, he'd definitely become paranoid.

As feelings of jealousy snaked through his system, Rylan kept his tone cool and aloof. "I'm not a fan of the combination." He nodded toward the mint-mocha flavored Kahlua Kady pointed to. "Perhaps you might want to consider a Latin-type flavor, like this one." With thoughts of Kady and her Antonio Banderas lover, he pointed to the chili-chocolate Kahlua. "I'm sure some men like Latin flavors."

"I suppose." Shrugging, Kady gifted him with one of her bright smiles. "Chili and chocolate is such a popular combination now, in candies and drinks, but I'm not a fan. Is that what you like, Rylan?"

"Me? Chili in my chocolate? Ha! Hell no. Not this guy." He thumbed his chest. "Nope, uh-uh, not me." Turning away, he rolled his eyes. Shit! What kind of stupid, irrational, dumbass comment was *that*? It would have been a perfect opportunity for him to shut the hell up but did he? Nope. Glancing at the bottle of ginger brandy Kady held, he plowed on, seemingly unable to stop himself from being a categorical jerk.

"Planning a special night with your special someone, I see." Appalled, and apparently consumed by jealousy, which he'd never experienced to this extent before, Rylan couldn't believe what was spilling from his mouth.

So this, *this* is what jealousy generates.

"Special someone?" Giving him a strange, teasing look, Kady said, "And who might that be?"

"On second thought, maybe it's a continuation of a special night last night...with that special someone. The ginger brandy will cap off your, ahem, breakfast together, hmm?"

*Omigod, shoot me. Just shoot me right now.* He had to keep his damn mouth shut before Kady had him correctly pegged as an imbecilic asshole.

"My goodness, Rylan..." Kady's beautiful smile had collapsed into a frown, an expression he hadn't seen on her before. He hated himself for being the one responsible for putting it there.

"What in the world are you talking about? Aren't you feeling well?" Kady lifted her free hand. Rylan thought she was about to feel his forehead the way Lorraine had in the restaurant. He'd welcome the feel Kady's skin on his, even if it was only to check his wellbeing. Dropping her hand, she told him, "You look a little green."

Yeah...with envy, he thought.

Moving close enough for him to smell her luscious lavender scent, close enough for him to plant a kiss on her graceful neck, Kady sniffed him.

Cupping her hand to her mouth, she whispered in his ear, "Rylan...are you drunk?"

"Drunk? I haven't had anything to drink. You think I'm drunk because I mentioned your special someone might prefer the chili-chocolate flavor?" At this point Rylan all but gave up wondering why his brain and mouth insisted on rattling off one jackass comment after another.

"Rylan, you really have me confused. I have no clue who you're talking about. Care to fill me in?"

From the sound of her voice as well as her vexed expression, it was clear Kady disliked the accusatory tone of his voice almost as much as Rylan detested it. But thinking about her and her Antonio Banderas, drinking together, talking together—and all the rest they did together, had obviously turned him into a consummate jerk. A real blockhead.

"Hope you have fun," he said before turning on his heel and heading for the cash register. He couldn't wait to get out of there.

"Rylan?"

*Aw hell...*

He heard the sound of her strappy shoes hurrying across the stone floor as she tried catching up to him. He was tempted just to leave the damn Scotch on a shelf and walk out...but that might strike Kady as even odder than he'd already acted toward her.

He couldn't help it. He knew he had no damn right to be jealous, seeing as how he was destined to be attached to Lorraine for the rest of his natural life, and probably in the afterlife as well if she had any say in it. But he *was* jealous just the same. Big time. Enough to turn him into a clod.

"Rylan?" Kady said again, touching his sleeve as she stood behind him in line. "Have I done something to make you angry with me?" She peered around him to look up into his face. Even angry and confused, she looked incredibly kissable. If only he'd followed through at the soiree and had completed that kiss. He knew he'd never get the chance again. If it ever got back to Lorraine that he'd kissed Kady, or even looked like he *wanted* to, she'd make life miserable for Kady...and Kady's chili-chocolate-loving Latin lover.

"Angry?" He lifted an eyebrow, going for one of those arrogant looks the Devingtons did so well. "Why would I be angry? I couldn't care less about what you do or who you see. Your love life is none of my business."

"My...Rylan, really, I don't understand what, or who, you're talking about. I really don't." Wide-eyed, she hugged the bottle of ginger brandy to her chest. "How about enlightening me?"

On the verge of mentioning Ramon Gustavo Taramino, Rylan remembered he was sworn to secrecy—remembered that Kady had confided in Lorraine about her relationship in strict confidence. Giving her a hard glance, he noted she was the picture of innocence, pretending she had no idea what or who he meant. She did such a good job he almost believed her. It was an academy award-worthy performance.

"Yeah," he huffed a humorless laugh, "sure you don't have any idea." Feeling his lip curl into a sneer, he tacked on, "The lady doth protest too much, methinks." After paying for the bottle of Scotch, he said, "Adios, muchacha. See you around," and left as quick as he could.

While walking to his car, he swore under his breath, remembering that Brazilians spoke Portuguese, not Spanish, so he'd just added another dumbass comment to all the rest. No wonder she'd looked at him like he had a few screws loose.

At least he'd accomplished something positive by ensuring that if Lorraine had anyone following him, they'd report to her that Rylan seemed to have zero interest in Kady. Hopefully his sicko fiancée would leave Kady alone now instead of cooking up some vengeful scheme designed to make her suffer.

He loathed the idea of Kady with another man, but at the same time sent up a silent wish that she and the man she loved would be happy together because that's what Kady Malone deserved—regardless of how much the idea irked him.

Running into Kady put a cap on an already stressful morning. Driving Quinn to the airport was like riding in a funeral procession. They were mostly silent during the ride. Quinn told Rylan he'd gone through some of his keepsakes, setting some aside for Saffron so she'd think of him when she saw them.

It was weird and kind of creepy. Almost like Quinn was talking about dying with Saffron being his widow. That was the last damn thing Rylan wanted skipping through his mind right now. It was rare for him to get so uneasy but, hell, when his brother and best friend was headed for a remote area of a foreign country, most likely without them able to be in contact, he decided there was just cause for some anxiety. And, yeah, for the first time he could remember, aside from when he was a kid, Rylan found himself feeling kind of lost and alone.

He and Quinn had always been able to talk about most everything. They'd always been there for each other, helping each other out of multiple jams. So Rylan's first instinct was to tell Quinn every damn thing Lorraine had said to him, all the innuendos, the sarcasm, blackmail and threats. But he couldn't. If he did, he knew Quinn would cancel his flight and rebook it for another day, just so he could help Rylan fix things.

He knew because if the situation was reversed and Quinn was the one in trouble, it's the same thing Rylan would do for his brother.

Not only wouldn't Rylan allow his problems to put a kink in Quinn's extraordinary Medicine Without Boundaries opportunity, he certainly wasn't going to invite Lorraine's wrath upon his brother. While he didn't know how much of what Lorraine threatened was just talk and nothing more, Rylan wasn't willing to gamble with Quinn's career. Quinn had worked too long and hard for everything to come crashing down because of some unstable woman.

He stopped at his apartment before heading for the university and his first class of the day. Oddly enough, one of the students in his environmental science class was named Ramon. Nice kid and a good student. Rylan vowed not to give him the evil eye, just because his name happened to be the same as Kady Malone's Latin lover.

Setting the bag from the liquor store on the kitchen counter, Rylan smiled. He'd never tried drowning his sorrows before. Respected award-winning, professors didn't engage in such weak-willed, unacceptable behavior. But, he decided, there's a first time for everything and tonight seemed like a good night to give it a try.

Since Lorraine had something or other going on with her women's club, that left the evening open for the esteemed professor Kilpatrick to have a date with a bottle of single malt Scotch...and a science fiction romance novel titled *Immortal Among the Stars*, right after he dropped off Quinn's keepsakes at Saffron's place.

# Chapter 19

~<>~

"I KNOW YOU'RE trying to be helpful, Kady," Saffron said, opening her front door, "but if you really want to help, just let me be by myself for a few days, okay? I don't feel like talking about Quinn. I just want to curl up with a good book, or ten, and lose myself in them until I feel like facing the world again."

"I understand completely," Kady said, eyeing her cousin who looked like hell. Her face was puffy, her eyes were swollen to slits and drippy, her nose was red and runny. Her half-matted, half-flyaway hair looked like she'd styled it with an electric whisk. And her voice was nasal and stuffy.

"Now get yourself a sweater or light jacket," Kady instructed, "because it's chilly out there this morning."

Saffron tried to laugh but it came out more like a cough. "Kady, I'm not going anywhere with you. Didn't you hear me? I'm not leaving my condo. I made sure both Sasha and Erin are scheduled and covering for me at the bookshop for the next few days. So please just leave me alone. I'll be fine."

Ignoring her, Kady walked into Saffron's bathroom, returning with a hairbrush. While Saffron groused and flailed, Kady smoothed out the tangled mess until it looked less like she'd been in a windstorm.

"What are you doing?" She tried pushing Kady's hands away. "Stop that, Kady."

Kady returned to the bathroom, then headed for Saffron's coat closet where she yanked out a long, comfy looking cardigan that she threw at Saffron.

"Don't even bother trying to fight with me, Saffy. Not after the shit encounter I've just had with Quinn's asshole brother."

Stilling, Saffron's mouth dropped open. "Whoa, shit and asshole together in the same sentence coming from a woman whose idea of off color language is saying hell? What happened?"

Taking Saffron by the elbow and tugging, Kady said, "I'll tell you in the car. Let's go Sad Sack Saffy."

"Where are we going," Saffron asked, stuffing her arms into the oversized cardigan as they walked to the elevator.

"To get something to eat."

"But you said you were bringing breakfast and coffee."

"I lied."

Tsking, Saffron said, "I can't go out anywhere looking like this."

Shrugging, Kady told her, "You had your chance. I told you in my text to get ready. This," she waved her hand over the frumpy-dumpy pajama-like getup Saffron wore, "is apparently your idea of getting ready."

"My look matches my mood. Seriously, where are you taking me?"

"Someplace you'll feel better."

A few minutes later Kady pulled up to Bekka House, parking in the driveway that already held a few other cars, aside from the ones parked out front.

Her tear-swollen slit eyes opening as wide as possible, Saffron said, "Oh no...is everyone here? Kady, I can't see people today. I told you that. I—"

"Stop your infernal complaining and move your pajama-clad ass out of the car and into the house." Kady reached into the back seat for the brown paper bag holding the ginger brandy.

"I don't know how I feel about your new alpha-personality, Kathleen," Saffron teased, laughter apparent in her tone. "It's belligerent, yet strangely appealing. I'm gonna kill you if the whole clan is gathered inside for a sadness and depression intervention."

"No weapons allowed inside Bekka House," Kady playfully warned.

Saffron laughed again. It was a good sign. If Kady and the others could get Saffron to laugh, she'd feel a lot better soon—whether she wanted to or not.

Before they'd reached the front door, it opened wide, with Astrid running out to greet her niece with a hearty mom hug.

"Oh you poor baby. Come inside. We have food, drink, and we all brought our listening ears so you can tell us all about what happened." Taking inventory of Saffron's appearance as they walked up the steps, Astrid said, "Aw, you look like absolute hell, honey."

"Thanks, Aunt Astrid. Your daughter was kind enough to let me know."

"Cute PJs though." Astrid winked.

Once inside the house a flurry of women gathered around Saffron, with each of them wrapping their arms around her one by one, telling her how much they loved her and how she looked like hell.

Izzy hobbled close, making her way through all the pairs of long legs standing around Saffron to give her own greeting. Kady smiled as she watched Izzy repeat what she'd done in the past, hugging one of Saffron's legs with her paws. That caught Saffron's attention. She bent down to pick Izzy up, holding her close and speaking baby talk while her tears ran freely.

Closing her eyes for a moment, Kady listened to the lovely music filling the space. It was like being carried away on a cloud to a magical, mystical place where difficulties were absent. She'd entrusted Reen to make sure the playlists Kady had selected were playing at the time of Saffron's arrival. She hadn't let Kady down.

This particular playlist Kady created offered a variety of healing sounds, like angelic chants accented by tinkling chimes in the background, and ocean waves with dolphin songs. There was also renaissance-era music, baroque music, Debussy's Clair de lune, and Pachelbel's Canon in D. Each piece was carefully selected by Kady for its calming, relaxing, tranquil qualities.

Complementing the celestial sounds was the incense and scented candles Kady brought to Bekka House early this morning, setting them in the spots she'd deemed perfect for everyone to enjoy their therapeutic scents. The main scent she'd chosen was lavender for its ability to reduce anxiety and depression. Accompanying the lavender was the herbaceous patchouli, to calm the senses, and earthy, warm sandalwood to promote a sense of peace and calm.

Bekka House smelled and sounded simply magnificent.

"Got the ginger brandy?" Astrid asked, snapping Kady out of her reverie. Kady handed the bottle to her mother, who went to the kitchen and was back in two minutes with an oversized mug, handing it to Saffron.

"It's a ginger brandy-spiked chai latte," Astrid told Saffron. "I made a big batch of chai latte that we can heat on the stovetop or microwave as needed—then add the ginger brandy or Baileys...or both, after heating. By the way, did you know the flavors of chai and Baileys complement each other perfectly?" Astrid went on, nodding as she draped an arm around Saffron's shoulder. "Try it sometime. Well, as a matter of fact, we can try it with your next mug of chai."

Kady and the other women glanced at each other, smiling as they listened to Astrid rattle on and on about whatever popped into her head as she strived to take Saffron's mind off what happened with Quinn.

"First take a sip of a plain chai latte, then take a sip of Baileys," Astrid continued. "You'll notice the Baileys tastes nearly identical to the chai latte. It's amazing. And when you mix the two together? Mmm, sheer heaven. Have I mentioned that before, dear?"

"I've probably heard you say the same thing at least sixty times, Aunt Astrid," Saffron chuckled, "but that's okay. I know you're just marathon-talking to make me feel better. I appreciate it. I also appreciate the taste of chai and Baileys together, almost as much as I adore chai with ginger brandy." She took a sip and ahhed. "Delicious. Thanks." She gave Astrid a kiss on the cheek.

"We're all set up for boozy coffee too." Delaney rubbed her hands together. "You'll find all the fixings in the kitchen for that as well." Lifting her own mug, she said, "Mine's got strong coffee, Kahlua, Frangelico and a smidgen of dark rum. I topped it with a splash of cream. Today is clearly not a designated diet day." She laughed.

"Speaking of non-designated diet days," Laila said, gesturing to the huge spread on the long dining table they'd set up with all the leaves, "I brought three types of scones, baked fresh early this morning. I made the triple ginger in your honor, Saffron. Ground ginger," she counted on her fingers, "fresh grated ginger, and chopped candied ginger. There's not a damn thing on this table today that's fat-free, low calorie, or weight conscious because sometimes you just gotta treat yourself to the real deal, you know?"

Everyone murmured their agreement. "And this is one of those times," Laila finished, giving Saffron a hug.

"Definitely." Saffron helped herself to a ginger scone. "Oh...so, so good, Laila. Thank you."

"I've got French toast sticks with freshly made maple butter," Annalise said. "Not just whipped maple, there's real butter whipped in it too." She licked her lips. "And I know you're an omelet lover, Saffron, so in the kitchen," she gestured, "I've set up an omelet station. Whatever you like, I've probably got there. I'll be manning the station so guess that means I'd better be careful about how many liquored-up coffees or lattes I have, otherwise I might start getting too creative." She laughed and pulled Saffron in for a hug.

Kady loved seeing how everyone was overly-chatty and upbeat, determined to keep Saffron from slipping too deep into a depressed state. While they always enjoyed talking about food and drink, they'd turned the volume up to high this morning, with all of them rattling off all matter of food-related discussion. Coming together like this for a cause is what the Malone women and friends did best.

"I baked a batch of Grandma Bekka's pepperkaker," Delaney gestured like a TV gameshow model, "with extra ginger. While the cookies were baking, I had to remind myself I was the one doing the baking each time I got a whiff because the first thing I thought of was—"

"Grandma contacting you all the way from Valhalla," Astrid said with light laughter as Laila nodded in agreement. "I can't tell you how often I sense my mother right there at my side. It's usually when I'm in the kitchen, or right before I close my eyes at night. It's so comforting when I hear her faint tinkle of her laughter, or maybe a whispered word or two."

Wiping tears from her eyes and cheeks, Saffron said, "I can't believe you guys went to all this trouble for me. It's not my birthday or anything. And I haven't done anything to deserve all this very kind attention. I-I used to be so awful to all of you. I'm so ashamed."

Making a raspberry sound, Reen gave a dismissive wave. "You don't have to do anything but just be you, Saffy. The past is the past. We all make mistakes. What's important is that we recognize them, learn from them, and move on to better, brighter horizons. You, my cousin-friend, are one of the best people I know. I love you, Saffy."

Through a flood of new tears, Saffron told Reen, "I love you too, Reenie. Thank you."

"We know how much you must be hurting, Saffron," Delaney added. "We know we can't make the hurt go away, but at least you'll know you have all of us here to love and support you as you go through the worst of it."

"Izzy tells me she understands too." Aladee kneeled next to the little dog, her hands positioned on Izzy's temples. "Izzy felt the same way when she lost her beloved Wolfgang many years ago in the first world war. She said the hurt never completely goes away but it gets easier with time. Plus she added that, unlike her and her German soldier, she feels you and Quinn will see each other again one day. She says I should tell you not to lose hope."

"God, I love that sweet, adorable little dog," Saffron said, with everyone else voicing their agreement.

"Hey there, Saf." Monica Sharp Griffin waddled through the front door, with Sabrina, her husband's sister, at her side.

"Holy Toledo!" Saffron said, mouth agape. "You're huge! I only just saw you two weeks ago and—"

"I know." Monica rubbed her extended belly, smiling down at the protrusion. "It happened just like that." She snapped her fingers. "Time's getting close."

"Should you even be here today?" Saffron asked her.

"I've still got another month or so. And I love you, Saf, and wouldn't miss this loving comfort intervention even if they had to wheel me in here while I was in labor."

"As a mother of six, I wouldn't be so sure about that," Astrid teased.

"She insisted on being here," Sabrina said. "Hud has given me strict instructions to make sure Monica is extra careful and to call him immediately at the first sign of anything out of the ordinary." She laughed. "I've never seen my brother so concerned for another person. Ever."

Monica and the other women laughed. "Hudson's been sooo attentive and sweet," she said. "I'm thinking maybe I should just stay pregnant all the time." She laughed again. "Ooh, feel that?" She grabbed Saffron's hand, placing it on her belly. "The baby's kicking. Isn't that the best thing ever?"

"Wow." They remained silent for a moment while Saffron kept her hand over Monica's baby bump. "I'm so damn happy for you," Saffron said, pulling Monica in as close as she could for a gentle hug once the kicking stopped. "Thank you for being here for me." She glanced around the large room and started crying again. "Thank you all. I swore to Kady that I didn't want to see anyone or even leave the condo today but...I'm awfully glad she wouldn't take no for an answer and bullied me into coming here this morning."

"In case you haven't noticed," Astrid said, "my trusty Kodak Instamatic has not left my tote bag. I know the last thing you probably want right now, sweetie," she said to Saffron, "is your photo-happy aunt snapping pics of you in your PJs, with that puffy pink face."

"Wow, that means you really rate, Saffron," Kady said.

"I will admit my fingers have been a little itchy," Astrid said, which was met with laughter.

"Aunt Astrid?" Saffron said.

"Yes, dear?"

"Do it!" Along with everyone else, Saffron made a series of silly poses, allowing her aunt to gleefully take photo after photo of their gathering.

"Those will be wonderful," Astrid said. "Believe it or not, one day you'll be glad to have a nice remembrance of—"

"Of The Great Saffron Intervention!" Saffron called out with ample laughter, flailing her arms wide. "It will be the perfect reminder of how much we all love each other. Even if I'm red-nosed, swollen, greasy-haired, and pajama-clad, I know I'll love every one of those photos, Aunt Astrid. Thank you."

Wiping happy tears from her eyes, Astrid linked arms with Saffron, leading her to a seat. "Now, my sweet niece, it's time for you to let it all hang out. We want to hear everything you're ready to share. It's best not to hold it in. A good cry, some healing laughter, and a nice, long talk will help. I promise."

During the morning, Saffron talked and cried and talked some more, telling them all of her grief at losing Quinn so soon after finding him. She said he wouldn't allow her to come to the airport to see him off early this morning because it would be too difficult for them both, so they spent the night professing their mutual love and expressing all the words they had inside.

"I must have closed my eyes, ever so briefly," Saffron said, "around three in the morning. I think Quinn was waiting for that because I'm sure that's when he took off. I never heard a peep." She sighed. "He was right, of course, I would have been a blubbering mess, hanging onto his ankles, begging and pleading for him not to go if I'd been there at the airport." She indulged in some teary chuckling.

Saffron told them Rylan had taken his bother to the airport. Quinn gave Rylan instructions about which of his belongings he wanted Saffron to have, like some photos of Quinn as a child, Quinn's first stethoscope, and his first pocket knife, awarded to him when he was in Boy Scouts, along with a few other sentimental items.

"Rylan texted me this morning, shortly before you arrived at my condo, Kady, letting me know he'd be bringing everything by later this evening if that was okay. Speaking of Rylan," Saffron glanced around the table, "did you hear what happened between him and Kady this morning at the liquor store?"

"They didn't," Kady said. "It happened right before I picked you up so I haven't had a chance to tell anyone else yet."

"What happened?" Astrid asked. "Is he very upset about Quinn leaving?"

"Frankly, I have no idea." Kady shrugged. "I suppose so, but Rylan didn't even mention his brother. He just said all these weird kind of nasty things to me, almost like he was accusing me of something, but I have no idea what, other than it seems to have something to do with a man he thinks I'm seeing."

"Ooh, who are you seeing?" Reen asked.

"Do tell," Sabrina said, sitting forward in her seat. "I didn't know there was a new man in your life."

"Me neither." Kady chuckled. "I'm not seeing anyone. That's just it. Rylan gave me kind of a *so long, have a nice life* speech. Really sarcastic, and even angry. It didn't make any sense. I thought he might be drunk but I don't think that was the case."

Both Monica and Astrid said, "Lorraine," at the same time, and Saffron nodded. "Same thing I thought," Saffron agreed.

"Lorraine?" Kady's expression scrunched. "What about her? He didn't mention anything about her."

"I hope you won't mind, Kady." Saffron reached across the table to place her hand over Kady's. "But I told Aunt Astrid about our conversation regarding Lorraine the other day. I shared my suspicions with your mom, who already has plenty of her own suspicious." Astrid nodded at that. "Monica already knows all about this Lorraine stuff because the poor thing has had to listen to me grouse about my sister incessantly."

"Amen," Monica said with a smile.

"Lorraine knows something's up," Saffron said. "And she's putting damage control into motion, the same as she's always done. It's how she manipulates people and situations. Trust me, I've been on the receiving end of her scheming countless times."

"I'm sorry, but I'm totally confused," Kady said. "What is it you think Lorraine knows?"

"You being crazy about Rylan," Saffron told her.

"What?" Kady felt like a neon sign flashing GUILTY just beamed over her head. "I am *not* crazy about Rylan." She slunk down low in her chair. "That's ridiculous. He and my cousin are engaged. I would never, ever do anything to jeopardize their relationship. So if Lorraine is thinking *something's up*, as you say, it's all inside her head because—"

"Exactly." Saffron tapped her temple. "That's what I'm trying to tell you. It's all in her head. I'm betting she said something to Rylan about you that got him rattled for some reason. Probably because he's crazy about you too."

"Oh no." Putting her hands over her ears, Kady shook her head from side to side. "I don't want to hear this. Do you know what kind of awful, terrible person this would make me? Rylan is in love with Lorraine and I am over the moon happy for them both." Looking around the table, she loudly insisted, "Well I am!"

"Aw, you poor thing," Astrid said, giving her daughter a compassionate look.

"What do you think Lorraine might have told Rylan?" Kady's oldest sister, Delaney asked.

"Something about Kady being a bitch, probably," Monica answered. "You'd never believe all the awful things she's done to Saffron over the years. Lorraine just isn't who she seems."

Kady had heard that several times now from different people.

"Lorraine is cruel and vindictive...and," Monica gave Saffron a contrite look, "I'm sorry, Saf, but your sister has some serious problems." She tapped her temple.

"The lady doth protest too much, methinks," Kady muttered, suddenly remembering Rylan saying that to her during their strange conversation, if you could call it that.

"I didn't think you were a Shakespeare fan, honey," Astrid said.

"I had no idea it was Shakespeare." Kady chuckled at her own lack of knowledge about one of the great playwrights—especially when she owned a bookshop that had several of his volumes on the shelves.

"From Hamlet." Astrid nodded. "Does that have some special significance?"

"No idea." Kady's shoulder lifted. "It's something Rylan said to me this morning. It had to do with me and some other man, I think."

"Knowing my sister," Saffron said, "I'll bet Lorraine planted a lie in Rylan's mind about Kady being involved with someone else so he'd forget about her."

"Oh, Saffron, I really don't think Lorraine would do something like that," Kady said, only to hear a collective groan of disbelief, apparently at her naïveté.

"Thirty-something and she's still such a babe in the woods," Delaney said.

"I am not!" Kady protested.

"Everyone's always good and kind in Kady Land," Laila said, batting her eyelashes.

"Kady's our walking-talking Pollyanna, always seeing the good in everyone," Reen said.

"That's my sweet, trusting little sunshine girl," Astrid said.

"Um, hello?" Kady laughed. "I'm sitting right here, you know. I can hear you all. You're talking about me like it's my eulogy or something. I haven't croaked yet, guys."

With an audible gasp, Astrid said, "Hush, Kady. I don't want to hear that kind of talk from one of my children."

Every so often Kady enjoyed shaking everyone up by engaging in a bit of unexpected wickedness, designed to get a laugh or break the tension.

With her best guiltless expression in place, Kady said, "Gee, Mom, you make it sound like I just called you guys motherfuckers."

All wide eyes were on Kady as the women joined in communal gasps and laughter at Kady's startling declaration. Sisters Annalise and Sabrina both had chai latte spraying out of their noses, while Laila choked on one of her scones and Delaney clapped her hard on the back, collapsing with laughter and nearly choking herself.

Aladee spread her hands over her mouth, sitting back in her chair and laughing so hard tears streamed down her cheeks until...her wings suddenly popped open, causing a sharp intake of breath around the table. A few of the people at the table hadn't yet witnessed the nymph's wing's opening and spreading, so there was a real sense of awe.

"Oops! Sorry," Aladee said. "It's Kady's fault for making me laugh so hard."

"Kathleen Doolan Malone, shame on you!" Astrid chastised, wagging a reprimanding finger but failing to keep a straight face. Soon she was laughing harder than anyone else.

Still laughing, Reen leapt from her seat shouting, "Omigod, I have to pee!" and running out of the room.

Reen wasn't the only one making her way to the bathroom. Monica struggled to her feet, waddling toward the first floor powder room, saying, "Yes, shame on you, Kady. Pregnant women eight months along already have a hard enough time as it is, making it to the bathroom in time, much less when they're laughing this hard. You'd better hurry up, Reen," she called to Reen's back, "I've really got to go!"

Turning quickly, just before making it to the bathroom, Reen headed for the staircase, growling as she raced upstairs to one of the second floor bathrooms. "Go, Monica! It's all yours!" she yelled before disappearing.

Kady smiled wide. Mission accomplished. There was relaxation, smiles, laughter, and friendly chitchatting all around, just as it should be. She loved being surrounded by laughter because it increased and released endorphins, the body's natural feel-good chemicals. Happily, her surprise off-color statement caught them all off guard, including Saffron, who laughed right along with the rest until tears flowed down her cheeks—happy tears this time.

Kady was elated to see Saffron already looking better. Tears of sadness weren't as frequent. One good thing stemming from their gathering and conversation this morning is that it helped take Saffron's mind off the heartbreaking situation with Quinn.

It had been months since they'd all gathered together like this. The last time was when Kady and Saffron announced they'd become business partners in Cherished Pages, and Kady had introduced her darling Izzy to everyone.

Speaking of Izzy, the little psychic dog lapped up all the laughter and positive vibes. Kady honestly couldn't imagine life without her beloved little bocker. She'd truly become a member of the family.

After more upbeat conversation, Kady noticed Astrid fidgeting in her seat and looking quite serious. "You okay, Mom?" Kady asked her quietly, and Astrid nodded, patting Kady's hand.

"Saffron, dear," Astrid said nervously nibbling her bottom lip, "I'm going to take a chance and tell you something I probably shouldn't. Something negative. It's about your mom..."

# Chapter 20

"IT'S OKAY, Aunt Astrid, go ahead," Saffron said. "Please. You've known my mother a lot longer than I have. If something about her can shed light on what's happening with Rylan and Lorraine, tell me. I know how she is, believe me, so there's not much that would surprise me. I mean, look how my mother has been to her own son."

"Well..." Astrid indulged in a lengthy sigh, "your sister, Lorraine, is very much like her mother. I remember Sean, my late first husband," she explained for the few at the table who weren't aware, "telling me about the vindictive things Colleen did to him when they were growing up. Colleen had resorted to blackmail and threats to keep Sean in line. He said much of it was just hot air but some things Colleen came up with really gave him pause, making him afraid she'd do something terrible to hurt him or someone he cared about."

"My brother and I suspected as much," Saffron said. "When we were young, Red and I used to talk about how it was almost like he and I were adopted because we were so unlike our parents, or our sister. In fact," Saffron chuckled, "Red and I always hoped that one day our real parents would come rescue us and take us away to live happily ever after. Oh..." Saffron's eyes grew wide as her hand clutched her necklace pendant. "Is that what you want to tell me? I'm adopted?"

"No, honey." Astrid gave her niece a sweet smile. "I know for a fact that Collen carried both you and your brother herself so I'm afraid there won't be anyone riding up on a white charger to carry you off and save the day." She looked apologetic.

"Too bad." Saffron chuckled. "Well the good news is that my brother got his well-deserved happily ever after. And maybe one day I will too."

"You will, sweetheart, I'm sure of it," Astrid assured her.

"Tell Saffron what Dad told me and Gard about when he and Aunt Colleen were kids," Delaney said. "I mean the stuff she used to do to win arguments."

"Oh..." Astrid wrinkled her nose. "I don't know, Delaney..."

"It's okay, Mom," Delaney encouraged, "you can tell Saffron."

Kady had no clue what Delaney was talking about and from the looks on everyone else's faces, neither did they. Delaney and Gard were the oldest of the six siblings and the only two who really remembered much about their father, Sean, because he died when the rest of them were quite young.

"I don't think that's a good idea, honey," Astrid said and Delaney rolled her eyes.

"Well whatever it is I have to know now!" Saffron laughed.

"Well if Mom's not going to tell you, I will." Delaney sat forward in her chair. "Once when Gard and I were little and had a fight about something or other," her hand flit through the air, "Dad sat us down and told us what sometimes happened when he and his sister, Aunt Colleen, were kids. It was one of those parental lesson-type talks about what can happen when brothers and sisters allow things to go too far."

All eyes were on Delaney as she shared her memory.

"When Dad and Aunt Colleen fought, she'd always blame him for everything, even when she was the instigator. She'd used to physically hurt herself, giving herself a bruise or some scratches, even cutting herself, then show her injuries to their parents as *proof*," Delaney used air quotes, "of what Dad had done to her and that he was responsible."

"Whoa!" Kady said, exchanging hard glances with Saffron, who gave a slow, confirming nod.

"What's whoa?" Reen asked. "What's that surprised look all about?" She mimicked their expressions.

"Saffron told me Lorraine used to do the same thing to her and Red when they were kids," Kady said. "To get them in trouble. She'd hit herself hard with a hairbrush handle until welts appeared."

"Sometimes Lorraine would use a wire coat hanger or," Saffron shuddered, "I remember one time she used one of her Barbie dolls to claw herself."

"Oh good grief, that's awful," Astrid muttered. "Well, abuse often begets abuse. Sean said both he and Colleen were beaten by their mother with whatever she had handy at the time, like the vacuum cleaner pipe, a wooden spoon, or a pancake turner. Their father, Seamus, generally used his leather belt. We're not talking about a little light hitting, we're talking about welts and deep bruises."

"Wow," Reen and Laila chorused.

"That's what a lot of families did then back then," Astrid said. "People who came here from *the old country*," she hooked quotes around that, "saw spanking and other physical punishment as being good parents."

"Too many still do." Monica caressed her baby bump. "My mom and dad raised us like that too. This little one," she looked down at her belly, rounding her hands over it, "will never know any physical abuse. Just lots and lots of love."

"None of our grandparents ever hit us," Laila noted. "Did they, Mom? Maybe I just can't remember."

"No, they never did," Astrid confirmed, sipping from her liqueur-laced coffee. "They were all model grandparents, Sean's father, Seamus, included. He was actually a wonderful man. All you kids loved your Grandpa Seamus, and I couldn't have asked for a better father-in-law. He and his wife were strict, old world Irish Catholics who would, as they said, *put the fear of God*, into their children when they needed it."

"I think my brother, Murphy, and I are half human and half fear of God," Monica noted with a laugh.

"Holy shit," Annalise said absently, covering her mouth and offering an apologetic, "Oops!" for what slipped out. "We never got anything like that from our parents."

Her sister, Sabrina, nodded. "All we got was a light slap on the hand to warn us not to touch a hot pan or an electrical outlet."

The worst they did," Annalise said, "was a fairly gentle hand-whack on the butt. It was more of a cautioning than something meant to hurt."

"Saffron," Astrid said, "did you, um, did you know your father was married before?"

"Yes. He didn't tell us much other than she died before he met and married our mother."

"Eh...not exactly. The first Mrs. Devington didn't die," Astrid told her, getting a raised eyebrow response from Saffron. "They were either divorced or the marriage was annulled. I'm not sure of the particulars. What I do know, because Colleen bragged about it to my husband, is that Walter paid his first wife off. He wrote her a hefty check. They broke up because your mom—"

"Oh brother..." Saffron huffed a humorless laugh. "Don't tell me. My mother broke up their marriage to get my father for herself."

"That's what Sean told me." Astrid's head bobbed. "Colleen was so proud of herself because, coming from a working class Irish family, she had to use considerable wiles, including some crafty blackmailing, to pull that off. Colleen Malone wasn't in the same league as Walter Devington. She studied everything about your father's life, social circle, and his first wife. Then she went to work on the first wife, as well as Walter, until Walter came to believe his first wife was a conniving gold digger, after the Devington wealth, when in fact—"

"My mother was the gold digger." Saffron nodded. "That explains so much. I can't wait until I can talk to Red about it."

"I'm truly sorry if what I said hurt you, honey," Astrid said. "I probably should have kept it to myself, especially with everything else you're going through right now."

"On the contrary, Aunt Astrid, I'm really glad you told me. I mean it."

Kady sensed that Saffron was genuine in her response. They'd talked many times about both Colleen and Lorraine, so Kady knew firsthand that nothing Astrid had revealed came as much of a surprise to Saffron, other than Walter's first wife being alive.

Kady also sensed that Astrid had purposely chosen this time to tell Saffron about her mother to provide a distraction from her grieving for her lost relationship with Quinn. It was unusual for Astrid to come out with such eye-opening information purely out of the blue. No, it was a carefully calculated decision on Astrid's part, designed to help heal rather than hurt.

Kady and her sisters had so often agreed that the best they could hope to attain in this life was to be as wonderful as their mom.

"What you told me substantiates so many of Red's and my suspicions," Saffron told Astrid. "We used to believe we were bad children for thinking bad things about our mother, often because she told us so herself. But now that I know it wasn't us, it was her, it makes it much easier for me. I know Red will feel the same way. I wish there was an easy way to contact him."

"I can get a message to him," Aladee said. "Using something we nymphs call *Nymph Mail.*" She laughed when she saw some odd looks around the table. "That's not the actual name, it's just something the other earthbound nymphs and I came up with. The actual name is..."

Aladee proceeded to speak in a foreign language, well not so much *speak*, it was more like *utter* an otherworldly sound, one Kady had never heard before. It was mysteriously beautiful, like what she'd expect to hear from angels singing. Once Aladee finished voicing the sound, she smiled at the awed expressions around the table, including Izzy's, who'd come to sit next to Aladee's chair, gazing up at her.

"That was beautiful," Astrid said. "What was that?"

"It was like it came right from heaven," Saffron said.

"The language of nymphs. It's called *Neonsolaya*," Aladee replied. "Our language is comprised of sounds humans are incapable of making because of a difference in the construction of our vocal chords. Some of the sounds are inaudible to the human ear, but certain creatures, like dogs, can hear them." She reached down, ruffling Izzy's fur. "Now you see why we just call it Nymph Mail."

"How cool is that!" Reen said.

"I can't give you an exact temperature," Aladee replied, taking Reen literally. "But I believe it's approximately the same as when I speak English."

At the sound of light tittering laughter, Aladee laughed as well. "Ahhh...it seems I have yet another bit of Earth slang to learn, hmm?" Reen gave her a short, simple explanation of the term before Aladee continued.

"We nymphs here on Earth are able to make contact telepathically with the nymphs who are still on Mount Olympus if we need to reach someone there. They can contact us the same way. So if you ever need to get in touch with Red, let me know. Messages can then be sent by MOC, Mount Olympus Courier." With a grin, Aladee finished by adding, "How cool is that?"

"Very cool!" Reen answered with a bright smile.

"It's kind of hilarious and wonderful at the same time," Saffron said. "You and I will definitely be having a talk later, Aladee."

It was wonderful seeing Saffron in better spirits. Initially, Kady felt bad about dragging her out when all Saffron wanted to do was stay at home, wallowing in her heartache. But her intuition told her the best thing for Saffron today was to be around people she loved, who loved her. Fortunately, her psychic insight was spot on.

They talked a while longer about the Devington and Malone families, as well as Quinn working in Nigeria with the Medicine Without Boundaries organization. Saffron said Quinn told her that being a part of MWB is something he'd long been hoping for. He was elated when they invited him to participate in the prestigious, award-winning program.

Something nagged at Kady. For some reason she couldn't understand, her psychic sense urged her to look into the MWB organization, telling her she'd find answers there. Answers to what—she had no idea, but Googling was definitely on her agenda for later this evening because her heartwish ring's stone had glowed with its blue light when the sense overtook Kady. Sooner or later she'd discover why she was meant to learn more about it.

Everyone present pitched in to make Saffron feel as loved, supported, and encouraged as possible. There was such tremendous unconditional love infusing the room that it became palpable for Kady. As a psychic, she could physically feel the magnificent outpouring of love and concern encompassing them, with Saffron at the core. The sensation was incredibly fulfilling.

Turning to Kady, Astrid said, "You haven't mentioned your heartwish for quite a while now. Have you been giving it some thought?"

"I have," Kady said, aware she hadn't really given her heartwish the attention it deserved. So much had been happening around her, including the mind-muddling problem of her misplaced preoccupation with Rylan Kilpatrick. But it wasn't a major concern because she'd known all along what she'd wish for.

"It's always been my intention to form a heartwish designed to make things right with Red, his parents and Lorraine," Kady answered. "I just have to figure out how best to word it so it covers everything."

"That's going to be one monumental heartwish," Reen said, shaking her head back and forth, "considering the depth of intolerance and narrow-mindedness involved."

"That's why I've been stalling," Kady said. "I know I need to phrase everything just right so it successfully fixes the issues and brings our families together, stronger than ever."

"Not that I really know much about the heartwishes," Saffron admitted, "other than the incredible miracle Reen put into motion with her beautiful, unselfish wish, but..." She paused, worrying her bottom lip as she looked at Kady. "But maybe you might want to focus on yourself and your own happiness instead of everyone else's—which you always seem to do, Kady. I honestly don't see how a ring can magically repair the complexities involved with Red. Besides," Saffron shrugged, "my brother is happier now than he's ever been."

"Complexities indeed," Astrid said. "Saffron is right. Think of yourself for a change, Kady, and make a wish that will bring you great happiness and satisfaction."

Kady said honestly, "I have my dream bookshop, my own little apartment, and the best business partner," she smiled at Saffron, "family, and friends I could hope for. I'm already happy and satisfied." As thoughts of Rylan intruded, Kady strived to push them to the back of her mind. Rylan had absolutely nothing to do with any heartwish she'd make.

"When I had the ring," Laila said, "it was like an instant knowing came over me, and I immediately knew exactly what I needed to wish for. Have you felt anything like that yet? With all those psychic insights you get, I'd imagine you'd have a powerful sense of knowing."

"It was the same for me," Delaney said, with Reen echoing her agreement. "The ring seemed to tune into what was already in my heart, making it crystal clear to me."

Gazing into the distance, Kady smiled at the question. She'd heard that from her sisters before, so she'd been waiting for something like that to happen. Some special knowing she'd be attuned to.

She was still waiting.

It was so odd the way she could zero in on others using her psychic abilities, but her insight seemed to fail her when Kady herself was the intended target.

"No, I haven't had that experience yet. It's one of the reasons I've been waiting to make my wish. I'm hoping for some sort of otherworldly guidance to help. I've tried talking to Grandma Bekka, but haven't received any signs or communication from her. Sometimes I do smell her pepperkaker baking, and I take that as a positive sign, but as far as inspiration or direction about my wish, there's been nothing."

She figured her mind had probably been too cluttered with thoughts of Rylan for her to fully focus on the wish she had to make. So much had happened in such a short time and she was feeling a little overloaded. She'd already decided to spend this evening composing her wish, wording it just right so it touched all the bases it needed to in order to achieve what Kady had in mind.

For some reason though...Kady's psychic sense kept telling her that the wish she'd planned wasn't the right one. That made things difficult.

Looking around the room from one woman to the next, this love-saturated room at the heart of Bekka House where the women she loved and respected more than any others in this world gathered together, Kady received a special, specific sense of knowing about several of them, foggy insight into a few others, and nothing for the rest.

She knew, for instance, that Reen would have good news for everyone soon. But Kady certainly wouldn't spoil anything because Reen didn't even know herself yet that she was pregnant. She'd been such a wonderful, loving stepmom to Drake's twins, and would make a fabulous mother to her biological child as well. Kady knew it would be a boy they'd name Sean Samuel Slattery, in honor of Reen's father and Drake's. Why she could so easily zero in on this very specific information was a complete unknown to her.

Then there was Annalise. Kady's insight was choppy on this one. She only knew there'd be a love interest on the horizon for her good friend soon. The knowing stopped there.

Next, Kady envisioned that her brother Gard's wife, Sabrina, was on the verge of making a major splash in the art community. She could feel an incredible sense of fulfilment and accomplishment on the horizon for Sabrina, which would include viral social media posts, as well as write-ups in local and national news. It was so well deserved. Sabrina was immensely talented and wholeheartedly deserved recognition and respect as a skilled artist.

Delaney, also was on the precipice of something sensational, regarding her writing. Her popular, wonderfully relatable and funny *Delaney's Diary* column and books would soon be drawing media attention, as well as a TV or movie offer.

The last fairly clear insight Kady had concerned her mother. She knew Astrid had a fascinating story to share with the family concerning Grandma Bekka. Kady couldn't tell what it was, only that it would be something quite astonishing.

There were other, cloudier and less explicit insights she'd received about others gathered here—fortunately nothing negative. No deaths or losses she could detect, aside from Saffron's loss...although Kady's psychic sense told to expect a positive outcome for Saffron's situation. Nothing would make Kady happier, but it wasn't her place to say anything to Saffron—or any of the others.

First of all, while Kady's insights were usually incredibly accurate, there were often signs that she misread, or perhaps something a person did in the interim might alter what Kady had sensed, How awful would it be for her to tell Saffron all would be well if Kady happened to be mistaken? Saffron would be crushed all over again.

Kady also chose not to reveal any of what she'd sensed because she felt, deep inside, that it was best for each person to discover their good news themselves. Kady eagerly blabbing to them about what she sensed would happen could rob them of that delicious moment of excitement.

She'd often wondered why she never received any insights about her own life. Kady supposed it was like the lottery. People often doubted psychics were genuine because they didn't successfully predict this or that, or because they don't win the lottery or other financial-related awards.

While Kady knew there were hordes of fake, scamming, unscrupulous so-called psychics bilking people out of money and belongings, she also knew that if true psychics could see and select winning lottery numbers for themselves, they'd be in danger of losing their sense of kind, sympathetic, helpful objectivity, and be concerned only with their own financial gain.

Interestingly, there was one person not present here today that Kady had received a rather clear inner knowing about. Lorraine Devington. The insight was strong but vague, merely telling Kady that Lorraine would be at the center of an important, major life-changing event soon. That's all Kady knew, the rest was purely conjecture on her part. She guessed it had to do with Lorraine's relationship with Rylan. She'd probably be Professor Kilpatrick's wife soon.

# Chapter 21

~<>~

"OKAY, THIS IS everything." Rylan set the medium sized box on the coffee table where Saffron had indicated. "Quinn's football trophy probably accounts for most of the weight." He smiled at the thought of his brother's prized award. "That trophy has always been his pride and joy, so the fact that he wants you to have it speaks reams. Trust me, Saffron, a guy doesn't hand over his high school MVP trophy to just anyone."

"Thanks for saying that, Rylan." Saffron gave him a friendly hug. "It really makes me feel good. I promise to treasure it and give it a place of honor in my condo. I appreciate you bringing Quinn's keepsakes over. Have a seat," she motioned toward a large gray tweed armchair, "and I'll get us something to drink. What would you like? I've got a fairly well-stocked bar."

"Just some sparkling water, if you have it," Rylan told her. The last thing he needed was alcohol with his after dinner treat waiting for him at home. "I can only stay for a short time. I've got class assignments to catch up on."

And a bottle of single malt Scotch calling his name.

"Lemon-lime or black cherry," Saffron asked. "You're free to go right after we finish our discussion."

"Lemon-lime." Rylan laughed as Saffron headed for the kitchen. "Having someone fire off a bunch of questions in an accusatory manner isn't my idea of a conversation, Saffron," he called after her.

"That's not fair," she said from behind the open refrigerator door. "I never accused you of anything. I'm merely looking for some answers, that's all. So, if I recall, we were talking about your interest in my cousin."

"No, *we*," Rylan pointed back and forth as Saffron came back into the living room, "weren't talking about that. You were. So I'll say it once again, because apparently you didn't hear me the first time." He added some levity so she wouldn't think he was angry. "You're mistaken, Saffron. I have no interest in Kady. None at all," he insisted, accepting the can of sparkling water she offered him and popping the top.

"The only woman I have eyes for is my beautiful fiancée, Lorraine. We're deeply in love and looking forward to getting married in a few months." He hoped the words didn't sound as empty to Saffron as they did to his own ears. "After the wedding we'll live in your uncle's little country house and—"

"Palatial estate," Saffron corrected him, nibbling on one of the sesame sticks she'd set before them in a small bowl.

"Estate," he amended with a groan as his eyes closed in a lengthy blink. Damn, living on her uncle's property was the last thing Rylan wanted. No, that's not true. The last thing he wanted was Lorraine...but evidently there wasn't a damn thing he could do about that. "I'll have a nice oak-paneled office," he told Saffron, "where I can develop assignments for my classes and work on—"

"Your science fiction novels?"

"I, uh, I'll probably be putting my writing on the back burner for a while. Until Lorraine and I get settled." If Lorraine had her way, he knew he'd never add another damn word to his nearly-completed manuscript, and it would never see the light of day. Unless he published it surreptitiously under a private pen name.

"It'll be ideal, Saffron. I'll enjoy being out in the country, and Lorraine will have the full staff she's used to. Best of both worlds, right? I'll split my time between Pacific Northwest University and Wisdom Harbor University until I segue into working fulltime for PNU. Sounds great, huh? We'll be very happy." Just thinking about the carefully planned future Lorraine had laid out for him made Rylan want to stab himself in the eye.

"Bullshit." Saffron folded her arms across her chest.

Half-choking on his sparkling water, Rylan coughed out, "Excuse me?"

"Oh for heaven's sake, Rylan, you sound like a damn robot carefully programmed by the Devingtons to say just the right thing at just the right time. Only an idiot would believe a word you're saying about your supposed undying love for my sister and your blissful happily ever after. And I'm no idiot."

"It's been a long hard day," he countered, tamping down his frustration and annoyance that she'd so easily pegged him. Was he really that transparent? "Starting with taking my brother to the airport so early, before heading to my first class. I'm overtired and, yeah, kind of blue about Quinn being gone. That's why I may not sound as enthused or on board as I would normally."

*Normally.* There's a word that no longer applied to Rylan's life. Nothing about his life would ever be normal again if Lorraine had anything to say about it. Saffron had no idea how spot on she was about his robotic soliloquy regarding his professed love for her sister. It turned Rylan's stomach to think of faking a happy life with the devious Lorraine Devington, pretending, for the express benefit of her family and friends, that he was head over heels in love.

Normal to Rylan was what he felt for Kady the night of Lorraine's soiree. It was the only normal, enjoyable sensation that came out of that silly party of hers.

He remembered noticing how the moonbeams danced through the trees that evening, spreading a glowing pattern over the grounds of Devington Manor. There Kady sat, on the window seat of Red's old room, moonlight sparkling over her coppery hair. Funny, he'd never been a romantic, so attaching those particular words to what he saw still surprised him. But then, everything he'd noticed and felt since meeting Kady Malone had taken him by surprise.

Itching to get the subject of Kady off his mind as well as Saffron's, Rylan asked, "So tell me, how are you doing, Saffron? I'm sure saying goodbye to Quinn wasn't easy for you. If it makes you feel any better, Quinn told me how hard it was for him to get on that plane this morning. He told me he loves you very much."

"Oh..." He hated seeing Saffron's eyes fill with tears as she gave him a sweet smile. "That's nice to hear." The last thing he wanted to do was make her cry. He had no clue how to make her feel better if she started bawling. A crying woman was one of the most difficult thing guys had to deal with.

Blinking back unshed tears, she said, "Let's just say that as of right now I can't imagine the pain and grief ever subsiding, although I'm sure it will...eventually." Saffron took in a deep breath, expelling it with a noisy whoosh. "Ours was a true whirlwind romance. Falling for your brother, especially that quick, was the last thing I ever expected and, according to Quinn, about the furthest thing from his mind too."

Rylan chuckled, remembering his brother's words during their drive to the airport. "That's about exactly what Quinn told me too. He said love came out of nowhere and hit him like a ton of bricks."

Looking wistful, Saffron said, "I guess there's nothing planned, organized, or even logical about the who, what, where and why of falling in love." Angling her head, she asked, "Wouldn't you agree, Rylan?"

"Oh yeah." Rylan bobbed his head. "Right. Sure."

"Uh-huh, so then tell me...why did you act like such an asshole when you saw Kady in the liquor store this morning?" She nailed him with a gotcha look.

He felt his face flush with color. "I don't know what you mean or what Kady told you, Saffron but I—"

"Well, Kady told me what you said to her," Saffron informed with an insincere smile. "And, honestly, you sounded like a real dick, Rylan. What was that all about?"

She caught him off guard. Rylan's initial instinct was to laugh because hearing such salty language from Saffron was unexpected. But this was too serious to laugh about. He had to play it cool so Saffron wouldn't get suspicious.

"I'm suspicious," she said, and now Rylan couldn't help chuckling. Planting her hands against her hips, Saffron said, "You think this is funny? I'm not trying to be funny here, Rylan. I'm looking for answers."

Clearing his throat, Rylan said, "Sorry." It was better than telling her he was laughing because it was like she was inside his head, reading his thoughts. "But I have no idea what answers you're looking for, and no clue why you're suspicious about anything. One minute you're talking about the who, what, where and why of falling in love, the next instant you're badgering me for some unrelated reason. In case you've forgotten, Kady and I aren't in love. I'm in love with," the bile rose in his throat and he swallowed hard, "your sister, Lorraine."

"Look, Rylan," Saffron's stance relaxed and her arms dropped to her sides, "you seem like a nice guy. You wonder why I'm suspicious. It's because I can only assume your sudden uncharacteristic Mister A-Hole demeanor is due to something Lorraine said, or something she's holding over you. My sister excels at that." Her smile was sympathetic.

It sounded like she knew. Of course she did. Why wouldn't she? Saffron and Lorraine were sisters. Aside from the usual sibling squabbles, Saffron had probably suffered numerous trials and tribulations because of Lorraine screwing her over all during their childhood.

Soundly tempted to open up to Saffron, Rylan couldn't. He wouldn't risk Saffron or Quinn getting hurt because Rylan had to go whining about all the shit Lorraine had threatened him with. He still had no idea just how lethal, or how hollow, Lorraine' threats of blackmail were. Better to be cautious and keep his mouth shut, rather than burdening either of them and taking the prize for Asshole of the Year.

"Are you going to say anything or just sit there giving me the silent treatment?" Saffron asked, making him realize he never responded to her suspicion that Lorraine was holding something over him. He liked Saffron and knew she was just trying to help. She didn't deserve him sitting there like an uncommunicative jerk, especially when she was feeling sad and depressed about Quinn.

He supposed he *could* share one particular tidbit of information with Saffron, just to get her off his back and keep her from nagging him about Kady. It might help her to understand why he'd been less than cordial to Kady this morning. She'd have to swear not to reveal what he was about to share with her because if Lorraine found out, she'd crucify him, and make life miserable for Kady.

"I apologize. I do have something on my mind," he told Saffron. "It's something Lorraine told me. Something I didn't expect and it threw me off kilter." Rylan scratched the back of his head. "Maybe upset me a little. If Lorraine finds out I said anything, she'll...well, she'd be angry." It was a more genteel way of saying Lorraine would clamp his balls in a vice and keep turning that lever until they burst.

"Lorraine had a slip of the tongue," Rylan said. "She accidentally told me something that Kady told her in strictest confidence and—"

"Nope."

Rylan's brow furrowed. "What do you mean, nope? You don't even know what I was going to say yet."

"It doesn't matter. My sister doesn't have accidental slips of the tongue Rylan. I guarantee that whatever she told you was planned and calculated, down to the nth degree. So go ahead and tell me." Rolling her eyes skyward, she made a cross over her heart. "I cross my heart and hope to die that I will not spill the beans to Lorraine. Is that good enough?" Her frustrated expression almost had him laughing again.

"Good enough." Rylan grinned. "Since you and Kady are close, you probably know about this already anyway, even if she doesn't want anyone else to know her secret."

"Secret?" Saffron's expression transformed from concerned to elated. "You mean Kady's expecting?"

"Expecting what?"

Saffron looked at him like he was a moron. "A baby, you big dolt. Is that Kady's secret? She's pregnant? Oh my gosh...you and Kady?" She bounced in her seat.

"What? Whoa, no!" Lifting both hands in surrender, Rylan repeated, "No! That's crazy, Saffron. Unlike her and her Antonio Banderas lookalike, Kady and I have never danced in the sheets. So, if she *is* pregnant, I have no idea. I mean," he shrugged, "she very well could be, but if she is, it's—"

Saffron's monumental groan interrupted his rambling. "Good God in heaven, Rylan, what on earth are you jabbering about? Spit it out, will you? You're rambling on and on and saying absolutely nothing. Just like my mother."

"Ouch." Rylan clasped his chest. "That hurt, Saffron."

"Ha-ha, very funny. Will you please get to the point and tell me the damn secret before I expire from old age? You're making me crazy here."

"Okay, okay..." He patted the air in a comforting motion. "It's about Ramon." His eyes closed in a long blink. Just thinking about the guy made him want to reach for the antacids to squelch the burn. "Ramon Gustavo Taramino." Yes, he had the guy's name committed to memory.

"Ramon?" Saffron gave him a curious look. "Kady absolutely adores him."

"Yeah." Rylan nodded. "So I've been told."

"I adore him too. He's such a darling. So charming. Everything he says in that deep Brazilian accent of his comes out sounding captivating. Makes him sound like a sexy Latin lover, even if he's just talking about trimming rose bushes." She laughed before her eyebrows arrowed down. "Wait...why would you get upset about something Lorraine said about Ramon? Oh no, he's not ill, is he?"

"I have no idea. But it sounds like you know him well, which means Kady's told you about the two of them."

"The two of who? Rylan you're not making any sense."

"Yes I am. You're not listening. I'm talking about them," Rylan said, twirling his finger in place, "Kady and Ramon." The way Saffron looked at him told Rylan she probably didn't know about it after all. "Look, I'm sorry if Kady hasn't taken you into her confidence about them being together but remember, you promised not to say anything. You'll make a lot of trouble for Kady if you do. Plus, Lorraine will have my hide for saying anything to you about them being lovers."

"Lovers...Kady and Ramon?" In an instant, the living room rang with Saffron's boisterous laughter. "My sister told you that? Lorraine told you Kady and Ramon are—" Another burst of laughter interrupted what she was about to say. "Oh this is just too rich."

Folding his arms across his chest while crossing an ankle over his knee, Rylan said, "Apparently there's more to this than meets the eye. What, pray tell, is so damned hilarious about your cousin and her Latin lover doing the horizontal mambo and keeping their relationship a secret from Kady's family?"

"Oh, Rylan, please...stop." Arms crossed over her belly now, Saffron kept laughing. "You're killing me with this stuff. Kady and Ramon doing the horizontal mambo." Her laughter grew more raucous.

Maybe Saffron wasn't as nice a person as Rylan had originally thought. As feelings of annoyance rose within, he said, "Saffron, I don't appreciate—"

"You poor big dopey, gullible, lovesick man." Her bout of laughter finally slowing, Saffron wiped the tears from her eyes. "She gazed at him with an odd combo of pity and absurdity while shaking her head from side to side. "I have no idea why my sister chose poor Ramon for her latest bit of propaganda. Lorraine doesn't even like him."

Rylan huffed a humorless laugh. "She's probably jealous that a guy who looks like Antonio Banderas prefers Kady instead of her for a lover."

Holding up her hand, fingers spread in a stop gesture, Saffron doubled over with laughter this time. "I told you to stop, Rylan. Seriously! For heaven's sake, Ramon Gustavo Taramino just celebrated his eighty-fifth birthday. And Lorraine dislikes him because he used to reprimand her for purposely chopping up the rose bushes he'd carefully manicured."

With a horrified look, Rylan said, "Kady's sleeping with a man old enough to be her great-grandfather?"

"No!" Saffron called out loud enough to interrupt the downward spiral of his thoughts. "For heaven's sake, Rylan, listen to me. Ramon was Devington Manor's head landscaper, their gardener, until he retired about ten years ago. He lives in that cute little ocean-front retirement village off Ocean Charm Boulevard now."

"I don't understand." Rylan's head throbbed with what could only be described as a classic Lorraine-style headache.

"I guarantee you that, while Ramon has always been, and still is, a handsome man, he and Kady have never done the mambo, either horizontally or vertically. Kady and I love the sweet old man like a grandpa. Nothing more."

"Holy shit, I don't believe it." Resting his elbows on his knees, Rylan bent, massaging his temples. "I mean, I do believe it, but I can't. Sorry, I know I'm not making any sense."

"Under the circumstances, you're making perfect sense," she assured.

His head still hanging low and cupped in his hands, he said, "What I don't get is, why would Lorraine make up a story about them being secret lovers? She had this whole elaborate tale laid out, Saffron. What's her logic behind this?"

"My first guess is she's afraid of losing you to Kady." Her shoulder hiked in a shrug. "Threats are my sister's forte. It's how she manipulates and controls people. You must have said or done something that didn't sit well with her and she's making a last ditch attempt to keep you in line. Am I on the right track?"

"Not only the right track, you're at home base. Since my talk with your sister, I've been operating under a litany of threats, Saffron. And fear. Me," he clapped his chest, "a grown ass man. I've always considered myself fairly brave but here I am, afraid of—"

"A sociopath," Saffron filled in. An instant later, she added, "Oh hell, I shouldn't have said that. I can tell by the way you're looking at me that you think I'm terrible for labeling my own sister that way. I love my sister, Rylan," she insisted, "I really do."

"I know you do. And on the contrary, Saffron, the only reason I may have a strange look on my face is because those were my thoughts exactly—about Lorraine being a sociopath. I hated labeling her that way too, but she's erased any misgivings I may have had. I spoke to Professor George Krakou about it. He's a former colleague of mine who taught Psychology 101 at WHU."

"Sure, I had Professor Krakou for Psych 101 myself." Saffron smiled. "Good instructor. He must be near retirement age now."

Nodding, Rylan said, "I was just at his retirement party last week. I told him my concerns about Lorraine. He said her traits are compatible with antisocial personality disorder. Sociopaths are people who might recognize what they're doing is wrong, but they just don't care—which makes psychotherapy difficult because patients have to recognize the issue and want change. Sociopaths don't think they have any problem."

"Lorraine to a T," Saffron said with a slow nod. "I suspect you told her you wanted to end your engagement."

"I did. I took her to breakfast, with the intention of letting her down gently, as kindly and easily as possible. I had it all planned out and, in my head, the conclusion worked out really well. But in reality, it turned into a nightmare when she flat-out refused to accept my decision."

"Aw, Rylan, you poor man. By trying to be gallant, you centered yourself in the middle of Lorraine's crosshairs."

It was uncanny how spot on Saffron was. She wasn't exaggerating when she claimed to know how Lorraine thinks, and what her sister is capable of doing.

"One by one Lorraine unfurled the rules and regulations of our relationship." He spread his hands wide. "Our whole damn marriage, Saffron, from the *I do* to the grave. Lorraine just sat there smiling, outlining each thinly veiled threat and the accompanying blackmail as casually as if she was reading a shopping list. I've never experienced anything like it before. Not even close."

"Believe me, I get it. It's what I've lived with my whole life."

"My biggest fear," Rylan went on, "is that your sister will hurt someone I care about." Saffron offered a confirming nod. "I worry Lorraine will misconstrue whatever I say or do, and make the people I care about pay."

"This is probably just the tip of the iceberg," Saffron said. "I've been on the receiving end of her threats so I understand your concerns. She's usually, but not always, blowing hot air. There were a couple times she followed through with the intention of causing trouble for me at school and, later, at work. She's probably made you fearful of talking to anyone. But if you do want to get it all off your chest, I'm a good listener. I'll bet you didn't even tell Quinn about any of this before he left."

"No way was I about to lay this on him before his trip. I know Quinn. He'd stall his Nigeria plans to help me."

With a sad, drippy-eyed smile, Saffron said, "That's one of the reason's I love him. Quinn, like you, Rylan, is truly a good man."

"I appreciate that. Thanks. I can attest that Quinn is the best. He's always been there for me."

"And vice versa, according to Quinn." She smiled. "So I assume Lorraine threatened to do something to ruin Quinn's reputation or otherwise screw up his affiliation with Medicine Without Boundaries."

"Bingo." Rylan's fingers raked through his hair. "I'm a respected professor. A man who prides himself in being intelligent and savvy, with a fair amount of common sense thrown in. So, tell me, how the hell did I manage to get myself caught up in Lorraine's intricate labyrinth of deceit? I feel like a calf, roped, tied, and being led to slaughter, unable to extricate himself from the sticky fingers of fate."

"Ah...I see the writer in you is coming out." Saffron chuckled. "Scotch, bourbon, gin or vodka?" she asked, rising from her seat and heading for the kitchen.

His head wrapped in fog, Rylan looked up at her. "Huh?"

"I figured you might be ready for something a little stronger than sparking water."

He thought about the bottle of Scotch with his name on it waiting for him at home. His father had always told him and Quinn, *Never drink alone, boys...it just leads to misery, depression, and ruin...even for the best of men.* Rylan could imagine himself getting stinking drunk by himself later—a drunken pity party. The unsavory image being generated wasn't who he was. No, Rylan Kilpatrick wasn't about to let a spurned woman's threats turn him into a hapless drunk.

"Scotch. Thanks. But only if you join me."

With Saffron's in depth knowledge of Lorraine's true character, Rylan decided it was safe to confide in her. It was time to lighten his burden by filling her in on his eye-opening conversation with Lorraine. Maybe she could even be of some help—advise him on the best way to deal with Lorraine's threats.

Taking the glass from her a few moments later, he studied it, swirling the caramel-colored liquid. "My first time having Scotch," he admitted to Saffron with a laugh before taking a swig. He wasn't quite sure what he thought about the unusual taste.

Saffron took her seat again, sitting with her legs tucked under her and holding a throw pillow in her lap. "I've only had Scotch once before. I bought it because—"

"Because it's a favorite of Quinn's," Rylan surmised. "Single malt, right?"

"Mmm-hmm. I'm still trying to decide if I like Scotch or not it's...different."

"Quinn said it's an acquired taste." He sipped from his Scotch, liking the herby taste better as he went along. "So I think it's time. If you're willing, I'll fill you in on everything."

If anything, Rylan hoped droning on about his monumental Lorraine-generated problems would help keep Saffron's mind off missing Quinn, at least for a while.

# Chapter 22

~<>~

"WOULDN'T IT be wonderful if he'd never met Lorraine? What if he'd met me first? Wouldn't it be sensational if I'd experienced the guilt-free deliciousness of his lips on mine? His tongue teasing, exploring as, at the same time, our legs tangled together? How extraordinary would it be if his fingertips pressed, just firm enough, gently raking, through my hair, across my skin, over and under each limb? Can you imagine the anticipation, the promise, the ultimate satisfaction of joining with a man so exquisite he makes my mouth water?"

With a monumental sigh, Kady grabbed her bath towel from the holder, wrapped it around herself, and stepped out of the shower onto the bathmat. Taking a second towel she scrubbed her wet hair and head with more vehemence than usual, as if punishing each guilty strand of auburn sprouting from the hard shell protecting her overstressed brain. When finished, she wrapped the towel turban-style around her head.

Once again, she'd thoroughly employed her favorite showerhead as she allowed her thoughts, for the final time, to wrap themselves in, out, over, under, and around Rylan Kilpatrick. Her cousin's fiancé. The man Lorraine Devington would marry.

Staring at herself in the bathroom mirror, Kady gave herself a contemptuous smile. Maybe it was more of a sneer. Oh how sorely tempted she was to use her magical heartwish for purely selfish reasons. How incredible it would be to wish she and Rylan would be a couple, forever, with Lorraine entirely out the picture.

She could do it. The ring had the power to do just exactly that for her.

Just a few carefully chosen words and Rylan would be hers, loving her, cherishing her, forever bonded to her. No one would ever have to know she'd made the wish. It would be her own deliciously naughty little secret.

Her shoulders slumped as her mind traveled to that very bad destination. Kady knew she'd go through life feeling like a cheater, a fraud, a pretender if she made such an opportunistic wish. Each time they kissed, she'd know it should be Lorraine Rylan was kissing, and the only reason his tongue danced with hers was because Kady had forced it to happen without his knowledge or consent. Without bothering to take Rylan's wishes into consideration.

"Everyone thinks I'm sweet, naïve, trusting...basically just shy of being a saint," Kady practically spit out because the words were bitter on her tongue. "They think I'm a good, caring, sympathetic person, always thinking of others. And I am. Sometimes. The rest of the time I'm a shameful, dishonorable woman who lusts after her cousin's fiancé. They don't know I'm a woman who dreams up the most explicit skin-on-skin fantasies about him. That I'm a woman so desperately in love with him that it hurts. *That* is the real Kady Malone."

Continuing to stare at her reflection, Kady looked deep into her violet eyes, searching, wondering when she'd become the reprehensible sort of woman who would, even for a moment, consider stealing the man her cousin loves by making use of a magical wish designed to make wonderful, positive changes for people.

"Kathleen Doolan Malone, you're pathetic." As she spoke the words, her eyes brimmed with tears. "No, stop it. You don't deserve to cry to make yourself feel better." She blinked away the impending waterworks, dabbing the residue with some tissues. Looking away from her reflection, she removed the turban-towel from her head and tossed it on the counter. Bracing her hands on the quartz countertop, her gaze was locked on her fingers as they turned red from exerting pressure on the hard surface.

"I'm am absolutely *not* wishing for a man, *any* man, in my life. I will *not* wish for someone to love me. I refuse to be a dismal, whiny, pitiable, pathetic woman who feels her life has been flushed down the toilet just because she had the misfortune to fall in love with a man she can never, ever, *ever* have. No, if it's meant to be, I'll find a man to love. A man who'll love *me*," she clapped the towel over her chest, "naturally, without the use of some undeserved magical intervention."

God how she wanted to cry, just for the cleansing effect. The emotional release. But she knew she'd be a snotty, drippy, swollen mess the rest of the day if she started—and those tears would be damned difficult to shut off once they began.

"Nope, I won't make my heartwish while I'm feeling sorry for myself. I'm going to fix myself up so I look decent and presentable and I'll sit there with all my wish making stuff carefully placed around me and I'll project a great big happy smile," she dragged her downward lips up into a creepy grin with her fingers, "as I make whatever the hell wish it is that I'm going to make."

Turning on the hairdryer she added, "And I'll make certain my wish includes ensuring that Rylan and Lorraine are happy. Happy, dammit! That'll be it. Done. Case closed. No more daydreaming, or night fantasizing...or pulsing showerheading."

A whine from Izzy caught her attention. The little bocker sat at the entrance to the bathroom, inclining her head left, right, and left again as she studied Kady. She usually kept her distance when Kady used the hairdryer, so the poor thing must have been pretty concerned about her mistress and friend to risk putting herself directly in the line of the frightening monster hairdryer.

Kady sucked in, then released, a deep breath, turning on a cheery smile for her furry little buddy's benefit. "Don't worry, I'm okay, Izzy. Really." She squatted, taking the dog's face in her hands and kissing Izzy on the forehead. "I think it's almost my time of month," she lied, "so my hormones must be out of whack, that's all."

The last thing she wanted was to make Izzy worry about her emotional health, which the little dog was probably doing right now if she overheard the rest of Kady's rambling, petulant lament.

She'd planned to make her heartwish after breakfast, a kale, spinach, collagen, matcha, and wheatgrass smoothie in a cashew milk base. Once the heartwish was made, she promised herself she'd never again torment herself with what ifs. She refused to dwell on what might have been if things were different. Rylan was taken...by her cousin, which meant there were no ifs, ands, or buts about it. The man was permanently off limits, even in Kady's most private fantasies. Thinking, dreaming, and fantasizing about him simply wasn't healthy, or right, or appropriate in any way.

A while later, she listened to her stomach growl and grumble. Her smoothie wasn't sitting well because she was vexed and uneasy. But, no matter, it was time to get everything together for her heartwish and that's what she'd do, feeling queasy or not.

After setting nearly everything in place for her heartwish, Kady stood in front of her small dining table, arms akimbo. Nibbling on her bottom lip, she eyed the setting she'd created in the middle of her small apartment and frowned. Something wasn't right. While it was lovely, serene, and inviting, something was missing. It was crucial that everything be absolutely perfect and it didn't feel that way.

"Why can't I see what's wrong?" she asked herself in a near-whisper. "It's so important that I don't mess up this one and only chance I have to make this heartwish." Shifting her attention to Izzy, she added, "Honestly, what the heck kind of psychic am I if I can't even figure that out for myself?" A moment later, she gave a humorless laugh. "Oh, I know what kind I am...a fake, a fraud, an imposter."

Izzy was nearby on the floor, playing with a chew toy. At the sound of Kady's muttered bellyaching, she got up, hobbled to the bookcase and stood there, resting both paws on one of the shelves. Placing her muzzle on the shelf, her nose pointed directly to the framed photo of Kady's late grandmother. Izzy looked up at Kady and again back at the photo.

Angling her head as she studied Izzy, wondering what she meant, it finally hit Kady. "Ahhh...I get it now. I understand." Smiling and petting Izzy's head, she nodded. "I'm not supposed to *see* what's wrong, I'm supposed to *feel* it. And what I feel is the absence of Grandma Bekka as well as all of my family. Although I need to be alone when I make my wish, I still need to be in the midst of their loving essence. Right, Iz?"

Izzy offered a companionable bark, which Kady interpreted as her agreement because it was accompanied by rapid tail wagging.

"Thanks, sweetie pie." Pulling Izzy close, she gave her a hug. "I know what we need to do. We're packing all my wish-making paraphernalia up and taking it to Bekka House so I can make my wish in front of the family's vintage aluminum Christmas tree. I swear, that old thing is magical."

The family room of Bekka House was the heart of the Malone family home. There were so many wonderful memories and so much love between the walls. Whenever she visited, Kady was left with the most amazing feeling of being enveloped in generations of affection.

Before leaving her apartment, she contacted her sister-in-law, Aladee, asking her to set up the Nymph Mail she'd talked about so Kady could communicate with Red while at Bekka House.

Within thirty minutes, Kady, along with all her wish-making accouterments, had arrived. She'd brought so much with her she needed her rolling carryon, plus the large tote slung over her shoulder.

"It looks like we're staying for a week, Izzy." She laughed.

Once she crossed the threshold to Bekka House and closed the door behind her, Kady was swaddled in the warm, gingery fragrance of her grandmother's *pepperkaker*, causing Izzy to lick her lips while sniffing the air. From experience, Kady knew the comforting spirit of Grandma Bekka was near.

"Mmmm." Closing her eyes, Kady took in a deep breath. "You're here, aren't you, Grandma?" she said. "I can feel you with me."

"I'm here, Kady, dear," Bekka's Norwegian accented voice whispered in her granddaughter's ear. "Your heart is in the right place. As you make this wish, trust in your feelings, child, they won't steer you wrong."

As her grandmother spoke those words, the metal ring band around Kady's finger grew faintly warm, while the heartwish stone glowed with a subtle blueish light.

Rebekka Eriksen, Astrid's mother, was one of three friendly Norwegian spirits who regularly visited Bekka House. The Malones weren't certain whether Grandma Bekka, her husband Jamie, and Anders, the grandfather of Delaney's husband, Varik, were technically ghosts or angels. They only knew their presence was soothing and most welcome. Kady and the rest of the family always thought of them as visiting rather than haunting.

Solely ensconced in the coziness of Bekka House, a sense of tranquility enveloped Kady as she prepared her heartwish backdrop on the coffee table opposite the family's retro aluminum Christmas tree.

Kneeling at the foot of the tree, Kady plugged in and turned on the rotating color wheel, watching it glimmer across the quirky collection of ornaments. Each time she saw the tree it had more ornaments, most of which were handcrafted.

It was the first time she'd seen the two newest ornaments Reen told Kady she'd created for her. With a contented sigh, Kady smiled while examining the cleverly knitted pair of women. One was Saffron, and the redhead wearing purple was Kady. They each held a stack of books. Across the backs of the ornaments were the words Cherished Pages.

"So, so adorable," Kady said, once again amazed at her sister's incredible knitting skill. "Oh my gosh!" Giddy, she picked the other ornament she'd just spotted. "Look, Izzy! It's you!"

Attentive at her side, the little dog seemed to study the ornament, touching it with her paw before turning to Kady and giving a soft bark. Reen had knitted Izzy wearing her fortunetelling costume, It was so stinking cute Kady couldn't stop giggling. She knew laughter was good for the soul so she was glad to preface her heartwish with a healthy bout of humor instead of the negative self-pitying attitude she'd been feeding all morning.

"This is it, Izzy." Kady's fingers gently scraped through the dog's fur as she glanced around her. "The perfect spot to make my heartwish."

Seated on the floor, she opened her laptop, set her phone in place, and neatened her stack of papers on the coffee table. The books she'd selected, containing passages of proverbs and positivity, poems of wisdom, love and acceptance, and her favorite optimistic affirmations, were easily within reach. A lavish number of her favorite scented candles, which took up the bulk of her carryon suitcase, were in position, surrounding the area.

Both cone and stick incense holders embracing compatible scents of lavender, patchouli, and sandalwood, were stationed in just the right spots for maximum sensory gratification. She'd turned on her oil diffuser, which she'd readied with lavender essential oil for the perfect aromatherapy addition.

Kady put on a pot of fennel tea with ginger, and essence of rose, complemented by her herbal honey containing more than a dozen healing herbs in a raw manuka honey base, providing an elixir effect.

"It's crucial that everything be as perfect as possible. Faultless. Splendid...so my heartwish will be exactly as I hope. This is a once in a lifetime opportunity, Izzy, so I need to make sure my heartwish is caring, unselfish, loving, positive, and made with scrupulous intention so it manifests the highest form of love, directly from my heart to those I cherish."

She'd set out a line of beautifully colored stones—her favorite crystals, choosing the ones that made her feel positive and happy when she gazed at their natural beauty. Her favorite large amethyst, meant to assist with a sense of calm for her nervous system; an obsidian to help protect her aura from negative energies; a moonstone to help her access her inner wisdom; a rose quartz to help manifest a sense of love; and a clear quartz for overall healing and to help Kady manifest a higher state of consciousness.

The perfect esoteric music reverberated throughout the family room of Bekka House. This playlist included her favorite Hildegard von Bingen's chants because she felt they'd encourage the most beneficial vibes—and she didn't have to worry about Lorraine complaining about listening to them.

Saging the family room left it with a subtle, familiar conglomeration of fragrances Kady enjoyed. She'd used her favorite mixture of white sage, lavender and cedar to create an uplifting, relaxing ambience as it cleared the space of negative energy. As fragrant clouds of pearl-gray smoke wafted up from her small saging pot, she'd waved a cluster of found feathers through the smoke, spreading it.

After saging, Kady meditated, beginning by focusing on gratitude for all her many blessings, before asking Grandma Bekka to help her formulate the correct wish. The most important element for Kady, was communicating with her beloved late grandmother. Bekka's presence had felt much closer the last few days, making Kady hopeful that the timing for her heartwish was right.

She asked for guidance in choosing her wish wisely, to help ensure the wish became a failsafe reality. The calming process, enhanced by the last vestiges of sage hanging in the air, helped her relax and let go of any stress clinging to her.

"What do you think, Izzy?" Gazing around her wish-making area, Kady gestured widely. "Have I achieved the perfect balance of mind, body and spirit for making my heartwish?" Ever faithful and caring, Izzy glanced around the room before placing a paw on Kady's knee. Her gentle bark was the answer Kady hoped for.

Kady's initial dilemma was that the heartwish she'd been focused on from the beginning didn't *speak* to her. It didn't feel right. The expected sense of satisfaction and fulfilment inside was missing. And she couldn't understand why. After all, a wish to heal the Devington family and have them become loving and supportive of Red, instead of ostracizing him for being gay, should be ideal. It should make Kady's heart glad. Shouldn't it?

But that wasn't the case.

It was only after she'd asked Aladee, to contact Red that Kady finally understood. Once Red had answered her questions with explanations that made perfect sense, Kady wondered why she hadn't realized the answer herself. It was so crystal clear to her now.

The Nymph Mail that Aladee made possible was astonishing. It could be used in various ways, including the face to face image connection Kady experienced today. The closest thing she could liken it to was using Zoom, but instead of a square with Red's image, she saw him in a sort of clear cloud with irregular borders. It was almost as if he was right there in the room with her—like she could reach through the cloud and touch him. In fact, she'd tried, but it didn't work because, no matter how tangible he seemed, Redmond wasn't physically there.

Kady was elated when Red told her he'd never been happier. He and Lonan had built a strong, beautiful, loving life together, a life they celebrated and enjoyed to the fullest. It delighted Red that Lonan was a fan of his mischievous spirit. Lonan told him he'd never laughed as much or as hard before knowing Red. It didn't hurt that Red was also a big ham, dressing up and playacting whenever he got the chance. He just loved making people laugh.

During their Nymph Mail conversation, Red had Lonan join him briefly. They spent some time playing with Red's fluffy white cat, Cupid, and Lonan's adorable mini unicorn. It was the first time Kady had seen the unicorn she'd heard so much about. The little guy was no bigger than a large dog. After being a bundle of nerves about her heartwish, it was good to let loose and laugh at all of Red's antics, including his self-effacing jokes about being a minor god.

Getting serious, Red and Lonan told Kady about their most enjoyable and rewarding pastime—finding kind, honest, good-hearted people around the world who were in need of help. Perhaps the people had lost everything in a tragedy, or they might be thinking of giving up after something deeply traumatic. Maybe they were in need of a safe place to eat and sleep.

Or they might have been shunned, disowned, abandoned, or rejected, and left out in the cold, alone and afraid—very much like what had happened to Red when he was disowned and all ties to his parents and sister, Lorraine, severed.

If Red and Lonan could improve the situation of any of those people by making use of their special gifts and abilities, they did so. It was fascinating listening to Red expound on the boundless abilities, the magic and wonder, available to residents of Mount Olympus. He and Lonan loved being able to make a positive difference in people's lives with relative ease, compared to the extent Red would need to go to if he was still living on Earth.

The recipients of Red and Lonan's acts of kindness weren't aware of how their good fortune came to be, only that their lives had become considerably better. The only clue the beneficiaries had about their secret benefactors was a note they each received, the contents of which was always the same, except for their names. The notes read:

...

Person's Name,

You've always been kind, compassionate, and giving.

Now it's your turn to reap some of what you've sown.

We know you will pay this kindness forward when you can.

Spread kindness, love, and joy always.

Love,

The Jubilation Factory

...

Loving the idea, Kady asked about the *Jubilation Factory* name. Red told her it's a foundation he and Lonan formed to anonymously help those in need. A network of assistants, located both on Mount Olympus and on Earth, shared their time and skillsets to assist them. It was the epitome of a win-win for all involved.

Once Lonan left the conversation, Red said, "You know how much I love kidding around and being the center of attention. Well, believe it or not I've got a grownup serious side too."

"Um...nope, I don't think I believe you," Kady teased and he chuckled.

"Well then, prepare to be dazzled with my adulting."

Kady couldn't help laughing. "Okay, my minor god cousin, you may hereby proceed to razzle-dazzle me with your coming of age tale."

"Okay, I'm putting on my serious face now." Red wiped his hand down in front of his face, erasing his smile and eliciting a giggle from Kady.

"One of the things I've learned is that not everyone is necessarily deserving of miracles, or to be the benefactor of magic wishes. At The Jubilation Factory, we carefully vet each prospect, using special technology available to us here on Mount Olympus to determine whether or not someone is pure of heart. We believe an ugly heart can't be miraculously made beautiful. That has to occur organically...or not at all."

"Hmm, you were right. I'm definitely feeling dazzled. And I think I know where you're going with this in relation to my heartwish." It was finally becoming clear why the wish she'd always intended to make never felt quite right.

"Yes..." smiling, Red confirmed, "my family. I love my parents and Lorraine and always will. And I forgive them for their draconian beliefs and actions. The wonderful wish you'd planned to make expressly for my benefit, Kady, is the embodiment of warmth, generosity, thoughtfulness, and selflessness, which is no surprise at all, considering it's coming from you, the sweetest, kindest girl I've even known."

"Aw, Red, you're going to make me cry. Thank you." She couldn't help wondering what Red would think of her if he knew how obsessed she was with Rylan.

"This is your wish, Kady, so it's entirely up to you, of course, but the reason I'd urge you to reconsider your initial wish is because, again, I couldn't be happier now. I'm eternally surrounded by, and infused with, love and acceptance."

"You have no idea how happy that makes me, Red."

"I'm fortunate enough to have a partner who treats me like the enviable god I am," Red put on a silly, arrogant air, "and has a unicorn for a pet. I live inside a fairy tale populated with mythical gods and creatures. I spend my time singing and dancing to Broadway tunes while arranging gorgeous flowers instead of crunching godawful boring numbers at the bank. I'm not being picked on, or made to feel guilty, or treated like a pariah. I'm having fun, enjoying life, and feeling gratified because I'm able to make a positive difference in people's lives."

"Wow..." was all Kady could say to that.

"Exactly. Now, taking all of that into consideration, I want you to ask yourself, Kady, if using this single opportunity you've been given to make a noble, unselfish, magnanimous wish from your heart, should be spent on absolving Walter, Colleen, and Lorraine of their ugly words and deeds."

Kady had never looked at it that way before.

"I know that, for my benefit, you wholeheartedly yearn to have my parents and sister realize the error of their ways and welcome me, as well as your mother and siblings, back into the fold so we're one big happy family, free of bigotry and unfair judgment. Kady, my sweet cousin, I adore you for your kind intentions. But, again, do those three deserve to have their slates wiped clean, without them having to put in the effort to learn such important life lessons on their own?"

Again, the first thing popping out of Kady's mouth was, "Wow." Red had just outlined exactly what she'd be doing—giving her aunt, uncle and cousin an easy way out and saving them from the consequences of their callous, unkind actions.

"I'm so thankful for Aladee and her Nymph Mail and the opportunity to talk to you, Red. You've opened my eyes and made such valid points. Honestly, none of that had even crossed my mind. All I cared about was wishing all the pain and heartache away so you'd finally receive the love and acceptance you deserve."

Thinking more about what Red said, she asked, "But what if your parents and Lorraine never come around? What if they remain narrow-minded, intolerant, and inflexible? How would you feel if you never had a relationship with any of them again, Red? Wouldn't you always have an inner sadness about it? A sort of hole in your heart?"

"While I'm a born idealist, I admit I'll probably always have a little spot of sadness at the back of my heart. But, believe me, Kady, the spot is shrinking each day. I know my parents and sister well enough to know they'll never naturally morph into openhearted, accepting people on their own. It would take years of therapy to bring them to a place of acceptance and understanding. But therapy won't work because they don't believe they have a problem that needs fixing."

"I agree. Well...except maybe for the part about your sister. You might not be aware that I recently had a long talk with Lorraine. It was very positive. She told me she never wanted to go along with your parents when they cut you out of their lives. She told me it's fine with her if you're gay, and that she misses you terribly and hopes you'll—"

"Kady..."

Gazing at Red's calm, happy visage, she angled her head in question.

"Lorraine wasn't being truthful."

Her shoulders slumping, Kady said, "That's the same thing Saffron and my mom told me."

"Listen to them. Saffron knows from firsthand experience. Lorraine's not a well woman, Kady. She'll expertly lie to your face in order to get what, or *who*, she wants. She'll hurt anyone she deems an obstacle in her path. And feel no remorse."

Red's words brought back the conversation she'd had with Saffron about Lorraine. "Saffron told me she thinks Lorraine is," she took a deep breath, "a sociopath."

"I can detect the pain in your voice, because you so desperately want to believe it's not true. I get it, I really do. It took me a long time to come to the realization about my sister too. You've always been so trusting and believing, looking for the best in people. That's one of the traits that makes you so special." Red gave her a kind smile.

"I'm not the nice person you think I am, Red."

His gentle laughter was evident. "Yes you are. Kady, I know how you feel about Lorraine's fiancé."

With a gasp, Kady uttered, "Oh my God!" She could have died on the spot. She had no idea Red knew. How did he find out? Did she have a *Shameless Hussy* neon sign flashing overhead or something? Maybe Nymph Mail could detect imposters!

"No, nothing quite that blatant." Red's laughter became wholehearted. "I know because I'm a freakin' minor god now with awesome powers of detection," he said with a smile, answering the thoughts she hadn't expressed verbally. "Which makes me special." His teasing grin spread from ear to ear. "Falling for Rylan doesn't make you a bad person. It just means you're human. You'll have plenty of time to be perfect when you're floating around with your wings and harp up in heaven, eons from now. Until then, give yourself a break, okay?"

Kady mustered a smile. "Okay...thanks."

"Getting back to Lorraine, like I said, listen to Saffron. She has a good, honest heart. She won't hurt you, Kady."

"That's one thing I already knew without you having to tell me." Kady chuckled. "Red?"

"Hmmm?"

"If you had the heartwish ring, what would *you* wish for?"

Red's hushed laughter felt like a tickle. "Kathleen Doolan Malone—"

"Yes, Redmond Edward Devington?" Kady mockingly cut in, increasing Red's laughter.

"You are blessed with insight, wisdom, and a heart bigger than the entire Pacific Northwest, but you're sorely lacking in confidence. I'm not telling you what I'd wish for because this is *your* special wish, not mine. It's *your* one magical chance to make a positive difference. What you fail to understand is that your heart has already made the wish. It's up to you now to recognize it and make it a reality. Treat yourself with the same kindness, trust, and generosity of spirit that you give others and all will be well."

A satisfied smile took hold as Red said, "So, how's *that* for adulting?"

"So good I'm considering hiring you as my new life coach. Thank you, Red." Using her palms, Kady wiped happy tears from her eyes.

"You and I will always be there for each other, Kady. I feel that clear to my bones. Now, my dear cousin, you know what I want you to do?"

"What's that?" Feeling so much better already, Kady offered her best smile.

"I want you to light all your special candles, play your female chants, burn that fragrant incense, diffuse that oil which, knowing you is lavender," he chuckled, "and discover your heart's wish."

He stopped talking for a moment and seemed to be taking in Kady's surroundings. "I see you've chosen to be in front of the retro tree at Bekka House to make your wish. It's the ideal location, infused with all the love from the people who've shared it there. I detect two good, kind spirits ready to guide you. One is your grandma, Bekka, and the other is your precious little Izzy, aka Madame Izidora Meszaros."

Nothing Red could have said would make Kady happier. The tongue-lolling Izzy answered Red's words with a congenial little bark before hopping onto Kady's lap and licking her face.

"I love you, Kady," Red told her. "Thank you from the bottom of my heart for always loving me for who and what I am, and for wanting to repair my life with your one and only heartwish. Be assured that I'm a *very* happy man. No repairs necessary." Red gave her a hearty smile.

"I love you too, Red. Thank you. You've been such a great help. All I ever wanted was for you to be happy and it looks like that's definitely the case, without the need for any wishes."

"Before we go," Red said, "I have a little gift for you. Something to add to the year-round family holiday tree. Watch the tree in three...two...one..." Red blew her a kiss and the Nymph Mail closed.

At the end of Red's count, a white light emanated from the silver tree, encircling a brand new ornament of two men garbed in white togas. It was Red and Lonan, smiling and holding a big red heart between them with "R + L" in white lettering bordered by gold. The satin figures had embroidered features and delicate gold trim enhancing the togas. The darling little ornament embodied the couple's love and happiness, warming Kady's heart.

"What a perfect addition to our tree." Looking skyward, Kady said, "Thank you, Red. I love it!" She had a feeling he was still able to hear her.

The more she considered Red's words, the more Kady was convinced of their merit. Using her wish as a sort of *get out of jail free card* for the Devingtons isn't at all what she had in mind when initially thinking about helping Red with her heartwish. People who were inherently dishonest, mean-spirited, and completely insensitive to the needs of others weren't the people who should benefit from a wish designed to make everyone involved happy and satisfied.

The Devingtons had purposely chosen their narrow path. It wasn't up to Kady to upset their applecart. And it certainly wasn't her place to exonerate them for all their egregious, hurtful acts.

As soon as that notion crossed Kady's thoughts, she heard the unmistakable tinkle of Grandma Bekka's loving laughter. An instant later came the welcoming ginger fragrance of her signature pepperkaker cookies again. It lingered longer this time before dissipating.

"You're here to let me know that Red's right and I should listen to him, right Grandma?"

Izzy hobbled close to Kady, looking toward the ceiling with an expression Kady could swear was a smile. Kady believed her sweet dog was attuned to the spirit world and could detect Grandma Bekka.

"Now that I know what I *won't* be wishing for," Kady said to her grandmother, "I need to put on my thinking cap, as you used to say to us, and figure out what my heart is telling me I'm meant to wish for. Please help me if you can."

"You already know what to wish for, my dear," came Grandma Bekka's ethereal voice.

Kady was never quite sure if she was actually hearing her grandmother speaking, or if perhaps it came from inside her head. In either case, it was very soft but clear as a bell.

"I'm so worried I'll make a mistake, Grandma, like the one I almost made wasting my wish on the Devingtons. Can you guide me, help me to make a wish that will bring the most happiness to someone deserving?"

"It's just as Red told you, and just as your mother has told you, Kathleen. Your heart chooses the wish. Open your heart, sweet girl, and search for the answer there. Clear your mind and pay close attention. You'll clearly see your heart presenting the wish to you, almost as if it's on a silver platter. Your perfect heartwish, Kady...your perfect heartwish..."

The last sentence trailed off, growing softer until it was gone and Kady no longer felt her grandmother's presence in the room.

And, *boom*, just like that, Kady realized her wish. It was right there as if her heart had installed a flashing neon sign six inches from her face so she couldn't possibly miss it. It really *was* the perfect heartwish!

To get all the details exact required Kady to do some in depth online research, to make certain she had all her facts straight and wouldn't muck up her heartwish. So she went to work. Finally, she opened a new document on her laptop, typing out the exact words she wanted to say as she made her wish so she'd be sure not to leave anything out. She saved the document as KDM-Heartwish.

Once ready, she closed her eyes, focusing on a mental image of the beneficiary of her heartwish. As she rested her ringed hand against her heart, her fingers warmed and Kady opened her eyes to witness the stone's glow encompassing her and Izzy, who calmly took it all in stride. Speaking confidently, with conviction, Kady uttered some of the most paramount words she'd ever speak.

"As I make this wish, my heart and soul make it as well. It is my truest, deepest heartwish." She was delighted and heartened by the light steadily radiating from her ring. "This deserving person has one of the purest hearts and charitable souls of anyone I know. She creates special, thoughtful little dolls for the sick children in the hospital's cancer ward, and spends what precious little personal time she has volunteering there, reading to those children. This is merely a tiny fragment of the boundless goodness that spills from Saffron Devington's generous heart."

As she spoke about her cousin, Kady felt vibration in her hand as an arc of blue-white light gleamed and glittered, jetting from her ring directly to the Saffron ornament Reen had knitted, surrounding the likeness with a soft glow. The changing colors from the rotating color wheel shining on the tree added to the overall lustrousness Kady saw before her.

It was wondrous!

"My cousin Saffron has been unlucky in love, until meeting Quinn Kilpatrick, the wonderful man I believe she's destined to spend her life with. The wish I make is to correct the terrible wrong that separated two people so very much in love."

Making sure to have her laptop open to the right page, Kady studied the information again before continuing.

"The wish I make is multidimensional. My heart indicates that this will work. I truly hope it does." She took a deep breath. "I've learned that Medicine Without Boundaries is in the process of creating a charitable affiliate, Libraries Without Boundaries, or LWB. It's just in the beginning stages. Their press release states they're about to begin vetting candidates to run and staff the foundation."

The blueish glow of her ring's stone amplified as she spoke, adding to Kady's confidence.

"With her business degrees, her extensive work experience in sales, real estate, administrative office positions, not to mention co-owning and managing a book store where she does all the bookkeeping." Kady stopped to take a breath.

"And Saffron's love of books and reading, her fondness for helping children, and her sincere desire to help improve people's lives," Kady went on, "Saffron is more than qualified to work with LWB in whichever capacity she pleases."

Kady drew in a deep, calming breath, hoping she was wording everything correctly. She followed that by sipping some of her healing tea as she continued reading the particulars posted by MWB about their new subsidiary.

"The first part of my multilayered wish is to have Saffron Devington secure whatever executive position with LWB that she would prefer most. A position that would provide her with the ability and financial means to travel back and forth to any of the umbrella organization's locations around the world. Including Nigeria, or wherever Quinn may be located in the future. And I wish the same for Quinn—to be happy and secure in whatever position he desires."

Prior to this part of her wish, Kady imagined an unhappy Saffron, with a horrified look on her face, saying, "Oh my God, Kady, you did what?! Why would you do this? It's not what I want." So Kady applied her psychic insight, followed by deep thought, meditation, and prayer until she knew without doubt she was safe including such specific career-related aspects for Saffron in her heartwish.

Her psychic discernment, as well insight from Grandma Bekka, and solid confirmation from Kady's own heart assured her this is definitely what Saffron would wish for herself.

The thought made Kady smile because, of course, Saffron would never make that wish if she had the ring. Nope, she'd definitely be wishing for something altruistic, to help someone else be happy instead.

Returning her full attention to the wish making process, Kady said, "The second part of my heartwish is to ensure that Saffron and Quinn are allowed to always be together, no matter where they are, and to be safe from harm, adversity, or illness at all times. I can't imagine two people better suited to one another. I wish them both love and happiness always in all ways."

As Kady's wish-making progressed, she found herself and Izzy comfortably cloistered in an expanding sphere of tranquil azure light. Izzy seemed to accept it as something safe and natural. Sipping from her honeyed tea again, Kady *mmmm*ed. The herby mixture was flavorsome, gently calming, and helped to strengthen her fortitude. She was closing in on the final part of her heartwish—perhaps the most difficult part of all.

"For the third and final part of my wish," Kady breathed a wobbly sigh, "I wish for Rylan Kilpatrick to be happy with the woman he loves. He's a good man and deserves it. I also wish for Lorraine Devington to be happy with the person she loves most, even though she may not deserve it. I wish for love and happiness for each of them always."

After what Red had told her about Lorraine, it was difficult for Kady to include a wish for love and happiness for her cousin, but she felt it was necessary in order for Rylan to be rewarded with the happiness he truly deserved. Maybe if Lorraine was happy she wouldn't make Rylan's life miserable. That's what Kady was banking on.

She believed an extra dose of love could only help soothe Lorraine, even if that love was unmerited. It would be a wonderful surprise if the results of her wish helped turn Lorraine into a more stable woman...if it helped her to be more loving, forgiving, fulfilled, and humane.

"We can always hope, Izzy, right?" Unlike the companionable barks Izzy had provided previously, this time she offered a whiny moan.

With the final portion of Kady's three-part heartwish complete, the vintage tree and area surrounding it was impregnated with glorious sapphire blue light. It was magical, mystical, and satisfyingly magnificent. She'd been awed and amazed before, but never like this. Not even close.

Her gaze on her still-glimmering ring, Kady was filled with gratitude for the opportunity to make a difference for someone she loved. "It's a true miracle in the making," she whispered as she took it all in, basking in the beautiful light of love, as she thought of it.

Scooping her dog into her arms, Kady hugged her. "We did it, Izzy. We did it!" She was compensated with a generous lick and what Kady had come to recognize as a hug from Izzy.

Having uttered the final words of her heartwish, Kady was aware that her entire system, from her skin to the deepest alcoves of her heart, her brain, her soul, all of it, seemed to coordinate to play one perfect clear as a bell note, assuring her she'd made the right choices for her heartwish and, most importantly, that all segments would come to fruition.

# Chapter 23

~<>~

NEARLY TWO HOURS after she'd completed making her heartwish, Kady's phone tweedled with a text alert: "I'm at your apartment, Kady, where are you?" It was from Saffron. After Kady told her she was at Bekka House, Saffron texted: "You made your heartwish, didn't you?" Bobbing her head with enthusiasm, even though Saffron couldn't see it, Kady confirmed Saffron's guess. Saffron replied: "Stay there. Don't move. I'm on my way over."

The last hundred and twenty minutes had been endless as Kady waited for some sign that her heartwish had succeeded. Until now, there'd been zip. Nada. Nothing.

She was nervous about it. It was so darned important and she wanted more than anything for her wish to be victorious. She was so full of angst she hadn't even called her mom or any of her sisters yet. While she knew her thinking was illogical and foolish, Kady didn't want to use her phone for calls or texts in case she missed an important communication from someone involved in her multidimensional wish.

Like the text she'd finally received from Saffron.

"Please, please, please let this be good news about my heartwish." She looked skyward, crossing all her fingers while hopping in place like a five-year-old. The nervous energy she'd built up during the whole wish making process was phenomenal. She wished she could be this alert and lively all the time.

She'd already neatened everything up that she'd brought to Bekka House, waiting to pack up all her candles and incense until they'd had a chance to cool—which was a good forty minutes ago now. The rest, including her vintage cream-colored ceramic teapot with the lavender flowers design, was in her carryon and tote bag.

The only thing she kept out were her notes about MWB and its new subsidiary foundation, Libraries Without Boundaries.

She was twitchy, squirmy and fidgety, waiting for Saffron's arrival. When the doorbell rang, she practically jumped out of her skin, letting out an involuntary *whoop!* before running to the door, yanking it open, and greeting Saffron with a mile-wide smile.

Arms extended with fingers spread wide, Saffron all but yelled, "Oh my God, Kady, why would you do this? It's not what I want!"

Momentarily unable to speak, Kady remembered those nearly exact words because she'd said them to herself earlier, thinking about how horrible it would be if she somehow made the wrong heartwish and Saffron confronted her because she'd ended up with something she hated—al because of Kady.

It was as if a thousand fire ants had gnawed through Kady's skull, breaching the covering of her brain and setting it on fire. Powerless to stop the immediate onslaught of tears, Kady covered her face and sobbed hard enough to make her shoulders shake.

She'd failed! Dear God, she'd really mucked it up good! What she did was wrong. Just as she'd feared, it's not what Saffron wanted after all. With the best of intentions, Kady had interfered in her cousin's life, inviting pain and grief. Maybe she'd even ruined Saffron's life.

Clearly concerned, Izzy sidled up to Kady, whimpering and hugging her leg.

"Kady! Oh my gosh. Kady!" Rushing over the threshold, Saffron grabbed Kady tight in her arms, patting and rocking and telling her it was okay. "Sweetie, why are you crying so hard? Are you hurt? Did something happen? What's going on?"

"I-I ruined your life," Kady said through hiccupping sobs. "I'm so sorry, Saffron. I thought I was being so careful. I mean, I did all the research and I-I...oh, Saffron, I never meant to cause you—"

"Kady, no, shhh-shhh-shhh." She rubbed her hand over Kady's back as she continued to sob. "I'm sorry, Kady. I'm such an idiot. I never meant to frighten or upset you. I've never been happier in my life, thanks to you. I only meant I never wanted you to waste your one, single, precious wish on me, especially if it meant leaving you in the lurch here at Cherished Pages, all by yourself. I'm thrilled and delighted with my astounding news but I also feel guilty as hell. You should have used your wish to benefit yourself."

Her chin still trembling, Kady took a step back, looking up into Saffron's eyes. Accepting the tissue Saffron dug from her purse and wiping her eyes and cheeks, Kady honestly insisted, "Seeing you truly happy does benefit me. So...you mean you're not angry about what I did? Heck, I don't even know exactly what I did—I mean how everything turned out. You need to tell me what happened, and how you knew it was because of my heartwish."

Shutting the front door and draping her arm over Kady's shoulder as they headed for the family room, Saffron said, "Even before you confirmed that you'd made your heartwish, I knew. I was certain. What's happened is too unreal, too strange and otherworldly for it to be anything but something magical. This is definitely no random happening. I have zero doubt about it. Honestly, it's just next to a miracle."

Izzy yapped a series of happy barks before twirling around in a circle. Her happiness for Saffron seemed to match Kady's.

"You have no idea how relieved I am to hear you say everything's okay. I love you so much, Saffron and I'd absolutely hate myself if I'd ruined your life by my decision."

"I love you too. Sit," she motioned to the cushy couch strewn with decorative throw pillows, "and we'll talk. I'll tell you everything that's happened in the last two hours. We'll polish off a bottle of pricy French champagne, and we'll eat expensive Belgian chocolate."

Kady chuckled. "That all sounds fabulous, except I'm afraid there's no champagne or chocolate in the house, unless you count my mom's giant stash of M&Ms. She keeps a ton of them in a big covered glass bowl in the pantry. They're her guilty pleasure. But as far as I know...they don't come from Belgium." She winked, feeling immensely better than she had a few minutes ago.

"Oh ye of little faith." Saffron snickered as she set the bag she carried, that Kady hadn't even noticed, down on the coffee table. Like a magician with his top hat and rabbit, she pulled out a bottle of champagne, followed by a silver-toned two-pound box of Belgian chocolates, tied with purple moiré ribbon, from the top chocolatier in Glassfloat Bay.

"Wow...I guess you meant it when you said you were happy," Kady said. "You just bought this?"

"Yup." Saffron nodded. "On my way over here. Want to know how much I love you?" Smiling, Kady nodded. "I love you enough to pay a premium price to get a chilled bottle of this stuff." She held the champagne aloft. Finally, Saffron pulled out a package of the special dog treats Laila made—the ones Kady and Saffron carried in Cherished Pages.

"You don't think I'd forget about my favorite little puppy dog in the world, do you?" she said to Izzy. Looking impossibly cute and endearing, Izzy sat, licking her lips and raising her paw to shake. Getting her treat, she scampered off to enjoy it.

"Oh, Kady, we have soooo much to talk about. Starting with, how in the world did you know I'd just heard about Libraries Without Boundaries and had sent in an application to be the Head Librarian? I never mentioned it."

"I didn't know. So, Head Librarian, that's the job you were offered? The one you wanted?"

"It's definitely the one I wanted. I've always wanted to be a librarian."

"I remember you telling me that."

"But it's not the only position I was offered." Opening her phone, Saffron pulled up her email. "Two hours ago my inbox was full of job offers from LWB for every damn job they were hiring for." She burst out laughing. "Once I opened the emails and saw what they were, I knew nearly one hundred percent that this is all due to your heartwish." Tapping the email with the offer of employment for the Head Librarian position, Saffron grinned. "Wait until you see what else."

She handed her phone to Kady. "Go ahead. Take a look."

Kady did, her eyes soon growing wide with surprise at all the attachments. "This is a copy of your MLS, Master's Degree in Library Science." She looked at Saffron, tilting her head. "I thought you said you didn't have a librarian degree...that your parents stopped you from getting one."

"Mmm-hmm," Saffron's head bobbed, "that's exactly what I told you. While I have taken a number of classes, I didn't take enough for a degree. I also told you I'd wanted to get a teaching degree as well, remember?"

"Uh-huh. I remember you taking a bunch of classes for that."

"Right, but I never finished." Reaching over, Saffron tapped another attachment. "And here you'll find a copy of my teaching degree—you know, the one I never got. Isn't that crazy? Oh, but that's not even the craziest part, Kady. Read the official email offering me the Head Librarian position."

Kady did, her eyebrows arrowing down as she read the part where they thanked Saffron for coming in to interview for the position, and telling her she was the overwhelming choice by the hiring and recruitment committee. "I don't understand...when did you go in for this interview?"

"How about never?" Saffron's smile was so wide, it bathed Kady's heart with delight. "There's all sorts of other stuff in there that makes no sense but, according to LWB, they think I'm the cat's pajamas!" She laughed.

Looking at the list of emails from Libraries Without Boundaries, Kady asked, "Did you delete all the other emails they sent you with the job offers for the other positions? I don't see them here. You should have kept them."

Spreading her fingers over her chest, Saffron responded, "*I* didn't delete them, but they were all deleted as soon as I decided I wanted the Head Librarian job."

"Poof, just like that?" Kady made a mushroom cloud effect with her hands.

"Yup. I'd got excited after reading each email, then went back to the librarian one and said aloud, 'Oh this is it. This is the one I want! Head Librarian!' *Boomshakalaka*, one by one, each of the other emails disappeared. Whoa, I'm telling you, Kady, the magic in that ring from Odin is powerful stuff! Make sure you look at this email," she pointed with the tip of her fingernail, "telling me where I'll be located for the next three years. Go ahead...look!" She outright giggled.

As soon as she saw the word Nigeria, Kady whooped, grabbing Saffron and hugging her so hard she feared she might crack her cousin's ribs. "Oh Saffron, this is fabulous! Sensational! I am absolutely, positively thrilled for you...and for Quinn! Ooh, does he know yet?"

"He does." Saffron gave a slow nod. "I called him right after sorting through all of this and making my decision. Nigeria's eight hours ahead of us. It was one o'clock when I called, nine p.m. their time. No one's been able to receive or make calls from Quinn's remote location since they arrived so when my call came in he couldn't believe it. He said his colleagues teased him about having a magic phone. Little do they know!" She giggled again. "I told

Quinn I'd fill him in on all the particulars when I see him in...ready?" Kady nodded. "In two weeks!"

"So soon? Wow!"

Clasping both of Kady's hands, Saffron gave them a squeeze. "Can you believe it, Kady? The timing is perfect. It gives me enough time to get most everything in order here before I leave."

"I'll help with whatever you need to do before you leave, and after too," Kady offered. "Just let me know."

"Thanks, I will. Want to know what Quinn asked me?"

Kady laughed at her cousin's over the top exuberance. "Of course I do!"

"Ooh, wait. What's the matter with me." Saffron jumped up, heading for the kitchen. "Kady, come help me find the champagne glasses so we can make a toast."

"Argh! I hate that you're keeping me in suspense," Kady teasingly accused, already having a darned good idea what Quinn had asked.

Once the champagne was poured, they held their filled glasses aloft.

"Quinn proposed, Kady! He proposed! As in marriage!"

"Omigod, I knew it. I *knew* it! A toast! Here's to my beautiful cousin and dear friend Saffron Devington, and my soon to be cousin-in-law, Quinton Kilpatrick!" After taking a few healthy glugs, they hugged each other, laughing and crying happy tears.

"I am beyond excited. I'm not even going to ask you what your answer was because I kind of have an idea." Kady and Saffron laughed together as Saffron slipped the wide ribbon and bow from the box of chocolates and opened it, displaying a luscious assortment of dark chocolate confections.

"I got the dark chocolate assortment. The chocolate and the fillings are all vegan. See?" She pointed to tiny writing on the box cover. "Certified vegan."

"Aw, thanks for remembering, especially when you were over the moon with excitement. Mmm, they look scrumptious." Reading the little descriptions of each filling, Kady plucked a decorated square from the box. "Coconut milk caramel with coconut pistachio crunch. Let's see if it's as amazing as it sounds." Her eyelids fluttered closed as she sank her teeth into sheer heaven. "Oh it is. Definitely." She laughed. "I must admit, this is a far better lunch than the breakfast I had this morning."

"Don't tell me, you had one of your gag-worthy green smoothies, right?" Saffron shuddered, making Kady laugh again.

"Maybe."

"I'm sorry, after you're just spent your one and only heartwish on me I should be much nicer...but every time I think about the taste you gave me that time." She shuddered again.

"It's okay. You're forgiven. Taste-wise, I'll admit champagne and good chocolate are far superior." Kady selected a chocolate with ginger mousse filling. "Mmm...absolute heaven. Kale can't begin to compete."

"I have a question though..." Saffron said. "You told me your wish was going to be about fixing Red's relationship with my parents and Lorraine. What happened?"

Kady told her all about her Nymph Mail communication with Red as they enjoyed more champagne and chocolate. Saffron said she agreed with Red's assessment but still felt guilty for Kady 'wasting' her wish on her.

During their long conversation, they examined each email and attachment Saffron received from Libraries Without Boundaries, marveling over the precise and exact manner in which each step of Kady's heartwish was conducted. The wish process left no sloppy remains that could raise eyebrows, such as multiple emails offering jobs, or other no longer pertinent information. All that was left is what was normal and necessary for anyone who'd just been offered a position with a company.

Saffron told her one of the most mind-blowing aspects of her experience was checking the university records from the dates she'd attended and, sure enough, the librarian and teaching degrees were both listed among the degrees Saffron had already earned. No stone had been left unturned.

"Please tell me you made sure to make at least some tiny wish for yourself too," Saffron said. "Honestly, Kady, I feel bad because you sacrificed to make me happy. I mean, God knows, I'm ecstatic, because I truly believed Quinn and I were over—that I might never see him again. I was beyond heartbroken. But then I think about you and how hard it must be because of the way you feel about Rylan and—"

"I made sure Rylan will be happy," Kady told her.

"Yay!" Saffron clapped. "Because I saw him last night. He came over to drop off Quinn's keepsakes for me and we had an absolutely fabulous, eye-opening talk. Mostly about you."

"You and Rylan talked about me?"

"Mmm-hmm." Saffron nodded. "*Veeeeery* important stuff! I tried calling and texting you a few times this morning to fill you in but you never answered. Was your phone on the charger or something? Ooh, Kady, once I tell you, you'll be smiling from ear to ear!" Her eyebrows danced while Kady's stomach flopped over and sank.

"I turned the phone off while I was preparing everything for my heartwish. I didn't want any distractions," Kady said absently, wondering what their discussion was about. She had the most awful feeling she'd made a mess of things. "I didn't turn it back on until after I made my wish...waiting to hear from you to make sure everything worked out all right."

"No problem. It all turned out okay anyway," Saffron assured, "since you made your heartwish about you and Rylan. Whew! I'm so glad you did. Honestly, one of the things Rylan told me will make you laugh your ass off, while making you angry as hell with Lorraine at the same time. It's about you and your Latin lover!" Saffron broke into laughter.

Kady sat there silent, her thoughts a blur. Nothing Saffron told her had really registered, other than it sounded like Kady may as well have drilled a hole in her own heart because she'd ruined the final part of her heartwish.

"Kady?" Saffron touched her arm. "Did you hear what I said?"

Looking up at her cousin, Kady said, "Hmm?"

"Aw, Kady...tell me you made your wish about you and Rylan. You did, didn't you? Please say yes, because—"

"Rylan and Lorraine," Kady said, shaking her head back and forth with agonizing slowness before downing the rest of champagne in her glass.

"No..." Saffron's face fell. "Oh no, Kady, you didn't. Lorraine doesn't deserve it, she—"

"I didn't do it for Lorraine, Saf. I did it for Rylan because..." she sucked in a weighty breath, "because I love him," she shrugged, "and want to see him truly happy. Lorraine may not deserve this part of my wish, but Rylan does. Since Lorraine's the person he's chosen for a lifemate, I wanted to ensure their union would be a happy, satisfying one. After this conversation of ours, I never want my feelings for Rylan mentioned again, okay?"

"But, Kady, you don't understand. It's not the way you think. You see, Rylan told me that he—" Saffron's phone rang and she frowned. "Speak of the devil...that's Lorraine's ringtone. She never calls me. Something must be wrong. Aw shit...not now...not now..." She sat there for a long moment, nibbling her bottom lip as she gazed at the phone.

"You're not going to answer?"

"I'm afraid." Saffron's voice sounded small and wobbly.

"Afraid?" If she hadn't heard the strange cadence of Saffron's voice just now, Kady would have laughed. But any notion of humor was squelched as soon as she caught the look of dread across her cousin's face. Kady had never seen Saffron look like this before. "Afraid of what, Saf? What do you think Lorraine's going to do?"

"Spoil my happiness. Rob me of my joy. The way she always does. She always finds a way, Kady. My sister can't stand to see me happy." She sucked in a deep breath, expelling it noisily as she quickly sat stiff-backed against the sofa cushion. "No, I'm not going to let her control me anymore. I'm not!"

Without another moment's hesitation, Saffron answered the call, putting it on speakerphone so Kady could hear Lorraine too. "Lorraine? What's wrong?" Her voice was bold and confident.

"Wrong?" Lorraine's giddy laughter rang out. "Don't be such a negative Nellie, Saffron. Nothing's wrong. Not a single thing in the world is wrong. In fact, I've never been happier."

Izzy let out a low, quiet growl at the sound of Lorraine's voice.

"The most amazing thing has happened," Lorraine continued, "and I want to tell you about it before I leave. I'm all packed and ready to go."

"Leave? What do you mean? Where are you going?"

"My all-time favorite place in the entire world."

"Paris?" Saffron's expression twisted into one of bewilderment. "You're going to Paris?"

"Of course! Paris, the city of love. For my honeymoon!"

Staggered, Saffron and Kady mouthed *honeymoon* at each other.

"Where are you?" Lorraine asked.

"I'm at Bekka House with Kady, but—"

"Perfect! I'll be there in ten minutes."

"No, Lorraine, wait!" But she'd already hung up. "Oh hell." Glancing up, Saffron gawked at Kady. "Oh my God, you sent my sister and Rylan to Paris? After everything Lorraine has done, you used part of your heartwish for her to go to her personal happiest place on earth? And did nothing for yourself? Dammit, Kady." She pounded the top of the coffee table, making their champagne glasses stutter. "*Damn it*! Why? Why would you do that?"

"No! My wish had nothing to do with Paris. I never said anything that specific."

Her head spinning, Kady was unnerved at how fast the heartwishes were granted. "Do you think they got married already?" She did her best to keep her expression calm and even. It wouldn't do to let on that her world had just imploded at the thought of Rylan and Lorraine being married. After all, this is exactly what she'd wished for, right? Well, not the Paris honeymoon part exactly, but it was all close enough to fit into the careful parameters of her heartwish—the wish Saffron led her to believe she never should have made.

"With the cost of that extravagant wedding Lorraine planned that rivals the national debt?" Saffron enjoyed a robust laugh. "Are you kidding? Unless..." she covered her mouth, "holy shit, Kady, maybe they're eloping and will have the big ceremony here for the family in October."

Caught in the midst of this unexpected conundrum, Kady nodded slowly. "Well...I guess we'll find out soon, won't we?"

"Kady..." Saffron had a pitying look across her pretty face.

"Aw, sweetie," Kady said, "this is no time to be feeling sorry for me. I'm fine. Really. If I screwed up my heartwish, it's my own damn fault, no one else's. Come on now, Saffy, this should be a time of ultimate happiness for you. Don't you dare go spoiling the superb results of the Saffron and Quinn part of my heartwish by worrying about me. That, more than anything, will really make me sad."

"No, I'll leave the spoiling up to my sister," Saffron said without a shred of humor in her voice. Rising from the couch, she grabbed the half-finished bottle of champagne. On her way to the kitchen, she called over her shoulder, "Grab the box of chocolates, Kady. I don't care how super thrilled Lorraine is about whatever her ultra-fabulous news is, she won't be celebrating it with our champagne and chocolate. Before Lorraine gets here I should have enough time to tell you what else I found out from Rylan last night...about you and Ramon Taramino."

Saffron's lips quirked into a smile as they safely stashed the wine and candy out of sight.

"Me and Ramon?" Confused, Kady's scrunched her face. "I don't understand."

"You know, your Latin lover."

"My what?!"

With a questioning whimper, Izzy's head tilted back and forth as she looked at Kady.

The doorbell rang.

# Chapter 24

~<>~

"I'LL FINISH telling you later, along with the rest of the eye-opening stuff you need to hear." Grabbing Kady's hand, Saffron gave it a firm squeeze. "Ready?"

Kady's teeth dug into her bottom lip. "As I'll ever be." She wasn't sure which one of them was more nervous. They walked to the door together, with Izzy between them.

Pausing before opening it, Saffron checked once more. "You going to be okay?"

"Yeah." There's no way Kady would give Lorraine the satisfaction of seeing her cry, or appear heartbroken about Rylan. "Just peachy. You?"

"Peach-a-rific." Saffron nodded with a smile. "Let's do this." She opened the door and Lorraine burst in, grabbing them both into a three-way hug so vigorous Kady wondered if her cousin had taken wrestling lessons.

"I'm doing it!" Lorraine belted out. "And I want the two of you to be the first to know...well, after Mother and Daddy, of course. They're positively euphoric. The three of us are on cloud nine!"

Izzy growled, receiving a narrow-eyed sneer from Lorraine in response.

"You're doing what, Lorraine?" Saffron asked, enthusiasm absent from her tone.

"Getting married!" She twiddled her fingers, flashing an impressive engagement ring Kady hadn't seen before. The huge diamond definitely fit Lorraine's penchant for glitz and showiness.

"Well that's nice, Lorraine, but it isn't actually news, is it?" Saffron pointed out the obvious. "You already sent out the invitations, remember?"

"Oh that." Scrunching her features with a *who cares* expression, Lorraine gave a dismissive wave. "I'm not talking about *that*. About *him*." She shuddered.

Kady and Saffron exchanged perplexed looks at the same time Izzy slanted her head in confusion.

"Could you be more specific?" Kady said.

Walking ahead of Kady and Saffron, Lorraine headed for the family room, taking a seat at the far end of the sofa, while Kady and Saffron sat next to each other at the center and opposite side.

"Ugh, who turned that garish old thing on?" Lorraine complained, glowering at the silver tree's rotating color wheel. Kady had decided to leave it on for a while after making her wish because she enjoyed the celebratory feel it gave the room.

"I don't understand why you people insist on having that dilapidated tree standing front and center in the family room when it's not anywhere close to Christmas," Lorraine griped. "Aren't you embarrassed to have that hideous eyesore prominently displayed? Even when it *is* Christmas, that old thing couldn't be less festive with its—"

"Lorraine!" Saffron interrupted her sister's endless flow of grousing. "Focus and tell us who and what the hell you're talking about." Izzy punctuated Saffron's statement with a bark.

"Oh, right." Her expression speedily morphed from cranky to blissful. "I'm talking about me getting married, of course."

"Yes, we've already established that," Saffron noted. Looking at her sister's ring finger, she said, "That's quite a rock Rylan gave you. Must have cost him a year's salary."

Aghast, Lorraine said, "Rylan?" She gaped at her sister as if Saffron had lost her mind. "Who's talking about Rylan? I'm talking about me and Reginald."

"Reginald?!" Kady and Saffron chorused, while Izzy made a curious noise too.

"Indeed! Isn't it fabulous? We're flying to Paris in about," Lorraine checked the diamond-band wristwatch she always wore instead of looking at her phone, "two hours. On Reginald's private plane. We'll exchange our vows tomorrow at sunset, floating along the Seine River on his family's private yacht while enjoying superb views of the Louvre, Notre Dame Cathedral, the Musée d'Orsay, the Eiffel Tower, etcetera." Her hand flit through the air.

Kady felt like a cartoon character that shakes their head so fast, trying to understand the incomprehensible, that screws fly out of their brain every which way.

"I don't understand," Kady said. "What are you talking about? I thought you and Rylan were getting married in October."

"Reggie Von Austerly," Saffron said, narrowing one eye. "The guy you used to be engaged to and dumped because you got sick of him? You're marrying him instead of Professor Kilpatrick?"

"What can I say?" Lorraine replied with a dazzling, un-Lorraine-like smile. "I was rash and immature. While Reginald—"

"Hold that thought," Saffron said, holding up her hand. "Sorry, that time of the month. Gotta make a change. Be right back. Don't say another word without me. I want to hear absolutely everything, Lorraine. All of your fabulous news."

"My lips are hermetically sealed until your return," Lorraine said with good humor. "I'm delighted you're so excited, Saffron."

"Oh, I am. Back in a few minutes!" Giving her sister a wink and a thumbs up, Saffron grabbed her purse and scurried off.

Somewhat skeptical about Saffron's sudden need to flee, Kady spent the next five minutes listening to Lorraine gripe about everything, starting with the cluttered décor all over Bekka House. She was referring to the wonderful handmade items, the gallery of memorable photographs from trips and events, the cozy, overstuffed furniture, and anything else that made Bekka House the perfect gathering place for loving family and friends.

Izzy was on her belly, her paws over her head and ears, looking like she'd had enough of Lorraine's endless beefing too.

After what seemed like a small eternity, Saffron finally returned. A good thing because Kady had run out of small talk and patience listening to Lorraine's malicious gossip about people who were supposedly her good friends.

"Did you just open the front door on your way in here from the bathroom?" Kady asked Saffron.

"Yeah. Just checking because I thought I heard something," Saffron answered. "Everything's fine."

Sitting on the couch again, Saffron stuffed her purse beside her, next to the armrest. "So, Lorraine, you left off at the part about you being rash and immature." Hands neatly folded in her lap, Saffron smiled.

"Oh yes," Lorraine went on without skipping a beat, "while Reginald may not be blessed with Rylan's matinee idol looks, he comes from a distinguished family, has tons of money and connections, and he's considered the prize catch in my social circle. Ooh," Lorraine's eyes popped wide, "just wait until they find out I've bagged Reginald! They'll be sooo envious! They're always talking about how the Von Austerlys have more money than God." Lorraine let out something sounding like a giggle.

"Wait a minute..." Clapping her hands on either side of her head, Kady shook it, which was no help. She was still baffled. "None of this makes any sense, Lorraine."

"On the contrary, it makes perfect sense. I'd be a fool to give Reginald up for someone as mundane and ill-connected as Rylan. Reginald and I have *so* much in common, whereas, Rylan..." Lorraine gave a disgusted huff.

"Granted, he may look striking and Bond-like in a dinner jacket, but the man's simply not Devington material. Imagine me married to a man itching to leave his professorship so he can," she shuddered, "write genre fiction. I'd be a laughing stock. No thank you."

Leaping onto the couch between Kady and Saffron, Izzy growled at Lorraine.

"Can we please muzzle that creature?"

"What the hell kind of heartwish did you make," Saffron whispered in Kady's ear.

"Not this one," Kady whispered back as she stroked Izzy's fur. "Something must have gone haywire."

"Careful," Saffron cautioned with another whisper, "Lorraine's in one of her manic moods. It can turn on a dime." Kady nodded.

"Hey now, no secrets allowed," Lorraine said in a teasing manner, shaking a chastising finger at them.

"So you and Rylan aren't engaged anymore? You're not marrying him." It was almost too much for Kady's overtaxed brain to process.

"Correct. Daddy's been urging me to reunite with Reginald ever since he first met Rylan. As if revealing an intriguing secret, Lorraine added, "Daddy's not one of Rylan's biggest fans." She wrinkled her nose with a smile.

"Well duh," Saffron quipped.

Lorraine's sideways glance at her sister was anything but friendly...or sisterly. Seems her mood was shifting. "Reginald's been calling me at least twice a week all along since I called off our engagement. We've been seeing each other for some time now."

"Seeing each other?" Kady asked, nearly exploding. "Behind Rylan's back? Lorraine, that's terrible!"

Sitting at attention, Izzy offered a supportive growl.

"You shouldn't be surprised, Kady." Saffron huffed an ironic laugh. "Red and I have been trying to tell you."

"Red?" Lorraine bristled. "Keep his name out of this conversation. No one cares what that perverted queer thinks or says. He chose to be a homo. Now he has to pay the price. His fault. Not mine."

"Aaand," Saffron said, turning to Kady, "I tried to tell you about that too, didn't I? Lorraine only pretended to be accepting of Red because she knew that's what you wanted to hear. Isn't that right, Lorraine?"

"Oh Lorraine..." Kady furrowed her brows. "Please tell me that's not true. I really believed you were being open and honest with me about your feelings for your brother. About missing him and hoping to see him again. You-you even got teary-eyed when you said it."

With a dramatic roll of her eyes, Lorraine tsked. "Isn't it time you ditched the rose-colored glasses and stop being so gullible? Honestly, you're such a baby, Kathleen. Or maybe I should say a Pollyanna. Yes, that's it. From now on you'll be known as Pollyanna Malone!"

Lorraine laughed and Izzy barked several times.

"I'm reaching the end of my rope with that damned dog," Lorraine said through clenched teeth.

Saffron took Izzy onto her lap, comforting her. "Shhh, shhh. It's okay, sweetie."

Lorraine's words hit Kady hard. She should have believed Saffron and Red when they tried to warn her about Lorraine's true nature. But she stubbornly continued believing the best about her cousin. Lorraine was wrong. Kady wasn't immature, she was a positive, optimistic, hopeful woman. Perhaps too trusting, but she was nobody's fool.

"Stop it, Lorraine," Saffron reprimanded. "Don't listen to her, Kady. Her words can poison your mindset."

"So you're Kady's self-appointed protector now? How pathetic." Lorraine's chin elevated as she looked down her nose at her sister and cousin. "I can say whatever I damn well please." She turned her attention to Kady. "As for my performance when we spoke, yes, thank you, I'll gladly accept the best actress award." Acrid laughter ensued.

Lorraine had always been snooty, irritable and negative, but this? "I'm so awfully disappointed in you, Lorraine," Kady told her.

"Well boohoo, that breaks my heart. Whatever will I do?" Lorraine pretended to squeegee tears from her eyes with her fists. "Grow up. The world isn't all sunshine, daisies and silly hippie peace symbols." She snickered. "Now scrape your jaw up from the floor and close your mouth before you attract flies."

"In one ear and out the other," Saffron coached Kady, making the gesture. "Just remember the source."

"Yes indeed, listen to Miss Logic and Wisdom," Lorraine said. "You can see how well she has *her* life in order." Mocking laughter followed.

"Why are you even here, Lorraine?" Saffron asked, sounding weary.

"I told you. Because I want to share my happiness with both of you." Lorraine's smile was bright and sincere—as if another woman had swapped places with her. "Two hours ago Reginald surprised me by coming to Devington Manor, getting down on one knee, right in front of Mother and Daddy, and proposing." She flashed her ring again. The diamond looked almost big enough to be mistaken for a small Christmas ornament.

"What a cruel joke to play on Rylan," Saffron noted. "You should have been honest with him so he could have moved on without any strings."

Kady couldn't help adding a boisterous, "Amen to that!"

"Nonsense, he's a big boy. He'll get over it. Daddy told me not to worry about the scheduled October wedding. Reginald and I will do the ceremony together instead of me and Rylan. That way we'll be married in front of all our friends and family so we don't miss out on any gifts. Household staff will change the invitations and do whatever else is necessary."

"You don't want to miss out on raking in all that dough and those gifts," Saffron said sarcastically.

"Precisely." Lorraine pointed at her sister with a smile. "You're still a Devington, Saffron. I knew you'd understand. I haven't told you the best part." With stretching grin, Lorraine wiggled with glee. "Reginald and I will be making our permanent home in the Paris countryside. A far cry from what Rylan means when speaking about living in the country." Lorraine laughed, all by herself.

An instant later, she turned angry expressions on Kady and Saffron. The woman changed guises quicker than flipping a light switch.

"Actually, maybe the best part is that I won't have to pretend anymore, now that I'm moving away for good. I won't have to see either of you or pretend to be cordial any longer. I'll also be rid of my cloying parents. Yes indeed, life is good, and I'm finally getting what I deserve."

As Lorraine buried herself, deeper and deeper, Kady found herself getting a crash course in *Sociopaths and their Personalities 101.*

"What did Rylan say when you broke the engagement?" she asked.

"He doesn't know about it."

"You haven't told the man yet?" Saffron asked. "What the hell, Lorraine?"

"Oh, get off your high horse, Saffron. Of course I haven't told him. Why would I want to deal with angst or drama before taking off for Paris and my fabulous new life there? I'll send the professor a *Dear Rylan* letter," she made a jotting motion in the air, "from France, letting him know."

"Poor Rylan will be devastated," Kady said. On the one hand she was thrilled Lorraine was leaving to marry Reggie, but on the other hand, her heart broke for Rylan. It would be a long time before he'd be ready for another relationship. But she could wait...no matter how long it took.

"Devastated?" With an uncharacteristic snort-laugh, Lorraine said, "Hardly. That weasel had the audacity to try to break things off with me. But I succeeded in...shall we say *intimidating* him enough to make him rethink his decision." She laughed at that, apparently finding it quite funny. "Devington women don't get dumped. We're the ones who do the dumping. Isn't that right, Saffron?"

"That's part of what I wanted to tell you earlier," Saffron told Kady, ignoring her sister's question. "I learned about it last night from Rylan," she clarified.

"He was talking about me behind my back?" Lorraine's eyes bugged.

"Only in the kindest way," Saffron lied. "So, Lorraine, exactly when did you start seeing Reggie again? Before or after the dinner party at Kady's apartment a few months ago?"

"Before." Lorraine brushed at some invisible lint on the sleeve of her dress.

Saffron gave Kady a sharp glance. Kady took it as a look that said, *see, what did I tell you about Lorraine?*

"I suspected Reginald was about to propose soon. So the morning Rylan took me to that awful place for breakfast to have a *talk*," she bracketed the word, "I stalled him, laying a guilt trip on him about Daddy spending a fortune on the wedding. I told Rylan he'd be humiliating me." Looking into the distance, Lorraine engaged in nasty laughter. "Poor dopey Rylan. He's such a man of honor and principle that he backed down immediately. He's amazingly simple to manipulate. Nearly as gullible as you, Kady."

Addressing Kady, Lorraine added, "I easily convinced Rylan you were deeply in love and having an affair with Ramon Gustavo Taramino." Her laughter increased. "And he believed me. Isn't that hilarious? Rylan looked angry as a hornet's nest. It was incredibly difficult for me to keep a straight face as images of Kady and Ramon raced through his mind. Just too funny."

"I can't believe this," Kady softly muttered, mostly to herself. "Why, Lorraine?" she said louder. "Why on earth would you do that?"

"Because I can." She offered a proud shrug. "I remembered how you used to say Ramon looked like an elderly Antonio Banderas. That gave me the idea. Brilliant, hmm?"

"All done to make Rylan jealous," Saffron told Kady before turning back to her sister. "In case you didn't know, Reggie and I are good friends, Lorraine. We talk fairly regularly. He never mentioned you two were seeing each other behind your fiancé's back."

"Friends." Lorraine tittered a laugh. "Aw, how cute that you think that, Saffron. Reginald are I are cut from the same cloth. Two peas in a pod. He knows exactly what to say and do to get the information he wants, or that *I* want, while throwing off suspicious people." Lorraine's gaze narrowed. "Like my own sister. Like a good boy, Reginald kept me fully informed about your numerous heart-to-heart conversations. We've had some good laughs over it while enjoying our mojitos."

Mocking Reggie's voice, Lorraine said, "Oh Saffron, I'm so in love with Lorraine. What can I do to get her to take me back?"

Her laughter was wicked. "And you, sister dear, readily believed every word he fed you, and answered every question he posed. So Saffronesque."

The color draining from her face, Saffron murmured, "That son of a bitch." She fisted her hands at her sides.

Kady's heart went out to her. It turns out Lorraine truly was as nefarious as she'd been warned. She reached over and took one of Saffron's fists, holding her hand as lovingly as possible until Saffron's fingers loosened. Izzy contributed by snuggling close to Saffron, licking her hands and making a sound almost like purring.

"I'd already grown tired of Professor Kilpatrick, whose annoying folksy ways and dry as dust interests are so frightfully different from mine it isn't even funny. I told Mother and Daddy about me and Reginald the day after my soiree, after Kady had visited. Daddy had already spoken to Rylan, finding him a major disappointment. Rylan's stubbornness and unwillingness to change proved he was nothing more than a handsome doll to toy with."

It was no wonder Kady had a hard time believing the warnings about Lorraine. She'd wondered if perhaps Saffron and Red were exaggerating, without meaning to. Now, after witnessing Lorraine in action for herself, Kady understood. Lorraine Devington was intolerable. Unstable. Unhinged. It was crystal clear now why Saffron used to be frightened of her sister...and perhaps still was.

"You should have seen Daddy, Saffron. The old codger was so relieved I'd chosen Reginald over Rylan that he cracked a smile and broke out his best cognac. We toasted to me having a successful future with Reginald."

This was like being a character in a movie where Kady hadn't read the script. All this time she'd felt like a shameless hussy because of her feelings for Rylan. Little did she know Lorraine was discreetly balancing two men at the same time.

"Had I decided to marry Rylan, I would have looked the other way if he chose to dally with a mistress, say...someone like you, Kady," she offered a perverse smile, "while I continued to carry on with Reginald behind his back. You don't honestly believe I wasn't aware of your interest in my fiancé, do you, Kady? You should really work on your poker face, cousin. I could read you like a book."

"I doubt that," Saffron said. "You'd have to know how to read first."

"You're malicious, Lorraine." Dropping her head into her hands, Kady willed herself not to cry. She'd been so careful not to reveal her attraction to Rylan. So cautious about not hurting anyone. "You're incredibly insensitive and mean-spirited. It's difficult to believe how cruel and unkind you are. All these years...how could I never realize it?" She felt her cheeks burn, probably turning crimson, as Lorraine's merciless gaze seared into her.

"Don't think I didn't notice Rylan's interest in you as well," Lorraine said, continuing her berating diatribe. "Apparently he likes the Rebecca of Sunnybrook Farm type. Oops," Lorraine's hand flew to her mouth, "I mean the Pollyanna type. Your science-fiction-writing hero is so naïve and trusting he never even suspected that I was seeing Reginald all this time. He automatically believed me each time I told him I was meeting with my women's club." She laughed openly.

"The part about you and whoever you marry having trysts with other people while you're married is just plain sad," Kady said. "Is that what you think love is, Lorraine? Why even bother getting married?" Even as she asked, Kady realized it was useless trying to have a normal give and take conversation with Lorraine.

"Having paramours is quite common among the wealthy, as well as royalty," Lorraine pointed out. "It's a simple matter of purposeful ignorance, that's all."

Kady wasn't surprised to hear Lorraine make comparisons with royalty, with her being the pampered Princess of Devington Manor.

That was enough. More than enough. Kady wouldn't allow Lorraine to blather on with her appalling ramblings and accusations when today was supposed to be Saffron's special day. Saffron said she was afraid Lorraine would try to steal her joy...and Lorraine was succeeding. She was sucking the life, love, and joy out of both of them and out of Bekka House itself. That took some powerful negativity.

"I'm glad you decided to visit this afternoon, Lorraine." Sitting tall, hands neatly folded in her lap, Kady transmitted a bright smile. "You see, you're not the only one with good news today. Remarkable news, in fact."

"Don't bother, Kady." Saffron placed a hand over Kady's. "My sister couldn't care less."

"Nonsense. I want to hear all about my sister's remarkable news so I can be as happy for her as I'm sure she is for me."

"Sure you do." Saffron chuckled.

"Saffron and Doctor Quinn Kilpatrick will soon be married," Kady announced, catching an almost imperceptible flash in Lorraine's eyes. "Saffron will be joining the esteemed neurosurgeon in Nigeria for the next three years thanks to Saffron's enviable new position as Head Librarian for Libraries Without Boundaries."

Lorraine nearly doubled over with laughter while Kady and Saffron exchanged stunned looks.

"I told you," Saffron said to Kady.

"Oh...oh wait." Lorraine wiped tears of laughter from her eyes after regaining her composure. "You were serious? I'm sorry, I didn't realize. I felt certain when you said my sister is planning to go live in the jungle among the Blacks that you were joking. But," she offered an indifferent shrug, "if that's what you perceive to be remarkable news, then bully for you, Saffron."

"Oh my God..." Kady said in utter disbelief. "Lorraine, I can't believe you said that. Shame on you."

"Don't go there with your ugly prejudice, Lorraine," Saffron warned. "I mean it."

"I can only imagine," Lorraine shivered, then briskly rubbed her arms, "how utterly embarrassed our poor parents will be when their friends ask what's happened to you, Saffron. They won't be able to let on that their daughter has thrown her life away so she can follow a man to deepest, darkest Africa where you two can romp around like naked jungle bunnies together."

Kady and Saffron gasped.

"Lorraine! For God's sake, please stop!" Kady pleaded.

A quick glance at staggered Saffron told Kady she was on the verge of tears, struggling not to give in to the sobbing that threatened. Saffron usually appeared so confident and strong. It was terrible to see her close to cowering now. It was no wonder, after a lifetime of her experiencing such cruelty from her sister. The slight sniffle and whimper coming from her broke Kady's heart.

Lorraine was intent on destroying one of the happiest days in Saffron's life. Saffron was right, Kady never should have shared Saffron's wonderful news with Lorraine. It was partially her fault that poor Saffron was so shaken now.

Seemingly in her own world, Lorraine cackled to herself.

Keeping her voice moderate, Kady said, "You're an intelligent, cultured, well-bred woman, Lorraine." She was well aware those qualities were absent today. "I'm asking you, please, to be civil. To treat your sister with kindness and decency. If you can't, then I'm afraid I must ask you to leave Bekka House."

While Kady maintained a cool, calm exterior, she could feel herself shaking—feel her insides agitating. Those were probably the most difficult words she'd ever said to another person.

Entirely ignoring Kady, Lorraine barged ahead. "I wonder what Quinn will think when he sees how pathetic and homely you are without your makeup, Saffron. The ugly duckling Mother always said you were when you were a teen, remember? And then came your real estate days. Will you revert to wearing your standard mortician-like clothing? Your dowdy, frumpy, undertaker suits, once you've ensnared the good doctor?"

Leaning comfortably against the sofa cushions, arms crossed over her chest, Lorraine offered a tongue-in-cheek smile.

"My God..." Kady muttered, appalled by Lorraine's words. Poor Saffron looked like she wanted to melt into a crack in the floorboards. "Please don't, Lorraine," Kady began, only to be ignored yet again by Lorraine.

"What happens when Quinn sees that plain, dull, blemished face? When he sees your untoned body, with the flabby belly and wide hips every day? You won't be able to hide all your flaws in the stifling African heat as you're drenched, stinking with sweat, and your clothing clings to your rolls and bulges. Your handsome neurosurgeon may find himself more turned on by the natives." More cackling punctuated her verbal abuse.

Rage, unlike anything Kady had ever experienced, roiled inside her, fermenting in her gut before gurgling up into her throat. Saffron had been through so much. She deserved to revel in this wondrous turn of events for her and Quinn. She should be celebrating, rather than cowering in fear and shame as her sister merrily provoked her with one stinging insult after another.

No...*no*! Kady wouldn't allow this blisteringly horrid woman to steal even one more second of Saffron's bliss.

Before Kady could speak, Izzy let out a low, menacing growl, inching slowly toward Lorraine on the sofa. A quick glance showed Kady that her sweet, loving little dog was baring her teeth. She'd never seen Izzy look or sound like that before. The dog had been so quiet, Kady had almost forgotten she was even there.

"Keep that lame, wretched flea bag away from me," Lorraine demanded, tucking her legs beneath her to keep them protected from the furious Izzy. "I mean it, Kathleen. Don't force me to further cripple that little toad you call a dog, because I will. I'll break her good legs if she even touches me. I promise you I'll—"

"Dammit, Lorraine, stop! Just fucking *stop*!" Leaping to her feet, Kady stood in front of her cousin, pointing an accusatory finger. Her face on fire, red hot with anger, Kady raged, "That's it! You are fucking done, you vile, contemptible, hateful bitch! Don't even think about spewing another brutal, toxic word from your venomous mouth. Not another ugly fucking word about your sister or my dog, or you'll be sorry." Her unexpected outburst had both Lorraine and Saffron staring at her, agape.

Neither of them were nearly as gobsmacked as Kady.

Apparently her harsh, once in a lifetime profanity-laced tirade didn't have quite the effect Kady hoped it would because a moment later, Lorraine blithely snickered at her. She snickered!

"Why am I not surprised to hear filth belching from your mouth, Kady? A clear sign of your limited vocabulary. Sweet Pollyanna who never speaks an unkind word, hmm? Ha! Nothing but an act." Her eyes narrowed into hostile slits. "You've always been the slow one in the family, the one everyone tolerates because they feel sorry for poor backward, challenged Kady."

Kady steeled herself against Lorraine's well-targeted verbal assault. Reminding herself the insults were callously designed to wound, crush, and paralyze her, Kady disregarded them, turned a deaf ear to the derision. If she didn't, Lorraine would get the upper hand, and things could get far worse for herself as well as Saffron.

"Lorraine, stop it!" Saffron shouted. "You can taunt me all you want, Lord knows I'm used to it, but leave our cousin alone. There's nothing phony about Kady. She tried to help you and Rylan get back on track. She doesn't deserve your venomous animosity."

"Keep quiet, you worthless, inconsequential waste of oxygen," Lorraine seethed at Saffron through clenched teeth. "What an asinine pair you two make. Two simpleminded, witless specimens of mediocrity. Two—"

"Shut. The. Fuck. Up, you cruel, heartless excuse for a human being," Kady growled, baring her own teeth as she spoke in a manner that was unfamiliar yet deeply satisfying. "How dare you rain on your sister's parade, you obnoxious, repulsive bitch! How dare you ridicule and rebuke your own flesh and blood." She gestured toward Saffron. "You disappoint me, Lorraine. Disgust me. You make my skin crawl. You're nothing but a pissant wannabe. You're not even fucking fit to breathe the same air as your wonderful, incredible, kindhearted sister."

Kady had uttered the F-word more often in the last five minutes than she had her entire life.

Dumbfounded, Lorraine blustered, "I beg your pardon!? How dare you speak to me that way. Saffron's parade? Don't be ridiculous. It's mine. *Mine!*" She clapped her chest hard. "*I'm* the fortunate, blessed, deserving one, not Saffron. It's always been me. I'm the favorite daughter. I'm not the one my mother tried to abort!" Spittle flew from Lorraine's mouth.

Aghast, Kady had a sharp intake of breath.

Her gaze shifting to Saffron, as silent tears rolled down Saffron's cheeks, Kady could only imagine how her bitterly wounded cousin must feel hearing Lorraine's cruel revelation—if it was even true. Kady herself felt as if her own heart had been mangled.

Once again, Izzy made her feelings known, clearly scaring the shit out of the unexpecting Lorraine with her hound from hell roar. Truth be told, it scared Kady too, as well as shaking up Saffron. Kady didn't need Aladee to explain how Izzy must be feeling. Kady understood—and felt the same way.

"You don't have to worry about Izzy, Lorraine." Kady grabbed Lorraine by the collar of her dress, yanking her forward. "Izzy won't have to harm you because, I swear to God, if you utter one more ugly, vicious word, I'll fucking break both your legs myself."

Reaching for her purse as Kady maintained her grip on her collar, Lorraine threatened, "I'm calling nine-one-one. I'm letting the police know you threatened my life, you maniac!"

"Lorraine!" Saffron yelled. "Enough!"

"No, it's okay, Saffron," Kady said, smiling at Saffron before showing Lorraine the same smile. "Go right ahead, Lorraine. Be my guest." Fishing the phone out of Lorraine's purse, Kady threw it at her. "The Glassfloat Bay police and all the emergency services people Gard works with know me and Saffron well from our charitable work in town and at Wisdom Harbor Hospital. Everyone knows us from our bookstore too."

By now, Kady had pulled Lorraine so close they were nose to nose as Kady spat her words directly into her cousin's face.

"You think *I'm* the gullible fool, Lorraine? Think again. You think you're so smart? So manipulative and deceitful? Well once I break your legs no one, not a single soul, will ever believe that sweet, innocent, gullible, naïve *Pollyanna* Malone could possibly be responsible for such a heinous, violent act."

Lorraine's mouth flew open and she gasped.

"The delicious part? You'd never be able to prove it, Lorraine," Kady continued, "without a witness to back you up. Saffron and I will swear you did it to yourself and should be put away where you can no longer be of harm to yourself or others. How's that for being manipulative, dear cousin? Can you relate to me better now?"

Amazed at the unfamiliar adrenalin rush and sensation of strength, Kady singlehandedly hauled her cousin to her to her feet as Lorraine stumbled off the couch, sputtering and blustering.

"You don't belong here, Lorraine," Kady said, her tone calm. "Bekka House is a sanctuary of love, light, and goodness for the pure of heart. For good, kind, caring people, and pets, who gladly celebrate each other's triumphs. Cruel, malevolent creatures like you have no place here, tainting the power of love and kindness." Releasing Lorraine's collar, Kady finished, "Now get out, Lorraine, or I'll throw you out."

Kady didn't have to say it twice. Sheet white, Lorraine gathered her phone and purse, hightailing it out of the family room, grumbling, swearing, bitching and cursing all the way...until she was a few yards from the front door. With agonizing slowness, she stopped, then turned toward Kady and Saffron, with a menacing look that would give children nightmares.

"You think you're going to ruin everything?" Lorraine said. "You think you're a match for me? *Me*!? Think again, Pollyanna!"

"Holy shit, Kady!" Saffron screamed. "She has a gun! Watch out!"

The gun was so small, Kady didn't see it at first.

As Lorraine aimed her pistol at Kady, Izzy barked, barreling forward, as fast as her little lopsided legs would allow. A few feet from Lorraine, Izzy leapt into the air, still barking. Lorraine fired the gun and Kady screamed in anguish when Izzy collapsed with a whimper at Lorraine's feet.

"Izzy! Oh my God, my poor Izzy!" Momentarily forgetting that Lorraine was brandishing a gun, Kady rushed forward to her little dog, lifeless on the floor. "Lorraine, what have you done?"

"Now it's your turn, Pollyanna."

"For God's sake, Lorraine, have you lost your mind?" Saffron screamed, her voice a good octave higher than usual as she rushed toward Kady. "Don't! Please!"

At that instant, the moment Kady feared might be her last, and Saffron's, the front door of Bekka House flew open, and Rylan barged in.

"Rylan, watch out!" both Kady and Saffron screamed.

Another shot rang out.

# Chapter 25

~<>~

"FUCK!" RYLAN yelled, gripping his shoulder and slumping halfway down the wall, trailing a smear of blood as he sank.

"Oh no! Rylan! *Rylan*!" Kady shouted. "Are you okay?" She realized it was a stupid question. Of course he wasn't okay. Her psychotic cousin just shot him at point blank range.

"I think so. It just hurts like hell. Move! Get away from her, Kady!"

At the same time, Kady saw Saffron tiptoeing toward Lorraine, behind Lorraine's back, causing Kady's heart to race with worry. She didn't want to call out a warning to Saffron because Lorraine might swivel around and shoot her.

Lorraine's gun-toting arm lifted. Her smile was maniacal.

In a rapid blur of activity, Rylan, Kady and Saffron clearly all had the identical idea because the trio jumped at Lorraine to restrain her.

Lorraine managed to fire another shot and they all screamed, including Lorraine. A quick assessment showed none of them had been hit...at least as far as they could tell. Kady had learned from her EMT brother, Gard, that sometimes when people get shot they don't even realize it until later.

During the commotion Rylan was able to secure the gun and toss it well out of reach, while Kady and Saffron sat on Lorraine's back as she writhed, screaming obscenities.

Getting to his knees, Rylan crawled to Izzy. Ever so gently, he scooped her into his arms, bringing the wounded dog to Kady. "Here's you're brave little protector. I checked...she's still breathing."

Kady took Izzy, cuddling her gingerly, speaking baby talk into her ear. Thank God in heaven, her sweet little Izzy was still alive. Izzy even made a barely audible little murmur as Kady spoke to her.

"Why didn't you move away when I told you to, Kady?" Rylan shouted, his voice full of angst. "She could have killed you. Saffron, same goes for you. Seriously, what were you two thinking with a crazy woman here brandishing a gun?"

"Shush, Rylan, be quiet!" Kady admonished. "You'll lose too much blood if you yell like that."

"What?!" Rylan and Saffron cried in unison.

Good grief, could she be any more idiotic? What the hell did that even mean? Kady didn't have a clue—it just spilled out of her mouth, seeming like the right thing to say at the moment. Apparently not, because both Rylan and Saffron were laughing now—causing a chain reaction because now all of them, including Kady and Lorraine were laughing. It was nervous laughter at its creepiest.

"I can't believe you're making us laugh when we're fighting for our lives here," Rylan accused, wiping tears from his face with bloody fingers, making him look like a grisly, goofy but still handsome as hell clown.

"Yeah, careful not to make Rylan laugh too hard, Kady," Saffron said. "He'll lose too much blood."

Kady realized their raw nerves must have taken over, making them laugh in an intense, entirely unfunny situation. Kind of like what happens in church when an old lady belts out off-key hymns while standing next to you. Or when you get the urge to laugh at someone's funeral. So, so inappropriate to succumb to laughter...the way Kady did a few times as a kid.

Holding up a finger, along with his phone, Rylan said, "Give me a minute." From the brief conversations Kady heard, she could tell he dialed 911, and the Glassfloat Bay Police Department, as well as a good friend and neighbor who was a veterinary surgeon. He'd apprised them all of the situation. They'd all be there soon.

After ending the call, Rylan took Kady's face in his hands. His lips met hers with a kiss that spoke volumes. It would have been even better if Lorraine hadn't been cursing a blue streak and bucking so hard while still laughing. Her movements kept Kady bouncing as she strived to keep Lorraine restrained.

"I've wanted to do that since the first time I ever laid eyes on you. This might not be the time, place, or circumstances I would have chosen but I couldn't wait a moment longer. I love you, Kady Malone."

"You do? Oh, Rylan, I love you too. I wish I could hug you, but..." Her gaze fell to the squirming figure she sat on, then to little Izzy, limp in her arms.

"We'll have plenty of time for that," Rylan told her. "Aw, hell, sorry, I got blood on your cheeks."

"No problem," Kady said. "I probably needed some color in my cheeks after what happened anyway."

Hands down, it was the most beautiful, special, romantic, and completely weird, moment in Kady's life. She held Lorraine's arm tighter behind her back as her cousin fought to get free.

"See that?" Saffron offered. "We're both getting our happily ever afters. But I still want to know what the heck kind of heartwish you made, Kady. I have a hunch it wasn't for all this." She laughed.

"Heartwish?" Rylan asked.

"I'll explain everything later," Kady promised. "Saffron, the wish is in a document on my laptop. I typed everything out so I wouldn't forget anything while making the wish. We'll take a look after all this is over to see what the heck I managed to do."

"Rylan," Saffron said, "did you hear everything on the call?"

"Every word, clear as a bell." He kept his hand pressed against his wound to help slow the bleeding.

"What call?" Kady asked as she and Saffron sat, shoulder to shoulder, struggling to hold down Lorraine's arms and legs. Damn, she was strong! At least her laughter had finally stopped.

"Remember when I got up to go to the bathroom?" Saffron asked, and Kady nodded. "It was just an excuse so I could call Rylan to tell him what was happening here with my crazy sister. I told him I was going to put us on speakerphone so he could hear the rest of the conversation. I wanted him to hear Lorraine's sneaky subterfuge firsthand. I also told him I unlocked the front door so he could get in if he needed to."

Saffron shrugged. "I don't know why I did that. I just had sort of a sickly hunch something might happen."

"As I listened, I got an uneasy feeling," Rylan said. "A prickly sensation told me I needed to be close by...just in case. I was in the car, parked nearly a block away, listening to everything, which is why I got here so fast. I'm only sorry she shot Izzy before I could stop her."

As Rylan spoke, Kady noticed a thin stream of blood on the floor. "Oh no...I think one of us was shot." The three of them checked themselves as well as checking for the source of the blood. It was coming from Lorraine. Their investigation showed Lorraine had inadvertently shot herself in the foot near her big toe. The wound looked minor. Rylan tore at the bottom of his shirt, using the strip of fabric to wrap around Lorraine's foot.

Looking up at Rylan again, Kady noticed the blood, trailing from his shoulder to his waist had increased. "Oh, Rylan, you're bleeding something awful!"

Looking down at himself, he chuckled. "Must be all that bloodsucking laughter."

With everything happening, Kady was too frazzled, frightened, and stunned to even cry. She wanted to examine Rylan's injury to see how bad it looked, but Lorraine, still lying on the floor on her belly, was bucking hard against Kady and Saffron. There's no way they were going to let her up until the police and paramedics arrived.

"Seriously, do you think you're okay?" Kady asked Rylan. "Are you feeling woozy or anything?"

"I've been better," he said with a crooked smile. "But I don't think it's too bad. Not that I have anything to compare it to. I've never been shot before." He chuckled. "But as they say in the movies, it's just a flesh wound, ma'am. At least that's what I think it is. If she'd hit an artery I'd be gone by now. I learned that from my brother when I had him read a scene in my book." He shrugged, which, his immediate grimace told Kady, was a very bad idea.

His voice sounding more pained, Rylan continued, "Quinn said writers often make the mistake of doing a supposedly non lethal gunshot to the shoulder. There's some major artery there. If hit, the victim will drop and die—fast. Often within fifteen seconds or so. Since I'm still here, I guess I'll survive...as long as I don't laugh too much of my blood out."

If Kady's hands weren't occupied holding Lorraine down, she would have covered her face in embarrassment.

"As soon as we see to the Wicked Witch of Glassfloat Bay here," Rylan said, gesturing to Lorraine, "I'll get myself checked out by the EMTs."

"Rylan, darling, when did you arrive?" Lorraine suddenly said in a sweet, calm voice that gave the three of them pause as they exchanged uneasy looks. "I'm so glad you're here. Oh, darling, it was just awful. I was telling my sister and cousin about how much I love you when they both flew into a jealous rage and attacked me. Kady was so vicious. Don't trust her. She's not who she appears to be."

"Thanks for the warning, princess. I heard the whole conversation. All of it. Every damn word you said, Lorraine. Sorry but it looks like you might be missing that flight to Paris, sweetheart. You won't be going anywhere for a while, with or without Reggie."

"Paris? Why on earth would I want to go there, especially with Reginald, when the man I love is right here in Glassfloat Bay? Oh, Rylan, I can't wait until October. We'll be so happy together, darling."

Lorraine turned her head until she could see Kady and Saffron. "Oh I'm so glad you two are still here. I was just telling Rylan that we had the loveliest chat here together at Bekka House this afternoon. Me, my beautiful sister, and my sweet cousin. We shared all of our good news. It was just like old times. We had such fun, didn't we Saffy?"

"Shit..." Saffron said, tears rolling down her face. Kady knew she'd be wiping at them if her hands were free. "Yes, Lorraine..." Saffron responded in a wobbly voice, "we had a lovely time together."

Lorraine had stopped struggling. She remained still and peaceful now as she chatted just like they were all enjoying a cup of tea together. It was so sad. And odd. And heartbreaking.

"Did you hear, Rylan?" Lorraine asked him. "My sister is going to Nigeria to be with Quinn. Isn't that wonderful news? I'm so happy for her. Your brother seems like a good man and Saffron deserves the best. She really does. I love her so much."

"Shit, shit, shit..." Saffron's shoulders shook from crying so hard.

"I wish I could hug you right now," Kady told her.

Nodding, Saffron attempted a smile.

"Yes, Lorraine. I heard the good news," Rylan said gently. Rather than sounding angry or belligerent after being shot by her, he showed Lorraine kindness...compassion.

That's when Kady finally began to cry.

Listening to her cousin's calm but bizarre talk was incredibly sad. Strange and absurd. She could only imagine how difficult it must be for Saffron to realize her sister was sinking further into madness, or whatever it was that made her the way she is. Kady had never experienced anything like this before...and prayed she never would again. She hoped Lorraine would be able to get the help she so obviously needed.

In a flash, the police, EMTs, and vet arrived, almost as if coordinated and in the same vehicle.

As a frenzy of people entered Bekka House and Lorraine was handcuffed, she smiled at Saffron, who stood a few feet away.

"I love you, Saffron," Lorraine said, her smile sweet, genuine, loving.

"I know, Lorraine...I know," Saffron responded, her face a waterfall of tears as she endeavored to smile. "I love you too," she said softly as Lorraine was led out of the house on a stretcher that had been folded into a transport chair.

Kady had never witnessed anything quite so heartbreaking.

# Chapter 26

*Two Weeks Later*

~<>~

CHERISHED PAGES Bookshop was closed to the public for a private event, Saffron's farewell party. She'd be leaving Glassfloat Bay for Nigeria tomorrow morning. The shop was bustling, full of family and friends, eager to give Saffron the celebratory sendoff she deserved.

One of her closest friends, Monica, wasn't in attendance, having given birth to Reenan Saffron Griffin early that morning. She, Hud, and their precious newborn were doing well and sent their love and good wishes.

Among those in attendance were some of the children from the hospital's cancer ward, and their parents. Saffron had made such a wonderful, positive difference in their lives and they were determined to be there to wish *Aunt Saffy* well.

The children had created individual bon voyage cards for Saffron—some in crayon, some with tempera paints, and some using colored pencil—all of which made her cry happy tears. In addition, more of the young patients, and their nurses and doctors, had prepared a giant farewell card with all of their signatures, little sketches, poems, good wishes, and thank-yous for all the happiness Saffron had brought to patients and staff. The card included a profusion of hearts and big glowing suns, drawn with bright, happy faces.

Clearly enjoying themselves, guests milled about, sipping their libations and munching on hors d'oeuvres and sweets.

Rylan's friend and neighbor, the veterinary surgeon, was able to save Izzy's leg by inserting rods into the area where the bone was shattered by the bullet. Since no major arteries were hit, she'd make a full recovery—although now she'd have two wonky back legs instead of one. Her leg would remain in a cast for another two weeks or so. The sweet little bocker remained in good spirits, managing to get around without too much trouble. She was delighted by all the attention she received from everyone.

Through telepathic communication with Aladee, Izzy wanted everyone to know she was doing well and they shouldn't worry about her. She said she felt truly blessed to have so many kind, caring people concerned about her. She only wished she had been able to do more that may have prevented Lorraine from shooting Rylan.

The gunshot to Rylan's shoulder was on the non-dominant side. The doctors told him he'd most likely end up with severe arthritis in that shoulder, and may possibly be dealing with a frozen shoulder in the future. Worst case scenario was he might be looking at a shoulder replacement if healing was problematic. Mirroring what Quinn had told him, the physicians stressed how fortunate Rylan was that the bullet hadn't hit a main artery in his shoulder. He probably wouldn't be here now if that had been the case.

Saffron's guilt-laced worries about leaving Kady to run Cherished Pages alone were mostly alleviated when Kady's mother, Astrid, announced she'd be stepping in, for as long as needed, to take Saffron's place. It had been a long time since she'd worked outside the home, which she'd done out of necessity while raising her six children as a single mother after Sean died. She was looking forward to a new challenge, spending her days working in a bookshop, one of her favorite places to spend time...and money.

Reen and Drake Slattery were in attendance. Just as Kady had foreseen a few months earlier, they shared the wonderful news that Reen was pregnant, that the baby was a boy, and his name would be Sean Samuel Slattery. Reen joked to Kady that the belly bump she had wasn't due only to her sister Laila's delicious scones after all.

Kady and Rylan had been seeing each other ever since that fateful afternoon at Bekka House. It seemed they had all the necessary ingredients for a true happily ever after. Kady was so happy her cheeks hurt from the constant smile plastered across her face.

She and Rylan had spent hours in each other's arms, talking about their future together, which included the particulars they both enjoyed, like getting that little house in the country where they'd build a happy home and family together—and Rylan could write his science fiction novels.

Just as Kady had suspected, the professor was the real deal, an impossibly sexy and hunky man who embodied an enviable combination of humor, bravery, intelligence, creativity, kindness, and compassion. Kady couldn't dream of a more perfect life partner. It was as if she'd had access to a happily ever after laboratory and had created Rylan herself, right down to the most crucial DNA strands required for developing the ideal dream man.

Soon after all the calamity of the shooting episode had died down, Kady and Saffron remembered to look at the heartwish document on Kady's laptop to see what the holy heck had happened with her wish.

The conundrum was solved when they read the exact heartwish Kady had made:

...

*For the third and final part of my wish, I wish for Rylan Kilpatrick to be happy with the woman he loves. He's a good man and deserves it. I also wish for Lorraine Devington to be happy with the person she loves most, even though she may not deserve it. I wish for love and happiness for each of them always.*

...

"Well the part about Rylan turned out perfectly," Saffron noted. "You wished for him to be happy with the woman he loves and, *voila*, that woman is you, Kady!"

Rereading the rest of the wish, Saffron engaged in quiet, mirthless laughter. Tears brimmed in her eyes when she said, "Your heartwish worked for my poor sister too. The person she loves most is, and always has been, herself. Did you see how happy she was when we saw her at the treatment facility the other day?"

"I did." Kady nodded. Perfectly calm, Lorraine seemed to be content in her tranquil new surroundings.

Following the frightening incident, Kady and Rylan decided not to press charges, even though authorities urged them to do so. But they, as well as Saffron, only wanted Lorraine to receive medical treatment.

Kady and Saffron figured that was all there was too it, but Rylan explained it's not legally up to them to decide Lorraine's fate since shooting someone is a criminal action. Actually, a prosecutor reviews the allegations and evidence and decides whether or not to file a criminal complaint.

Fortunately, Rylan knew John Humboldt, the head prosecutor for the City Prosecutor's Office in Glassfloat Bay. John's son, one of Rylan's students, was in danger of failing Rylan's class, as well as several others. Due to Rylan working with the boy, he passed with a good grade, avoiding college expulsion. John was especially grateful for Rylan's time and patience. Once Rylan contacted him about the shooting incident, John readily agreed to drop the charges as long as Lorraine would be admitted to a psychiatric hospital.

After miles of red tape and paperwork, as well as bickering from her parents, Lorraine was checked into the clinical residential treatment program at Wisdom Harbor Psychiatric Hospital, the top mental health treatment facility in the Pacific Northwest. The private facility provided a stable, long-term living arrangement in an attractive home-like atmosphere, which reminded Kady of a beautiful college campus of a private university.

The residential program also offered a healthy sense of community, helping residents build self-esteem, develop relationships, and improve life skills. Lorraine would receive mental health treatment daily on the premises. She'd also be attending group therapy sessions.

As lovely as the surroundings were, and even though the program was one of the most well-respected and successful in the country, Walter and Colleen Devington balked at the idea. They argued to keep Lorraine at Devington Manor, insisting their daughter must have been stressed and simply had a bad day.

They believed she'd be back to her old self after resting at home for a few days so she could resume her social life, and continue with her plans to fly to Paris with Reginald. They said they'd consult with a private doctor regarding outpatient mental health services.

Even the Devington's high-priced attorney couldn't keep Lorraine from having a criminal record. Under the circumstances, he strongly urged them to cooperate with the prosecutor who was being uncommonly lenient. Once they fully understood all options and possible ramifications, they finally agreed to cooperate with the prosecutor's office.

Saffron believed that while her father would cooperate, he'd most likely try to pay off a judge to get his daughter's criminal record expunged. With all his money he'd likely succeed.

It was also agreed that once Lorraine was deemed well enough, she could continue with her plans to be with Reginald in Paris. Kady gave Reginald a lot of credit. He obviously loved Lorraine because he'd immediately cancelled his flight to France when Saffron contacted him, letting him know what had happened. Reggie urged Lorraine to let the doctors at the facility help her, promising her he'd be ready and waiting for her release, regardless of how long it might take—and then they'd carry on with their plans to be married and move to Paris.

Glancing around the shop, Kady didn't see Rylan. She hadn't seen him for at least thirty minutes. "Saf, have you seen Rylan? Sheesh, I hope he didn't get bored and leave." She laughed.

"Kady, it's your shop, and you're here. Rylan's not going anywhere." Saffron winked. Motioning across the large room, she added, "He was just over there a minute ago. He's probably just being sociable and talking to everyone."

Saffron stood still for a moment, gazing at Kady. "I'm having the best time ever." She brushed a kiss across Kady's cheek. "I'll never forget this wonderful bon voyage party you put together for me on such short notice. I know how much effort you put into this, with so little time before my departure. Thank you so much. I've taken tons of pictures so I can show Quinn when I see him."

At four o'clock, the official bon voyage party had come to an end and guests filed past Saffron on their way to the door, saying their goodbyes, wishing her well, and giving her hugs.

Once the bookshop had cleared out, only family and close friends were still in attendance.

Clapping her hands for attention, Saffron stood at the center of the shop. "Hey everybody, get ready for a fun conclusion to our evening together. As promised, one of the romance novel cover models will be here soon so get your questions ready for him and prepare to have your fortunes told."

"Wait...what?" Kady asked Saffron quietly, tugging at her sleeve. "Fortunes? What cover model?" As Saffron's attention flitted this way and that, Kady gave her a whap on the arm. "Saffron! What are you talking about? This is all news to me...and I'm the one who organized the event." Her laughter was incredulous.

Covering her mouth with her hand, Saffron said, "Oops...well, color me embarrassed. I could have sworn I told you about it. Things have been mega-hectic the past two weeks with all I had to do to get ready to move, plus filling your mom in on the shop's daily operations, all the stuff with Lorraine and my parents...whew! It obviously slipped my mind. I'm sorry. You know how much I've always wanted to have a cover model here in the store. So I planned it to happen just before I leave. Hope that's okay."

"Oh my gosh, Saf, of course it is. But...I don't understand. When did all this happen? What book are we talking about? How did you have time to do this so quickly?"

"Oh...um, I set it all up before I had any idea you'd be throwing a going away party for me," Saffron said.

"Which book?" Kady asked again.

"Uh, I forget. I can't recall its name right now." Squatting, Saffron drew some shimmery purple material from a box on the bottom bookshelf. "Here, put this on." She handed Kady a flowing Lurex cape.

"What?" Kady laughed. "A cape? Why? What for?"

"Ugh! Kathleen Malone, you're the woman of a thousand questions tonight. Just do it. That way you'll match the cover model and you two can give psychic readings together."

Kady just stood there, looking at the shiny, metallic-looking material in her hands.

"Seriously," Saffron near growled, "do I have to do everything? I swear, you won't even be able to tie your own shoes once I'm gone." While talking, she put the cape on Kady, stood back, and gave a bright smile as she made a rapid little clapping motion. "Perfect!"

Catching movement out of the corner of her eye, Kady watched Astrid and Reen setting a life-size standalone cardboard poster next to the round fortunetelling table Kady regularly used. The table had just been dragged into place by her sisters, Delaney and Laila. Instead of the fringed velvet table covering Kady usually used for her demonstrations, the table was topped with sparkly emerald green material. A deck of tarot cards rested at the center. Next came two wire-framed chairs.

The poster looked familiar. "*Immortal Among the Stars,*" Kady read aloud, slanting her head left and right until it finally dawned on her. "That's the title of the book I gave Rylan to read!" With light laughter she said, "I'm sure he's never bothered to even open the book, much less read it."

"Probably not," Saffron agreed before scooting off. Her attention was elsewhere with whatever it was she had to do to prepare for the cover model's arrival.

Kady still hadn't spotted Rylan, even though the crowd had really thinned.

Aladee carefully set Izzy, who looked simply adorable in a sparkly emerald green Lurex costume and matching turban, on a large square floor pillow. Aladee said Izzy was very agreeable to wearing the costume and it didn't bother her leg to do so. She also said Izzy had a feeling something special was going to happen this evening and she was looking forward to being a part of it.

Kady was suddenly overcome by an odd, slightly woozy sensation. She paused for a moment, supporting herself against a bookshelf, trying to focus her thoughts as a flood of fragmented messages flitted across her mind. She often felt this way when her intuition was at its strongest. Izzy was right. Kady sensed something special was on the horizon, she just didn't know what.

"Ladies and gentlemen," Saffron said, "take a seat and get comfortable. She gestured to the folding chairs that had been set up by Kady's brothers and brothers-in-law.

"Where did all those folding chairs come from," Kady asked Saffron quietly.

"Shhh!" Saffron tapped her finger against her lips. "I'm about to introduce our guest cover model and his dog."

"Dog?" Kady said. "The guy brought his dog?"

"Yup. Cute little German Shepherd puppy. He's part of the act."

Planting her hands on her hips, Kady slanted Saffron a puzzled look. "What act?"

"You know, like Izzy is part of your act."

"Wait a minute...you're saying this other dog is supposed to be psychic, too?"

"Yes indeed. Wolfgang the psychic German Shepherd. He'll be in costume as well."

At the sound of the other dog's name, Izzy's head popped up from her pillow and she whimpered. It's no wonder Izzy jerked. Wolfgang was the name of Madame Izidora's German soldier—her long lost love.

Folding her arms across her chest, Kady said, "Saffron, what the heck is going on?"

"Shush," she made the gesture at her lips, "too many questions while I'm trying to get things ready."

"This cover model sounds like a bona fide flake. Are you sure he's legit?"

"Hmmm...could be a flake, but he's definitely legit. You can check out Amzeran Zorazich and Wolfgang for yourself and decide."

"Amzer what?"

"Amzeran Zorazich, the title character from *Immortal Among the Stars*. The cover model said he likes to stay in character when he tours."

"Wow." Rolling her eyes, Kady shook her head cautiously. "Definitely a flake." But Kady imagined all would work out and

Saffron would be happy to finally have a cover model at the bookshop before she had to leave.

"He's in the backroom," Saffron told Kady. "He'll be here in a minute with Wolfgang." Saffron returned her attention to arranging chairs and making sure people were comfortable.

"Amzeran Zorazich and his psychic German Shepherd, Wolfgang, indeed," Kady muttered beneath her breath. Poor Saffron was so busy with everything she'd probably allowed herself to be suckered by this cover model guy. Hopefully he wasn't too much of a kook.

In the blink of an eye, an ornately costumed German Shepherd puppy came racing toward Kady, stopping at her feet. Sporting one of those goofy dog smiles and panting, he looked up at her, his tail whirling like helicopter blades. An instant later, Izzy came hobbling over, making little bark sounds that sounded for all the world as if she were talking. Wolfgang did the same before wrapping Izzy in a hug.

"Oh my gosh..." Kady said, hands on knees as she bent to give the pups a better look. "This is about the cutest thing I've ever seen."

A murmured *awwww*, was heard around the room. It was impossible to keep from smiling at the two elaborately costumed canines who'd clearly become fast friends.

Kady held out her hand to greet the German Shepherd pup. He happily presented his paw in return and she shook it. "How do you do? You must be Wolfgang." Inclining his head, he offered a soft, cheerful bark and turned toward his canine companion, Izzy, to lick her face. Izzy gleefully lapped up Wolfgang's attention.

"Well, Izzy, it seems you have a new boyfriend," Kady noted, only to be met with more of the quick barky sound that seemed like speech.

"Wolfgang Von Ludwig, Amzeran Zorazich's immortal psychic German Shepherd from outer space."

Kady jerked straight up at the sound of Rylan Kilpatrick's deep voice coming from behind her. Her heart leapt as she saw him standing there, a few yards away, resplendent in a costume nearly identical to the one the model on the book cover wore...except for the shimmery green sling Rylan wore because of his injured shoulder.

A smile curled at Kady's lips as she took in his magnificent appearance. He could have stepped right off the cover of *Immortal Among the Stars* in his fabulous futuristic emerald green vestments. The professor really and truly could be a romance novel cover model.

"Rylan," was all she could manage to say as her heart beat a rapid tattoo.

Cocking his head, Rylan held his finger aloft in an admonishing manner. "Mind your manners, Earth woman. I am known as Amzeran Zorazich, if you please...the great immortal among the stars." He gestured widely with his good arm.

Forgetting they had a seated audience, Kady whisked her head in surprise as her family members cheered and whistled.

"Rylan...er, I mean Amzeran Zorazich, what are you doing?" Kady asked.

"Wolfgang and I are here to answer questions and portend future events. Be seated, bookshop owner." He motioned to the chair next to him as Rylan sat in the other chair.

Kady had so many questions, but before she could ask, Rylan spoke out in a deep, commanding voice. "Does anyone in the audience have a question?"

"Yeah, me!" Standing in place, Kady's brother and Aladee's husband, Nevan, cleared his throat. "I have a question, Americano Zach."

Amidst background giggling, Rylan grumbled. "Proceed, Earthling who has not learned his lines," he said with a dramatic flourish.

"I hear my little sister loves some professor guy. I wanna know...will they have a happily ever?"

Seated next to Nevan, Reen elbowed her brother's thigh, whispering "After. *After!*"

"Oh right, sorry. Will she get her happily after after?" There were groans around the room. "Hey, easy, guys." Nevan patted the air before him. "I'm doing my best here, you know?"

Her elbows propped on the table, Kady rested her chin on folded hands, enjoying the playful scene unfolding before her. She was amazed and impressed as Rylan went through the tarot card ritual with perfection, right down to the interpretation of the cards he turned over for Nevan. Somebody had clearly coached him during the last two weeks.

"I see many positive signs in the cards," Rylan said. "I foresee answers among the books."

Rylan clapped twice and Saffron immediately appeared at his side, spreading a small selection of paperback romance novels on the table in front of Rylan and Kady.

"I shall now consult with my psychic partner from outer space." Whistling, Rylan patted his thigh. "Wolfgang, come here boy." Involved with his furry new ladylove, Izzy, Wolfgang ignored Rylan. "Pssst, Wolfie." Nothing. Rylan reached inside his arm sling, pulling out a dog snack and holding it at his knee. "Wolfie, come on, pal, you've gotta help me look good."

Wolfgang abandoned Izzy and was at his master's side in an instant. "That's a good boy." Rylan picked up the little German Shepherd, positioning him on his lap, facing the books on the table. "Okay now, Wolfgang, I need you to—" Wolfgang busied himself searching for another snack in Rylan's sling. "That's all I've got, buddy. You cleaned me out. Okay now, pay attention," Rylan said to the drooling, tongue-lolling dog.

Before Rylan could speak another word, the German Shepherd pup turned in Rylan's arms, facing him and wrapping himself at Rylan's neck while lavishing him with licking kisses as he *spoke*. Laughing, Rylan hugged the dog, petting and patting him. "I love you too, boy. Good boy."

Izzy was clearly eating this all up. She looked happy and content.

"All right now, Wolfie, time to get down to business." Rylan cleared his throat. "And now, ladies and gentlemen, Wolfgang Von Ludwig, Amzeran Zorazich's immortal psychic German Shepherd from outer space, will choose a book that will answer Nevan's question about his sister's *happily ever after*." He put emphasis on the words. "It is time to make your selection, Wolfgang." Rylan gestured to the books on the table.

Everyone dissolved in laughter at Rylan's vain attempts to have the easily distracted Wolfgang choose a romance novel for Nevan. He'd already leapt down from Rylan's lap a few times to check on Izzy, and happily mingle with his rapt audience in the folding chairs. Because of his shoulder, it was difficult for Rylan to pick the hefty German Shepherd puppy up into his arms. Sensing the problem, Saffron snatched Wolfie up, bringing him to Rylan and plopping him in his lap.

"Aladee, we need you," Saffron called. Rising from her seat next to Nevan, Aladee came to Rylan's side, bending low to whisper in Wolfgang's ear.

"*Was für ein guter Junge du bist, Wolfgang. Guter Hund. Hmm? Ja, ich werde Rylan alles erzählen, was du mir gesagt hast,*" Aladee said to him, speaking German. It translated to, "What a good boy you are, Wolfgang. Good dog. Hmm? Yes, I'll tell Rylan everything you told me."

Looking from Wolfie to Rylan, Aladee grinned. "Wolfgang wants you to know he thinks you are a good man. He loves you very much and is thankful that you and I were able to rescue him from the tierheim, the animal shelter, in Germany. He also is eternally grateful to be reunited with his one true love, Izidora Meszaros. He promised to do his best to perform for you and all the people here that you care about."

"Oh my God..." Kady said in astonishment. "So this really is *the* Wolfgang Von Ludwig? Izzy's love—her World War One German soldier?"

"It is indeed," Aladee confirmed. "They're both elated to be reunited after so many years."

Surprised and enchanted by this wonderful revelation, Kady asked, "How did you find him?"

"Through Izzy's help and my Nymph Mail network," Aladee said. "Izzy told me she sensed that, like her, Wolfgang was also a canine in this lifetime. Last week, when Saffron and Rylan contacted me about tonight, they asked if it was possible to search for this particular dog. After giving all the information we had about Wolfgang and Izidora's human existence, Wolfie was located in Germany. We were able to have him transported here immediately."

"Before I left for Nigeria," Saffron said, "I wanted to do something extra special for little Izzy who's been such a brave, sweet little soul." She squatted next to the pillow where Izzy reclined, stroking the dog's fur as she spoke to Kady.

"I spoke to Rylan and he was fully on board with the idea. He said he's wanted a dog for a long while. Only my sister's dislike of pets kept him from visiting a shelter before. Little Wolfie here is my thank you to you, Kady, and to Izzy, for being so important in my life."

Rising to her feet, Saffron went to Kady, giving her a hug and whispering that she loved her, promptly bringing happy tears to Kady's eyes.

"This is a good excuse for me to brush up on my college German," Rylan said. "Let's see if I can remember a little...*Wolfie ist mein neuer bester Kumpel, nicht wahr, Junge?*" Rylan told his dog, massaging him behind the ears as he spoke. Rylan received an enthusiastic tongue-licking, along with love nips to his good hand.

Looking up, Rylan smiled. "Hopefully I told him 'Wolfie is my new best buddy, aren't you, boy?'" Wolfie barked in response, followed by Izzy's bark.

"Okay, boy, let's try this one more time," Rylan said. "Then you can go join your Hungarian Gypsy fortunetelling sweetheart." He nuzzled the top of Wolfgang's head.

"Yeah, time's a wastin. Let's get this show on the road," Nevan jokingly complained, tapping his wrist where a watch would be.

"Nevan Malone, behave yourself," Astrid chastised, and everyone chuckled as he sank down in his seat.

Rylan plunged ahead. "Wolfgang Von Ludwig, Amzeran Zorazich's immortal psychic German Shepherd from outer space, will now choose a book revealing the answer to Nevan's question."

"It's been so long since I asked, I forgot the question," Nevan joked, only to get a lively whap in the back of his head from Astrid. "Ow!"

With Wolfie settled quietly on Rylan's lap, he spoke in the dog's ear. Almost instantly, Wolfie placed his paw on one of the books, *Immortal Among the Stars*. Next, he pushed the book in front of Kady, licking Kady's hand when she reached for the novel.

"Well that's a very good choice, Wolfie." Kady ruffled his fur. "Thank you."

"Wolfie wants you to open the book and read what's on the title page," Rylan said.

Kady did so, gasping as she read the handwritten inscription aloud, *"Promise you'll stay with me always, my darling, beautiful Kady. Marry me and make me the happiest man on earth. All my love, Rylan."*

It was then that she noticed Rylan was no longer sitting in the chair next to her, but was on the floor now, on bended knee, holding an open ring box out to her.

Clapping her hands against her cheeks, Kady sat there in a euphoric state of shock, willing herself to remain calm and not fall off the chair in a dead faint. Taken by complete and utter surprise, she wondered how she could possibly miss any psychic signs that this was going to happen.

Silence hung in the air like a thick fog.

"Well don't leave him hanging...answer the poor guy," her brother Gard called out.

"Tick-tock, tick-tock," Nevan said.

"Tough crowd," Rylan muttered. "You're not making this any easier, guys," he called to Kady's brothers.

"Boys!" Astrid reached over to give both her sons a smack on their arms. "You're incorrigible. Go right ahead, son," she told Rylan, "you're doing just fine."

The realization finally hit Kady. "Omigod Rylan! I'm sorry. You just caught me completely by surprise and...yes! *Yes*! Of course my answer is yes!"

"Whew!" Plucking the ring with its large amethyst stone from the box, Rylan slipped it on her finger, and the room exploded with whoops and hollers and congratulatory wishes.

Kady sprinkled Rylan's face with kisses. He grabbed her tight and kissed her until her toes just about curled. Aside from the moment being exceptional, something about it seemed so familiar...almost like déjà vu, but Kady couldn't quite figure out what it reminded her of.

"We're here too," came Red's voice. A quick bit of maneuvering from Aladee adjusting her Nymph Mail had Red, his partner, Lonan, their white cat and mini unicorn, visible to everyone there. Just as when Kady was preparing for her heartwish, the images appeared in the air, as if on an invisible screen. "We've been here for the whole thing," Red said, "but we purposely stayed out of sight so we wouldn't steel your thunder, Rylan, you handsome devil. Congratulations, you two lovebirds! Kady, darling, I'm sure you know how elated I am for you."

"Thank you, Red!" Kady said, followed by Rylan's thanks as well.

"And, Saffron, my beautiful, sweet sister," Red continued, "you know I wish you every happiness with Quinn and your exciting new career. I love you my dear Saffy, and miss you. Quinton Kilpatrick, who's also quite the handsome devil, is indeed a fortunate man. Adorable Aladee will help us keep in touch."

"Aw, Red, thank you." Saffron blew her brother a kiss. "Love you!"

With Red's partner Lonan now standing shoulder to shoulder with Red, Lonan said to everyone, "I want all of you wonderful people to know that we love you and that you don't have to worry about Redmond because, and I think he'll agree, he's never been happier."

"Definitely true," Red said. "Lonan and I have a gift for Rylan and for Izzy. Rylan, please go to Izzy and take her in your arms."

Rylan did so, finding himself and Izzy encased in an ethereal pink vapor. An awestruck gasp sounded throughout the room. Astonishment was etched across Rylan's features, and he looked rather uneasy.

"Through the myth and magic of the gods and goddesses here on Mount Olympus," Red said, "and my great honor to be counted among them as an immortal minor god, I, along with my partner, my dearest love, Lonan, bestow upon Professor Rylan Kilpatrick and Madame Izidora Meszaros full and complete healing. Within twenty-four hours, your shoulder will be healed, Rylan, as if you were never shot. And Izzy's legs, *both of them*, will be healthy, uninjured, and without any signs of infirmity. We've arranged for the physicians to accept it all in stride."

"Oh Red!" Kady cried. "That's such wonderful news. Thank you!"

More wonderstruck gasps echoed around the room.

"Redmond," Astrid said, "what an amazing gift. It's so nice to see you again, sweetheart."

"You too, Aunt Astrid," Red said, blowing her a kiss.

"I-I'm flabbergasted, Red," Rylan told him. "I don't know that to say, other than thank you so much. And it's nice to meet you." He laughed. "Wow, it's, um, it's going to take me a minute to get used to being part of a family that boasts minor immortal gods, genies, nymphs, ghosts and angels but I—"

As soon as the word *angels* left Rylan's lips, the large space was permeated with the delightful gingery fragrance of Grandma Bekka's pepperkaker.

"*Ja, ja*, I'm here with you all too," came the soft, distant sound of Bekka's Norwegian-accented voice. "May God bless you all, children."

"Wow." Rylan scratched his head. "Just...wow."

"It was the same for me at first too, Rylan," Nevan admitted. "You'll get used to it all in time."

"You're most welcome Rylan," Red replied. "In return, I trust you'll take good care of my darling, starry-eyed cousin."

"Always," Rylan said, his arm around Kady's waist.

"Before we pop off," Red said with a bright smile, "I want you to know, Saffron, that we'll monitor Lorraine's progress, doing what we can to help bring her to a healthy, stable point. Healing the mind is far more difficult, and takes much more time for us, than healing a physical ailment. Rest assured, Lorraine will be making it to Paris with Reggie within the next year, where she'll reside permanently, which," Red's smile grew broader, "if we're all honest, will be a relief, and the best for all concerned."

Crossing her hands over her heart, Saffron thanked her brother as tears rolled down her cheeks. "I can't tell you how much better that makes me feel before I leave, moving so far away from everyone...from Lorraine. Thank you for being so incredibly kind after all she put you through, Red."

"My pleasure. And I mean that, Saffy. Understanding the positive role forgiveness plays in our lives is so important. I don't believe we can be truly free or happy unless we learn to let go of the hurts, the grievances, the pain caused by others. That's not to say we'll forget it, but we can move on and leave anger and heartache in the past where it belongs—where it can no longer hurt us. Safe journey, Saffy!"

And with that, Red and Lonan were gone.

Once the excitement died down, Rylan leaned toward Kady. "The only person I don't know here is the elderly gentleman sitting in the back, talking to your mother. Is he a relative or a friend."

"A good friend. That, my dear fiancé," Kady said with a warm smile, "is Ramon Gustavo Taramino."

# Chapter 27

~<>~

THE WALLS of Cherished Pages Bookshop were surely laminated thick with layers of love, happiness, healing and laughter as, one by one, everyone there enveloped Saffron in their arms, wishing her well on her exciting and extraordinary journey ahead. Full of glee mixed with sadness, Saffron promised she'd find a way to keep in touch once she was established. Aladee vowed to do whatever she could using Nymph Mail for added communication as well.

Kady was...well, she was simply in seventh heaven.

While getting better at admitting she was a bit gullible, and maybe too trusting, she'd never been prone to being a fatalist. Kady honestly believed with all her heart that her life, as well as the lives of those she loved so deeply, would indeed have their happily ever afters. Bumps in the road? Roadblocks? Yes, of course, but each roadblock overcome only makes the happier times, all the good parts, more cherished, treasured, and appreciated.

Everyone stayed to help clean up before leaving the bookshop. Kady was immensely thankful because the place was a cheerful, well-partied mess, and she, Saffron and Rylan had to be up before the crack of dawn to get Saffron to the airport in time. In a pleasant turn of events, Reggie had arranged for his private plane to fly Saffron to Nigeria.

Saffron told Kady she thought Reggie had probably suspected that Lorraine had spilled the beans about the kinks in Saffron and Reggie's supposed friendship. She believed he felt guilty and this was his way of making a peace offering. Whatever the reason, she was grateful for the opportunity to have a more comfortable, pampered travel experience.

At the end of the evening, once everyone had gone home, Kady and Rylan went upstairs to her apartment. She still hadn't gotten over the remarkable fairytale-like sensation of all that had happened in the last few hours. So many wonderful things. Such good news. There was an abundance of contentment mixed with exuberance—an odd combination but a good, potent one, full of enchantment, hopes, and dreams for the future.

"I had no intention of proposing this early in our relationship," Rylan said as they brought their glasses of wine to sit at the couch in Kady's living room.

"I know. Saffron told me she practically begged you." Kady laughed. "She apologized, claiming she absolutely *had* to be here to see you propose."

"It was so important to her to have this happen before she left," Rylan said, chuckling along with Kady. "Not that I didn't *want* to propose," he assured her, "it's just that I thought it might be best if I waited a reasonable length of time after Lorraine and I...well, until after our fractured relationship wasn't such recent history. I was afraid your family would be concerned if they thought I was on the rebound, hopping from one engagement to another so quickly. So I talked to your mom and stepdad, Tore."

"You did?"

"Yup, and they were behind me one hundred percent, already welcoming me to the family and giving me their blessing. In fact, right after our talk, as I was about to leave, Astrid made me stay there while she pulled out her camera to *log the happy memory*, as she put it." Rylan chuckled. "Between all those photos and all the ones she took today, especially as I proposed," he rolled his eyes, "your mom will be able to fill an entire album of just me, myself, and I."

"You know what that means, don't you?" Kady teased, and Rylan shook his head from side to side. "It means you're a bona fide Malone now."

Rylan burst out laughing. "Seriously, doesn't anyone want to be a Kilpatrick?"

"Mmm-hmm." Kady kissed him. "Me, myself, and I do." This kiss lasted longer. "I'm just still amazed at everything all of you were able to do in such a short amount of time. It seems everyone was in on it but me."

"Everyone," Rylan confirmed. "We all worked overtime to make sure today came off without a hitch. You'd already seen to that as far as Saffron's bon voyage party. Fortunately, that kept you busy enough not to notice much of what was going on around you."

As Rylan spoke, both Wolfie and Izzy leapt up onto the couch between them, nuzzling each other.

"Oh my gosh, did you see that?" Kady said, amazed. "Did you see how fast Izzy moved? It looks like it won't even take twenty-four hours for her to heal. I'm so happy for her." She ran her fingers through Izzy's fur as she spoke. "And you, of course. How does your shoulder feel?"

Removing his sling, Rylan gingerly rotated his shoulder.

"Well hell..." He increased his range of motion and grinned. "Apparently Izzy's not the only one who won't need the full twenty-four hours. What's it been, three hours or so."

"Something like that." Kady nodded. "That means you'll be able to sleep on your side with more comfort."

"It also means I'm hale and hearty enough to engage in other pleasurable activities." His eyebrows wiggled as he snaked his arm around Kady.

Holding his arm, Kady rested her head against Rylan's chest. "Oh, Rylan, look at us. Together. Engaged. Talking and planning a life together. I still can't believe this is happening. I was so sure I'd have to resign myself to you being totally off limits because—"

"Because I was your cousin's man," he interrupted with a smile. "I, on the other hand, had no doubts we'd eventually end up together. None whatsoever."

"Really? How could you be so sure?"

"I'll show you rather than tell you." Careful not to disturb Wolfie and Izzy canoodling together, Rylan got up, returning in a few minutes with Kady's crystal ball, placing it directly in front of him on the coffee table. Making circular movements over the sphere with his hands, he said, "I see an image coming into focus."

"Oh you do, hmm?" Kady laughed. "Tell me, immortal Amzeran Zorazich, what do you see?" Kady leaned forward, playing along with Rylan's cute scenario.

"Yes, I see it clearly now. The merging of two souls, locked in a passion-filled lover's embrace. They're dressed like the man and woman on the cover of a futuristic science fiction romance novel."

Kady's eyebrows scrunched. It sounded like he was describing the image she'd spotted in the crystal ball the night they met. But that wasn't possible.

Still peering into the crystal ball, Rylan said, "The image is of us, Kady...the same image you saw at your dinner party the night we met."

"Wait...you mean..." Uttering a gasp, Kady locked gazes with Rylan. "You saw it too that night?"

"I absolutely did." He nodded slowly. "I knew exactly why you were so distraught that evening. I also knew there wasn't a damn thing either of us could do about our feelings at that time. What's more, I knew, felt it deep inside," his fingers thumped over his heart, "that you and I would replicate that cover one day. And today is that day. I remember the exact moment we mirrored that image...do you? Let's see how much of a romantic you really are, Kathleen Doolan Malone." Drawing her closer, he brushed a kiss across her lips.

Kady thought for a moment, then her eyes grew wide. "Oh my gosh, yes. Yes! I do remember! It was just after you proposed. After you slipped the ring on my finger and we embraced, kissing. I had this strange sort of déjà vu feeling and wasn't sure why." She smiled at the man she loved. "And all this time you knew. You saw the image in the crystal ball but never said anything. Why?"

"Because we were in such a precarious position and I respected that—respected your feelings. You see, I'd already fallen in love with you, Kady. It was immensely evident you were having a difficult time coming to grips with the idea of us, of you and me together, while I was engaged to your cousin. Why? Because you're such an honorable woman, Kady. Because you put your own feelings, thoughts of your own happiness, second to your cousin's. And I loved you enough not to—"

"Upset the applecart," Kady said the same instant Rylan did.

"Exactly." Rylan's head bobbed slowly. "Then, when I attempted to break up with Lorraine, I'd planned to come directly to you afterward so I could confess my feelings for you. But, well, we know what happened with me trying to break my engagement to her."

"I'm so glad Lorraine will be getting the help she needs."

"I am too," Rylan agreed. "When Quinn and I were kids, my mother had a bunch of favorite quotes she'd tell us. One of my favorites was, *If you love something, let it go. If it comes back to you, it's yours forever. If it doesn't, then it was never meant to be.*"

"Grandma Bekka used to tell us a variation of that," Kady said.

"So," Rylan shrugged, without wincing this time because of his shoulder, "I had to let you go, or at least let the idea of you and me go. I knew, I honestly believed, one day we'd find our way to where we are today, looking forward to our very own forever. Together."

"I have a feeling," Kady smiled, "that you read that romance novel I gave you. You did, didn't you?"

"Every spicy, sexy, steamy, bootylicious word." He planted kisses around her face with each word. "I even learned some fascinating new things from that book." He gave her a promising smile.

"About outer space and the future?"

"Nope. About lots of sensual, arousing, stimulating things I want to do to you. Things I want the two of us to do together. Things men don't really think much about, but obviously women do—which I learned from reading that book. I want to spend hours pleasuring you, Kady, exploring every intimate nook and cranny of your succulent body. I want to learn what makes you purr, what makes you moan, what makes you gasp with pleasure, or scream out my name." His smile was deliciously wicked.

"I want us to replicate all those erotic pretzel-like positions described in the book...in the shower, the tub, the bed, the car, standing against the wall, hanging from a basket suspended from the ceiling." He chuckled. "All of it. I don't know if they're actually possible to achieve but I guarantee you we'll have a hell of a lot of fun trying."

"Mmm...that sounds sensational," Kady said, barely able to get the words out because she was so turned on, experiencing agreeable sensations coursing through her system...gathering at her sweet spot. "And naughty. And erotic. And delicious."

"I hope you have whipped cream in your fridge."

"Nope, sorry, it's not vegan. However, I do have the most sinfully rich and delicious dark chocolate sauce you've ever tasted...which would add another layer of delectability to our sensual explorations.

"Ahhh, Kady, my love, we're going to create our very own love story, our own scintillating romance novel, which we'll write sentence by sentence, paragraph by paragraph, chapter by chapter as we journey along our forever road together. How does that sound, my lovely fiancée?"

*Fiancée.* The word caused Kady to glance at her beautiful amethyst ring. He paid attention. He knew she was partial to purple and amethyst. This man was a keeper and she'd make certain to never let him go.

"It sounds perfect, Rylan, like my innermost dreams and fantasies. You, Professor Kilpatrick, are my Prince Charming." She kissed him, thoroughly enjoying the taste of him.

"And you, Kady Doolan Malone, soon to be Kilpatrick, are my fairytale princess." He returned her kiss, making her feel almost drunk with delight.

"If I had a crystal ball," Rylan said, "I'd see you on our wedding day wearing a crown of flowers on your long auburn hair. You'd wear a long wispy white dress with angel sleeves that move like soft, flowing veils as you step barefoot through the grass, to the melodious tune of chirping birds, and your favorite chants. The angelic dress, of course, concealing a body made for sin. The best part is that I'd be waiting for you beneath the flower-entwined arch at the outdoor altar, waiting to exchange our vows as our loved ones watch."

Rubbing her arms, Kady shivered.

"Cold?"

"No...I just can't believe you so perfectly detailed the nearly identical image of us that I've held close to my heart ever since we met. My ideal wedding. Really, Rylan...it's uncanny." Tilting her head, she looked at him with awe. "Are you sure you're not psychic?"

Laughing gently, Rylan threaded his fingers through Kady's hair. "I'm psychic enough to know that you and I will spend our lives loving each other, enjoying and satisfying each other. And that we'll have a matching set of rocking chairs where we'll sit, hand in hand, our dogs there beside us, when we're old and gray and even more in love than we are today."

He swept her tight against his chest, covering her mouth with his. The sensuous kiss was laced with more love and emotion than words could express. It shook Kady to her very core as she savored the sweetness, the light, the passion of Rylan Kilpatrick's heart and soul communicating with her own.

Rising from the couch, Rylan scooped Kady up into his arms, gazing into her eyes with such ardor it made her shiver.

"Yes, my darling Rylan." Her head rested against his chest, her fingers investigating, caressing, as he carried her to the bedroom. "We'll write our romance story together, treasuring each step along the way of the loving, impassioned journey my heart promises me will spread across the pages of our very own happily ever after."

**Turn the page for a special 2-chapter sneak peek** of book 7 in the Heartwishes series, **THE DAUGHTER'S HEARTWISH.** This book will be available before the end of 2024. I've had so many readers request Bekka's love story. I can't wait until you can read it because, even though I'm a teensy bit biased, I happen to think it's a really beautiful tale. This book features the WWII era story of Kady's Norwegian grandmother (Astrid's mother), Rebekka Johannesen Eriksen (Grandma Bekka), who meets Jamie, the American soldier who will become the love of her life!

# The Daughter's Heartwish: Chapter One

*Bekka House*
*Glassfloat Bay, Oregon*

~<>~

"OOH, WILL you look at that," Astrid Malone Thorkelson said as her daughter, Laila, crossed the threshold into Bekka House with her husband, Zak. One by one the guests arrived with tempting dishes for her very special brunch in celebration of Astrid's late mother, Bekka. "What, pray tell, are those two glorious mounds you're so proudly showing off?"

Looking down at her chest, Laila grinned. "They're the same size as always, Mom. I'm just wearing a bra today so they look more glorious than usual." Everyone sitting around the fully-leafed dining table broke into laughter while Astrid's cheeks turned pink.

"Oops," she muttered with a shrug before she joined the others laughing.

"The two glorious mounds I'm so proudly showing off are cranberry walnut bread." Laila presented two sizeable round loaves of crusty bread resting on a large stoneware platter. "Just baked this morning." Bending, she closed her eyes and sniffed. "Mmm, hope they taste as good as they smell."

"Oh puhleez," her sister, Delaney, said. "As if anything you've ever made doesn't taste like awesome sauce."

Zak, her Mediterranean husband turned to his wife with a questioning look. "Have I tasted your awesome sauce? If it is as delicious as your other offerings, I would like very much to taste it."

Now it was Laila's turn to get red-faced as more giggling transpired around the table. Zak, the former genie, was doing great with his mastery of English but sometimes...

Glancing around the table as muffled laughter overtook the guests, Zak tsked and nodded. "Ahhh...so I see I have yet again misunderstood something and created awkwardness."

"Don't you worry about it. Pay no attention to them, sweetie," Laila kissed him on the cheek, "they're all just immature. I'll, um, I'll let you taste my awesome sauce tonight, okay?"

"I look forward to it." He flashed a white-toothed smile. The teasing gleam in his eye told Astrid her son-in-law may not be quite as ill-informed as he led them to believe.

"Yeah, *we're* the immature ones," Reen cracked.

"Anyway," Laila continued, "I added some nutty whole grains to these loaves, which makes them perfect for slicing thick and toasting. I recommend slathering the toast with copious amounts of butter, and perhaps a dab of spreadable honey. I've got some other stuff to bring in from the car, so can one of you do the honors?"

"I'm capable of doing that," smiling, Kady Malone raised her hand, happily volunteering to the sound of groans around the table. Laughing as she got up, heading for Laila, she said, "Aw, come on, guys, it's not like I'm cooking it myself. Laila's already done that. I'm just going to toast it and spread it with—"

"Oh...Kady...sweetheart..." Rylan Kilpatrick said with a hopeful smile. "Maybe you should just sit and relax and let someone else prepare the food." Snickering could be heard from most people present as Kady's fiancé ventured cautiously, obviously trying to avoid hurting his fiancée's feelings.

"Poor Rylan," Reen said, shaking her head. "I see you've already been exposed to the hazards of your fiancée in the kitchen."

'Well, I..." Caught, Rylan looked more like a kid called to see the teacher than the esteemed science professor he was.

"Yeah, once you're married plan on eating out a lot," Kady's brother, Nevan said. "Don't worry, pal, you'll get the family discount at Half Potato Pub," he told Rylan with a wink, referring to his popular Irish pub.

"Fess up, Kady," her brother, Gard, said. "We all know you'll just try sneaking some of your weird, *healthy*," he bracketed the word with his fingers, "vegan stuff onto the toast."

"No I'm not," Kady said with a dismissive wave before reaching out to take the platter from her sister, Laila. "I'd only make one teensy change," she claimed, holding fingers an inch apart.

"Here we go," Reen's husband, Professor Drake Slattery said, chuckling. Sitting back in his chair, he crossed his arms over his chest. "And what might that *teensy* change be?"

"Well I just thought it might enhance the bread," Kady said, "if I spread it with some coconut oil instead of butter because it's—"

"Nope." Kady's oldest sister, Delaney, rose from her chair, taking the platter before Laila could hand it off to Kady. Heading for the kitchen, she said, "Thanks but no thanks, Kady," as she walked.

"Okay but no butter on mine," Kady said. Turning to her fiancé, she asked him, "What about you, Ry?"

"Butter!" Rylan said so fast the word nearly came out a blur.

"Fine." Nursing a little pout, Kady said, "I'll use some of the coconut oil I brought for myself then, which will keep my skin young, smooth and supple." Playfully patting her cheeks, she tried in vain to hide an emerging smile. "While the rest of you get mummy skin."

"Look at Mom," Reen said, pointing to Astrid. "She's been a butter eater all her life and doesn't look like a mummy."

Astrid nearly spewed her Kahlua-spiked coffee as laughter tangled in her throat. "Mummy? Jeez, Maureen, I'm not *that* old."

Reen gasped. Her face turning red, she sputtered, "Oh, no, Mom! I meant...I mean..."

Laughing louder than the rest, Astrid reached over and clasped her daughter's hand. "It's okay. Your old mom knows what you meant." She gave Reen a wink.

"Never old, my love." Astrid's husband, Tore, stepfather to her children, leaned over to plant a kiss on her cheek. "You'll always be forever young and beautiful to me."

While the women chorused *awwwws*, the men teased Tore about making points.

As Astrid glanced around the room, watching her children, their partners, spouses, and friends chatting, laughing, and swapping stories, her heart was filled with gladness and gratitude. There was nothing more satisfying than being surrounded by the people she cared most about in this world.

The key words were *in this world*...because what much of what she'd gathered them to relay this morning was *otherworldly* related.

Today's brunch topic was special, which is why Astrid made a few changes to the routine. While the guys usually got to escape the women by huddling in front of the sizeable wall-mounted TV, watching football or whatever other sport, drinking their beers and chomping down on an array of snacks, today would be different.

Although the dining table was huge with all the leaves in place, it still wasn't large enough to accommodate everyone Astrid had invited. Folding chairs and TV trays were set up around the room's perimeter.

"This is quite a feast you've set out, Aunt Astrid," Red Devington, said. He and his partner, Lonan, had traveled from their home on Mount Olympus to join them today. "Your invitation," Red, held up the engraved card, waving it, "says this brunch is in celebration of Bekka. While she wasn't technically my grandmother, I've adopted her as mine." He flashed a grin. "She was always so fabulous to me. Kindness personified. And she was very funny too! Do I sense a special announcement coming our way? Is the city dedicating something to her? They certainly should."

"I like the way you think, Red. Bekka loved you very much," Astrid answered with a smile. Angling her head to the side, she added, "The reason you're all here today is to hear a unique story about my mother, rather than an announcement. But, yes, it's very special...and magical, which is why I'm so glad you two could be here with us when I share it."

"*Magical...*" Kady's fiancé, Rylan, chuckled. "Here I thought, when I fell in love with Kady and asked her to marry me, that I'd become a member of her large, loving, typical, ordinary family. Little did I know that her *typical, ordinary*," he added finger quotes, "family is riddled with magical happenings. I'm sitting at a table with gods, a nymph, a genie, and people who have performed miracles through the powerful magic of a pair of heartwish rings...from Odin, no less. And then there are the angels and ghosts." Rylan's eyes closed in a long blink as he shook his head in wonder.

"Don't forget Sabellius," Red reminded Rylan.

"Who?"

"Our pet mini unicorn," Lonan explained. "We call him Sabby for short."

"Your pet unicorn...of course." Rylan's stifled chuckling followed. "Yup, I'm still falling down the rabbit hole and not quite sure when, or if, I'll ever reach the bottom—or come up for air again." He held up both hands. "Not that I'm complaining, mind you. The entire extended Malone clan has given me plenty of inspiration for my sci-fi books." Rylan's chuckling morphed into laughter and the others joined him.

"Well buckle in, son," Astrid told him with a wink, "because you'll be falling even deeper after you hear what I have to tell you this morning."

Peering around the room, Astrid smiled. Thank goodness they kept building on to Bekka House because everyone Astrid had included on her guest list was in attendance. She'd invited everyone who loved Bekka...everyone who'd been touched by her. She never took for granted the shared feeling of love and good humor when people spoke of Bekka. How fortunate she was to have been blessed with a woman like Rebekka Johannesen Eriksen for her mother. And how rewarding for her six children to have had Grandma Bekka in their lives.

After giving everyone time to catch up and chat, Astrid began, "So, the reason I've asked you here today involves a heartwish. Kady and Nevan, I know you two still have your heartwish rings and haven't received information about who will get them next, but the heartwish I have in mind is an old one. It's *my* heartwish, in fact."

"Mom, you never told us you had the heartwish ring," Delaney said, clearly surprised, as her sisters and brothers muttered their own surprised reactions. "When was this?"

"A long time ago, when I was a teen. The ring came to me from Bekka's mother, my grandmother, Helga. Once I made my own heartwish, my ring was passed to my mother, Bekka."

"And Grandma Bekka gave it to me," Delaney said. "She had it sent to me after...after she passed away."

"Right." Astrid smiled. "As your grandma told you when you were little, she always knew you'd be the next in line for the ring." Delaney nodded with recollection.

Platters, casseroles, bowls, and soup tureens were passed as they all chatted. A tempting array of savory and sweet foods were scooped, sliced, plated, and eagerly enjoyed. As always, the delicious dining options were topflight.

"Does this have to do with the something wonderful and mysterious that you hinted at during our phone conversation when I first moved here to Oregon from Chicago?" Delaney asked.

Astrid nodded. "Yes it does."

"That was before you made the move here to Glassfloat Bay," Delaney said to her mother. "You told me it had to do with your visit here just before Grandma died." Delaney looked at her sisters. "I tried to pry it out of Mom but she wouldn't budge." She and her sisters laughed. "Mom said she had to wait until everyone was together."

"At that time," Astrid said, "you were still traveling overseas, Kady, and Gard was still working in Antarctica. I had the most wonderful, memorable time with my mother when I visited Oregon to see her. I got to meet all the wonderful people who were so important to her." She looked around the table, returning smile for smile. "Bekka, died just before the end of my visit. I was here with her at Bekka House just moments after it happened."

"That must have been so hard for you, Mom," Kady said.

"You would think so," Astrid said with a warm smile, "but it turned out to be beautiful and happy as well as sad. You'll understand once you hear my story...well," she shrugged, "Grandma Bekka's story, actually. Literally. You see, along with a long, loving letter that she wrote to me the day she died, I have a manuscript that she wrote. She called it Bekka's Story, in Bekka's Own Words, by Rebekka Johannesen Eriksen." Astrid smiled. "Isn't that sweet? I have it here in my tote bag...right next to my cherished Kodak Instamatic." She patted the large leather and canvas bag at her feet.

"Something wondrous happened on Bekka's last day with us. That, my dearest ones, is what I'll share with you this morning. Mom told me her story so many times I know most of it by heart, but it's good to have her manuscript here for reference."

"So Grandma actually wrote a book?" Kady asked.

"She did. It's more of a short story or maybe a novella," Astrid told her. "Grandma Bekka's story begins many years ago. She grew up in Norway with her parents, my grandparents, Helga and Gerhard Johannesen."

"He's the one Gard was named after, right?" his wife, Sabrina, said.

"He is." Astrid nodded. "Gard was named after a true hero. I never got to meet Grandpa Gerhard. He was killed during the occupation of Norway by Nazi Germany, which began in April of 1940. My grandfather was a brave, wonderful man who gave his life to help Norwegian Jews escape."

"He was part of the resistance?" Reen asked.

"Yes, the armed branch...I can't remember the name," Astrid said.

"That portion of the Norwegian resistance movement was known as *Milorg*," Reen's husband, Professor Drake Slattery offered. The multi-degreed Drake was a walking fount of knowledge. "About sixty percent of Norwegian Jews managed to escape to Sweden during the war."

"With a lesser number escaping to the UK," Varik, Delany's Norwegian husband said. "My grandpa told me Hitler and the Nazis believed Norwegians were racially superior to Germans. Not culturally," he smiled, "just racially. Hitler thought he could win Norwegians over to his worldview."

"Hitler had very skewed views," Astrid's husband, Tore added. He and Varik were cousins, both from Oslo. "Nazi architects and planners began building a model Aryan society in Norway during the war. Fortunately, they didn't succeed."

After thoughtful silence settled around the room, Astrid said, "Giving assistance to Jews during the war meant the death penalty. My grandfather, Bekka's dad, is one of the unfortunate ones who were caught and executed." She gave a small shudder. "Sometimes at night I would catch poor Grandma Helga holding a photo of her husband, and crying as she talked to him. I'd often see my mother, Bekka, doing her best to comfort my grandmother. It broke my heart."

"Did your mother and grandmother come to the United States before or after that?" Nevan's nymph wife Aladee asked.

"Grandpa Gerhard arranged for Helga and Bekka to immigrate to America in 1939, a year before the Nazi occupation," Astrid said. "Neither of them wanted to leave him but my grandfather insisted he could see the signs clearly and it was important for them to leave their beloved Norway to ensure their safety. They weren't Jewish, but Grandpa feared what might happen to his wife and daughter, both beautiful women with very fair skin and flaxen hair, once the Nazis arrived."

"Oh how sad," Kady said.

"It's hard to imagine," Astrid said. "Grandma Helga begged him to let her stay there with him. She proposed they send their daughter, Bekka, to safety in America. But my grandfather, who sounds like he was very much like Varik's grandfather—"

"Loving and caring but old-world stern and immovable," Varik interjected, and Astrid readily nodded.

"Yes, exactly." Astrid gave her son-in-law a warm smile. "So my mother and grandmother arrived in Chicago in 1939. There was a sizeable Norwegian community there who helped them get settled in their new country."

"Did they speak any English?" Gard asked.

"Yes, enough to understand and be understood. Today, English is the primary language in Norway, but most schools didn't make it part of their curriculum until the mid-1970s. Bekka was lucky enough to learn some English in school and she taught what she knew to my grandmother. It's my understanding that my grandfather insisted on speaking only his native tongue."

"Just like my grandpa, Anders," Varik said. "He was adamant that we speak only Norwegian at home, telling me if I wanted to learn English I could move to America." He laughed. "Which I eventually did. Since Grandpa Anders and I lived in a remote area in the mountains, I was homeschooled until college and didn't have the opportunity to learn English."

"Varik has some great photos of his grandpa hanging in our library-slash-office at home," Delaney said. "He's got the beard and pipe and he's wearing lederhosen—and a gruff expression. Honestly, he looks just like Heidi's grandfather in the Shirley Temple movie."

"He did," Varik agreed. "But, like Heidi's grandpa, Anders was kind and fair, with a true heart of gold."

"Aside from quickly learning to improve her English, my mother also had a lovely singing voice," Astrid said. "I remember her singing along to all her vinyl record albums as she cleaned the house. I tried to imitate her but I sounded like a sick croaking goose." She laughed.

"Don't be silly," Laila said. "I think you have a great voice, Mom."

"That's why you're my favorite daughter," Astrid teased, to the expected ruckus from her other three daughters.

"Anyway, when Bekka sang, you could barely distinguish her Norwegian accent. After moving to the US from Norway she got a job as a salesclerk at the great Marshall Field's store on State Street in downtown Chicago which, sadly, no longer exists. It's a Macy's now."

"You used to take us to Field's for lunch at the Walnut Room each year at Christmastime," Delaney said. "We'd sit beneath their world famous gigantic Christmas tree."

"It was sheer magic," Laila said.

"Then we'd go stand in the long maze to see Santa and Mrs. Claus," Reen said.

"Such precious memories," Astrid said with a faraway look. "In 1942, when your grandma worked at Field's, her manager heard her singing as she worked, in between customers. She suggested Bekka would be a perfect choice to help entertain the soldiers at the USO functions."

"USO?" Aladee asked.

"United Service Organizations," Astrid clarified. "They provided recreation and aid services for the men and women of our armed forces."

"It was created by an order of President Franklin D. Roosevelt in 1941 to help keep the morale of military personnel high," Drake explained.

"The USO was the organization Bob Hope traveled with during the war with many of the top entertainers at that time," Astrid told Aladee. "And from the blank look on your face, it looks like my son will have to fill you in later on who the heck Bob Hope was." She laughed.

"Sounds like we'll be doing some streaming this weekend," Nevan told his wife. "You'll like Bob Hope. Funny guy."

"Mom loved the idea of helping out at the USO and entertaining. She'd always wanted to be like Ginger Rogers, or Betty Grable, or one of the other song and dance female entertainers of that era."

"Sounds like Grandma Bekka was quite a ham," Delaney said, chuckling.

"Oh she was," Astrid confirmed. "She worked really hard trying to learn American vernacular, along with a midwestern accent so she'd blend in with the other women at Chicago's USO as much as possible. There were a few times she'd had problems because she'd forgotten and answered a soldier with *ja* instead of yes. Some were rude, accusing her of being a Nazi. Can you imagine? The accents and sound of the languages aren't even similar."

"The boys in service were so indoctrinated to hate everything Nazi-related during the war that German Americans often had a difficult time," Drake said. "Wartime was hard for them and terribly tough for Japanese Americans too."

"I almost forgot about Grandma Bekka doing her American accent for us," Gard said with a pop of laughter. "It was cute because she really thought she had her Chicago midwestern accent down pat when, in reality—"

"She sounded almost exactly the same doing that or talking in her usual Norwegian accent," Laila said, wiping tears of laughter. "Oh my gosh, she was so funny and all of us heaped all this praise on her, telling her what a good job she was doing because—"

"Because we all loved her so dearly," Delaney said, nodding enthusiastically.

"And we wouldn't hurt her feelings for all the world," Nevan said.

"Is it any wonder practically the entire town of Glassfloat Bay grew to love Grandma Bekka?" Kady asked. "I recently came across a stack of cards and letters she sent me. I kept them all."

"The letter she wrote to me on her last day included some vintage black and white photos." Astrid handed the pictures to Kady, asking her to pass them around.

"Listen to what Mom said here. 'People used to tell me I looked like Betty Grable,'" Astrid read aloud. "'Funny, at the time I never thought I was very attractive, but looking back at the photos now I can see I was a looker. Hubba hubba! I used to worry that I was fat which, I know now, is ridiculous. I wish I could go back and tell my foolish young self not to be so darned self-critical. That's a good lesson for my beautiful granddaughters to learn while they're still young."

"Young." Delaney made a raspberry sound.

"Oh puhleez," Astrid said. "Spare me, whippersnapper." Once laughter subsided, Astrid continued reading from the letter. "'Now I guess I look more like Mrs. Santa Claus than Betty Grable.'" Glancing up again, Astrid told them, "Mom doodled a bunch of what we'd call laughing-emojis today. Then she said, 'But that's okay, because I've decided Mrs. Claus is beautiful.'"

"Oh, wow, Grandma Bekka really did look like Betty Grable," Delaney said, looking at the photos. "And she didn't have an extra ounce of fat on her either."

"Let me see." Reen took the photos from her sister, laughing silently while studying them. "Boy I wish I was that fat. She looked like a movie star the way she was leaning against that pillar. Like a wartime pinup."

"Mom told me she did some modeling on the side back then. I think that's what these pictures are from."

Reen tsked. "Things sure were different in the forties. I'd bet none of us supposedly average-sized women at this table could fit into the dress grandma's wearing here." With a pointed look at Monica Sharp Griffin, Reen amended, "Except for skinny-minny Monica, of course."

"Maybe pre-baby. I'm afraid my skinny-minny-ness has left the building," Monica joked back good-naturedly.

"Tell me about it." Reen lovingly rounded her protruding belly. "Sean Samuel Slattery, who some of you may have mistaken for a beachball I swallowed, is going to be a big boy. But even at my thinnest, I could never close those buttons over my waist." She tapped a black and white photo of her grandmother wearing a simple fitted A-line dress with boxy shoulders, a slim-belted waistline, and a hemline below the knee, before passing them to her sister, Laila.

"Fat?" Laila said with genuine surprise. "You've got to be kidding. And, yeah, there's definitely a Ginger vibe going on. Make Ginger a flaxen blonde, and they'd almost be twins. Grandma Bekka was a stunner when she was young, and a beauty as she aged. I think that's the first time I ever saw her without the thick crown braid on the top of her head."

"See her shoes in that picture?" Astrid said, finding her place in the letter. "Mom said, 'These were my favorite shoes. Since leather was needed by the military during wartime, shoes often came with velvet or suede uppers. These were velvet. They had short, thick heels and a peep toe. Cute, *ja*? My stockings came up to the thigh and were fastened on by garters attached to my girdle. This was long before pantyhose, or the trend for women to go barelegged. Those women were thought of as promiscuous.'"

"Wow, women really have come a long way," Reen noted.

"Not nearly far enough," Delaney offered.

"After that," Astrid said, "Mom wrote, 'Did you notice my hair? It has victory rolls on either side and a chignon in back. Those were the days before I let my hair grow long and plaited a crown braid.'"

Looking up from the handwritten letter, Astrid smiled. "Listen to this. Mom wrote, 'My sweet granddaughter, Kady, showed me how to make playlists for Alexa. She helped me find many of my favorite forties wartime tunes. I've been humming along with Glenn Miller's "In the Mood" as I write this. It was recorded in 1940, so I feel almost as though I've been transported to another time and place. I've been nostalgic all morning for some reason.'"

Astrid paused her reading, saying, "Alexa, play Bekka's 1940s playlist." A moment later, Bekka House was filled with a medley of Grandma Bekka's wartime favorites, both vocals and instrumentals, all by the original artists. "I thought I'd set the mood for us as I finish reading this letter," Astrid said with a wink.

"I found this letter in her knitting satchel. Mom had tucked the letter into an envelope addressed to my old suburban Chicago address. Since I was here in Oregon visiting her at the time, she must have intended to send it to me once I left to go back home. It gives a lot of insight to how Mom was feeling that last day. It's as if she knew it was her time." Astrid breathed deeply, letting out a wistful sigh.

She continued reading aloud, "'If I allowed myself to indulge in sentimentality, I could easily close my eyes and linger in memories of myself as a young woman back in Chicago, singing songs for the troops at the local USO. The older I get, the harder it becomes to extricate myself from those mental journeys back in time.'"

"Aw, I can only imagine," Delaney said.

"This part is interesting...and unusual," Astrid said. "'See my seemed stockings in the photo where I'm looking over my shoulder? Those seems were drawn with eyebrow pencil to mimic the look of seamed silk stockings. We even used tea to dye our legs so they'd have some color like real stockings. When we didn't have tea, believe it or not, we used watered down leftover gravy to darken our *gams*, as we called our legs back then.'"

There were cringing looks around the table.

"Bekka went on, 'Times were different then. Most everything was rationed and we were desperate. Of all the fashion items we girls had to part with during the war, I think silk and nylon stockings were probably the most difficult.'"

"It must have been next to impossible to draw those lines straight unless she had a friend helping," Red noted.

"That's what she says here," Astrid told him. "'We all pitched in to help each other, to make sure we weren't walking around with squiggly lines snaking up our skirts. The stocking shortage was due to silk being used to make parachutes. With the military's silk and nylon production, stockings were terribly expensive and eventually banned, so we had to get creative. It's so much fun to reminisce about my younger days. But it can also be painful. I choose to push the bittersweet thoughts from my mind, keeping my smile in place.'"

"I don't think I ever remember Grandma Bekka without a smile," Gard noted, and the rest agreed.

Astrid continued reading. "'Right now "Don't Sit Under the Apple Tree" is playing, and I'm blinking back unexpected tears at the poignant memories flooding my thoughts. Can it really be possible that so many decades have passed since the end of the war? One minute I was a young woman filled with hopes and dreams for the future. Then, in the blink of an eye, I'm in the winter of my years.'"

Astrid worked to hold back her own tears after reading her mother's words. "'Ah, I can't help but smile when Alexa plays "Mairzy Doats." Don't you worry about your old mama, my sweet Astrid. Everything's jake.'" Astrid laughed at the clueless looks around her. "That's forties lingo for everything's hunky-dory, or a-okay. Bekka finished that part with, '*Ja*, I may be geriatric, and sometimes I have aches and pains from the arthritis, or maybe I get blue because I miss my Jamie, but I've still got plenty of spunk left. *Ja*...I'll be just fine.'"

As bittersweet memories flitted across her mind, Astrid smiled. "As she always did, my mother signed her letter, *Jeg elsker deg*, Mamma." She looked up from the letter. That's Norwegian for *I love you*. It was one of the phases I heard most often from my mother, going back to my earliest memories."

Astrid took Bekka's manuscript, placing it in front of her and patting it as she smiled. "This isn't the original. I copied it and printed it out so nothing would happen to the original, which has handwritten notes and some doodling in the margins."

Astrid rubbed her hands together, surveying the sizeable family room of Bekka House, along with all of Astrid's invitees, "So now it's time to share Grandma Bekka's love story with you all, just as she told it to me so many times throughout the years. We're starting in Chicago. It's Christmastime, December of 1942..."

# The Daughter's Heartwish: Chapter Two
## *Chicago, December 1942*

~<>~

"HIYA, FELLAS! Welcome to the USO Christmas party. I'm Bekka, and..." At the outbreak of wolf whistles she paused, savoring the appreciative din for a moment. Speaking into the microphone again, Rebekka Johannesen continued, "And this is Rita and Margo." She gestured left and right, beaming a smile as she and her two best friends were treated to more whistles, cheers and clapping.

"We may not be pinups like Betty Grable or Lana Turner," Rita said into her microphone, smiling at the vigorous disagreement of the servicemen.

"And we may not be the Andrews Sisters," Margo added.

"But, brother," Bekka continued in her best American midwestern accent and 1940s lingo, "we sure know how to swing!" She kicked out her leg, slapping her knee and a cheer went up from the enthusiastic audience of uniformed men. "And we do a mean rendition of "Boogie Woogie Bugle Boy.""

Looking out over the sea of servicemen, she hoisted the bugle in the air. "Which one of you big lugs is gutsy enough to come up on stage with us and do a little pantomime on the horn while we sing?" Several hands went up, with some guys hooting and hollering like gangbusters.

"My pal Jamie here can ape Harry James better than anybody I know," one soldier called out, grabbing his buddy's hand and thrusting it into the air. "And he doesn't even have to pantomime." Clapping his friend on the back, he added, "Ain't that right, Jamie?"

"Well..." With a confident grin, Jamie shrugged. "They tell me I'm not too bad."

Bekka had locked gazes with the handsome soldier earlier. She'd been manning the industrial sized coffee urn when she felt the heat of his gaze on her. Dashing in his army uniform he'd stood there watching her for a long moment before ambling up to the table and requesting a cuppa joe. Tall with a head of wavy nutmeg-brown hair, he had a velvet smooth voice, hypnotic brown eyes and a smile that tugged at her heart.

When their fingers brushed as she passed him the cup, something electric sparked between them.

Now here he was, right up front, flaunting the same devilish smile he'd given her earlier.

The men around Jamie nudged the guy, urging him to get on stage. "Sure," he said, "what the heck." He climbed on stage and took the bugle from Bekka. Putting the horn to his lips, he blew out a jazzy version of reveille. Another cheer went up from the packed room.

"Hey, this boy can blow," Bekka said to the men. "You're a real killer diller on that horn, soldier."

"Thanks!" Leaning closer, he said for her ears only, "Love that Norwegian accent, blue eyes."

*Blue eyes...* Bekka liked that, much preferring it to the usual doll, babe, honey, sugar or sweetheart. Their gazes connected and she stifled a dreamy sigh.

"How did you know I'm Norwegian? I thought I'd covered up my accent pretty well."

"Oh, um..." Jamie chuckled. "Sorry, but it's kind of obvious. My parents are from Norway, so I'm familiar with the accent."

"Hey mac, you can go fishing later, let's get to the jive," one of the soldiers in the audience called out, as the others backed him up with cheers.

Before putting some distance between them, Jamie gave Bekka a wink.

"Who needs Harry James when we've got Jamie!" Margo offered, followed by another rousing cheer from the men.

Focused entirely on Jamie, Bekka felt her cheeks color as he flashed his charismatic smile, just for her. The timbre of his voice and sensuous linger of his gaze were unsettling. For an instant, she could almost believe they were alone, and she found herself wishing they were.

Jeepers creepers, this boy was a looker! Aware she needed to return her attention to the crowd and her job of entertaining *all* the men instead of just one, she drew in a deep breath and cleared her throat.

"So, Jamie, what's your last name and where are you from?" Bekka asked, easing herself back into her playful stage persona.

"Private James Eriksen of the United States Army, by way of Portland, Oregon, at your service, ma'am." He saluted. A few of the men whooped a holler and Jamie laughed. "Sounds like my buddies from Camp Adair near Corvallis." At the mention of the Oregon base serving men from the Northwest region, another round of cheers were heard.

Rita asked, "Can you play "Boogie Woogie Bugle Boy" on that horn?"

"Can I!" He demonstrated a few bars and the crowd went wild.

"Hot diggity dog!" Margo said, while Bekka remained silent, happily drinking in his presence. She'd met a lot of fine-looking servicemen at the USO functions but Private Eriksen succeeded in capturing her attention like no other.

The foursome entertained the audience with an upbeat performance of "Boogie Woogie Bugle Boy," complete with exaggerated gestures and plenty of humor. As Jamie left the stage Bekka and the girls treated the men to Irving Berlin's hit song, "This is the Army, Mr. Jones," followed by several other tunes on the hit parade. Although she tried hard, it was difficult for Bekka not to keep her eyes glued on Jamie as she, Rita and Margo performed.

As soon as they'd left the stage, and the dance music resounded over the speakers, Jamie snagged Bekka's arm. "Hold on there, blue eyes. You don't think you're getting away from me that fast, do you? How about a dance?"

Bekka felt a rush at the touch of Jamie's hand on her elbow. Before she had a chance to answer, he'd whisked her onto the dance floor and they were jitterbugging. He was as impressive with his feet as he was with his mouth. As the dance ended, her fingers smoothed over the sleeve of his olive-drab jacket. She longed to feel the warmth of his skin beneath the rough layer of wool and his khaki shirt.

The USO events were always chaperoned. Dating the soldiers was strictly forbidden. Even so, romance often blossomed. She and the other volunteers were there to dance with the servicemen and make their visit enjoyable, to help boost their morale. As a rule, Bekka avoided getting personally involved with the men. Why chance getting hooked on a guy when she'd probably never see him again?

Falling under the charming, dark-eyed soldier's spell, Bekka reminded herself that rules were meant to be broken.

"Another jitterbug?" Bekka lamented three dances later, wrinkling her nose as the music started. She loved swing dancing but had hoped for something slower this time so the handsome soldier could hold her close in his arms.

"It's getting warm in here," Jamie said, as if he'd been reading her mind. "I could go for a walk outside to cool off, how about you?"

"Sure." After grabbing her wool coat and scarf Bekka grew nervous about spending time alone with the soldier. Not because she was afraid of Jamie, but because she was worried she'd bore the poor guy to tears.

It wasn't like she led an interesting life. Entertaining servicemen at the USO and doing smalltime performances locally, it wasn't as if she, Rita and Margo were celebrities. The everyday plain old Rebekka was nothing more than a salesclerk downtown at Marshall Field's. Maybe the soldier was just lonely and wanted to be reminded of his Norwegian parents when he heard her familiar accent.

Most of what Bekka said and did onstage was scripted to help her come across as more American. Dear Margo and Rita had spent plenty of time coaching her so she'd have a better grasp of popular words and phrases that were part of American slang. It was more difficult than she thought it would be. English wasn't the easiest language to learn, and so many of the slang terms were difficult for her to understand.

Among all the terms to remember, there was anchor clankers, which meant sailors. Bald men were chrome domes; cute girls were cookies; a bad dancer was a dead hoofer, while good dancers were jive bombers. If you're cooking with gas, that meant you're doing something properly. To leave is to take a powder. And so many other strange sayings it made her head swim.

Bekka's fondest hope is that Jamie wouldn't be whistling dixie...which meant wasting his time. Honestly, what could she talk to him about to keep him entertained enough not to think she was a complete dud?

A smile took hold when she came up with an idea.

"You mentioned you liked Abbott and Costello," she said, thinking a movie would be a great way to be close to him without having to carry a conversation. "Their new movie is playing just down the street if you're interested. I think this one has the Andrews Sisters in it too."

"Normally that would be swell." Jamie hugged Bekka close. "But right now I'm more interested in getting to know you better, blue eyes." He winked at her.

She tried to act nonchalant but the way he kept calling her *blue eyes* forced Bekka to swallow a wistful sigh. The most delicious sensation zipped through her when Jamie gazed at her with those glittery eyes. It was like she'd never been fully alive until she met him.

"Is there someplace we could grab a cuppa joe and something to eat around here?" Jamie asked as they left the dance and stepped into the chilly early evening air. His stomach growled so loudly Bekka heard it and they chuckled together.

"There's plenty to eat back at the USO. They really put out a nice spread." She hiked a thumb over her shoulder. She hoped that wasn't what he wanted. She'd like nothing more than to keep Jamie all to herself.

He gave her that mesmerizing look again. "I meant someplace more private where we could get to know each other better. Someplace where there's not a hundred other uniformed dogfaces hanging around making eyes at you."

"Oh." A ripple of excitement made her shiver. At that moment Bekka felt so buoyant she expected to look down at her feet and find herself walking on air.

"Cold?"

"No." Bekka shook her head. "In fact the temperature is surprisingly mild for December."

"Really?" He gave a strangled laugh. "You call this mild?" Crossing his arms over his chest and grasping them, he made an exaggerated shudder. "It feels like it's twenty degrees."

"Close. It's about twenty-five. The wind makes it seem colder," Bekka explained.

"I guess they don't call Chicago the Windy City for nothing." He clapped his arms.

Looking up at him, she laughed. "Gee, Jamie, you really are cold, aren't you? Your teeth are chattering."

"I'm not used to this. Back home in Oregon we'd call this a deep freeze." He rubbed his hands together, blowing on them. "There wouldn't be a living soul out on the streets."

"In the winter when it goes from below zero to thirty degrees," Bekka said, removing the wool scarf from around her neck and placing it around Jamie's, "we're sitting out on our porches and taking walks without jackets."

Shaking his head in bewilderment, Jamie said, "That's just plain nuts. Give me Pacific Northwest weather any day. Hey," he clutched her scarf, "there's something wrong with this picture. I'm the one who's supposed to be gallant."

"Yes but I'm not cold and you're the one with wimpy Oregonian blood." She winked at him.

It looked like Jamie was about to protest but he chuckled instead, saying, "You've got a point." He tugged the scarf close, inhaling her *Evening in Paris* scent. "Have you ever been out there, Bekka? To the Pacific Northwest."

"No. Since it's so far north with all those mountains in Oregon and Washington, I thought it would be even colder than Chicago."

"Lots of people think that until they experience our mild winters." Jamie smiled. "It averages between forty and sixty. We get very little snow but plenty of rain. My dad, who had immigrated to Minnesota, where there was a large Norwegian population, was used to bone-chilling-cold winters. After we moved to Oregon he always said 'at least you don't have to shovel rain.'"

"True. The thing I hate most about Chicago winters is trying to walk on ice," Bekka said. "I'm forever falling on my *baksiden*." She rubbed her butt. "But I'm not sure if I'd give that up for lots of rain and cloudy skies. Too much makes me feel kind of blue."

"Our rain is different. It's soft and gentle. No whipping winds like here in Chicago. Heck, most people in Portland don't even use umbrellas. Once you get used to it, all that rain is peaceful. Aside from plenty of moss, the rain means we have a really colorful spring and summer."

"Moss...sounds like Ireland."

"I understand it's very similar."

"So there are lots of plants and flowers? I can barely get anything to grow here," she complained.

"Tons," Jamie assured her. "Flowers that bloom this big." He formed his hands as if he were holding a basketball.

Bekka gave him a skeptical look. "Mmm-hmm. Whatever you say, Jamie."

"No kidding. I'm on the level, Bekka." He gazed at his hands, bringing them closer together. "Okay, most of them are closer to softball size," he admitted. "And big, towering evergreens, thick as a forest all around the houses." Catching the look of disbelief on her face, he crossed his heart. "Honest."

"You make the Pacific Northwest sound like paradise. Very...uh...*magisk*." She frowned, trying to recall the word in English. "What is the word?"

"Magical?"

"*Ja*, that's it, magical! But if it's so grand, why doesn't everyone want to move there like they do California?"

"The only reason it's not as popular as California is because of the winter rain. But, brother, our summers beat California's any day. All that rainfall gives us beautiful foliage the rest of the year, along with plenty of sunshine."

"Chicago summers are hot and humid." Bekka wrinkled her nose, remembering how much she grumbled on those sweat-soaked days. "I'll definitely have to visit Oregon one of these days."

"You'd love it. There are no glacial temperatures in the winter or hot, sticky days in summer. We'll go there together after the war. That way I can give you the official ten cent tour." Jamie's smile looked sincere and eager.

"So you and your family live in Portland?"

"We did at first, in a small apartment. Later, we moved to Glassfloat Bay, a small coastal town that's about a hundred miles from Portland. It's a two and a half hour drive. Dad bought the house about twelve or fifteen years ago. It's small, more like a cottage, but he plans to build on to it little by little and I'll help him with that once I get home again. The ocean's just a nice, short scenic walk from the house."

"Oh, Jamie, it sounds *akkurat som himmelen*—oops, sorry, that means—"

"I know." He flashed a smile. "It means just like heaven. I think it is...a little patch of heaven. The streets and buildings in the center of town are a quaint blend of old and new architecture. The main drag is Ocean Charm Boulevard. It's the sort of picturesque town you see in movies, where everyone knows everyone and they're like one big family. It's a great place to live."

Jamie made it sound so charming and appealing. Bekka would like nothing more than to visit there after the war and have Jamie give her that ten cent tour he mentioned.

"Okay, so where to?" He offered a teeth-chattering smile. "Someplace with a heater might be nice."

Happily, conversation with Jamie was easier than she thought it might be. Since he clearly enjoyed talking about his hometown, that was a perfect subject. "Well, Bullard's is a couple of blocks that way." She pointed to her left. "It's a corner drugstore with a great soda fountain. They make the best *sjokolade* malts, vanilla phosphates and black cows." Realizing what she'd said, Bekka said, "Oops, I meant to say chocolate. I'm still learning English and have a habit of slipping into Norwegian more often than I'd like. But I think I'm doing pretty well, *ja*?"

"*Ja*," he answered her with a wink. "You're doing great. My Norwegian isn't as good as it could be, but I'm fairly familiar. I should have paid closer attention to my family speaking the language when I was a kid."

"I have to make a confession." She cupped her hand at the side of her mouth. "Just about everything I say when I'm entertaining at the USO is scripted. I have to study it hard so I don't come across as too foreign. It's helped me learn more English too. Lots of the military men don't want to hear foreign accents now, you know?"

Jamie nodded. "I understand. There's a lot of uh...opinionated thinking right now because of the war. In any case, I think you do a great job with your part at the USO. It all sounds very natural."

"Really?" Jamie nodded and Bekka wiped her forehead. "Whew! That's good to hear. I really do try hard."

"So this corner drugstore you mentioned...lots of booths, and stools at the counter, right?"

"Plenty," Bekka answered. "Sound good?"

He shook his head from side to side. "Not private enough."

He was hinting at coming back to her apartment. She could sense it. "I don't know, Jamie..."

"Oh, I get it." His smile faded. "Hey sugar, are you rationed?"

Familiar with the lingo she'd recently learned from Rita and Margo, Bekka recognized Jamie was asking her if she was taken by anyone.

"I mean, that would be okay," Jamie continued. "There's no reason we couldn't still have some nice conversation over a soda. But," he gave a boyish shrug, "I was kinda hoping..."

Bekka smiled at his presumption. "No, I'm not going steady, or engaged or otherwise involved with anyone."

"Whew..." Mirroring Bekka's gesture, he mopped his forehead with his hand. "That's what I like to hear."

The mention of rationing gave her an idea. She opened her handbag and plucked out a folded paper.

"Speaking of sugar, look what I have." She waved it under Jamie's nose.

Holding her hand to still it, his eyes brightened when he opened the paper and read it. "A sugar rationing coupon. No kidding! Hey, those are like gold." He licked his lips in exaggerated fashion.

"Believe it or not, I traded a beef coupon for this," Bekka admitted. With the coupon an inch from her lips, she smooched the air. "Ever since some of the markets began selling *hestekjøtt*...eh..." She tried like heck but couldn't remember the word in English.

"Horse meat?" Jamie offered and she nodded.

"*Ja*, thanks, horse meat. Because of the meat shortage I've been leery of buying beef." She winced. "I mean, what if the butcher accidentally slaps a beef hamburger label on a package of ground horse." Now she shuddered.

"Whoa, Nellie!" Jamie made a neighing sound.

"Exactly." A wide-eyed Bekka nodded. "People who've tried it say it's supposed to be pretty good, but I'm not too keen on chewing old Nellie. I'd much rather take my chances on the sugar."

"I'd have to agree. I like to think I'm a somewhat adventurous eater but that's going too far for me. So then, we're off in search of sugar?"

"We are." Bekka smiled at the slightly wayward idea she was about to suggest. "Maupon's Market is a couple blocks from here. They should still be open," she said with a quick glance at her watch. "If we hurry, I'm sure we can make it. We'll stop in, pick up my eight ounces of sugar and go back to my apartment." Giving him a quick glance, she caught his smile and her heart pounded.

"I've got some flour," she continued, "and just enough chocolate and butter to make a small batch of those popular new chocolate chip cookies."

"Chocolate? You've got chocolate? And butter?"

"Mmm-hmm. Just a little of each." Putting her finger to her mouth she made a secretive shushing gesture. She'd never been happier for carefully limiting her apportioned food. If a few special ingredients could make this soldier so happy, it was worth her going without for a while.

"Butter..." he shook his head slowly, "imagine that. I'd almost forgotten what it tastes like. I knew I liked you the first time I set eyes on you, blue eyes." Jamie winked.

"It's not like before the war when we took all those ordinary foods for granted," Bekka noted. "On one of my trips to the grocery store a few months ago I had my allotted quarter pound of butter in my shopping cart and believe it or not, someone fetched it."

"I think you mean filched it," Jamie said.

Oh, *ja, ja*, filched." Bekka laughed. "There's often no butter to be had and I'd been lucky enough to grab one of the last quarters. All it took was one quick look away from my cart and phffft! Gone."

"Whoever stooped that low deserves a knuckle sandwich." Jamie socked his open hand with his fist, making Bekka aware of the slang's meaning without further explanation.

"I was furious at first," she said, "but then I wondered if maybe the young woman I saw with the four *barn* in tow might be the one who took it. I decided she and those children needed it a lot more than me. Besides," she patted her belly, "me losing a few pounds certainly couldn't hurt."

"You look perfect to me." Placing his arm around Bekka's shoulder as they walked, Jamie gave her a squeeze. "You're a good gal, Bekka."

She bit her bottom lip. A good gal? On the contrary, she felt like a sinful, wanton woman. After all, good girls shouldn't be inviting virtual strangers up to their apartments just a few hours after they'd met. Neighbors would surely talk and her reputation would most likely suffer, but right now it didn't matter.

She felt something almost magical with him at her side, something that made her feel whole and complete. To heck with gossip, she decided. She *had* to be with him...had to spend some time getting to know him before he was off to war again, and out of her life...probably forever. The melancholy notion made her sad.

"Chocolate chip cookies at your place sounds swell." Jamie linked arms with her. "Got the coffee too?"

"*Ja*, you bet I got the joe. And a percolator and two *forklær*." This time she corrected herself. "Aprons!" she smiled.

"Two?"

"Well *ja*, of course." Bekka giggled at the confounded look on his face. "You'll need one if you don't want to get your uniform full of flour when you help me bake those cookies. So, what do you say?"

"Howdya like that? Here I get a short leave and some doll puts me on KP." He laughed. "Well I guess that's better than LD. Just point me to the kitchen." He gave a salute.

Bekka thought for a moment. No matter how much American lingo she learned, something new always popped up. "Okay, I know KP is kitchen patrol, but what's LD?"

Cupping his hand over his mouth Jamie leaned in close. "Latrine duty."

"Oh, *nei*, I wouldn't do that to you." She laughed to herself as the wicked thought of engaging in a little BD, bedroom duty, with

Jamie came to mind. Bekka felt herself flush as succulent images of her and the gorgeous soldier, naked, hot and sweaty jitterbugged across her mind.

"My place is about a ten-minute bus ride from the grocery store," she told him, grateful she'd taken the time to neaten her apartment after work and before heading for the USO.

Less than an hour later they were bustling around Bekka's kitchen, talking up a storm about anything and everything as they tossed cookie ingredients into a big glass bowl. Jamie was so masculine that he still looked every inch the man all dolled up in the ruffled over-the-head apron.

"Did you make this recipe book?" he asked, flipping through the pages of the three-ring binder notebook.

"My mother, Helga, and I put this together. We keep adding to it." Smoothing her fingers over the yellowed recipes, she smiled at the warm recollections coming to mind.

"Looks like a lot of love went into making this," he said, examining the tabbed sections dividing the recipe categories. "Is your mom here in Chicago too?"

"*Ja*, Mamma's staying with some good friends and family in the Norwegian community in the Logan's Square area. Just temporarily, just until they get settled here. They arrived here from Norway a short time ago and, unfortunately, the mother has fallen ill, so Mamma is there helping take care of her and her seven children."

"Your mom sounds like a good, caring woman," Jamie noted.

Bekka gave him a warm smile. "Honestly, she's like an angel. *Alle sier det*, um sorry, I mean everyone says so. Mamma is always watching out for and taking care of others. She felt guilty about leaving me alone here at *Juletid* but I convinced her I understand and not to worry about me. We'll have many more Christmases together."

"Sounds like you have your mom's angel genes." Jamie's smile lit up his handsome face.

"*Takk for komplimentet*, oh, that means—"

"Thank you for the compliment," Jamie translated. "That's one of the phrases I remember. And you're very welcome."

"Mamma and I actually share this apartment, but she's so much in demand because she has such a good, helpful way with new immigrants that she's usually gone more than she's here. She knows how difficult it can be because we went through it ourselves when we moved here in 1939."

Bekka felt her cheeks warm. "Oh dear...I'm sorry for so much *snakker*, er, talking. I can just go on and on." Her voice trailed off with light laughter. "Enough about me. Tell me about you, Jamie."

"I love hearing you talk," he said, fixing his big brown eyes on her. "I want to know everything about you. How about your dad? Is he here too?"

Bekka's face warmed for an entire different reason at the mention of her father. "No, he...um, Pappa fought in the *Milorg*."

Jamie's eyes went wide while Bekka shook her head in frustration. "I can't recall the right word. Can you help?"

"The armed branch of the Norwegian resistance," Jamie said.

"Resistance." Bekka engaged in a slow nod. "*Ja*, Pappa was killed by the Nazis two years ago, after they invaded and occupied Norway."

"I'm so sorry. That must have been tough on you and your mother."

Bekka's head bobbed again. "*Ja...ja*...it still is. We miss him so much. It was hard leaving our home, everyone we knew and loved, and coming to a new country to live without him." She broke into a natural smile then. "Oh, Jamie, Pappa would have loved it here. If only he would have come with us. But he, well, he insisted that Mamma and I leave before the Nazi's arrived."

"Your pappa was a wise man." Jamie brushed his thumb against her cheek.

"Mamma and I love our new home. We're both American citizens now." Elevating her chin, she gave a gratified smile. "Proud Norwegian Americans."

"Same for my parents. They've been here in the US since shortly before I was born." Returning his attention to her cookbook, Jamie told Bekka, "Mom used to have a similar recipe book. She'd spend hours clipping recipes from the newspaper and magazines and was always making us something new." His eyes lit up and he chuckled. "My least favorite were the recipes that had the word *surprise* in them."

"Oh *ja*, I can relate." Bekka gave a knowing nod. "Like Mamma's *kjøttkake* surprise recipes. Meatloaf," she quickly clarified. "You never know what will be hiding in the center of that ground meat." She shuddered. "The one I liked best had a tunnel stuffed with peas and mushrooms. I even make that myself now and then."

"At least that sounds normal. My mom's stuffed meatloaves tended to be somewhat less conventional." He arched an eyebrow. "Even after all this time, she's still trying to adapt, and be more American. Making popular recipes she comes across in the paper makes her feel patriotic, I guess." Jamie and Bekka laughed together.

"Worst of all are Mom's gelatin surprises," Jamie continued. "Boy she'd end up sticking all sorts of strange things into those wobbly dishes...I mean stuff that should never, ever even be on the same plate. Like chopped ham, olives, pineapple and grapes, all held together with gelatin and marshmallows."

The narrow-eyed sour face he made while demonstrating a shaky plate of gelatin had Bekka laughing.

"That must be a thing with moms," she said. "Sometimes Mamma makes those too. Unfortunately, I'm too old not to do what I did as a child—hide the *special*," she hung invisible quotes around the word, "ingredients under the rim of my *tallerken*...eh, plate."

"I did the same. So how'd that work for you?" Jamie asked with a snicker.

"Just fine until it was time to clear the table, revealing my neat little circle of inedibles." Bekka smiled. Returning her attention to her thick notebook, she told Jamie, "This is a collection of favorite recipes mostly from Mamma and my *bestemor*...um...."

"Grandma," Jamie said before Bekka had a chance to translate. Giving her a broad smile, he told her, "I guess my Norwegian isn't too bad after all."

"It's good! And I'm glad for that."

"I'd say we make a pretty good team, *ja*?" Jamie said, boasting a smile.

"*Ja*, I think so too." Yes indeed, Bekka could see them together as a team for a long time. Forcing herself from her dreamy thinking, she cleared her throat. "The cookies we're making now are from Mamma's recipe. The chocolate chip is a new type of cookie, so I haven't made too many batches. But I think I do a good job with them. Mamma's gingery pepperkaker was actually my favorite cookie as a kid. It still is."

With more than a spark of interest, Jamie asked, "You know how to make pepperkaker?"

"Oh *ja*, of course I do. It's our traditional holiday gingerbread cookie." With a teasing smile, she elbowed him. "You know that. I watched Mamma make them every year. When I was about eight, she let me help for the first time, and I've made them every year since. But," sighing, Bekka shrugged, "it seems Americans prefer the new chocolate chip cookies."

"Well this boy with Norwegian roots," Jamie thumbed his chest, "loves chocolate chip, but nothing can compare to pepperkaker. They're definitely my favorite. My mother has never been much of a baker, so the last time I had them was when my grandma was still alive. Maybe we can make them next time we see each other." He looked hopeful.

Unable to keep from smiling at the thought, Bekka nodded, probably too enthusiastically. "*Ja*, I would like that very much...*soldat gutt.*"

"You called me soldier boy." Lifting an eyebrow in amusement, Jamie chuckled. "My mom calls me that too."

"*Ja*? But I bet your mamma doesn't do this when she says it." For humorous effect, Bekka angled her head, batting her eyelashes at him in dramatic fashion, which clearly amused him.

"Definitely not. Blue eyes, you're a real dolly."

Stilling in place, she thought for a moment before scurrying around her kitchen, opening cabinets and checking the pantry.

"What are you doing?"

"Checking to see if I have what we need to bake pepperkaker. Do you want to make those instead? Because of rationing, I only have enough ingredients to make one type of cookie today."

"Could we? With extra ginger?" Jamie asked, his eyes lighting up. "I'm salivating just thinking about it."

"Plenty of ginger is just the way I like them too," Bekka told him. "I have fresh ginger root as well as powdered ginger. Before the war I had a supply of candied ginger too, which is a wonderful addition to the cookies. But with rationing, that's something I haven't been able to get for quite a while."

Rubbing his hands together, he said, "I can't even begin to tell you the last time I had homemade cookies." Enthusiasm was evident in his expression. "We haven't even started and this is already the best experience I've had in a *very* long time." He watched as she pulled out additional mixing bowls, utensils and ingredients. "Do you want some help?"

"*Nei takk*...eh, no thanks." Holding his gaze for a long beat, Bekka, nibbled her bottom lip. "Um, you know..." she said as she sifted the dry ingredients, "I've never done this before."

His lifted an eyebrow as he looked up from his task of measuring the salt. "Bake cookies?"

Her gaze dropping to her feet, she shook her head. "No, I mean invite a man up to my *leilighet*, um, I mean apartment," she corrected, looking back up at him. She slipped into Norwegian more often when she was nervous. "I just don't want you to think I'm, you know...a—"

"A *skjøge*?" Jamie asked with a teasing smile. The word basically meant harlot.

"*Ja*, exactly." Bekka felt her cheeks grow warm. They were probably peppermint pink. "A loose woman."

"And you're not, hmm?"

She gave a meek side to side shake of her head again in response. "In fact, Mamma would have a conniption fit—that's a new phrase I just learned—if she knew I'd invited you up here." A hiccup of her nervous laughter followed.

"Oh." With a disappointed look, Jamie untied his apron. "Well in that case I'll be going." Saluting her, he added, "See ya, sister." He yanked the apron over his head, tossing it over a chair and headed out of the kitchen.

Uttering a surprised gasp, Bekka watched him retreat. Her jaw dropped and her shoulders sagged. That definitely wasn't the response she'd expected.

~<>~

# And So, Dear Reader,

You've finished reading The Psychic's Heartwish, a Daisy Dexter Dobbs book that (*fingers crossed and hopeful sigh*) you were sorry to see end. Meanwhile I, author DDD, am gleefully clacking away at my keyboard, writing yet another sensational, utterly phenomenal (*please don't burst my bubble*) book. I'd like to conclude our time together with a heartfelt THANK YOU for choosing to read this book, the 6th in my Heartwishes series.

I hope this destined-for-love story of bohemian bookshop owner Kady Malone, and science professor Rylan Kilpatrick added a smile to your day. I imagine some of you have known people similar to Kady's toxic cousin Lorraine. I have. It's often easy to be fooled by people because they don't always show you who they really are. But other times? *shudder* They're *exactly* as they seem and you have to learn to trust your first gut instinct. Both Kady and Rylan, two trusting souls, were dangerously caught off guard by Lorraine's menacing deceptiveness. But, delightedly, my books only have happy endings!

I have also had the good fortune to know so many truly good-hearted people like Kady in my life. As I wrote this book, I found myself inwardly cheering for her kind, compassionate soul and boundless, resolute determination to heal the terrible rift in her family, specifically where it concerned her ostracized gay cousin, Red Devington. (If you haven't read The Nymph's Heartwish (book 5) yet, you'll learn all about what ultimately happens to Red in that story.)

~<>~

If you enjoyed The Psychic's Heartwish I'd be delighted if you left a positive review or rating on the site where you purchased it. (Not that I check daily for new reviews, or ever Google myself, or do anything else indicating I'm an insecure creative person craving validation. Nope, nothing like that.) Your review can be long, short, or just a star rating. Reviews help other readers find my books, and keep my stories from getting lost in a site's complicated algorithms. Plus, it gives me encouragement to keep on writing!

Speaking of other readers, you can help them find this book by recommending it to your friends, neighbors, relatives, coworkers, your dentist, doctor, mail carrier, all the strangers you meet in the grocery store, at the mall, the neighborhood pub, your favorite coffee shop, and, of course, everyone you know online. (I'm ready with additional suggestions if needed.)

Thanks again! Wishing you love, laughter, romance and happy reading!

—*Daisy Dexter Dobbs*

~<>~

# DAISY DEXTER DOBBS BOOK LIST

Bold, opinionated Greek men, the Drakos brothers star in this hot, hot, HOT laugh out loud romantic comedy series featuring lots of hunky, delicious Greek men and the women who capture their alpha male hearts. (Can be read as standalones but better appreciated when read in order so you can get to know all the characters.)

Trained by the Greek (Book 1: Jordan and Riley)
Vexed by the Greek (Book 2: Dino and Sophie)
Bossed by the Greek (Book 3: Sebastian and Ardine)
Conned by the Greek (Book 4: Benedict and Angel)
(additional stories for more brothers coming)

~<>~

## STANDALONES

Don't Even Think About It (Mindy and Archer)
*Laugh-out-loud Romantic Comedy (spice level: scorching-hot and hilarious)*

Avowed chocoholic Mindy handles her upside-down life with as much grace and aplomb as possible—by attempting chocolatcide.

This steamy, spicy, laugh-out-loud, award-winning romantic comedy novel is brimming with love, snappy banter, sexy inventive scenes that sizzle, and numerous naughty words.

~<>~

## MORE SERIES AND STANDALONES COMING SOON FROM DAISY

Daisy has written close to 100 novels and numerous novellas and short stories over the last few decades. She certainly can't have novels full of pay phones, answering machines, landlines, no email, or the internet, or social media now, can she? Nope, nope, nope.

Of course not. So now that she has the rights back to all of her books and stories from her previous publishers, she's been hard at work rewriting and updating her books for release as an indie author. Revisiting umpteen stories featuring gorgeous, handsome, oh-so-sexy hunks is a tough job, but somebody's gotta do it. So here's a sneak peek at just some of the dozens of titles Daisy's been maniacally, um, I mean, *diligently*, working on (check her website and newsletter for updates!).

~<>~

Visit DaisyDexterDobbs.com[1] for a full, up-to-date listing of Daisy's books. Sign up for Daisy's newsletter and mailing list to get notifications for new book releases, contests, and more.

~<>~

---

1. https://www.daisydexterdobbs.com

## About the Author

A born storyteller, Daisy Dexter Dobbs started writing stories at five, satisfying her inner ham by reading them aloud, using a toilet plunger as a microphone. Today, Daisy creates written voyages of the imagination, infused with love, laugh-out-loud comedy, friendships, family and guaranteed happy endings. Some of her books include paranormal and fantasy elements. And some books are scorching HOT on the spice scale.

Having worked at more than 40 different jobs provides Daisy with a ridiculous amount of questionable experience to draw on for her characters. She's been: a ghostwriter for politicians; a library art director; a weight loss counselor; mayor's executive secretary; a Realtor; travel agent; editor; and a butcher's meat wrapper, quitting after she spotted a big eyeball coming toward her on the conveyor.

A Chicago native, Daisy and her husband, now live in the Pacific Northwest. Happily, Daisy no longer feels the need to use a bathroom plunger as a microphone when entertaining.

You can find Daisy here:
Facebook: DaisyDexterDobbs
Instagram: DaisyDexterDobbs
TikTok: @daisydexterdobbs
Amazon: Daisy Dexter Dobbs
Goodreads: daisydexterdobbs
BookBub: Daisy-Dexter-Dobbs
Twitter/X: DaisyDDobbs
Threads: @DaisyDexterDobbs
Pinterest: DaisyDDobbs
Email: DaisyDexterDobbs@gmail.com
Read more at www.DaisyDexterDobbs.com.

www.ingramcontent.com/pod-product-compliance
Lightning Source LLC
Chambersburg PA
CBHW022236020726
47496CB00004B/930